The Wou1

Copyright © 2022 by Alex Amit
All rights reserved. This book or any portion thereof
may not be reproduced or used in any manner whatsoever
without the express written permission of the publisher
except for the use of brief quotations in a book review.

Printed in the United States of America

First Printing, 2022
Line Editing: Grace Michaeli

Contact: alex@authoralexamit.com
http://authoralexamit.com/

ISBN: 9798434379342

The Wounded Nurse

Alex Amit

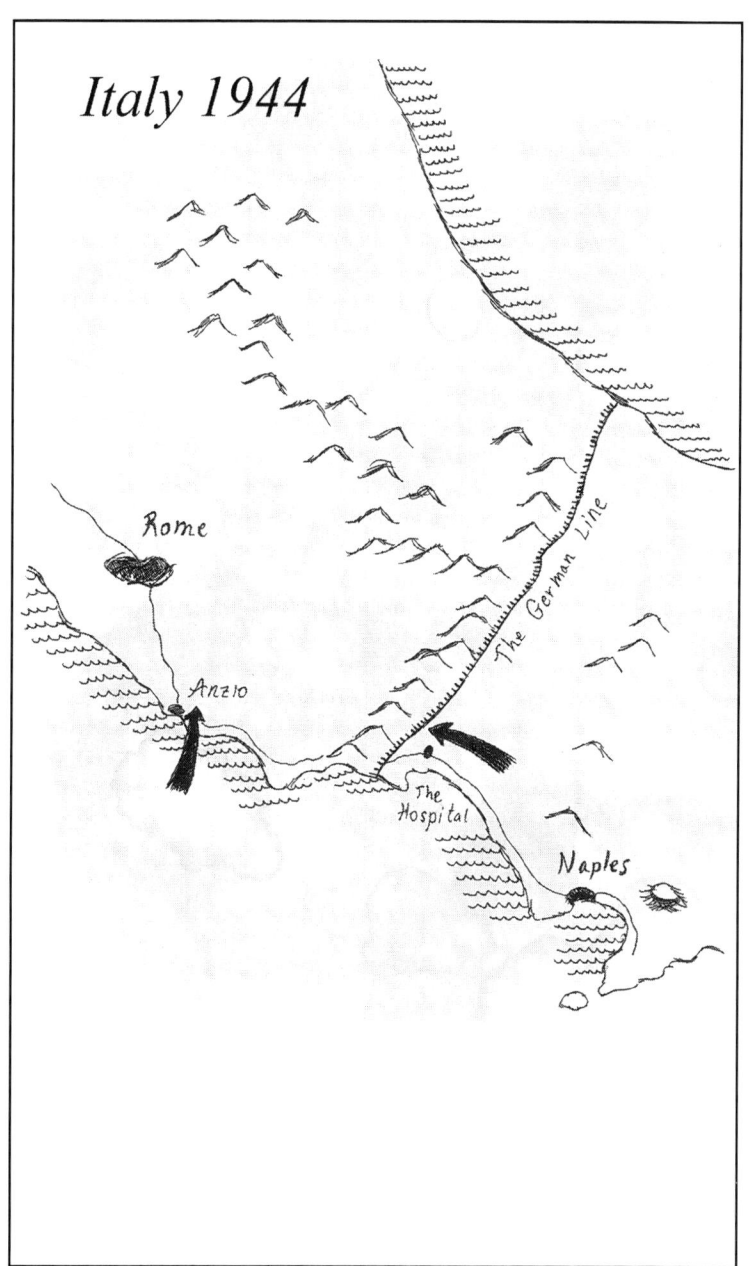

Italy, front line south of Rome, field hospital, April 1944

"Are you the new nurse? Put your finger here," the doctor instructs me, and I press my fingers to the open wound in the chest of the wounded soldier as he lies on a stretcher placed in front of us on the simple wooden operating table.

"My name is Grace," I answer, ignoring my blood-soaked fingers as I try to stop the wounded man's bleeding as best I can.

"Vascular Scissors." He speaks quietly, and I collect them from the metal tray next to me, placing them in his hand. The tray is full of surgeons' chisels, sewing materials, and syringes. I must not make mistakes. The tent is lit by dim yellow light from a lamp hanging from the tarp roof. It sways from side to side in the wind that shakes the tent sheets. In the weak light, I struggle to find the right spot to tack my fingers while the wounded soldier continues to bleed. I must succeed. The faint sound of raindrops that have been hitting the tarpaulin for three days interferes with my concentration. It is only disturbed by the sound of the scalpel blades or scissors I throw onto the stainless steel tray with sharp rings of metal. I can also hear the constant growl of cannon batteries firing in the distance, their muffled voices continuing unabated.

"Now try to take your finger off," the doctor instructs me after finding the point of injury and blocking it. I move my fingers away as he quickly stitches the exposed skin. "Cut another strip off his uniform and disinfect immediately afterwards."

I take my hands off the wound, hold the scissors, and quickly cut his torn uniform. It's soiled with mud and blood that have mixed together, until it's impossible to tell what's what. I throw the strips of cut cloth onto the muddy ground, then grab the bottle of alcohol and some cotton wool. I start cleaning the wounded soldier's skin, feeling his body shivering at the sting of disinfectant. I have to hurry, soon they'll be bringing in another wounded soldier. This one was also waiting to one side, lying in his stretcher, until we were finished taking care of the one before him. I've lost count of the number of wounded soldiers I've treated in the last few days.

"How long have you been with us?" the doctor asks me.

"This is my fourth day." I stand proudly. I've hardly slept for the last three nights, working in this tent since I arrived at this hospital and the attack on the German lines began.

"The wound has reopened. Put your fingers on it again," the doctor speaks a little louder, and I toss the alcohol-soaked cotton swab and the scissors onto the metal tray, ignoring the jarring sound of metal hitting metal. My fingers are tucked into the open wound again, trying to stop the flow of blood staining the soldier's pale skin crimson.

"Where's another nurse?" He looks to the sides. "I need another nurse now, and two units of blood, stat."

"Nurse," I shout hoarsely, "we need two more units of blood now." My eyes are fixed on my wet fingers and the dripping stretcher full of blood. I can feel drops hitting my feet.

"Two units of blood on the table." Someone arrives and places two glass bottles filled with crimson liquid before disappearing in the direction of another operating tent. I have to get some rest.

"Now, to the vein, as you learned in nursing school," he tells me while my fingers are tucked inside the wound, and I feel the pulse through the throbbing artery and the pool of blood. "Do not take off his sleeve. Cut it off." I turn my head towards the scissors thrown onto the metal tray. "Hurry up." His fingers replace mine.

"I can't find the vein," I whisper as I struggle with the needle, shoving it in over and over. I must succeed. He must live. I stop for a moment, wiping the sweat from my forehead and rubbing my eyes as I grab the wounded man's hand where it lies on the table, and try again.

"Good, now hold the bottle as high as you can, like you learned." He guides me as I find the wounded man's vein, and I lift the glass bottle high, ignoring my tired hands. Despite the cool breeze, I feel all sweaty; at least the rain has stopped, and the spring sun is shining between the tent sheets.

"Will he live?" I ask the doctor.

"I hope so." He smiles at me wearily. "What did you say your name was? Grace?"

"Yes."

"You're doing fine. Start binding his wound."

I carefully attach the blood bottle to the metal rod, and use the scissors to continue cutting off the wounded man's uniform, ignoring my tired and trembling hands. My fingers clean off the remaining blood with a cloth, and I disinfect his body again, opening a clean bandage and starting to cover his body.

"Is this okay?" I look at the doctor, who is leaning back and watching my hands.

"Yes, it's okay."

"Is this treatment tent three? I'm looking for the new nurse, Grace," I hear a male voice.

"That's me." I turn my gaze to the two uniformed soldiers entering the tent, carrying a stretcher with an unconscious, wounded man, placing him on the table at the side of the tent. One of the soldiers has a bandage on his forehead, and they're both dirty with dust and mud.

"We've brought you another two wounded, one with a chest injury and one with head and chest injuries."

The doctor approaches and looks at the wounded soldier, collects a stethoscope from the tray and checks his pulse.

"Take one of them. I can only treat one." He turns to the soldier with the bandage on his forehead and the Red Cross symbol on his arm.

"I can't. I was told to bring them both to tent number three, to ask for Grace. The rest of the operating tents are full," he says in a tired voice as two more soldiers enter, carrying another wounded man on a stretcher and placing it on the ground. The wounded man's eyes and chest are wrapped in bandages that were once white, and now are filled with ugly red spots. Since the attack began three days ago, they've been coming in an endless stream.

"Grace," the doctor instructs me, "take the one we treated to the recovery tent, and we'll start with that one," he points with his hand, "give him an injection of morphine."

"Help me carry him," I instruct the soldier while holding the wounded soldier as carefully as I can, and we both place him on the operating table. I need to rest, to get out of this suffocating tent, breathe some air that doesn't carry the smell of blood, and close my eyes for just a few minutes.

I go to the bucket of water standing to one side of the tent and dip my hands in the cold water, rinsing my face and eyes. I have to keep them open. My fingers grip the scissors again, and I start cutting the bandages covering the new wounded chest, ignoring his sigh of pain and the bloodstains on his once-khaki uniform.

In the distance I again hear the thunder of cannon batteries, getting louder, and maybe the howling of fighter plane engines, and a strange whistle accompanies the ticking noise of machineguns.

"Get down." I hear someone shouting, and I see round holes forming in the tent tarp. I reach my hand forward, trying to protect my face from shards of glass from the shattering lamp, or maybe it's the blood bottles hanging on the metal rod.

"What's happening?" I hear someone shouting, and maybe that's me who's screaming. I see the sheets of the tent being torn apart, and through the gray sky I see a huge flame at the spot where Surgical Tent Two had stood.

"German planes." someone yells from outside, and I pull the wounded man from the operating table and carry him down into the mud, shouting at him that he'll be fine, but he doesn't answer me, and my ears are filled with the noise of drums until I can't hear my screams, or the screams of the people outside or around me in the tent, I don't know. It's just flames all around, and people are running, and maybe they're yelling too, and I grope on the muddy floor looking for the other wounded man who was in the tent, to pull them to the floor, but I can't see anything, mud or maybe blood is covering my eyes.

"They're shooting at us," I whisper, crawling on the floor, managing to find someone lying down, maybe one of the wounded from before, maybe it's the doctor. I'll clear the blood, and then I'll see.

"Don't worry, I'll protect you," I think I tell him as I lie down on top of him, but I'm not sure he's answered me. It's all flames, and the noise of aircraft engines and the constant ticking of machine guns, and my whole head is full of screams. I can't feel my leg, but it doesn't hurt at all.

"Don't worry, I'll take care of you," I whisper to him again, placing my head on his chest. I'll close my eyes for just a moment. Just a moment. "I'll take care of you."

Italy, a military hospital south of Rome, four months later, August 1944

"Good morning, Grace, how are you this morning?" I hear Nurse Audrey, and feel her palm resting on my shoulder.

"Same as I'll feel tomorrow," I answer as I continue to lie on my white metal-framed bed, turning my back to her and looking at the yellow wall of what was once a magnificent mansion, now serving as a US Army hospital. My eyes examine the thin cracks in the plaster as if they were arteries bringing life to this place. But the plaster is peeling. Maybe this place should have died by now.

"How did you sleep?" She keeps talking to me, even though my gaze is turned to the yellow wall and I'm not looking at her. Maybe she should leave me here in the corner of the hall, and help the other wounded.

"Grace, sweetie, are you okay?" She strokes my shoulder.

"Like a corpse, I feel like a corpse," I answer. For two months now she's been asking me the same question, and for two months I've given her the same answer. But she still keeps coming every morning to take care of me, walking around my hospital bed in her white nurse uniform. I hate the white pajamas I wear, announcing who I am. Even prisoners are given unique uniforms, just in different colors and appropriate sizes. My pajamas are too big on me, and they're the smallest size they could find in this place. All the others around here are wounded male soldiers. I'm here by mistake. I'm a nurse who should be taking care of them instead of lying on this metal bed.

"Are you in pain?"

"Do you have anything to give me?" I keep staring at the wall. She's no longer willing to give me morphine. At first, when I was crying in pain, she would soothe me with a dose of morphine, coming to my bed at night and injecting me, and I would sigh in relief and manage to sleep. She's not willing to do that for me anymore.

"Don't you want to get out of bed?" I hear her bring my wooden crutches, placing them by my bed. "Grace, you'll feel better if you get up and go out to the garden with the others in recovery."

"Do you think a missing leg can be recovered?" I whisper to the wall, hoping she doesn't hear me.

"At least you're alive," she answers, and pats me on the shoulder, continuing to talk to my back.

"Yes, at least I'm alive." I smile at the wall. Wall, do you hear? I survived, so it's okay to keep me in pain and not give me morphine when I ask for it. Maybe this whole staying alive thing was a mistake.

Only Audrey and the Italian cleaning woman come to my corner every morning. Audrey changes my bandages while I try to ignore her, and the Italian cleaner in the black dress scrubs the floor and ignores me. Still, I don't need them. I get along fine myself.

"Grace, are you excited?" Audrey keeps talking to my back.

"Excited for what?" I ask the wall, wondering what's so exciting about staying alive. "Are you organizing a dance competition, and inviting me to participate?" What should I be excited about? That she's being forced to take care of me?

"Excited about going home." She brings the crutches closer and places them in front of my eyes, blocking my view of the wall.

"Who's going home?" I slowly get up and try not to look at her face, I don't want her to notice my surprise. Are they sending me home?

"You're going home," she answers as she hands me the crutches. "You have to get up and start getting ready."

"Am I on the list?" I struggle to stand by the side of the bed, holding the white metal frame for support and refusing to take the crutches from her. I'm not disabled. I never was.

"Yes, you're on the list. Your stay at Military Hospital 12 ends today. Soon they'll start reading the names of all the wounded who are going back home. Happily for you, you're on that list. The ship is already waiting at the port of Naples." She quickly replaces the sheet on my bed before I go back to lying in the position I've been in for the past two months. "From now on, you'll be taken care of in America."

"Are you sure?" It's probably a mistake. Does she think I've been cured?

"I'm sure you're going home," she replies as she places the rejected crutches by the wall. "You've received an exit ticket from the war back to our beloved nation. New York Harbor is waiting for you." She smiles at me. "I'll miss you, even though you were stubborn."

"But I'm not recovered yet." I look down.

"For you, the war is over." She smiles at me as I lie back in bed, turning my back to her again and staring at the old wall, searching for a new crack that's been wandering through the plaster for centuries.

"Grace, you'd better arrange your belongings. They'll be picking you up soon. You'll continue your recovery back home, along with the rest of the disabled." She puts her palm on my shoulder one last time, and I hear the sound of her shoes walking away down the hall. Now she's probably crossing the curtain separating my corner from the large hall where all the wounded men lie, going to tell someone else he's starting his journey home today.

"Grace, for you, the war is over," I whisper to the wall, looking down at where I once had a leg.

"Edward," I hear one of the nurses after a while. She's standing in the center of the hall, among the other wounded soldiers. I scrape the old plaster from the wall with my fingertips, exposing more grooves within. I've been doing this for two months now, peeling the wall and examining it, looking for shapes within.

"Here," I hear Edward answer.

"Stefan," she reads another name.

"Here."

Maybe Audrey was wrong. Maybe this is another list of the wounded, not those returning home.

I quickly get out of bed and sit down, standing and supporting myself as I grab the crutches leaning against the wall. I hate them, they hurt my armpits every time I try to use them to walk, as if reminding me that from now on I depend on them and the pain they bring. But I must know. Was Audrey wrong?

I carefully try to jump towards the window, leaning against its wooden frame and looking out at the wide parking lot in front of the hospital. She's not wrong.

A convoy of clean white ambulances stands on the road leading to the hospital, entering one by one and passing by the metal gate that was once the estate's barrier, and was now thrown to one side of the road. They slowly drive in and park at the entrance next to the large Red Cross flag spread on the ground, signaling to the sky and enemy aircraft that this complex is a hospital.

Maybe she was wrong after all? Maybe she won't call my name?

"Philip," the nurse continues to read off the list of names, and I turn around, looking at the great hall full of white metal beds and wounded soldiers.

"Going home." Philip sits down and answers while his friends greet him, wishing to be on the list next time. I stifle a scream of pain as a piece of wood gets lodged in my finger while I try to peel off the whitewashed window frame. She wasn't wrong.

"Owen," she continues, "going home." Some of his friends are clapping, and two approach and hug him.

"Malcolm." Another name on the list.

"I hope you can handle the German submarines," I hear someone laughing with him.

"If the Germans failed to kill me with their planes, nothing will kill me on my way home," he answers the one lying in bed next to him before getting up on his crutches, opening his metal locker, and packing his things. I can see Audrey approaching and helping him.

Soon the nurse will read my name. I should start packing my things, but how can I return home if I haven't recovered? Why are they sending me home for treatment with the other disabled wounded ones? I'm so young. I'm not disabled, I can't be disabled, I came here to save lives, I'm a nurse.

"George."

"We'll meet back home," he laughs, and I look at him

shaking hands with his friends. I have to do something. I have to stay here, I'm too young to be in a wheelchair.

"Robert." She doesn't stop reading, walking through the great hall as she approaches me. I have to stay here. I have to go back to being who I was. I have to talk to someone to get me off the list, I'm only twenty-three years old.

"Grace," I hear my name.

What should I do?

"Grace."

I'll talk to someone. Surely there's someone who will listen to me.

"Grace!" she raises her voice and approaches me.

"Going home," I answer.

"Pack up your things. The ambulances are already waiting."

"I'm packing my things," I answer her, and hobble back with the crutches to my bed, looking at my belongings. They are tucked inside a small metal locker on the side of my bed. A hairbrush Audrey once gave me as a gift, some feminine things, and a small bag with my clothes. I'm not going to pack them, they're going to take me away from here. I'll talk to the head nurse on the second floor.

"Gilbert," the nurse holding the list walks away from me, back to the aisle between the men's beds. I have to hurry.

I hold the crutches again with both hands and start walking between the other wounded ones lying in the white beds in the hall. I'll talk to the head nurse, and she'll take me off the list. Click-clack, click-clack, I mustn't delay now. I lower my eyes as I walk down the passage between the straight rows of white beds. Click-clack, click-clack, *don't stop walking, pass by the wounded man standing by his bed and arranging his belongings, don't look at him, keep your eyes down, he must be staring at me, him and all his friends,* ignore their stares. I have to concentrate on my next step, keep my eyes on the floor. They must be whispering behind my back, pitying me and my leg. I have to ignore them. I'm not as injured as they are, I'll recover. I just have to reach the doorway. Just a few more steps, pass by the nurse standing in the center of the hall, holding the page and reading from it. I have to be careful not to fall.

"Grace, where are you going?"

"I forgot something. I'll be back in a second," I answer without turning my head, and try to walk out of this hall as fast as I can. I have to keep on walking, ignoring the pain in my armpits caused by the crutches that hate me, ignoring the whispers I can hear. They're probably talking about me.

"Did you pack your things?"

"Yes, they're already packed. I'll be back in a minute."

Why isn't she continuing to read the names from the list? She's probably watching me, she and all the other men in the hall, scrutinizing how I hobble while holding my crutches. It's not me. It's someone else. I have to climb the stairs to the second floor and reach the head nurse. I'll explain it to her, she'll understand.

"There's been a mistake," I tell her as soon as I enter her office at the end of the hall, coming through the door with the golden brass plaque attached: "Head Nurse".

"Sorry?" She raises her head and looks at me. She sits behind a large wooden desk covered in papers. Will she kick me out because I didn't knock and wait for her to call me inside?

"There's been a mistake on the list." I stand as steadily as I can in the center of her office, trying not to gasp from the effort of climbing the stairs. It took me a long time to climb the stairs, stopping several times to rest, trying not to think of my hurt leg.

"What kind of mistake?" She puts down the paper she's holding in her hands and looks at me, but even though I try to examine her, I can't tell if she's angry with me or will let me talk and explain. Her nurse's cap is tightly fastened to her black and silver striped hair.

"They're accidentally sending me back home."

"I don't think there's been a mistake here," she answers and goes back to reading, holding the paper at a distance. In a few years she'll need reading glasses. At least she isn't scolding me and kicking me out of her office.

"Please check your lists. An error has occurred here. They're sending me home." She must listen to me.

"I don't have to check my lists. I know your case. You're the only wounded female in my hospital. Your name is Grace. You recently came here from a hospital in Chicago where you started working as an intern nurse. You volunteered for the U.S. Medical Corps and joined a convoy from New York Harbor to Sicily, and from there you continued here to Italy. Four months ago you were injured in the major attack south of Rome. Fortunately for you, you survived the attack, and fortunately for you, your leg was amputated below the knee and not above it. And for you, the war is over," she says indifferently and goes back to reading the paper she's holding.

"Eight days," I whisper.

"What?" She doesn't raise her eyes from the paper.

"I just arrived," I want to shout at her that I had only been in Italy for eight days. "I need to recover. I can't stay like this."

"We gave you the best care we can here." She finally puts down the paper and looks at me. "They'll continue to treat your disability in America."

"But I still need to recover, to overcome my pain. I'm in pain," I say quietly. I hate that word she uses. I'm not like them.

"I'm sorry, but we can't arrange our schedule around your requests, we are at war, and it takes time for wounds to heal and for the pain to go away," she goes on, uttering the words from her pink lipstick-painted lips.

"I need more time."

"Everyone needs more time, but we need your spot. There was another massive attack north of Florence. For some reason the Germans keep fighting, they don't want to surrender. There are a lot of new wounded on the way, and you know how it is. You also wanted to be a nurse once."

"Yes, I wanted to be a nurse too," I quietly answer, and I want to shout at her that I once was a nurse, not just wanting to be one. I was a nurse for eight whole days here in Italy, where I hardly slept and treated wounded soldiers coming from the front. And once I also smiled a nurse's perfect smile, with red lipstick matching my white uniforms, and it was just a few months ago that I boarded the ship at New York Harbor heading into the war in Europe.

"You'd better hurry. The convoy won't wait for you all day. The ship is already waiting at the port of Naples. They did us a favor sending us a ship to evacuate the wounded back home. Who knows when the next ship will arrive?"

She answers politely and goes back to reading the paper she's holding, hinting to me that the conversation between us is over.

"But there are German submarines at sea," I try, knowing it will no longer affect her. Nothing will change her decision, not even one injured woman who was once a nurse, or German submarines trying to sink any ship that crosses the Atlantic.

"Don't you think you should trust the Lord, who is watching over you? I'm sure He's the one who kept you alive, or made your injury be below the knee. It's a much easier disability than above the knee." She looks up from the paper again, and I lower my gaze, examining my bare foot. Once I had two, but now instead of my feet there is only a blank piece of ugly white hospital pant leg. Even though God kept me alive, and even though I have a knee, my leg is gone. Maybe he shouldn't have tried so hard.

"Thank you, head nurse," I answer and turn to leave.

"Blanche, my name is Blanche," she answers as she begins writing something on the paper. "And please close the door behind you."

"Yes, head nurse Blanche," I whisper, and lean on my crutches, releasing my hand and closing the door. I have to hurry, the convoy is leaving soon. I must do something.

"Where did Grace go?" I hear the voice of the nurse, the one reading the notes. I lean against the wall near the on-call nurse's door, trying to catch my breath. I'm not used to walking so much with the crutches. In a moment they'll start looking for me.

How can I go home like this, a lame rag doll on crutches that everyone is staring at with pity? Wheelchairs are for older people who can't walk anymore, not for young women like me.

"She went up into the hallway," I hear someone answer. What should I do?

I'm not disabled. I must get out of this convoy.

"She said she'll right back." The nurse from the hall is talking to someone else, maybe Audrey, the nurse who likes me. Will she help me escape?

"I'll help you look for her." It seems that it's her, and after a moment, as I peek from the hallway towards the stairs, I see her climbing towards me.

"Grace, you have to pack, the convoy is leaving soon. I'll help you down the stairs."

"I can't go with the convoy. They'll make me disabled in a wheelchair at home." I start to cry.

"I'm so sorry," she approaches and hugs me. "But there's nothing we can do, you have to go."

"Please help me stay." I hug her. "Please, just some more time." She's the only one here who cares for me.

"I'm sorry, I can't, you'll be fine back home. They have a special place where they'll teach you everything you need to know."

"But I'm twenty-three," I whisper to her in tears.

"Come down with me. I'll help you pack." She stops hugging me.

"I'll be right there," I whisper to her. "I'll just wash my face and I'll come."

"Shall I help you down the stairs?"

"No, it's okay," I wipe my eyes. "Can you start packing my things?"

She gives me a little hug and goes down the stairs, disappearing into the main hall. I have to hurry, they're going to take me. I can't go home and be crippled.

I hold the crutches firmly and try to walk down the stairs leading to the entrance, but I stop and look down. After my injury, I've never gone down stairs. How will I go down without falling?

I reach out and try to hold the railing with my hand, supporting my body with my hand and jumping down the first step. But the crutches loosen and fall noisily down the stairs to the bottom. I've lost my support. Did they hear the noise in the hall? Will they come looking for me?

"I'll try jumping one step," I whisper to myself, gripping the railing tightly, jumping down and almost falling.

"And one more," I whisper and grab the railing, hoping Audrey won't come looking for me again.

"And one more." I'm panting.

"Help me," I beg the Italian cleaner in the black dress who's starting to go up the stairs.

She stops and looks at the crutches lying at her feet on the floor, then looks up at me.

"Please," I whisper to her. In all those months she cleaned my corner every morning, I never spoke to her. Maybe in the beginning, when I was in so much pain and yelling, not remembering who I spoke to. But I don't think she understands me now.

She starts going up the stairs and looks at me with her dark eyes. She doesn't understand. But when she gets close to me, and I think she's going to pass me by, she takes my hand and wraps it around her shoulder, holds my hand tightly, and hugs my body with her other hand, supporting me as we slowly go down together, me leaning against her body, trying not to gasp at the jumps down the stairs.

Would she be helping me if she knew I was running away?

"Thanks," I smile at her when we reach the first floor, and she helps me lean against the wall. She bends over, collects the crutches lying on the floor, and hands them to me, not saying anything. She just turns her back and goes up the stairs, ignoring me.

"Thank you," I whisper to her again, and hurry as much as I can, passing the building's large front door and ignoring the pain that's started in the amputated leg. I have to hurry. If I can just manage to go to the hospital's garden without them noticing, they won't find me there, and the convoy will go without me.

The white ambulances are parking in front of the hospital entrance with their back doors already open, ready to welcome the wounded, and all the drivers are gathered around one of them, talking to each other and enjoying the warm morning sun. Will they notice me? I have to act like I'm a regular injured person, it's a hospital, there's a lot of wounded people here.

I slowly hobble towards the back of the building as I lean on the crutches, careful not to slip and fall. I mustn't rush, I'm not used to them, I never agreed to go out to the garden before.

"Let's go outside, the garden is in front of the sea, the warm air will make you feel good," Audrey used to tell me every morning, smiling at me with her big eyes and red lipstick. But I refused, and insisted on lying in bed in front of the wall, looking at the plaster lifelines of the cracks in the wall. Now I have to cross the parking lot, they want to take me away from my wall.

Just a few more steps, I count the line of clean white ambulances, they're not like the ones we had at the front, which were khaki and filthy with mud. I mustn't think about it, but then my thoughts break through, flames and shattered glass and machineguns and people screaming and shouting. There is a burnt smell of fire and gasoline in my nose, I need to vomit.

Breathe, breathe slowly, these are different ambulances, everything is okay, look in a different direction, don't think about that day, these are clean white ambulances, and the soldiers driving them don't shout that there are more wounded. Just a few more steps to the end of the parking lot, you can make it.

"Excuse me, are you with us?" One of the drivers is approaching. He probably wants to help me. I don't need help.

"No, I'm with the next convoy." I continue to walk, trying to keep smiling even when my bare feet step on the sharp stones, does he notice that I don't wear shoes?

"Good luck. Do you need help?"

"No thanks, I'm fine." I keep walking, hoping he won't try to be a gentleman and escort me, and to my relief he returns to his friends who are gathered around a wooden box with the medical corps emblem on it. Some of them bend over and hold cards, place coins and gamble, while the rest stand around and watch them, attaching money to the game. Just a few more steps up to the path that leads to the garden.

The garden behind the hospital is empty in the early morning hours, and the white deckchairs on the grass are empty by now, arranged in straight lines ending at the cliff facing the sea, waiting for the wounded. Later they'll stroll through the garden, supported by the nurses, or just sit motionless in the wide chairs and look to the horizon, waiting for evening, for the nurses to pick them up and take them back to their beds. To this day I sometimes stand at the window, looking at them in the garden, refusing to go out. I'm not as they are.

The grass feels soft to my bare foot, but I must not stop here and sit, not even to rest, they must be looking for me already. I keep crossing the green path, careful not to slip on the grass still wet with the morning dew. I have to keep moving forward, find a place to hide. I direct my steps to an old stone shed at the end of the garden. The gardener must have used it before the war came. A few more steps and I'll be safe.

Just behind the old shed wall, I allow myself to stop and rest for a moment. Even though it's early in the morning, I'm all sweating; my bare foot is bleeding from the sharp stones that injured me as I crossed the hospital parking lot. I should have put my shoe on, but then the nurse with the list of names would suspect me. What will I do now?

I carefully lean against the shed wall and sit down, feeling the rough stone wall scratch my back through the hospital pajamas, but I have no choice, the crutches fell to the floor as I try to lean them against the stone wall for a moment. I'll stay here. They won't find me here. The ambulances will go on without me.

"Grace!" I hear the nurses calling in the garden. Did the ambulance driver tell them he saw me? Will they come pick me up? I cling to the wall and try not to move or make noise, but I know it doesn't matter. If they just get behind the shed, they'll find me. Maybe I should give up and go home, what does it even matter? How long will I be able to run from the convoy?

I try to crawl and hold the crutches, but it's too hard. I have to rest, just a few more minutes, but the voices calling my name are coming closer.

I take a few breaths, crawl to the crutches again, hold them, get up and keep on moving, stepping towards the stone wall surrounding the mansion and the grove of cypresses and olive trees behind it. I must reach the grove, it's the only place I can hide from the voices crying out my name. My bare foot is scratched by sharp stones as I climb the wall, but I have to cross it and get out of the garden. I hold onto the stones with all my might. I have to succeed, I have no other choice, I've already thrown the crutches over the stone fence, I have no way back.

The engine noise from approaching planes makes me cringe, and I feel exposed while holding myself to the stone fence, unable to escape or even bend without falling. All I can do is lower my gaze and close my eyes and wait for the machinegun noise to hit me while I try to shrink and become part of the stones, as the sounds of aircraft engines get louder. But the noise passes over me, and when I finally open my eyes and look at the sky, I see the large green bodies of two bombers with the blue circle and white star of the U.S. Air Force painted on their wings. These are not German planes. Slowly they drop and disappear behind the treetops, approaching the military airfield behind the hill.

"Grace!" I hear the shouts in the garden again. I must cross the wall. I manage to pull myself over the stone wall and fall on the other side, trying to support myself as much as I can. Still, my amputated stump hits the ground, and even though I try to stifle my scream, I fail, and scream in pain, looking at my pants and seeing a red stain spread on the white cloth, dirty from the ground. I've opened the wound that had healed.

Get up, ignore the pain, keep walking, do not look at your pants. I have to get away.

I keep walking in the woods, supported by my crutches, looking for a place to hide. Please don't hear me. Between a row of bushes, I lie on the hard ground and tuck the sleeve of my shirt into my mouth, biting it with my teeth, holding my shouts back. I don't care about the tears of pain flowing down my cheeks. Please don't hear my cries. Please don't take me from here and make me crippled.

Hours later, after I see the ambulance convoy leaving the hospital and heading south on the road to Naples, only then do I get up from my hiding place in the bushes and try to stand upright. My whole body hurts, and I walk slowly, looking for a passage through the stone fence through which I can return to the hospital. I can't jump over the wall again, I'm too afraid to stumble and hit my stump on the ground. My leg is full of scratches and blood, and my arms are scratched from my fingernails. I've hurt myself, doing anything to keep quiet when I heard them searching for me.

It takes me a while to find a spot where the stone fence is ruined, with a big hole in it. It's probably a remnant of the war fought here and passed on north, a tank shell or a bomb from a plane, and I slowly step through the gaping opening in the wall, careful not to slip on the sharp stones. I hobble to the old shed, leaning against its wall that hides me from the hospital. I have to rest again, I'll try to be as quiet as I can. When the day is over, and the injured men in the garden go inside, I'll try to sneak in with them. I have no idea what I'll say to the nurses, but I'll think of something, they'll understand. I was like them too, once.

"What about the amputee nurse? Did they find her? I think she managed to escape." I hear two nurses talking to each other across the wall, and smell their cigarette smoke. They must be close to me.

"She didn't get on the convoy. She shouldn't have joined the war at all," the second one answers her. "She wasn't even really a nurse, just an intern." That sounds like Audrey.

"They shouldn't have sent her to the front."

"I don't know why they sent an unprofessional person like her to the front lines. She's just arrived and now she's returning home."

"At least she wants to stay."

"She needs to know her place. She's disabled. She needs to be taken care of. She can't become a nurse again." I hear Audrey and cringe.

"Who would want her like that at home?" the other nurse answers Audrey. "Luckily I'm not in her place."

"Yeah, no one would want her at home. Too bad for her. I feel sorry for her. She could be so beautiful if she hadn't lost her leg." My fingers tightly grip the sleeve of my shirt.

"She just didn't realize she had to stay away from German pilots," one of them laughs.

"Yes, better to choose our pilots." The other one also starts laughing.

"Where were you? We're looking for you," I hear another voice. "New casualties from the front just arrived, we need your help." Their speech fades away with bursts of laughter.

My fingers slowly crumble the reddish terracotta plaster off the old wall. I'll stay here a little longer, I'm comfortable here when I lean against the shed wall. I can handle my pain here.

The cool night breeze blows in my face as I finally rise and walk toward the dark hospital building, passing the garden between the empty lounge chairs. I have to drink and eat something, I didn't eat anything all day, and the pain in my amputated leg has intensified from prolonged sitting. I need some help from the nurses.

In the silence that surrounds me, I can hear the sound of the waves in the distance. My hands ache from holding the crutches all day, but I ignore the pain and approach the old mansion-turned-hospital. In the dark all around, only a few windows in the building shed light into the night, like eyes staring at me accusingly. Still I ignore them, I must go inside, I must find Audrey, maybe she'll agree to take care of me, even though I don't know my place and shouldn't be here, and I'm no longer beautiful without my leg. I have no one else to ask for help. After that, I'll return to my corner and wait quietly until the next ship takes me home. I promise myself that I won't shout, even if I'm in pain.

The parking lot at the hospital entrance is empty of ambulances, and only a few military vehicles are parked on the side next to each other like a black mass. In the distance I notice two large cypresses at the entrance near the ruined gate. Step by step I pass the vehicles in the parking lot, past the large canvas of the Red Cross flag spread out in the center of the parking lot. It looks almost black in the faint light of the moon, but I ignore it and look towards the entrance to the mansion, praying no one will see me at such a late hour and that everyone is asleep except the nurse on call.

I have to sit and use my hands to go up the entrance stairs, climbing them one by one, dragging the crutches behind me and trying not to make noise. I have no more strength to stand and jump, but it doesn't seem to bother anyone. The great hall is dark, and only a faint light emanates from the nurses' station, where one of them sits and listens to the radio quietly playing jazz music. But it's not Audrey. A few more steps, and I'll get to my corner.

Even the wounded are quiet in the dark room, and no one tells me anything as I walk between the rows of straight beds towards mine, occasionally stopping to breathe and rest while looking at the floor with downcast eyes, careful not to stumble in the dark. With a few more steps, I'll reach my corner, and I can lie down and go to sleep, I'll give up on food.

But when I get to my corner and feel the metal frame of the bed, I quickly pull my hand back. My bed is no longer mine.

They gave my bed to someone else, they've left me no place to be. Another soldier is lying there. Even the small locker that was once mine stands next to the bed that is already his.

What was I thinking? That they would save my place for me? Those nurses who thought it was a pity I didn't go, that I don't belong here? Why didn't I go with the convoy? How will I stay here now?

As I hold onto the bed frame so as not to fall, I approach the wounded man and examine him in the dark, but I can hardly see his face, only the bandages covering his head and eyes. I can't even hear his breathing, even when I bring my head closer to him. Is he still alive? Shall I call the shift nurse?

I gently touch his lips with the tip of my finger. They are hot. He is alive.

I'll wait here until morning, by my bed. I'll take care of him, see that he's alive. I sit on the floor at the foot of his bed, holding myself from drinking the glass of water next to his bed. Putting my back to the wall, I try to ignore the pain in my leg, but it gets harder, same as it was after they removed my leg, and I scratch the wall and my thighs, trying not to cry.

"Soon the morning will arrive," I whisper to the wall. "Soon they'll give me something for the pain. Wall, do you hear? Does it hurt you when I peel pieces of plaster from you?"

Unwanted

"Good morning, Gracie, how do you feel this morning after everyone was looking for you yesterday?" I open my eyes and see Audrey smiling. She leans over me as I sit on the floor under my occupied bed, my back against the wall while I raise my eyes to her. Her smooth brown hair is neat and collected, and she smells of soap. I touch my head, feeling my messy hair.

"Are you thirsty?" she asks, and I just nod my head while she strokes my arm. Then she gets up and walks away, coming back after a moment and serving me a glass of milk and a bowl of porridge.

"Thanks," I hoarsely whisper to her as I sip from the bowl, continuing to watch her as she rises and stands over me, checking the sleeping wounded man in my bed. She has a beautiful body with an ample chest, and I lower my gaze and examine her clean white nurse's dress and her two legs standing safely on the floor by the stranger's bed. She's not as ugly as I am.

"Grace."

"Yes," I look up at her.

"The head nurse wants to talk to you." She smiles at me with her red lipstick.

"Yes," I answer as I chew the porridge.

"Now, she wants to see you now." She takes the bowl from my hands, even though I haven't finished yet. I wipe my mouth with my palm and comb my hair with my fingers, trying to fix it. I also try to wipe the soil residue and bloodstains from my dirty pajamas, a reminder of yesterday's scratches. I need to be tidy, the head nurse wants to see me.

Click-clack, click-clack. I cross the hall and look down, knowing that all the previous wounded ones are watching me now, the amputee who escaped from the convoy yesterday. They're explaining who I am to the new ones. I should ignore them, I'll explain everything to the head nurse.

It takes time for me to go up to the second floor, it also takes time for me to stand by the closed door to her room and catch my breath. It also takes time for me to knock on the door and wait for her to call me inside.

"What am I going to do with you now? I have a whole hospital to manage, and one wounded woman who thinks she's above military rules and deserves special treatment," head nurse Blanche talks to me, but I don't look at her. I'm standing tall and looking ahead to the window behind her, from which I can see the blue sea spreading from her window to the horizon. The crutches hurt me when I lean on them, but I keep standing still.

I was wrong. I was so wrong. No one will take care of me anymore, she doesn't need someone like me here either.

"I have nowhere to put you. I don't need you here." She keeps talking, and I look for a moment at the white nurse's hat attached to her silver hair, and her bright eyes staring at me, lifting my chin back and looking at the blue sea again. No one here will help me recover.

"What will I do with you?" she asks me again, but she does not seem to intend that I answer her. I have nowhere to go, I have no bed to sleep in either, what can I say to her?

"I can help in the hospital in the meantime. I'm a nurse," I whisper. Or I used to be one once, at least.

"Help me in the hospital? Doing what?"

"I'm a nurse." I try to stand as tall as I can.

"You mean an inexperienced intern nurse."

"I'm a nurse," I repeat, wanting to tell her how many wounded soldiers I treated in those few days before I was injured. At some point, I stopped counting.

"What kind of intern were you? An OR nurse?" She looks at me, checking my dirty pajamas.

"Yes, Head Nurse Blanche."

"And can you treat my wounded in the operation room, with your leg?"

"No, Head Nurse Blanche." I keep standing straight but I know it won't help me.

"So you're no longer a nurse, you're a cripple who should have been sitting on the deck of a U.S. Army hospital ship, on your way to New York Harbor, drinking hot American Army milk and being excited to see the Statue of Liberty appear on the horizon."

"Yes, Head Nurse Blanche," I answer, remembering that time I left New York Harbor a few months ago, on our way to war. I'd stood on the deck and watched the proud woman holding the torch of freedom in her hand, and I felt so proud to serve our nation. Though it was raining as we sailed, I remained standing, holding the railing, looking at the copper statue as it slowly shrank, uniting with the skyscrapers behind it until they became a stain on the horizon. That was my first voyage, and I was so excited. But I mustn't think of it now. It was so long ago. I'm so redundant now.

"And now you're holding up a bed I need for a wounded soldier, I have no extra bed to give you." She keeps looking at me, as if reading from a list of accusations.

"Yes, Head Nurse Blanche." I don't answer that someone else has already taken my bed.

"Go to the nurses and ask them to try to arrange a place for you to sleep."

"Yes, Head Nurse Blanche." I make sure to stand straight, even though it's hard for me to lean that way. I won't show her that it's difficult for me, even though she doesn't care.

"And return to your corner, you're going home with the next convoy."

"Yes, Head Nurse Blanche." I don't want to tell her that I have no corner anymore either.

"And find someone to take care of your leg. You were injured. You must be treated."

"Yes, Head Nurse Blanche."

"And get out of my office."

"Yes, Head Nurse Blanche."

"And call me Blanche."

"Yes, Head Nurse Blanche." I take one last look at the sea inviting me to come visit, so blue in the summer morning sun. Then I turn around and hobble away, leaving her office.

"Audrey, I apologize, Blanche asked that you help me find a place to sleep." I enter the nurse's station, which is just a small room in the corner of the hall. Maybe it used to be the servants' waiting room before the war, when they used to have balls or receptions at the mansion. Now it's been converted into the on-call nurse's room, full of pills and medicine shelves, syringes and morphine vials.

"Gracie, you should call her Head Nurse Blanche," Audrey answers as she continues to read the book she's holding, sitting behind a small wooden table in the center of the room.

"Sorry, Head Nurse Blanche asked that you help me find a bed." I stand up straight and look around, examining the shelves laden with pill bottles in all varieties of color, as if from a sweet candy store.

"One moment," she raises her head from the book for the first time and looks at me. "In the meantime, please wait outside," she smiles at me. "The entrance to this room is only for nurses."

"Yes, Nurse Audrey." I step outside the small room and stand at the entrance, watching her eyes pass over the pages while she mumbles the words to herself until she reaches the end of the chapter, moves the bookmark to its new place, closes the book, stands up and smiles at me.

"Let's find you a place to sleep." She passes me, walking down the aisle between the beds. "We don't want you to sleep outside in the garden like you tried to do yesterday."

The main hall is full of the newly-wounded, to the point that the beds almost touch each other, barely allowing the nurses room to move and take care of them. All the wounded men sent home yesterday have been replaced by new ones, as if they had never been here at all.

"The Third Division failed to break the German lines," Audrey turns around and tells me as she stops for a moment next to one of the new ones, helping him sit up in bed. "A lot of wounded arrived yesterday." She keeps walking as she talks to me: "You should have gone home, even if you think you're in pain and that you need more time to recover. We must obey regulations." She smiles at another new one, stroking his black hair gently. "Isn't that what you were taught in the nurses' course?"

"Yes, obeying regulations is what we were taught in the nurses' course," I answer and feel the pain in my leg, remembering the woman who recruited me back in Chicago.

"You're volunteering for the war," the recruiting nurse told us then, in Chicago. She was standing on stage in a hall full of excited nurses like me. Above our heads hung a sign spread from side to side, calling for war volunteers. "You will be sent overseas," she continued to speak as she raised her voice. It was unnecessary, we were all fascinated by the war and willing to contribute to our nation. "You will take care of the war wounded in Europe and the Pacific. You will see blood." She paused for a moment and looked around with her red lips, reviewing all the nurses who had come to the conference. "The main thing you should take with you to the war from Chicago is your professionalism." She paused for a moment, "This is not a game, this is war. You'll be in the army, and the army works according to rules. You must be more professional than you are here in Chicago. You can't feel pity for combat soldiers. The wounded mustn't think that you feel sorry for them, or sad about what's happened to them. You must be professional. They, like you, volunteered to serve our nation. They are proud, like you are now." She finished and came down from the stage to shake our hands, and we all got up from our chairs and hurried to the registration booth.

"We'll have to re-register you. I deleted you from our lists yesterday." She continues walking down the aisle, searching for a bed.

"Thanks," I whisper, wanting to shout that she shouldn't have erased me, that I just want to recover here like any of the other wounded around us, the ones she's so kind towards. I'm not to blame for the Germans fighting so hard. They cut my leg off too, I didn't do it to myself.

"Grace, you'll have to share your corner with the wounded man who's already there. The main hall is full," she tells me when she finally comes back. She pushes a white bed, carefully maneuvering it down the aisle, and placing it by the bed of the wounded soldier who took my bed last night.

Now, in the daylight, I can finally see him. He is lying in bed like all the others, but unlike them, his eyes are also covered with white bandages wrapped around his head. Only his lips and unshaven chin are visible, and his black hair sticking through the bandages.

What will I do? How will I be next to him? Our beds are so close to each other, only the small metal locker that was once mine separates us. I have never slept so close to a man, feeling his presence, even if he's injured and his eyes are covered with bandages.

"What about intimacy?" I ask Audrey. Before today, I'd had a curtain to hide me from other eyes, my private corner that protected me from all the other men in the hall. How would I clean up next to him? And what about the rest?

"I'm sorry, you really should have gone back home with the ship and not stayed here." She pushes the wounded man's bed even further, placing him by the wall that was mine, the one I always used to talk to and scratch at night.

"You'll have to get along with him. It doesn't really matter to him," she continues to talk as she spreads clean sheets on my new bed. "He can't see, his eyes were injured, and even if he lives he'll remain blind." She turns to him and gently strokes his black hair before talking to me again. "Let me help you clean up."

"It's okay. I'll clean up on my own."

"Are you sure?"

"Yes, thank you, Nurse Audrey."

"As you wish." She places bandages and iodine on the small metal locker, and again strokes the hair of the quiet wounded man now lying next to me. "I'll come by soon to see how he is doing." She turns her back to me and walks away, drawing the curtain separating us from the rest of the wounded soldiers in the hall.

I look at him again, examining his chest that peacefully rises and falls under the white sheet, looking at his eyes covered with thick bandages. Everything is fine, he can't see me, he's badly injured and fighting for his life.

I sit on my new bed and turn my back on him, opening button after button as I take off my pajama shirt and slowly clean my body with the sponge, shivering for a moment at the touch of the cold water.

"He can't see me," I whisper to myself as I roll down my hospital pants. I won't look in his direction. *He's not here, it's just me and my wall that already knows my body.* My hand gently rubs my thighs as I clean myself, keeping my back to him.

After that, I keep quiet when I put iodine on my wound and cover my amputated leg with new bandages, feeling no pity for myself like a proud nurse. But the tears keep flowing down my cheeks, and I can hear my heavy breathing as I hold myself back from screaming in pain, so glad he's unconscious and can't hear my sighs.

"Did you manage?" Audrey asks me later when she pulls back the curtain and comes to check on him.

"Yes, thank you." I lie in bed, waiting for the pain to go away, scratching my hips.

"Next time," she smiles at me, "try to stay here and not run away when the ship arrives. You just injured yourself again. You have to remember that even though you're not a nurse anymore, obeying the rules is always good for the wounded as well."

<hr />

I'm in pain. The hospital is quiet late at night, except for the soft music coming from the nurses' room. I can't fall asleep while I lie all sweaty in my bed, trying to overcome the pain in my leg that has come back. I scratch my hips with my fingernails, sighing and trying not to shout for help.

I must have something to help with the pain, a shot of morphine, just one shot to let me fall asleep like before, when the nurses agreed to help me.

I'm trying to get up, sending my hand towards the wall, but the bed of the silent wounded man prevents me from reaching it, keeping me away. I can't even peel the plaster from the wall, and my fingers scratch my arms as hard as I can while I bite my lips, but the pain in my amputated leg continues.

"Please stop, please stop," I whisper to the pain. I can't go on like this, and I feel the tears in my eyes when another wave of pain comes.

"Please go." I bite the white sheet spread out on the bed,

trying not to whine, but when the next wave of pain arrives I can't hold myself back from sighing, tucking my face into the mattress. Maybe it's good that there's music in the hall, so no one hears me.

I think it's an opera, maybe from the BBC radio broadcasting from Naples or a station in the north, the area still under German occupation. But the pain hurts so much, and I can't concentrate on the music. What should I do? I'm scratching my leg, trying to hurt myself elsewhere, anything to stop feeling those waves of pain, but it doesn't help. I can't hold myself back anymore, I have to ask them to give me something. My whole leg burns with pain and the scratches I've made with my nails.

As quietly as I can, I grope for the crutches placed by my bed, trying to hold them with my trembling hands, getting off the bed and crossing the quiet hall and the sleeping wounded, hobbling to the nurses' room. But as I approach their station, I see that the nurse on call is not alone. A few of them are standing in the small room, laughing with each other, and I stop where I am and turn around, hobbling back to my place. They're probably laughing now about the one who wanted to be a nurse and ended up crippled. I'll handle the pain by myself.

A new wave of pain arrives, and I grab the bed's iron frame as tightly as I can, trying to stop my shaking hands.

Breathe, breathe, don't shout. I won't cry now. Everyone else is asleep or suffering quietly, except for the nurses who laugh in their little room, even the silent Italian cleaner walking through the hall and cleaning the floors probably suffers from something. I'm no longer sure if I really see her walking in her black dress, or maybe I've started to hallucinate.

"Help me," I whisper to her when she nears me, "please help me."

She turns to me and says nothing.

"Please, I need you to help me," I whisper to her as she approaches, and I look at her, trying to see her face in the dim light. Does she understand what I'm saying?

"I need you to help me move something," I whisper to her again, not wanting the nurses to hear over the music coming from their room. Even though I'm not sure she understands me, she comes closer while I get again out of my bed and stand by the silent wounded man.

"I need you to help me change our beds," I say to her. "I need to be by the wall." I lean my crutches against the peeling wall and support myself with the metal bed frame, starting to pull and move it.

"It doesn't matter to him," I explain to her as we move the beds, even though she doesn't ask why I'm doing it. "He's blind and silent, he doesn't see anything anyway." But she says nothing. She just finishes moving the beds with me and hands me the crutches, ignoring my sweating face and my sighs. Maybe she didn't notice, maybe she just didn't understand.

"Thanks," I whisper to her as she walks away and returns to her cleaning job. I follow her with my eyes as she bends over between the wounded beds in the dark, disappearing with her black dress, leaving me alone with my pain and the silent wounded man.

"Sorry," I explain to him, sighing as my fingers crumble the plaster. "I needed my wall. To you, it doesn't matter at all." But he doesn't answer me.

"It hurts so much," I whisper to him, wiping tears of pain from my cheeks, reaching out my hand and tightly gripping his bed's metal frame. "Does it hurt for you like that too, even though you're silent?" In the dark, I can't tell if he's breathing at all. "Are you alive?" I ask, not expecting an answer, but I manage to get a little closer, reaching out my hand and feeling his lips. They're still warm.

"You're alive," I whisper to him, wiping away another tear. "They must have given you morphine for you to not suffer, and now you're in dreamland." My fingers wet his lips with some water from the glass next to his bed. "Don't get used to it. When they quiet you down, the pain will make you want to die."

<hr />

"Audrey, I'm in pain. I need morphine." I stand in front of the little nurses' room the next day, tightly gripping my crutches so she won't notice my shaking hands, though she'll probably notice the sweat on my forehead. I just need one dose until my wound heals again. If only I hadn't fallen that day when I tried to jump over the stone fence.

"Gracie, I'm sorry, I can't give you any." She looks up from the book she's reading.

"I need it. It hurts so much."

"Gracie, you know you were addicted to it."

"But I'm in pain, just one shot, I'm not addicted," I search for the narcotics shelf in her little room. "I'm strong enough for that." My hands grip the crutches tightly.

"No, you're not." She closes her book. "I've seen strong soldiers get injured, you're not one of them."

"I am. I'm a nurse like you, I've treated injured soldiers like you. I've seen things."

"Gracie, how long have you been an intern nurse?" She gets up from her chair and approaches me.

"A long time, from the time I landed in Italy until I was injured," I answer her, not wanting her to know it had only been eight days.

"Italy wasn't a long time too, although to you it may seem like an eternity." She looks at me. "A few days isn't a long time. Two years is a long time. I was in the first wave that landed in North Africa in '42, when it all started. Back then, in '42, no one thought we'd still be fighting in Italy two years later. Back then we just thought that we had to beat them," she slowly says. "I'd already seen too many wounded in this war when we fought the Germans, and when we fought the Italians; I've seen enough wounded for a lifetime. And I know you're not strong enough to get morphine without getting addicted. You don't even understand that you were injured yet." She looks down at my missing leg, and I lower my eyes, wanting to turn around and hobble back to my place.

"Aspirin, that's the most you'll get from me," she keeps talking, and I reach out my hand to her like a beggar. I don't like her calling me Gracie.

"I'm glad you understand." She smiles and turns her back to me, taking a handful of pills from one of the glass jars on the shelves and placing them in a small jar for me.

"Thank you," I whisper to her, holding the pills tightly. "They'll help me." But I know that by nighttime they won't be enough.

"Gracie," she calls me as I turn around and start my journey to my corner.

"Yes?" I turn back to her.

"Do you smoke?"

"No." I want to tell her my name is Grace.

"Start smoking," She walks over to me, taking a box of cigarettes out of her white uniform and stuffing it in my pajama pocket. "If you havne't seen enough injured soldiers yet to start smoking, then maybe you should look at yourself and realize it's time for you to start. Who knows, maybe it'll calm you down."

"Thanks."

"You're welcome," she smiles at me. "And if you're bored, you can always read a book." She goes back for a moment, takes the book lying on the table, and gives it to me. "We nurses have too much work anyway, we don't have free time to read. Now get back to your bed and get some rest, I see you're sweating."

"Thanks," I answer her quietly, but she's already turned her back on me and gone to talk to one of the other nurses who's entered the hall.

"Are you coming to the pilots' club tonight?" I hear the other nurse ask Audrey as I slowly hobble away, supported by my crutches and careful not to drop the book and the jar of pills.

"Sure I'm going, are you coming too?" Audrey answers. "I like one of them, and I need a break from all the work here."

"I hope it's not the handsome one I like," the other nurse laughs, and they approach each other and whisper.

"Pick me up in the evening. I'll be ready." I can still hear Audrey answering her when the other one leaves the hall.

"I'll be ready tonight too," I whisper to myself. I have a book and aspirin pills to fight the pain.

"Wall, it hurts. What should I do?" I whisper to it at night. I must do something before I start sweating again.

My fingers fumble for the jar of aspirin standing on the metal locker, and I open it, pour its contents out and swallow some pills, feeling them burn in my throat. I don't care that I have no water, I won't touch the glass of water belonging to the quiet wounded man, not even one small sip.

How much time has passed? I feel the sweat on my back, I should count the minutes to give the pills time to take effect. "Please, pain, stop," I whisper. I have a book, I can read the book.

My shaking hands hold the book she left me. I'll try to read. "Wall, do you hear? I will read to you." Maybe even the silent wounded man will listen. I need light.

I have a candle in the drawer, but I don't have matches or a lighter. Maybe the silent man has one? "Do you have a lighter?" I ask him, knowing he won't answer. Would it bother him if I looked for a lighter in his bag? I don't think it would bother him at all, he's almost dead anyway. All the soldiers have lighters in their bags, they usually engrave sentences on them for luck, believing it will keep them from reaching this place.

"I apologize, I have to," I whisper to him as my hand searches for his bag, which has been thrown inside the locker. I feel the remnants of mud covering the bag peel off and fall to the floor. "I'm only searching the bag pocket. I only need your lighter for a moment, my leg hurts so much."

"Thanks," I whisper to him as I feel the cold metal touch of the lighter, and I pull it out and light the candle, place it on the locker, lean back and open the book.

"Do you want me to read to you?" I ask him, and start reading without waiting for an answer. If I stop for just a moment, I won't be able to continue. I must try not to think about the wave of pain that has just arrived in my leg, as though it were waiting for the dark night. I must keep reading, mumbling the words and thinking of something else. "Do you hear?" I ask the wounded man after a while. "The heroine has a beautiful dress, and now she's on her way to prom, but all that interests her now is that she's really in pain, but the author didn't dare write that in the book, he thought they would think she isn't a heroine. What do you think about dances? Do you live at all, or are you like the wall?" But the wounded man doesn't answer me. Maybe he's not alive anymore? Every now and then I put my fingertip to his lips, feeling their heat or wetting them with some water, just to avoid thinking about the pain.

"Nurse Audrey, do you hear?" I whisper when a new wave of pain strikes my leg, and my fingers crumple the pages, gripping them tightly. "I've overcome the pain, I'm reading your book." I wipe the tears with my fingers, trying to straighten the wet and crumpled pages. Soon the pain will pass.

But the morning isn't coming, and I read page after page to the wounded man, I mustn't stop.

"Head Nurse Blanche, do you hear?" I stifle a shout as I scratch the book cover during the next wave of pain. "I am a nurse, I'm taking care of someone, I've read him a story." But I can no longer hold on anymore, and I grab the book and toss it against the wall, bending over the bed and filling my mouth with the white sheet, suffocating my sobs.

"Here, you can see, I'm a trained nurse. I can treat another wounded person," I keep whispering to the silent man as I wipe away my tears.

"I've even managed to wet your lips with some water, or maybe those are my tears, but you don't mind," I whisper to him as I stroke his lips with my wet fingers.

Breathe slowly, let the wave of pain pass, get out of bed, and look for the book on the floor. I will read to him a little longer, maybe the wounded man is in pain too.

"I'm glad you took my advice," I hear Nurse Audrey's voice the following morning, and turn my eyes from the wall. She stands by the silent man's bed and looks at the open book thrown onto our shared locker.

"That really helped." I sit up in bed and hold the book, not wanting her to notice its crumpled pages. I also take back the crushed cigarette box thrown onto the locker, trying to straighten it after clutching it last night.

"I'm glad it hurts less." She begins to change the silent wounded man's bandages.

"Last night I had almost no pain at all." I gently caress my scratched knees, careful not to accidentally touch the amputation below. I'll have to ask her for iodine for the scratches.

"You know," she continues talking to me, "I also wanted to be deployed to the front as a nurse. But I decided I wanted to be by their side when they wake up in the hospital, to be the one helping them recover." She bends down and gets close to him, her white dress and chest almost touching his body. "John, how are you this morning?" Her fingers stroke his hair.

"I wanted to save lives," I whisper to the crumpled box of cigarettes I hold in my hand. "I wanted to be the one who kept them alive until they got here." I tuck the cigarettes deep inside my shirt pocket and look at Audrey. She sprinkles sulfa disinfectant powder on his chest, making sure not to soil her white uniform with the powder.

"Don't you think those are decisions we should leave to God?" She smiles at me and turns back to him. "John, how are your wounds today?" She takes his open pajamas to the sides. "Gracie wants to take the Lord's role on the battlefield, she wants to be the one to decide whether you should live or die. But it seems to me we should leave that decision to the true God, don't you think?"

"That's not what I meant," I answer, wanting to crumple the pages of the book I'm holding again.

"I know," she smiles at me. "I was just kidding, but it doesn't matter to John anyway, does it, John? Did you know his name is John?"

"No, I didn't know that." I look at the silent wounded soldier, trying to imagine him as John. She hadn't told me.

"It's written on the board by the side of his bed. You can see it for yourself." She looks at the bandages she's replaced for him with satisfaction. "Now let's see how you are. It'd be best if you didn't go running around again. Does the amputation hurt now?" She smiles at me.

"It doesn't hurt at all." I grab the sheet tightly and smile at her. "Can I replace the bandages myself? I want to practice."

"Are you sure you can?" She looks at me.

"Yes, I have to study."

"Less work for me." She places the jar of sulfa powder and bandages on the white locker. "If you fail it, call me." She strokes John's hair again. "Bye, John, and make sure to rest."

She turns her back and walks away to the hall where all the wounded are.

"How long should I rest?"

"About a month, until the next ship arrives."

<hr />

"John?" I get closer to him after she leaves. "John, can you hear me? I'm Grace, the one who was in pain last night." I examine his lips and the bandages over his eyes. "Nice to meet you." I extend my hand and touch his fingers, shaking his hand.

His fingertips are warm, but he doesn't respond to my touch, and I can only notice his chest rising and falling with every breath he takes.

"John, did you hear Audrey?" I speak to him a little later. "If you live, you have a month to be by my side while I rest, a month to hear my sighs at night." But he does not respond.

"I wanted to be a nurse and take care of the wounded," I whisper to him, even though we're both alone in the corner of the hall, separated from the others, and I don't have to whisper. "But I probably won't tell anyone I'm a nurse anymore, certainly not like I did that time in Chicago, before I boarded the ship that brought me here."

"I'm going to the war in Europe," I shouted to the soldier holding me in his arms while dancing, at the ball in Chicago.

"Can I see you again before you go?" he shouted back, trying to overcome the music in the huge hall.

"Soon I'll be leaving."

"What are you going to do there?"

"I'm a nurse," I smiled at him. All around us soldiers with neat uniforms and medals held their girls and danced.

"Will you take care of me if I get injured?" he brought his lips close to mine, trying to overcome the loud jazz music that the band was playing.

"I promise," I laughed, placing my hand on the back of his neck and stroking his hair as we danced close together. But I did not let him kiss me.

"Do you hear, John? I didn't let him kiss me, and now I won't dance or kiss anymore. I'll just rest and wait here for the pain to arrive at night, until they send me home. What would you do if you were me?"

※

"Give me something to do." I stand next to Audrey, who is changing a bandage for a wounded soldier in the hall.

"Gracie, you should return to bed, your job is to rest." She pauses for a moment and turns to me.

"Give me something to do. Let me help you." I try to stay stable as I lean on my crutches.

"You can't help me. You're injured. You need to lie down and rest."

"I'm a nurse like you."

"Gracie, you're no longer a nurse like us, you never were, even if you really wanted to be," she says, before returning to hold the wounded man's hand.

"But you have a shortage of nurses, don't you?" I hand her the scissors, trying not to lose my balance, careful not to slip in front of the other wounded men watching us now.

"Thank you." She takes them. "We're at war, we always have a shortage of nurses, but we know how to manage with the ones we have." She begins to cut his bandage, exposing the wound.

"So let me help you." I hand her the bandages. "I don't want to lie down all day. I'll do whatever you need."

"Is there something wrong with your corner? John's company shouldn't bother you. He's blind and barely alive." She looks at me again for a moment. "Or does it bother you, and you want your privacy? Do you know we're at war?" She hands the scissors back and puts iodine on his wound.

"No, he's not bothering me at all, and yes, we're at war, and I came to the war as an intern nurse. I want to learn."

"You came to this place to rest and wait for the ship back home, not to be an intern nurse. We don't need you to help us here. We get along." She looks at me for another moment. "Maybe the Italian cleaner who usually curses everyone is looking for help." She smiles at me before turning her back and moving on to the next wounded soldier, asking him how he's feeling, leaving me standing alone in the center of the hall. All the wounded are watching me.

Keep on going back to your place, don't lift your eyes, just a few more steps to your corner, ignore all the wounded looking at you. They must be whispering to each other and pitying you. Just a few more steps.

I'll wait quietly in my bed, just as Audrey wants me to, and I'll read in my book as Audrey wants, and I won't be in pain as Audrey wants. Just a few more steps, just another month of waiting for the ship.

When I get to my corner, I firmly hold the scissors still in my hand and mark a line on the plaster of my wall. Tomorrow I will mark another, just as she wants.

"John, do you hear? They don't want me. Without my leg I'm unneeded," I tell him as I sit on my bed and hold the book. "They want me to lie here in bed next to you and wait for the ship to take me home. They want me to be crippled at home.

"Do you think a disabled woman like me can dance and kiss?" I keep talking to him, and thumb through the book pages for no reason.

"I wanted to be a nurse, John, and now Audrey wants me to be a useless rag doll who rests and waits for the pain at night and for the ship to arrive, whichever comes first." I look at the book in my lap. "I'm not even good enough to help the Italian cleaner who curses everyone."

My fingers search for the page I'd stopped reading yesterday.

"I don't want to be a rag doll, and she hasn't cursed me yet," I tell him, and close the book.

It takes me a while to find the Italian cleaner who curses everyone, but finally, when I go out into the garden, I see her walking among the wounded in her black dress. She passes between them and hands them glasses of sweet juice made of synthetic orange-flavored powder.

"I want to help you." I approach her, but she walks away from me to the next wounded soldier sitting in a white garden chair, looking over the cliff to the sea.

"I want to help you." I follow her, but she just looks at me for a moment and walks to the next wounded soldier. Maybe she didn't understand me.

Without asking her, I begin to move between the wounded ones sitting in the garden chairs, taking the empty glasses from their hands. It seems they only hand them to me out of surprise, and I hobble on my crutches and chase the Italian.

"Please take them." I place two empty glasses on the tray she's holding. I can't take more than two glasses, and even then, I'm panting from the effort of chasing her through the large garden, my healthy leg still sore. My amputated leg bothers me too, but I won't give up.

"Please take them," I say to her again, giving her another two empty glasses, but she keeps ignoring me and continues to walk among the wounded. I won't break, not now, I'll have enough breaking moments at night in front of my wall, when the pain arrives and everyone is asleep, I'm scared of the night.

Again and again, I hobble between the wounded men sitting in their white chairs and enjoying the sun, taking empty glasses of juice from their hands and turning to look for her, but suddenly she's not there.

The garden is full of wounded men sitting in white deckchairs, and two nurses bend over and hold one of them, trying to help him walk, but when I look around I see no woman in a black dress walking around carrying a tray in her hand. I start to move between the wounded soldiers, searching for her, but she's gone, and finally I throw the empty glasses I'm holding onto the grass, I have no strength to keep carrying them. But I keep on searching for her. I don't want to go back to my corner, to let Audrey see that I'm resting. I am a nurse. At the end of the garden, I notice the edge of black fabric behind the old shed, and when I get closer, I see her.

She's sitting on the ground by the old shed wall, where I was sitting that day when I ran away, wiping her cheeks and not noticing that I'm standing there watching her.

I take a few steps forward, debating whether to tell her anything, but then she notices my presence and looks at me as if expecting me to say something, her eyes red from crying.

"Thank you for helping me then, when I tried to go down the stairs, and with the bed that night." I approach her slowly, but she keeps looking at me with her black eyes and says nothing. I don't think she understands me at all. I take one step closer.

"Thanks," I tell her again, and she answers me in Italian and wipes her eyes. Maybe she's cursing me like Audrey said she used to do, and after a moment of silence where we examine each other, I turn my back to her and start hobbling to the garden. She doesn't understand me anyway.

"I hate you all. You are the same as them," I hear her tell me in English with an Italian accent.

"I just wanted to thank you." I turn to her.

"I hate you all. You are the same as them," she repeats, wiping her red eyes again.

"What do you mean, the same?"

"You Americans, you're just like the Germans." She begins to speak English in her Italian accent and doesn't stop. "Why did you have to come here from New York to my village? Don't you have enough country of your own?"

For a moment, I want to tell her that I'm not from New York, but from Chicago, but she doesn't stop talking, and it seems to me that she is speaking more to herself than to me.

"Of all the villages in the world, why did you have come to mine and destroy it? You and your soldiers and your tanks and your planes, you come and occupy and destroy our houses, and take for yourself what is left and plant your flag, as if everything here belongs to you. You are just like them." She keeps on talking and wiping her tears.

"We are different," I try to explain to her. "We're not like them."

"Yes, you are different." She looks at me with her eyes black and red from crying. "They said danke and achtung, and you say thank you. You just think you're different. The only difference between you and the Germans is you have better cigarettes." She finishes talking, wipes her teary cheeks, and turns her eyes away from me, looking at the cypress trees surrounding the hidden corner behind the shed.

I want to answer, to explain to her that she is wrong and that we've come to free them, and I approach and stand over her, hearing her quiet sobs even though she's looking away from me.

She's about my age, maybe two or three years older, and has long black hair and light brown skin, tanned from the local sun, and her fingers tremble when she wipes her eyes.

"Cigarette?" I take the box of cigarettes I'd received from Audrey out of my pocket and hand it to her, and she takes one without saying a word, looking at me for just a moment with her dark eyes, turning her gaze to the treetops.

And I carefully lean the crutches on the wall and sit on

the ground next to her, watching as she lights her cigarette and smokes in silence, and we both examine the smoke curling in the air. I have no idea what she's thinking as the tears continue dripping down her cheeks.
"Francesca," she says after a while.
"Grace," I answer.

"It's my job, not yours, don't take my job," she says when she finishes her cigarette, throws it on the dry ground, wipes her eyes, and gets up.
"I want to help you," I say, but she doesn't answer me and walks away.
I look around at the dark green trees and the mountains on the horizon, hearing the wounded talking in the garden behind the shed. I won't continue to sit here waiting for the evenings and nights to come, even if she doesn't want me to help her. I've run out of other options. No one else wants me anyway.
I start to get up, trying to support myself, and reach for the crutches leaning against the wall. But when I try to grab the wooden sticks, I slip and fall, hitting the ground.
Breathe, breathe, breathe. I'm trying to stifle the scream of pain that emerges from my mouth, tucking my lips in the dirt and whimpering hoarsely into the hard ground. My aching hand that stopped the fall gropes and feels my injured leg, examining whether it has been damaged.
Just keep breathing. I slowly lift my head off the ground, looking around. Did anyone see me fall? Does anyone pity me?
I can still hear the wounded talking in the garden, and no one is coming to help me. At least no one saw what

happened, the Italian woman who walked away also didn't hear my scream. I just have to ignore what happened, it didn't happen, no one sees the tears. My nails scratch my knees and thighs again, gently touching my amputated leg. I must stop crying.

It takes time for me to sit back and lean against the shed wall, and it takes time to clean my mouth and lips from the dirt and dry leaves, and it takes time for me to take the cigarette box out of my hospital shirt pocket and tuck a cigarette between my lips with my shaking hand.

But I have no matches or lighter, and I stay seated, leaning against the wall with the unlit cigarette between my lips, feeling the smell of tobacco while my fingers crumble the plaster of the old shed wall. What will I do when I fall like this next time, and everyone sees and pities me?

Only when the sun starts setting, and the wounded are escorted into the building by the nurses, do I rise of my hiding place and walk among them, looking at the grass, careful not to slip again, raising my head every few steps and smiling at them.

"See you tomorrow," I say to Francesca, but she doesn't answer me.

I'll go back to my corner and clean myself, and I'll swallow the aspirin pills that don't help me again. And I again I won't sleep at night and read from Audrey's book to silent John, and tomorrow I'll again look for the Italian who hates me, running after her with empty glasses of orange juice.

Step by step, I cross the aisle between the beds of the wounded, my eyes on the floor, counting steps and trying to remember the last page I'd read yesterday, but when I get to our corner and sit on my bed, I see there's a bundle of letters on our locker, tied with a thin, coarse rope. No one has ever sent me letters.

A Bundle of Letters

I gently hold the bundle of yellow letters, inspecting the army stamps and addresses covering them before I turn the package around. Who sent me letters? But when I look at the name on the first envelope, I see they're not for me, they were written to silent John. I place them back on the metal locker standing between us, and go back to lie in my bed, turning my back to him.

But after a while, I turn from my wall and hold them in my hand again, feeling the thin paper and imagining they are mine. Since leaving home, I haven't received any letters, and I know I won't receive any either. No one from home would write to me, certainly not my mother or father, and I have no one else waiting for me. My mom works from dawn to dusk as a saleswoman in a clothing shop, coming home after sunset, preparing food for Dad, tidying up the house and going to bed. And my dad barely works and just goes out to the neighborhood bar every night with his Polish friends, drinking beer and cursing the Nazis. When he's home, he just sits next to the radio and listens to the evening news broadcasting the battles, cursing the Nazis. At the beginning of the war, he prepared a large map of Europe, ready to mark the liberation of Poland with small pennants; but after the Germans invaded Russia and the whole map was filled with small Nazi pennants marking their progress toward Moscow and Stalingrad, the map disappeared from our living room one day, though the cursing remained. I smell the letters I'm holding tightly in my hand, bringing them closer to my chest and imagining that they're mine, even though they're his. They have a faint and pleasant smell of flowers.

"I see you've received some letters, won't you open and read them?" I open my eyes and see Audrey standing next to me. How long has she been there?

"I'll open them soon. I'm resting now."

"You must have been waiting for them for a long time."

"Yes, I was waiting for them for a long time." I hold them tightly, hiding his name with my palm.

"Who's it from?" She smiles. "Do you have someone waiting for you at home?"

What should I answer her? Shall I tell her that back home, when I went to all those dance clubs, I didn't find the one I wanted, and now it's too late? Shall I tell her how they used to compliment me on my fashionable curly hair, like in the magazines, and now no one will compliment me anymore?

"I have someone at home," I say quietly.

"You didn't tell me that," she touches my arm and smiles. "Now you have a reason to recover and go home."

"Yes, I have a reason to go home." I try to smile at her. Why am I not telling her the truth?

"You should tell me about him someday." She turns her back to me and starts taking care of John, changing his bandages. "Do you hear, John? Our Gracie has someone waiting for her at home." I hurry to tuck the letters under my pillow. He doesn't care anyway, he's barely alive.

At night, when the hall is quiet and dark, and the pain in my leg comes back, I take out the letters from under my pillow and examine them, but it's too dark.

"John, can I borrow your lighter?"

He doesn't answer me.

My fingers rummage through his bag, and I pull out the lighter, light the candle, feeling the engraving on the metal lighter again with the tip of my finger. In the dim light of the candle, I can't see what's written.

"Thank you, John," I whisper to him, examining the bundle of letters, even though I know they belong to him and that I shouldn't do it.

The yellowish envelopes are dirty with dust and mud, but I can read the name John Miller in round handwriting.

"John Miller, nice to know, your name is John Miller." I stroke his lips and wet them with a bit of water, feeling his quiet breathing.

"Who's writing to you?" I ask him after a while, still looking at the package, even though I know he won't answer me. My fingers turn the envelopes over and look for the answer, but I must untie the thread binding them to see. Only his name is visible, and a stamp with sloppy handwriting in it: Military mail, Tunisia, Third Division, transfer to Italy.

"John, may I untie the thread?"

My fingers gently untie the knot, and the letters spread over my bed's white sheet. I take the last one, holding it in my hand and examining the stamp.

"Let's see," I speak to him. "Do you know someone wrote you a letter half a year ago? Where were you at that time? In Tunisia? I'm sure it's a woman, according to the round and neat handwriting, even though I haven't opened it, it's yours. Why didn't you receive it when you were in Tunisia?"

I try to imagine him in uniform, walking in the desert in all those places that barely made headlines at home. When I was still in Chicago and went to the cinema, they would show those places in the news once in a while, before the film. "Our brave soldiers," the announcer enthusiastically described the American soldiers fighting the Germans, "in Kasserine Pass, Marrakech, Casablanca," he'd say the foreign names.

I try to remember other places he mentioned, and failed.

"I was so jealous of those newsreels," I keep talking to John. "I also wanted to fight for our nation. The soldiers always seemed smiling and happy, unlike my parents at home. Did you smile at the movie cameras when you walked in the desert?"

I move slightly away from his bed and lean back in mine, looking at him. "What's your height?" I think he's much taller than me, but I'm not sure, I've never seen him standing. I pull back the blanket covering him, only for a moment, and examine him in the dark. He's taller than me, I mustn't do that.

"I apologize. I just wanted to know." I cover him again, arrange the blanket, and stroke his hair. I have to return the letters to him, they're not mine, but I need to imagine there's someone who loves me at home, just for a few more moments.

I wet his lips with some water and wet mine too, I'm not used to talking so much, even though he's just listening and saying nothing. I turn the envelope over, in a moment it'll no longer be mine, and I wonder about all the hands and mailbags it went through until it arrived in Italy and into my hands. It's time to say goodbye to my momentary letter. It belongs to silent John. I'm not allowed to view his personal belongings.

"Well, her name is Georgia, she lives in New York State, and she wrote you a letter. Are you from New York State, too?" I ask him, but he stays quiet and doesn't tell me if Georgia is the name of the woman waiting for him at home, or maybe his mother, or anyone else at all.

For a moment I hear the nurse on the night shift walking around the hall, and I stop talking to John, hiding the letters under the pillow, not wanting her to start asking me about them.

"What did Georgia write to you six months ago, when you were in North Africa?" I ask him after the nurse walks away, returning to her bright room at the end of the hall. "Aren't you curious to know? What's on your mind when you lie there with your eyes covered? Do you also feel alone? Or do you feel comfortable in the warm cloud of morphine and the knowledge that there's someone at home who loves you?"

I hold the letter in front of the candlelight, trying to see what's written inside the closed envelope. But I can't read anything, and the mud stains on the paper also interfere, though I try to gently remove them with my fingernails. Would he like to know? Would I want someone to read me the letter if I were in his place?

"John, would you like me to read you one of the letters, or read to you from the book? Which do you prefer?"

At first I go back to the book, trying to read it to him, but as I read it in a whisper, my eyes pass the same line over and over again until I finally put the book aside and take the first letter. Just one letter.

I gently open the envelope and start reading the long lines written in curly handwriting.

"My John,

It was snowing this week, and our school's basketball court was covered in white flakes, making it look like a soft white blanket waiting for us to walk and chase each other, as we did the winter before the war, that time that you kissed my frozen nose..."

I stop reading, look at the bottom of the letter for the signature, then look back at John, who listens to me in silence.

"Well then, Georgia is probably your girlfriend. I don't know yet, because I haven't read the whole letter, but you kissed her nose when you ran after each other in the snow."

I must not continue to read him the letter. This is his love, not the love of a crippled woman who happens to be next to him right now, doing something she shouldn't be doing. Still, I can't stop reading, and my lips whisper to him all the words written in the letter, until I finish with Georgia's kisses. He must be glad I read to him. If I were in his place, I would be happy if he'd read to me.

"That's it, that's the letter from Georgia who loves you, but there's more." I gently fold the paper and return it to the envelope, tucking the whole pile of letters under my pillow, even though they're not mine. I lie down in my bed and look at the dark ceiling.

"Tell me, John, what does she look like? Is she nice?" I can't fall asleep. "Maybe you have a picture of her?" I ask after a while.

I reach out and grope for his leather bag in the dark, and rummage through its pockets until I feel the hard paper of a picture, pulling it out, lighting the candle again and looking at her.

Georgia 1941 is written on the back of the picture in her curly handwriting, and when I turn it over, she smiles at me. She has short blonde hair, slightly curly and fashionable. I also had curly and fashionable hair, but brown, not golden like hers. And she has green or blue eyes, I can't tell in the black and white photo, not dark like mine; and she's wearing a floral summer dress rather than an ugly hospital uniform.

She smiles at John, who probably was the one photographing her leaning against a tree in a field full of weeds and bushes, where they lived, or maybe they went hiking before Pearl Harbor happened and it all started.

"You're lucky she loves you. You're lucky to have her," I whisper to him after returning the picture to his bag in the locker, but not before I smell it. The hard yellow paper of the picture no longer smells of flowery perfume.

I then fill my mouth with aspirin pills, blow out the candle, turn my back to John, and stroke the wall with my fingers, looking with my fingernails for more pieces I can peel. I hope the aspirin overcomes the pain tonight and I can fall asleep. And I hope someday someone will love me like that too.

The next morning I mark another line on my wall, even though I've decided not to do it anymore. I also hide John's letters in my bag, even though they are his. Then I pick up my ugly crutches and walk away from my corner filled with silent John and the picture of Georgia who loves him. I'm glad I told Audrey that I have someone, at least she won't feel sorry for me.

Bag, bag, bag, bag, my crutches hit the floor as I lower my gaze while walking through the hall among the wounded. Thirty-eight steps from side to side, I counted them yesterday. I have to raise my head so they won't feel sorry for me, but what if I don't pay attention, slip and fall? I deserve to fall. I'm a liar who reads letters that aren't hers. I deserve nothing more than working as an assistant to the cursing Italian.

And so the next day passes, and the next few. Every morning I mark another line, and every afternoon I chase after Francesca, holding empty glasses of synthetic orange juice, and every evening I read John a letter from the package sent by the woman he loves. And every night I swallow aspirin pills and sigh in pain in the dark.

John remains silent, and there are days I read him letters I've read to him before, choosing the parts I like most and trying not to stain the thin paper with my tears, ruining Georgia's curly handwriting, so I can read them next time as well. It seems to me there are parts I already know by heart.

And Francesca still ignores me, even though she lets me put empty juice cups on the tray she carries while walking through the garden in her black dress. And Audrey lets me bandage myself every morning, placing the bandages and sulfa powder on the metal locker before she goes to treat the other wounded men. This is the closest I'll ever get to being a nurse. I have to do more.

"John, do you hear?" I whisper to him at night when I finish reading one of the letters, folding it back up and returning it to the envelope. "Do you mind if I touch you?"

I wait a moment for him to respond, but he doesn't answer me, and I make sure the curtain is drawn, separating us from the other wounded before I pull back his blanket, examining the bandages and his breathing.

"I'm going to start here." I whisper to him. "Tell me if I'm doing something wrong." I carefully remove his bandage, setting it aside, and bring his lighter closer to his body so I can examine the wounds on his chest. I'd made sure to wash my hands thoroughly beforehand.

"Now tell me if this hurts you." I sprinkle the disinfecting sulfa powder on his body from the jar Audrey left this morning for my wounds.

"I think it's okay. You're not complaining." I open the clean bandages she'd left for me and start dressing his body. If I want to succeed at being a nurse, I have to practice. I'll change a bandage myself every few days.

"I think I did a good job." I run the lighter close to his body, checking the bandages I've placed and smiling at him. "I'm a nurse." I bring my lips closer to his, imagining I'm the good nurse from the movie, the one I saw then in the Chicago movie theater before the war started. But I don't kiss him, just hold my lips tightly and close my eyes despite the darkness, imagining the touch. He's not mine, he has a woman who loves him at home.

"Good night, John," I whisper to him as I return to my bed and cover myself, swallowing my aspirin pills. "Tomorrow I'll read you a letter and replace your bandages again."

"Your injury is getting better, the bandages are really clean," Audrey smiles at him the next day as I follow her with my gaze. My injured leg bothers me, but I'll get over it. Will she notice that I treated him?

"I'm glad you have less infection," she strokes his hair after she finishes cutting off the night's bandages and throwing them to the floor, waving for Francesca to come pick them up. But Francesca continues to clean among the wounded on the other side of the hall, turning her back to Audrey and ignoring her sign.

"Grace, please call the Italian to come clean here."

"One moment, I'll just finish getting dressed." I turn my back to her, opening and closing my pajama buttons.

"I don't know why we hired her. She's an ignorant Italian who doesn't know English at all. How do you even talk to her?"

"Maybe she needed a job."

"She should look for work elsewhere, not with us."

"But they're under our occupation, we need to take care of them, don't we?"

"Have you been to North Africa?" She stops taking care of John and comes to stand in front of me.

"No." I look up at her, continuing to hold onto the buttons of my open shirt.

"If you'd been in North Africa, you wouldn't feel sorry for them or think we should take care of them. I saw what they're capable of doing."

"Who, the Italians?"

"No, the Germans."

"But she's Italian." I keep looking at her and finish closing my shirt, wanting her to move so I can take my crutches.

"They fought side by side with the Germans, they're just like them." She throws my bandages onto my bed. "If you'd been in Tunisia and seen their planes bombing convoys of trucks, your opinion would be different." She puts the sulfa jar in my hand. "You think the plane that wounded you was an American plane? And the soldier who wounded John? And all the others here?"

"Yeah, you're right." I stand on my leg, jumping and pushing myself between her and the wall, taking my crutches. "I hate her as much as you do, but I have no other choice. She's the only one who lets me be with her." I turn my back on Audrey and start hobbling around the hall looking for Francesca, or the ignorant and cursing Italian as Audrey calls her.

"We didn't intend to destroy your village. It must have been a mistake," I tell Francesca later that day when I see her go to the corner behind the old warehouse. I wait a few moments, then follow her.

The pleasant morning sun is warming the garden full of the wounded, who sit in their white chairs waiting to recover, and for the ship that must be already on its way here to take us home. At least that's what the lines on my wall tell me.

"You Americans never mean to." She moves her gaze away from me to the blue sea on the horizon, and sits down on the ground, leaning against the wall.

I look at her and stay standing, afraid to sit and fall like last time.

"Did someone destroy your New York?" she continues speaking to the sea.

I look at her fingers, seeing them peel off the plaster of the warehouse wall, crumbling it and throwing the reddish powder on the dry ground.

"No, no one destroyed New York."

"Have you been to my village?" She peels another piece from the wall.

"No, I haven't been to your village. I haven't had the time yet." I try to imagine her village. I have to sit next to her. I carefully support myself on my crutches and get down on my knees, removing the dry leaves, sitting down carefully and leaning against the wall.

"Once, before the war, there was a movie theater in the center of the village. We used to go there every Saturday evening to see a movie. Now there is empty sky, a gift from a German bomber."

"I'm sorry," I answer, thinking of the ruined houses in Naples that I'd seen then, the first day I landed in Italy.

"And of the square and the fountain, where we used to drink water when I was a child, only stones remain. I don't know whose gift that was," she continues to speak in her Italian accent.

"I'm sorry." I don't know what else to tell her.

"No, you're not really sorry. You live here in this mansion you took for yourself when you arrived. You made a little America here, with an American flag and American food, and American music played on a turntable you brought from America or found in an abandoned house. You don't care about my village and my fountain. But at night you send letters back home to intact New York. I'm in Italy. It's so beautiful here."

I search for something to tell her while my fingers stroke the envelopes tucked in my shirt pocket. I need to return them to John, they're his. I couldn't resist and took them with me, even though I shouldn't have.

"Do you have a cigarette?" she asks me after a while, and I give her one, remembering the cigarettes I had and the bunch of kids that day, when I arrived by ship at the ruined port of Naples. I no longer remember the port we left in Sicily, I just remember the spring sun and that I'd had many cigarettes and two legs.

The grey landing ship slowly approached the city of Naples, back then in the early spring. I was standing on the deck, looking at the houses slowly growing in the distance, and Mount Vesuvius revealed itself through the morning mists. The city had already been freed from the Germans a few months earlier, and was considered safe and clear of German snipers and mines they'd left behind while retreating, hidden among the rubble of houses and under stone bridges. But still, the top deck was full of alert sailors standing behind anti-aircraft machineguns, searching the morning sky with their eyes for enemy planes that might attack the convoy. The yellow lifebelt that had been tied around my neck since we boarded the huge landing ship burned my neck, and now, as we got closer to the city, I loaded my duffel bag, laden with personal gear and cigarettes even though I didn't smoke, onto my shoulder.

"Take them, you'll need them after landing." The quartermaster threw cartons of cigarettes and food ration packs at us from a truck standing on the dock, as we boarded the landing ship.

"Uncle Sam is sending you to war. Take his presents." He kept throwing packs at every soldier standing in the line, and I watched all the senior soldiers who'd fought in North Africa and Sicily, and I wanted to be as experienced as them. They grabbed the packages thrown by the corporal and shoved them in their pockets and heavy duffel bags, and I liked them, filling my duffel bag too, even though I didn't smoke.

"Get ready to go down to the shore," the metallic sound was heard hours later on the ship's speaker, and we lined up again in straight rows, watching the ship glide over the filthy black, oily water, slowly entering the ruined port of Naples.

Like an angry boy scattering and overturning his toys, the retreating Germans had left the port of Naples as devastated as they could. Cranes were blown up and thrown into the water, and I watched their metal skeletons sticking out of the dark water in a mess. Capsized ships lay near some of the docks, exposing their red bellies to the sky as if they were huge, bleeding whales, painting the green water with patches of black oily fuel. But the striped and star-shaped flag was seen over one of the ruined buildings, and from the grey landing ships with us in the convoy that were decked out before us, I could see a steady stream of khaki trucks and soldiers going down to the shore.

"Lowering the ramp," the speaker announced in his metallic voice, and the ship shook as the anchor chains were tossed to stern, stopping the ship as it opened its metal mouth to the dock and lowering the heavy ramp.

"Beginning departure," the speaker on the ship's bridge said goodbye to us, and I started walking in line, following the backs of the soldiers in front of me, going down the ship with the noise of heavy trucks and the smell of diesel fuel all around us.

"All the new ones gather here," a sergeant called to us on the dock, waving with his hands and trying to overcome the noise of engines and driving crawler belts from several Sherman tanks that had just passed near us, shaking the concrete of the docks. "Wait here," he shouted, "we'll see how to arrange transportation north, to the front lines, for you."

"*Americano, Americano,*" a group of barefoot children ran carelessly in our direction, skipping briskly between the khaki trucks and a stack of diesel barrels, approaching the new soldiers gathered on the dock.

"*Cigaretta, signorina, cigaretta.*" They surrounded us and held out their hands.

"Andare via, go away," the sergeant shouted at them, and they ran from him while laughing, continuing to smile at us, keeping a safe distance from the sergeant.

"*Cigaretta, signorina, cigarette,*" they kept calling to us from a safe distance, smiling with their white teeth, and I looked at them one by one with their smiling faces. One child was smaller than the others, trying to push out his hand and imitate the older ones, but he stood a few feet away, afraid of the sergeant.

"*Andare via*, get out of here, *no cigaretta*," the sergeant tried to drive them away. "They use cigarettes as money on the black market. They exchange them for food," he explained to us while threatening them with his hands.

"*Gracia, signorina, gracia, signorina, viva America*," they yelled at me after I took the cigarette cartons out of my duffel bag and held them out in my hand. Like stray cats, they quickly approached and snatched them from my outstretched hand, while keeping a safe distance from the sergeant who was momentarily away, directing a convoy of trucks departing from one of the landing craft, and immediately running away. At a safe distance from the sergeant, I saw them stopping and opening the cartons, and the tallest boy among them lined them all up and handed them my cigarettes equally, even to the little boy who had barely reached out his hand.

"*Viva America,*" they waved goodbye to me one last time before disappearing towards the townhouses overlooking the harbor. I stood there, looking at the large buildings. Some were perforated with bullet marks, and some had simply disappeared into a huge pile of bricks, leaving only a single wall facing a blue sky.

"You're a good woman," the sergeant shouted in my direction after a while. "It suits you to be a nurse." He tried to overcome the noise of more Sherman tanks crossing our way, but though I only smiled back and didn't answer him, I just thought that I didn't need the cigarettes, even though almost all the soldiers around me smoked.

But now it's summer, with a warm August sun outside, and I'm no longer a nurse, and I have no idea what happened to the children who took my cigarettes in the port of Naples. The next time I visit there, the ship home will be waiting for me.

"Someday I'll come visit your village," I finally say to Francesca, feeling the stone wall at my back and looking for a piece of plaster to peel.

"Yes, one day you'll come visit my village, and one day you won't conquer us anymore, and one day my husband will return from the war in Russia," she answers, and it seems to me she's wiping away a tear. "Do you have a cigarette?"

Again she finishes smoking the cigarette I gave her and says something in Italian, getting up and returning to the garden. This time I don't try to get up and chase after her, but stay seated and follow her with my eyes, peeking at her from behind the warehouse wall.

She walks among the wounded and her black dress flutters with each step she takes, and I try to imagine her holding the hand of the man she loves as they'd walk hand in hand in the village square, where I've never been. How do you feel when you love a man and lose him in a war, so far away in the cold Russian winter?

"It has nothing to do with me. She's just an Italian cleaner," I whisper to myself, rising cautiously and starting to follow her among the wounded, smiling at them, ignoring the sweat and pain of walking with my ugly crutches. Soon the day will end, and I can return to my corner.

"Gracie, do you like to swing dance?" Audrey asks me at the end of the day, as I enter the hall and pass the nurses' station.

"What do you mean?" I stop and turn to her, all sweaty. I have to clean myself.

"I just wanted to know if you like to dance." She smiles at me, straightening her tight white dress with her hands.

"Yes, I love to dance," I answer, and hold my crutches tightly as I lean against them, remembering last summer.

"Where are we going tonight?" I'd ask my friends at the nurses' school every weekend, and we'd argue and laugh and pick a club, going inside and waiting on the sidelines, smiling at the handsome soldiers in their decorated uniforms who kept inviting us to dance with them, not giving up even when we turned them away.

I liked my light pink dress the most. I'd hold the hand of the guy I chose that evening and spin in his arms as quickly as I could, feeling the fabric fluttering around me like I was a flower just spreading its petals to honor the soldiers going to war. I'd say goodbye to him at the end of the night with a smile, promising that I'd never forget him. Then I'd go home by myself, knowing we would never meet again. But it didn't bother me. I knew another soldier would approach me the following weekend, excited to invite me to dance.

"Yes, I like to dance," I answer again, watching her arrange her lipstick.
"We're going to visit the pilots in the evening. They have a club at their airfield." She smiles at me.
"But how will she dance?" another nurse from the nurses' room asks her.
"Yeah, you're right," Audrey replies, "it's a pity you can't join us, you'd probably enjoy it."
"Yeah, it is a pity," I answer, turning around and hobbling away from them, looking down so I don't fall.
"At least you have someone waiting for you at home." I can still hear Audrey.
"Does she have someone at home? She's lucky, especially if he's already proposed to her," I hear the other nurse.
"I wonder if she's already written to him about her injury," Audrey answers her.
Bag, bag, bag, bag, bag, bag, thirty-eight steps across the hall with downcast eyes, to my corner so I can lie in bed and look at the wall. I've been played for small gossip between the nurses.
"Gracie," I hear Audrey and don't want to turn around.
"What?" I stop and turn around, looking at her from a distance.
"We didn't really mean to hurt you. It's a shame you can't come with us." She smiles at me as she arranges a lock of hair back in place, examining herself in the little mirror she holds in her hand.

"It's okay," I answer, and turn back. She didn't really mean to hurt me.

When I lie down in my bed, I take the pack of cigarettes out of my pocket and hold a cigarette in my mouth. Feeling the bitter tobacco taste, I play with John's lighter, opening and closing it again and again. My eyes watch the flame, but I don't light the cigarette. I have a few more hours to play with the lighter until night comes, and I can read him by the candlelight.

"John, do you hear?" I read him one of the letters late at night, after I've finished changing his bandages, holding the thin paper close to the dim light of the candle flame.

"She loves you, and she misses you, waiting for you to return home." I open another letter, reading her words of longing and feeling so sad.

"She asks why no letters have arrived from you. She looks at your picture every night, she keeps it in a drawer next to her dresser." I read him the following letter, written last fall. "It's raining again, and she was walking alone on the street, thinking of you." I wipe away a tear.

"John, are you asleep? Or will I keep reading you another letter?" I stroke his black hair, even though it belongs to Georgia. Maybe he'll imagine she's the one stroking his hair.

"She says there's a new teaching staff at school this year, and that there are almost no men left in town. Is she a teacher? She also writes that almost all the men have been drafted into the army, like you. And there are only two male teachers in the whole teaching staff, and she misses you so much. Why didn't you write to her?

"Was the ship carrying your letters sunk in the Atlantic

by a German submarine?" I keep talking to him. "Or were you not able to sit and write to her about love, with all the death around you in the North African desert?" I take a short break to sip from his glass of water. "What happened? Why did you let her miss so much?"

I start to feel the pain in my leg, and I open my box of pills, filling my palm and swallowing them, grimacing at the bitter taste.

"Shall I keep reading you?" I ask him, but then I hear a noise from the hall entrance and look up. Some nurses noisily enter the quiet, dark hall and approach the nurses' station, filling it with sounds of laughter, and it seems that they're a little drunk.

"They've come back from the pilots," I whisper to him. "There's a military bomber airfield nearby, behind the hill, and they invite the nurses to come visit them at the squadron's club. They say the pilots are handsome. It's nice to meet like that, but it doesn't matter to me. Who would like to meet me the way I am?"

The sounds of laughter from the nurses' station increase, even though the nurse on duty is trying to silence them.

"John, it seems to me that I'll continue to read to you tomorrow." I reach my hand out in his direction and stroke his lips.

"Please continue," I hear him whisper, his voice barely heard. But his lips move, and in surprise I blow out the candle and drop the letter on the floor.

John

"Nurse," I hear him whisper in the dark.

I have to call the nurses, tell them he woke up. I get out of bed as quietly as I can, holding its iron frame so as not to fall, and fumble on the floor with my fingers, searching for the letter I'd dropped.

"Nurse," he whispers again. That's not my job. I get up and place the folded letter under my pillow, careful not to make any noise. I didn't know he was listening to everything I'd said and read to him. How long has he been listening to me for?

"Nurse," his lips slowly move. I look at the light coming from the nurses' station; they're still laughing with each other, probably talking about the pilots.

"Yes, I'm here," I finally answer him.

"Where am I?"

"In a U.S. Army hospital south of Rome."

"How long have I been here?" He speaks slowly, barely mouthing the words.

"A few days." I wet his lips with my fingers after placing them in the glass of water on the locker.

"Thanks," he whispers.

"You need to rest."

"Have we taken the damned Florence yet?"

"Yes, we've taken the damned Florence," I quietly answer, and it seems to me that he smiles in the dark when he hears my answer.

"And you're the nurse who takes care of me and reads to me?"

What should I answer? I look towards the nurses' station again, and the nurses making noise. I have to call one of them.

"Yes, I'm the nurse who takes care of you," I whisper to him.

"It's very dark here. I can't see anything."

"Yes, you were injured. You need to rest. Don't speak now."

"Will you read me more?"

"Yes, I'll sit next to you and read to you, now rest." I stroke his hair and lean into his backpack, rummaging in his front pocket, looking for his lighter to light the candle again.

Now that he's alive, I allow myself to read the engraved inscription on the brass lighter by the light of the candle: Third Division, to Hell and Back.

"You've got a long way back," I whisper to myself as I open another letter from the bundle.

"What did you say?" I hear him.

"My beloved John, I miss you so much," I start reading him the letter from the woman who loves him and is waiting for him to come home.

<hr />

"Good morning, how are you?" I open my eyes and look at my wall, hearing Audrey by my side, but she's not talking to me.

"We were worried about you. How are you feeling?" I keep hearing her.

"I'm in pain."

"You were injured. You need to recover. It's going to take time." I roll over in bed and look at them, her hand stroking his black hair while she smiles at him.

"You have a different voice," he whispers to her, and I turn back to my faithful wall again.

"What do you mean?"

"When you read to me, you had a different, more pleasant voice." I smile at the wall.

"I didn't read to you."

"Some nurse read letters to me."

"You must have dreamed it. You were badly injured. There was no other nurse here who took care of you," she tells him, and I sit up. I have to get away from here before she figures out who's calling herself a nurse. My hands hold my crutches as I quietly walk away from them. I'll come back later, after she leaves.

"There's just a wounded woman lying next to you, but she's not a nurse, she's just a wounded woman." I can still hear her.

Bag, bag, bag, bag, I keep hobbling on the hated crutches, my new legs forever, bag, bag, bag, bag.

"Are you the one who read my letters?" he whispers to me at night as I sit down in bed and rummage through his bag, looking for his lighter. What should I answer? Maybe he'll believe I was a dream?

"Yes, it's me," I answer him after a while.

"Thanks."

"It was nothing," I look down at my missing leg, forgetting that it's dark and he can't see anyway.

"Why did you read to me?" he asks after a while.

"Because you were alone in the dark."

"It's dark here," he says, as if to himself. "Sometimes painful, sometimes pleasant." I want to stroke his hair and tell him not to get used to the pleasant morphine, but I know I mustn't, I'm not a nurse anymore and I don't have the privilege to stroke his hair. He also has a loving Georgia waiting for him at home.

"So you're lying here by my side?" he asks.

"Yes."

"How were you injured?"

"A minor injury. I'll recover soon." I don't want him to feel sorry for me. The pitying looks of the nurses and the other wounded are bad enough.

"And you wanted to be a nurse too? The other nurse told me when she replaced my bandages."

"I was an intern." I play with his lighter, flicking it on and off, enjoying the sound of the metal closing on the flame.

"An intern in this war is a nurse," he whispers.

"Yeah, isn't that ironic? A nurse gets injured instead of taking care of other injuries?"

"Yes, this war is full of irony." I notice his smile as he slowly turns his face towards me. "What is your name?"

"Grace."

"Nice name."

"Thanks," I answer, and shed a tear. But it's because of the pain in my leg.

"I didn't introduce myself. I'm John." He moves his fingers slightly while his hand rests on the white bed.

"Nice to meet you, John." I touch his fingers.

"Will you read me more letters? Or dreams, as the other nurse said?"

"I've read you all the letters you got."

"Then we'll have to wait for a new letter to arrive."

"Yes, we'll have to wait for a new letter to arrive. I can read to you from a book I have here."

"Grace?"

"Yes, John."

"Can you read to me from the book you have?"

"Yes," I smile to myself.

"I like reading books. Soon I'll recover and go home. It seems the war is over for me."

"Yes, the war is over for you," I whisper to him and open the book, reading to him by candlelight, not wanting to tell him that for him, the war has only just begun.

"Grace. Grace," I hear him sigh.

"Yes, John," I open my eyes and turn in his direction. I can see his silhouette in the dark.

"Grace, are you here? I'm in pain." He sighs again.

"Where does it hurt?" I sit up, leaning close to him. The hall is quiet tonight.

"Everything, the wounds, they hurt."

"Try to describe to me where it hurts."

"Waves," he sighs, "all over my body." I touch his fingers and he closes them tightly, holding my hand.

"Have you received any painkillers today?"

"A long time ago, the other nurse gave me a shot, Grace, I'm in pain. Please help me."

"I'm not allowed to give you painkillers. Only she takes care of you. I'll go call her."

"Thanks," I hear him sigh again, and I get out of bed, grabbing my crutches and crossing the quiet hall, walking towards the light emerging from the nurses' station.

"Grace, why are you awake at such an hour?" Audrey asks me, looking up from the newspaper she's reading.

"It's the wounded man next to me, John, the blind man. He's complaining of pain, he's asking for a shot of morphine."

"Is he complaining and wants morphine, or are you the one who wants the morphine?" She smiles at me.

"John." I look at her.

"And you don't want a shot too? I remember you're in pain as well."

"No, I'm not in pain at all. I don't need the morphine," I answer, looking down to my missing leg, wanting just one shot so much.

"Okay." She gets up and walks to the medicine cabinet behind her, unlocking it and handing me a small glass vial. I haven't held one like this in so long.

"Here you go, inject him. You were an intern, you should know how to do it." She sits back in her chair and takes the newspaper.

"But you have to inject him, not me." I hold the vial in my trembling hand until I'm afraid it will fall and shatter.

"I trust you." She doesn't even look up from the newspaper. "I don't hate you as you might think."

Thirty-eight steps through the dark and quiet hall to my corner and to John. I'm careful not to drop the vial and syringe in my hand. All I need is to stop for a moment and inject myself. He wouldn't know. No one would know. I'd inject half for myself and half for him, he wouldn't notice the difference, and I'm in pain too. The terrible pain was just waiting for this time to emerge, asking for the morphine itself.

"Nurse?" John asks me as I stand by my bed.

"It's me, Grace."

"Is she coming?" he moans.

"She's coming soon."

"Thanks."

"Try to fall asleep in the meantime."

"I'll try," he sighs again, his fingers clenching into fists.

Don't think, don't think, take the syringe, draw the material from the small vial, hold out your hand and inject. Don't think, you deserve to feel better.

"Thank you, nurse," he moans.

"Try to rest." I open the box of aspirin lying on the cupboard, trying to take a handful, but the box falls to the floor and I hear it shatter to pieces. My hands hold the iron bed tightly as I bend to the floor, searching in the dark for my pills, ignoring the shards of glass hurting my fingers. I must find my pills.

"Grace, are you okay?" I hear him.

"Yes, I'm fine," I answer, and shove two pills into my mouth. I must find more, to soothe the tremors and pains.

"John, are you still in pain?" I finally whisper to him after managing to swallow enough pills. I get back to my bed and try to bandage my injured fingers with the sleeve of my pajama shirt. I grope the metal locker, I might have leftover bandages. But he doesn't answer me, the morphine has already worked its magic and he's fallen asleep.

I'm still in pain. It'll take time for the pills to help, if at all.

"Good night, John, pleasant dreams." I wet his lips before lying in my bed and closing my eyes, trying to calm down. Even for me, the war is far from over.

"There are no new letters, just a newspaper." I return to our corner, holding the folded newspaper under my arm. For several days now, I've been going to the garden to work with Francesca, who refuses to talk with me about her missing husband, and after finishing my work, I pass through the nurses' station to find out if new letters are waiting there for him.

And every morning, when Audrey comes to take care of him and smiles at me as if on cue, I get out of bed and walk away, letting her treat him in private. I cross the hall with downcast eyes, ignoring the looks of all the other wounded men, returning only after she's said goodbye to him and continues to treat the rest of the injured.

Most of the bandages have been removed from his body and face, and he's already leaning back on his pillow, looking in my direction when he hears my crutches beating the floor as I return to our corner. Only his eyes remain covered in white bandages Audrey has changed for him.

"Did you go again?" he says when he hears my crutches, his hand buttoning his shirt. I notice that the shrapnel wounds on his chest are healing and slowly becoming scars, the same German cannon shell shrapnel that hit his eyes and took his sight from him.

"I don't want to embarrass you."

"Aren't you a nurse? You must have seen worse than me." He follows me with his head as I sit down on my bed.

"You're getting better every day." I smile at him,

remembering after a moment that he can't see me, so I touch his fingers resting on the white sheet.

"The other nurse told me you've been here for a long time."

"Yes, my recovery is taking more time than I thought."

"I don't think she likes you."

"I think she tries to help me sometimes."

"She has a smile that doesn't like you. Why does she hate you?"

"How can you tell? Are you listening to her smile?"

"I'm in a world of darkness and pain, what do I have left to do but listen?"

"Paris has been liberated after four years of German occupation," I read the headline to him, not wanting to keep talking about me.

John looks in my direction for a moment, as if thinking of what to say. "Four years of occupation," he finally says, "Four years waiting to be free."

"It's not over yet," I continue reading to him from the newspaper. The Germans have withdrawn from Paris, but they are reforming their lines on the Belgium border.

"It's over for the French, at least. Do you think you would've survived?"

"Survived what?"

"Four years of occupation."

I hold the newspaper, looking at a photo of the rows of American soldiers marching under the Arc de Triomphe, the masses of French people standing in the street cheering for them, and I wonder if I would have survived. How would I feel if I were a young Frenchman having to live under German occupation? What was it like to see a German soldier?

"Do you think they destroyed Paris?" I finally ask him, trying to read more in the article.

"They destroyed the bridges in Florence," John speaks slowly. "They blew up bridge after bridge to prevent us from crossing them. They only left the oldest bridge undamaged, for some reason. Maybe they didn't have time to blow it up."

"Have you seen a German soldier up close?" I ask after a while. How afraid would I be of German soldiers if I was in Paris under Nazi occupation?

"Yes," he quietly answers.

"How was he?"

"He was the enemy. He wanted to kill me, just as I wanted to kill him."

"Well, John, let's see if we can get you out of bed." Audrey stands between us and smiles at me with her perfect red lipstick, a cue that my time with John is over, and I smile back at her and get out of bed. She'll be all over him until evening.

"Have you ever killed anyone?" I ask when the hall grows quiet at night, and Audrey says goodbye to him and walks away.

All day, as I was walking in the garden with the empty glasses, I looked at the wounded soldiers sitting in their chairs and tried to guess which of them had killed German soldiers.

"Yes, I have," he finally answers.

"And were you afraid of them?"

"You know," he speaks quietly, almost whispering, "since landing south of Rome, at Anzio, I haven't been afraid." He pauses for a moment, and then continues: "We were on our way to the beach in small landing craft, and we all knew the Germans were waiting for us. We all held our weapons tightly." I can see his fingers closing into a fist in the dark. "We waited for the boat ramp to drop, so we could start running towards the sand and the German machineguns." He stops again for a moment. "In the distance I heard cannon fire from the huge warships firing at the shore, like thunder. I heard the engine noise of our small boat struggling against the waves. We were all trembling from the cold wind over the sea, and the foam of the waves splashing into the boat. But most of all we were trembling with fear. Some soldiers vomited, some prayed silently, one soldier held the cross on his necklace and closed his eyes." He brings his hand close to his neck as if to show me, and I unwittingly touch the small silver cross around my neck while he keeps talking. "But I was just trembling with fear. Can I have some water?" he asks, and I serve him the glass, placing it in his outstretched palm. He takes a few sips.

"Thanks," he whispers, and continues: "In that fear, I looked at the morning sky turning red in the east, and I wasn't afraid anymore." He pauses, taking a few breaths, and I look at his lips by the faint light of the candle, waiting for him to continue.

"You see," he continues slowly, "I always knew that one day, in a month or year, I don't know when, but the day would come when the war would be over. And at that moment, on the small landing craft making its way to the beach, I decided that when that day arrived and I went back home, Private John Miller of the United States Army would no longer exist. There's Private John Miller, and there's me. It's not me who fights and shoots people on the beaches in Italy. It's him."

"But you were injured," I whisper to him, looking into his bandaged eyes.

"It doesn't matter, I came through the landing at Anzio and the siege, I survived the fighting near Rome, I came through the battle for Florence. I was wounded, and I'll recover, and I'll return home, and everything will return to normal. John Miller of the Third Division of the United States Army will remain here on Italian soil. He won't return home with me."

"And who will you be when you get back home?"

"I'll be who I was, John Miller, from my small town of Cold Spring in New York. Who I've always been."

"Good night, John Miller of Cold Spring, New York," I say to him when I finish reading another chapter of the book and blow out the candle. Maybe he'll dream about home tonight.

"Good night, Grace from America," he answers. "I don't even know where you're from."

"I'm not from a small town. I'm from Chicago."

"Good night, Grace from Chicago."

"Pleasant dreams about home."

"You too," he says, and I think about home. Maybe I'll dream I have both legs tonight, or that the war is over.

"The Russians are advancing in the east. They've taken tens of thousands of German POWs," I read the newspaper headlines to him the next day, after Audrey replaces his bondages and leaves. "No new letter for you, I'm sorry."

"I have patience, a letter will arrive soon." He looks in my direction.

"You'll go home soon." I try to imagine his small town.

"We'll both go home soon." He smiles at me, and I wonder if Audrey told him about my escape from the convoy last time, but I'm ashamed to ask him what she's told him about me. Soon the ship will arrive again. I can already feel it, they're starting preparations. This time they won't let me escape. I won't be the nurse I wanted to be, not here and not at home.

"Tell me something about your hometown." I try to change the subject.

"Cold Spring? There's not much to tell, one main street, with a grocery store, a barbershop, a clothing store, a shoe store, all the stores a person might need." He smiles at me. "And everyone knows everyone. Lots of trees, a river, and the train station to the big city of New York." He leans back and looks at the ceiling as if imagining the main street and the cars driving through it. "One small town, so close to the big city."

I want to ask him about Georgia, but I'm embarrassed and look back at the newspaper, examining a picture of a long column of German POWs captured by the Russians under the same headline declaring Russian victories in the east.

"I'll be back later, John." I suddenly get up and say goodbye to him, reaching my hands out for the crutches leaning against the wall. I have to do something.

"Grace?"

"Yes, John?"

"You have a lot of grace in you," he smiles at me, and I look at him and think he wouldn't have said that if he knew I was lying to him about my injury.

"Francesca," I find and call her to come with me to our corner behind the shed, pushing the newspaper into her hands once we're there, showing her the headlines.

"The Germans are withdrawing from France. Why are you showing me this?" She looks at me.

"No, the second headline, the Russians are taking German soldiers as prisoners of war."

She looks at me and doesn't seem to understand what I want to tell her.

"Maybe your husband was also taken prisoner. Maybe he's alive."

Francesca looks at the newspaper and examines the picture for a long time. Maybe she's trying to find her husband in the huge curving column of black dots captured by the Russians, but suddenly she throws the newspaper on the ground.

"Do you think the Russians will keep them alive after what the Germans did to them in Stalingrad? Do you really think they will give the Italian prisoners food and coats for the winter, after they fought side by side with the Germans?"

"You have to believe that they will." I try to stand in front of her.

"To believe?" She looks at me angrily. "It's easy for you to tell me I have to believe, isn't it?" Her eyes blaze with rage, and the little silver cross around her neck shakes with every word she says. "And what about you? Do you believe? I heard you screaming at night when you didn't even know my name. I'd clean under your bed and hear you begging to die, or asking God to return your lost leg. I heard you cry to the nurses to give you more morphine. Do you still believe someone will let you go back to being a nurse, and not just pick up empty glasses after the Italian woman?" She takes a few steps away from me, her black hair scattering everywhere, but after a second, she turns back to me. "It's easy to tell others they have to believe in things that won't happen." She spits on the newspaper lying on the ground, steps on it and crushes it, tearing it to pieces with her shoes. "I do not believe the Russians or the Germans," she doesn't stop talking. "And you should stop believing that your leg will grow back and that you'll be a nurse again." She starts walking away from me, spitting on the newspaper again. "I didn't tell you I have a husband who disappeared in the Russian winter so that you'd pity me. If anything, I feel sorry for you, and out of pity I let you feel you're worth something by collecting empty glasses of orange juice."

"I don't pity you, and you don't pity me," I shout back at her, but she doesn't stop walking, and I start crossing the garden behind the hospital, passing the wounded men sitting in their deck chairs and the Italian woman collecting glasses of empty orange juice from them. I don't care whether they look at me or what they think of me, the crippled woman with the crutches. I don't care what the Italian in the black dress thinks of me either. I slowly approach the edge of the cliff overlooking the sea and look down, playing with the crutches on the edge of a rock, jamming the tip of the wooden sticks into the hard stones.

The blue waves at the bottom of the cliff cheerfully shatter on the black rocks, spreading white foam around them. Below me, down the narrow path going from the cliff to the beach, I can see two off-duty nurses dressed in fashionable blue and mustard swimwear, making their way to the white sand.

"The sea is beautiful from here." I hear a voice and turn around, careful not to stumble.

"Yes, Head Nurse Blanche."

"Do you like the sea?"

"Yes, I do," I answer, even though I don't like it anymore. I haven't gone to the sea since arriving here. Back then, at home, packing my things for the war, I placed a swimsuit in my bag. But now it's too late.

"When do you know it's your last time?" I ask her after standing together in silence for a while.

"You never know." She keeps looking at the horizon. "Or rather, it's for you to decide when the last time will be."

"Sometimes the war decides for you." I think of the red swimsuit I had. It was lying at the bottom of my army duffle bag, lost the day I was injured. Maybe it's better that way.

"And sometimes you decide for the war," she replies, still looking at the horizon. "There are those who aren't nurses anymore, yet they give wounded men morphine at night, or just read books to them, or help Italian women. It seems to me they're the ones deciding for the war."

"I don't think the Italian woman wants me to help her anymore." I keep looking down at the two girls who have reached the foot of the cliff and are now walking on the white sand, looking for a place to lie in the sun.

"Sometimes people are in pain even if their body looks unharmed," she says, and walks away. I follow her with my eyes and see her approach Francesca, taking a glass of orange juice from her and thanking her, gently touching her arm.

Francesca ignores me the following days as I try to help her. She proudly turns her back to me and walks among the other wounded, collecting their glasses and not smiling at anyone.

"Aren't you working with the Italian anymore?" Audrey asks me as I enter from the garden, panting and struggling with the crutches. "I thought you liked her." She smiles at me.

"No, I'm still working with her," I answer, turning towards my corner. I don't want to talk to her about Francesca.

"Right from the start, when you arrived, I knew you were the kind of person who liked them."

"Them who?" I stop and turn to her.

"Them, the Italians."

"What's wrong with liking them?"

"Do you remember that they're our enemies?"

"They're no longer our enemies, we occupied them, they've surrendered and banished Mussolini." I start hobbling away from her towards my corner.

"And do you think banishing Mussolini puts the past away? That's it, they're no longer our enemies?"

"Do you think Francesca is our enemy?" I stop walking and turn back to her.

"She surely doesn't like us."

"Yes, she doesn't like us," I quietly answer.

"They fought against our soldiers, the Italians. Now they deserve to suffer, don't you think?"

"Don't you think they've suffered enough?"

"We give her a job. I think we're doing pretty big favors for those who were shooting at us just a few months ago. I think that's more than enough."

"I don't think she ever shot at anyone. I think she's trying to survive, like the rest of us."

"It's their fault they chose to be fascists. I'm not sorry for them." She smiles at me with her red lipstick.

"I think nurses are supposed to like people."

"I think you're not a nurse, so you surely can't have an opinion about that."

"I used to be a nurse."

"No, you were an intern, now you're a cripple waiting to go home, even though the last time you managed to escape me."

"I apologize that it was during your shift."

"It seems to me you've recovered enough if you no longer need the lovely morphine. Soon the white ship with the Red Cross will come pick you up. You'll have to return to our beloved nation and stop connecting with our enemies."

"The ship is on the way?" I take one step closer to her.

"Don't worry, it's probably on its way somewhere in the Atlantic Ocean, trying to avoid German submarines. Maybe you like them too?" Why does she hate me so much? What did I do to her?

"Maybe I like people."

"Maybe it's time for you to go home, don't you miss home?"

"Yes, I miss home," I answer, turning my back to her and walking to my corner, not telling her that I miss my leg most of all.

"Is that you, Grace? I can recognize you by the walk." He smiles at me, and I stand at a distance from him, leaning my hated crutches against the wall. At least John and the wall are blind enough not to see my missing leg.

"Yes, it's me. Sorry, there's no letter." I sit down on my bed. "Say, John, what do you miss most?" I ask, and regret the moment the words came out of my mouth. I should be more sensitive.

"It's personal." He looks in my direction.

"Don't you have something you miss that isn't personal?" I can't hold myself back, I'm tired of being so alone with my pain.

"I miss the landscape," he replies after thinking for a while, and I feel ashamed for asking.

"I miss the view of Tuscany," he speaks slowly. "The hills that gently slope towards the dirt roads, the cypresses standing tall at the sides of the fields, marking our paths." He pauses before continuing to talk: "You know, I knew we were at war and that the Germans were hiding in front of us, in battle positions, and that I should be careful. But every night, before I closed my eyes in a ditch or an abandoned house, or just lying in the field under the stars, I imagined that one day after it was all over, I'd bring her here, to show her the hills of Tuscany."

I get out of bed and walk away from him, leaning against the wall even though it's uncomfortable for me and I have to hold onto the window. But I don't like being close to him when he talks about the woman he loves.

"You should really bring her here when the war is over."

"And here? Outside the hospital, how's the view?"

"Beautiful as the hills of Tuscany," I answer, even though I've never seen the hills of Tuscany, only the ruins of Naples and the hospital tent where I worked non-stop during the attack. Since then I've been here, in this large mansion that has been turned into a hospital.

"Describe the landscape to me, I can imagine what you see."

"I'm not sure I can describe what you want to hear."

"I've heard you read me stories and letters. I'm sure I'd like your words." He gets up in bed and sits as if waiting for me to start talking.

I hold my crutches, lean on the window frame and start talking to him. "We're in a hospital by the beach, but from our window it's impossible to see the sea. The sea is on the other side," I continue describing it to him, mixing reality with my imagination. What does it matter what's outside? He can't see anyway. "From here you can see the green hills stretching towards the mountains."

"What else do you see from our window?"

"The driveway at the front of the hospital. It's beautiful and well-kept and surrounded by trees." I look at the front driveway and the military trucks parked on the side, next to a stack of fuel barrels. "At the center of the front driveway is a patch of flowers." I look at the military jeep parked near the entrance, next to the big white flag spread out on the ground with the Red Cross marked in its center.

"What kind of trees?"

"Tall, upright cypress trees, on either side of the front gate." I see the two officers leaning against the jeep next to the front steps. They both have visor caps brown leather pilot coats. "Next to each of them is a beautiful bougainvillea." They talk to two nurses in white uniforms while standing in the same indifferent pose of the self-confident officer. "The bougainvillea is close to the cypress trees, literally flapping on them and climbing between their branches, filling them with flowers."

"Georgia loves flowers."

"The bougainvillea has a strong fuchsia color." I see the two nurses laughing, probably from a joke the pilots told them.

"She loves roses the most. I used to bring her roses. Do you think there are roses here?"

"I'm sure you can get roses here. There must be a rosebush here you can pick." One of the pilots places his hand on the nurse's arm, and it seems to me that she likes his touch.

"When I recover and return home, we'll get married." I turn to him and see him smiling in my direction.

"I know she's waiting for you." My fingers caress the window frame.

"She wanted to get married before I went to war, but I didn't want to. I was afraid something would happen to me, even though I didn't tell her that."

"So what did you tell her?" I look at his bandaged eyes. Why haven't any of the nurses had the courage to tell him he'll be blind?

"I told her we'd write letters to each other, and when I returned from the war, I'd propose to her. It'll happen soon."

"Yes, it'll happen soon. The ship is on its way." I look back at the window, seeing the pilots hugging and kissing the nurses goodbye as they get into the jeep.

"She's waiting for me," I hear him whisper to himself.

"Yes, she's just waiting for you." The nurses keep standing on the front stairs, looking at the jeep driving away through the broken gate.

"I miss her smell so much. Have you ever felt such a strong longing like that?"

"No," I whisper to myself as I look at the jeep moving down the main road towards the airfield, following it with my eyes until it disappears behind the hill. I'm lame like the other nurses, I also don't have the courage to tell him he'll remain blind.

At least I can try to get him roses so he can smell the flowers of the woman he loves.

"Where can I get rose perfume? Or rose flowers?" I ask Francesca the next day. It took me time to stand in the corner of the garden and wait for her to go behind the shed. When I saw her disappearing behind the wall, I crossed the garden and joined her, placing my crutches on the wall and sitting next to her. This was my corner first, and if she's still angry at me, she can find another corner for herself.

"You can go look in the village. Maybe the Germans left perfume after they withdrew and took everything to their dear fraus in Berlin," she answers, looking the other way.

"Can you try to get me some?"

"I'm busy. I don't have time to help you."

"Do you think I can go to your village like this?"

"You can ask one of the nurses to go instead of you."

"I can pay you in cigarettes if you don't have time to help me."

"Do you think you can offer me cigarettes out of pity?"

"I don't pity you," I raise my voice slightly.

"You're from America. You're spreading your cigarettes all around because you're sorry for us."

"Do you think I feel sorry for you?" I burst out at her. "Don't you think I'm busy enough pitying myself? Do you think I just don't want to see your village?" I raise my voice. "Do you think it's nice for me to stand on the edge of the cliff and watch the other nurses go to the sea? Or going to visit the pilots? When all I do is look down at the floor all day so I don't stumble." She keeps looking away from me. "All you think is that I'm a spoiled American who's full of cigarettes.

Here, take my cigarettes." I throw the box at her.

"*Americana*, I did not mean…" she whispers, and I notice that she is shedding a tear.

"Just don't you pity me." I try to get up, wanting to be alone, but when I place my hand on the wall my palm slips on the plaster, and I fall again and hit the ground. The wave of pain and offense breaks through my whole body, and I shove my face in the dirt and the dry leaves, whimpering into them.

"*Americana,* are you okay?" She gets up quickly and tries to hold me.

"Go away, don't pity me," I whisper to her while sobbing with my eyes closed. I can manage the pain by myself. "Leave me alone, please."

"*Americana,*" I feel her hand touch my hair.

"Just go, please go." I keep my eyes closed and don't raise my head.

Only after I can no longer hear the rustle of leaves around me do I open my eyes and lift my face from the dirt, carefully standing up and looking around, trying to make sure no one saw me fall. I don't want anyone to feel sorry for me. My hands clean the dry leaves off my clothes as much as I can. At least I wasn't injured like last time. The squashed cigarette box was left lying on the ground, and I want to pick it up, but I'm afraid I'll slip again. I'll leave it where it is, Francesca will probably take it next time she sits here.

Step by step, I return to the garden among the wounded, supported by my crutches and acting as if nothing happened. When I look around, I don't see Francesca, but when I enter the hall in the evening and reach my corner, there's an enamel mug standing on the locker, filled with red roses. Next to the flowers is a letter for John that someone left there.

Dear John

"*Dear John,*" I begin to read the letter to him by candlelight, and only my whispered voice is heard in the dark hall.

"*It's been so long since I've written to you, and frankly, it's been so long since I've received a letter from you.*" I stop for a moment and look at him.

"Please keep reading," John looks at me and smiles, reaching his hand out and groping for the rose in the enamel mug, holding the red flower in his hand.

"*I don't know how to write...*" I read quietly and stop, continuing to read the following lines without whispering the words.

"Grace, I can't hear you."

"Wait, I can't read it." I bring the paper closer to my eyes, continuing to read a few more lines.

"Is everything alright?"

"The light from the candle is too weak. I can't understand what she wrote."

"Is everything okay? I hear something different in your voice."

"No, everything's fine," I answer. "I fell in the garden today and it still hurts a little, but it's nothing." I remember at the last minute that I haven't told him about my amputated leg. "The candle's almost gone. I'm going to get a new one. Give me a few minutes." I get out of bed, my hands gripping the letter tightly.

"I'll be waiting," he replies, smelling the flower in his hand.

"Crippled Grace, what woke you up at this hour? You can't fall asleep because of pain, and you want more of my magic medicine?" Audrey asks as I approach the nurses' station, leaning against the door frame and wanting to keep reading the letter, even though I'm hiding it from her.

"No, I just can't sleep," I answer, wishing she would go for a walk among the wounded in the hall and leave me alone for a few minutes.

"I'm sorry, but this time I can only give you aspirin." She gets up to bring me some pills from the jar behind her, and I turn my gaze back to John. In the dark hall, only our candle continues to flicker in the corner. She won't leave the nurses' room.

"Thank you. I'll try to overcome my pain." I walk away from her with the pills in my hand, and sit on the stairs to the second floor, careful not to stumble, starting to reread the letter in the dim light of the lamp above my head.

Dear John,

It's been so long since I've written to you, and frankly, it's been so long since I've received a letter from you. I don't know how to write what I'm going to now. There's no easy way to say it, there's never an easy way to write such things, but I've met someone else, and we're together.

I've been waiting for you for months, for a letter that never arrived, thinking and fearing that you'd forgotten me.

The distance from you, the longing and the loneliness were unbearable for me, and he was by my side when I felt I was falling apart. And now we're together...

What shall I tell him? I look up from the letter I'm holding. It'll break him into pieces. Why couldn't she wait for him a little longer? I lower my eyes and keep reading.

When we parted, we said the war would never change us and tear us apart, but we were wrong, it's changed us, you went overseas and I found a new way... I stop reading for a moment and wipe the tears from my cheeks. Why was she doing this to him when he was so vulnerable? How would I read it to him?

I will never forget our love that has gone.
Georgia

And that's it. The letter is over. And I hold it in my trembling hands and don't know what to do. John is waiting for me. I try to breathe and think: what will I tell him?

"What happened? Is everything okay? It took you a long time," he asks when he finally hears the sound of my crutches by his bed.

"I apologize. It took the nurse on duty a long time to find me a candle."

"Is the night shift nurse the one who likes you? Audrey?" He smiles at me and keeps holding the red rose. I hate the smell of roses.

"Yes, it's her again." I smile through tears. "Give me two minutes, and I'll keep reading to you."

"Don't let her make you cry," he holds out his hand in my direction.

"*Dear John...*" I start reading to him again, skipping the lines I'd read before. *"Summer has just started, and I continue walking through the garden every day on the way to school, looking at the roses and thinking of you..."* I stop for a moment and look at him. Will he notice my trembling voice? Will he notice the words are mine and not hers? It took me a while to convince Audrey to give me a piece of paper and a pencil, and it took me a while longer to try and think of what to write for him as I walked away from her and sat on the steps again, writing to him in the dim light of the lamp.

"*I've been waiting for a letter from you for so long,*" I keep reading. "*Imagining myself opening it and reading your words…* John, why didn't you write to her?" I scold him in a feigned voice, though I know it doesn't matter anymore anyway. Georgia has already made her decision.

"I wanted to write to her," he tells me in the dark, his fingers gently stroking the flower in his hand. "I would sometimes sit at night in the desert, after the sun went down, and the sky would be filled with stars and cannon fire on the horizon, and I couldn't write to her. Or in Sicily, after holding my rifle for two days, protecting a ruined building against German attacks," he continues to speak to me from the darkness, "how could I write words of love at night, after all the war I saw during the day? Georgia seemed so far away to me, living in a peaceful world full of smiles and trees and flowers." He smells the flower in his hand, and I feel the tear running down my cheek. "You see," he continues, "there were those who wrote to their loved ones, but I wanted to keep our love clean and pure from the war around me. That's what we promised each other, that our love would go on even if we didn't hear from each other, no matter what. Can you understand why I didn't write to her?"

I lower my eyes, knowing I need to tell him. But I don't have the courage.

"*I'm waiting for you to get back to me. Love, Georgia.*" I finish reading the letter to him and fold the paper, carefully burning it in the candle's flame and scattering the ashes on the floor so no nurse will accidentally find it and the words I wrote to him.

"Thank you, Grace from Chicago, have a good night," he whispers to me later.

"Good night, John from a small town near New York City. She's waiting for you to come home, and get married," I answer and stretched my hand out to my wall, trying to peel off as much plaster as I could. I had to tell him the truth.

<hr />

"Who is the blind man?" John asks me a few days later, when I get to our corner and he hears the sound of my crutches.

"What does that mean?"

"Who is the blind man?"

"What do you mean?"

"Just answer me, who is the blind man?" He raises his voice slightly.

"Where did you hear that?"

"What does it matter where I heard it?" He looks in my direction, his eyes covered with white bandages. "Who is the blind man?"

"Where did you hear that?" I whisper, not wanting the other wounded men to look at us, though it seems to me that everyone is already watching us.

"From two nurses who spoke next to my bed this morning, they thought I was asleep. Who's the blind man? The nurse you like, Audrey. She said that." He follows me with his head as I step towards the window and look out at the front driveway and the ambulances parked there.

"Your vision has been damaged," I quietly say, unable

to look in his direction, even though it doesn't matter, he doesn't know where I'm looking anyway.

"Yes, I was injured, but my eyesight isn't improving. You're a nurse, tell me, will I see again? All the other nurses refuse to answer me."

I am silent, looking out the window again, examining the cypress trees outside the hospital and how they bend in the autumn wind.

"Will I remain blind?" he asks quietly.

I continue to say nothing, watching the empty road to the hospital, keeping my back to him.

"I thought you were my friend," he says after a while.

"I'm trying to help you." I turn from the window and start hobbling towards his bed, supporting myself with the metal bed frame. He's so alone now, and he doesn't even know how much yet.

"Please go. I don't want you to help me."

"Please. I want to help you."

"Please go." He turns his back to me, and even though I stretch out my hand to him, I stop myself and don't stroke his hair. I mustn't do that, he thinks he has a woman waiting for him at home.

"Please."

"Just go."

I slowly hop on one leg to my crutches and start moving away from our corner, lowering my eyes and looking at the floor, feeling the other wounded men and the nurses staring while I cross the hall.

The sound of the enamel mug hitting the wall makes me cringe for a moment, but I don't turn around and keep hobbling. I hear more bumps, maybe the book being thrown at the wall or other things from our locker.

Bag, bag, bag, bag, keep walking. *He's the blind one, not me. I have my own wounds to handle, and they're painful enough without thinking about the pain of others.* I look at my missing leg. Why did I even start helping him? Why did I read him the letters at night? I have to get out of here, the stares from the other wounded are suffocating me.

After sitting behind the old warehouse for most of the day, and playing with the box of cigarettes left on the ground, I return to the building in the evening, hobbling on my crutches.
"I thought you wanted to be a nurse and help the wounded, not break their spirits," I hear Audrey from the nurses' station, and stand at the entrance to the hall.
"This isn't a field hospital," she keeps on talking, "or wherever you were when someone decided you might be an intern nurse. This is a place of caressing and loving hands." I turn to her, thinking of something to answer her, but she doesn't let me.
"Why exactly did you tell him he'll stay blind? Do you have the authority to say such things?"
"No, I have no authority," I answer, thinking that I had no authority, but I had the courage.
"You have no authority, nor are you a nurse, and yet you act like a nurse."
"Yes, Red Lipstick Nurse."
"You know, I feel sorry for you. You wanted so much to be a nurse, and you failed. Maybe you should stay in your corner, where you do nothing."
"Yes, Red Lipstick Nurse." I straighten my chin and look at the calendar over her head, trying to see whether the ship's arrival date is marked.

"Or busy yourself picking up dirty glasses of orange juice with the Italian you like so much, though I realize you're failing there too."

"Yes, Red Lipstick Nurse."

"And stay away from John."

"I have no intention of getting close to John. You're doing a great job taking care of him, his sight will probably return soon," I answer and turn my back to her, not waiting for her answer, leaving the hospital. I don't want to be close to him, he also probably doesn't want to be close to me.

The cold breeze blows in my face as I stand on the cliff's edge and look down at the stormy sea hitting the rocks. I can barely see the white foam in the dark.

"Why is all this happening to me?" I scream at the wind, looking back at the hospital building and hoping no one heard my screams. But the building remains quiet, and only the lit windows look at me, accusing me with their yellow eyes. Why did I even start helping him?

"I'm not guilty," I shout into the sea as I slowly walk on the slippery rocks, holding my crutches for support. "I was just trying to be nice to him, so he wouldn't hurt so much. It's not my fault they put him next to me, it's not my fault he was injured, it's not my fault everyone thought he would die. I just felt sorry for him." I keep shouting at the rocks as I take the cigarette box out of my pocket and pull out a cigarette with trembling fingers.

"What did I do wrong? Wasn't I a good nurse? Didn't I try to help him?" I ask the waves, which crash on the black rocks at the bottom of the cliff, spraying the air with sea drops carried by the wind and hitting my body where I stand at the top.

"I was just trying to be a good nurse," I yell at the sea as I light the cigarette with John's lighter, looking at the flame fighting the wind. "Just one cigarette, I won't break. All I wanted was to be good to people," I cry to the sea.

The wind keeps hitting my face and scattering my hair, but I stay on the rock, inhaling the smoke and coughing, holding John's lighter in my hand. I have to give it back to him. For a moment, I look down at the sea and touch the small cross around my neck.

"God," I whisper to the wind that strikes me. "What do I have to do? I promise to give it a try."

But the wind doesn't answer me, it just keeps blowing in my face, and I keep coughing from the bitter smoke, and when I finally head back to the building, the lit windows keep staring at me with their yellow accusing eyes.

"I'll stay away from him, I'll recover, and I'll leave this place," I whisper to the yellow windows looking at me.

Rage from the sky

"I'll stay away from him," I whisper to myself over the following days when I see him sitting on the bench in the garden, looking at the sky.

Every morning Audrey takes him outside and seats him on the same bench overlooking the gray sea, stroking his head and leaving him there. Every day he sits on the bench for hours, looking at the horizon with white bandages covering his eyes. Sometimes I see him holding a book in his hand, and once I notice him flipping through the pages, moving them aimlessly while his gaze is aimed at the horizon.

Now and then she approaches him and puts a hand on his shoulder, whispering something in his ear and then walking away, leaving him to continue sitting in front of the autumn wind coming from the sea.

Even at night, we say nothing, I read from the book in silence, dog-ear the pages at the end of each day even though it destroys the book, and he lies there in darkness, maybe sleeping, maybe listening to the rustling pages as I read.

In the mornings I turn my back on them, hurrying as much as I can to get organized, say goodbye to the wall, get away from the corner, and go out to the garden to enjoy the autumn sun. I'm not a nurse, and I shouldn't approach him, or Audrey will complain about me.

Even today, when I look at him, he's sitting on his bench. Still later I see him going down on his knees on the grass, searching the ground with his hands, probably looking for the glass of juice that has fallen, his hands groping in all directions.

"Can you help me?" I ask him, and he raises his head.

"I don't think you need my help." He fumbles with his hands until he finds the bench and goes back to sitting on it, leaving the glass lying on the grass. "And I don't need pity."

"I don't feel sorry for you. I need help practicing with my crutches."

"There are many other wounded here who would be happy to help you. I hear them talking in the garden all day. You don't need to pity the blind."

"I miss our conversations."

"I'm a very bad conversationalist these days. It's hard for me to start small talk about the weather or the view around us."

"I thought Audrey was talking to you."

"She's just stroking my hair, as if it'll make my vision improve."

"Please help me, I miss your stories."

"I've told you all the stories I have," he answers, but he gets up and stands in front of me, and I raise my gaze and look at him. He is taller than me.

"Put your hand on my shoulder, help me walk with my crutches." I take his hand and place it on my shoulder.

"Audrey really doesn't like you."

"Yeah, she really doesn't like me. At least she just went into the building. So we have a few minutes of freedom. Help me walk, I have to practice."

"So you can run away from here?" he asks, and I cringe. Did she tell him what I did last time, when the ship arrived?

"Everything okay? Do you not like my touch?"

"Everything's fine. I like your touch."

"So why did I feel your body tense?"

"Tell me something. Tell me about Tuscany."

"Do you always change the subject when it's not right for you?"

"I miss your stories of Tuscany and the desert." I walk slowly, feeling his warm fingers on my shoulder.

"At one end of a dirt road we walked down, we came to an old oak tree. It had probably stood there for thousands of years." He quietly speaks as if wanting me to be the only one to hear him. "The thick tree trunk was wrinkled like an old man, and its green canopy cast a heavy shadow on the brown ground beneath it. As we approached it with our guns drawn, looking carefully and scanning for a German ambush, it seemed to me that it was looking at us, examining our steps, trying to see how determined we were to win this war." He continues to hold my shoulder gently. "Later that day, when we stopped to rest for a few minutes under its shadow, I thought that this tree must have seen the German soldiers before us cross the same dirt road at its feet, and the Crusaders and the Romans before that. This oak tree must have seen all that could ever be seen on Earth." John continues to tell me about the oak tree in Tuscany as we walk over to Francesca, and I place his hand on the tray so he can choose a glass of orange juice for himself.

"Tell me more," I ask, sitting next to him on the white bench overlooking the sea.

For the next few days, he waits for me in the garden with stories, and I patiently wait until Audrey disappears into the building before getting close to him, placing his hand on my shoulder or sitting next to him on the bench overlooking the sea. Sometimes I watch the seagulls flying above the waves. Still, most of the time I look at his lips as he describes the yellow North African dunes stretching like waves to the horizon, or the blue bays of the sea in Sicily, so clear you could toss a coin into the depths of the sea and dive and find it. I ask him questions, wanting him to tell me what his eyes saw before they were covered in white bandages forever.

Only at night do I keep quiet, forcing myself to sleep under the watchful eyes of Audrey, who walks through the dark hall.

"What's that noise?" I feel his fingers tighten on my shoulder one day as we walk in the garden, while he's telling me about a house in the middle of the battlefield and an old Italian lady who refused to leave it despite the bullets whistling around, explaining to them with her hands that she would not run away from anyone, certainly not from the war.

"It's okay. Those are the American bombers from the airfield beyond the hill," I answer.

"Something's wrong." I feel him tense up and stop walking.

"It's their engines."

"They don't sound like American bombers," he says, and I feel his fingers tighten on my shoulders even more until he's hurting me. I turn my gaze to the source of the noise, towards the sun, and see four black dots approaching us, growing with every second. Between their wings are glimmers of light and flashes, while the noise of their engines gets louder.

"Get down," I scream at John and release his hand holding me, pushing him towards the grass as we both fall. "Get down," I scream at him again, even though we're both already on the ground, and I hear the sharp whistles and screams around me. I also scream in pain when my injured leg hits the ground, while I lie on John and protect him. My hands cover my head as I try to make us both disappear into the ground, to escape the noise of the plane's engines that sounds like chainsaws, and the screams all around disturbed by machinegun thunder. When I raise my head for a second, I notice the black iron cross painted on the planes' gray wings, and the ugly swastika on their tails.

"Nurse." I hear screams from all over, and I look for my crutches. Where are they? They're lying on the grass a few yards away, but the wounded man shouting is closer than them. "Stay down," I shout to John, and start crawling to the groaning wounded man. I must take care of him. His pants are torn, and a stream of blood is dripping from his red leg.

"Your hand," I shout at him when I manage to reach his side. I tuck my hand against his bleeding femoral artery and place his hand on mine, pushing our fingers as hard as I can to stop the blood flow. "Hold on tight," I keep shouting even though I'm close to him and there's no need to shout. "Your belt," I struggle with my other hand to loosen his belt, pulling it with all the strength I have, and once it's loose I begin wrapping it around his wounded leg to make a tourniquet.

"A stick, I need a stick," I shout, and grope the grass for a branch, grabbing it and tightening the tourniquet. All around I hear screams and people running, and also more nurses and doctors in their white uniforms.

"Hold on and don't let go. You'll live." I place his hand on the stick tightening the belt. "Do not let go," I shout at him again, searching for the next wounded man lying still on the grass, looking at the sky and the planes that have already gone.

I manage to crawl to him, opening his shirt and trying to block the wound in his chest with a piece of cloth by ripping my shirt pocket. Then I support myself as much as I can and start resuscitating him. He can be saved. The screams around

me don't stop, but I just press my lips to his and breathe as much as I can, ignoring the sweat and the noise around me.
Keep resuscitating, keep resuscitating, keep resuscitating.
"Doctor," I shout, "I need a doctor here."
Keep resuscitating, keep resuscitating, keep resuscitating.
"Doctor," I shout hoarsely. How long has it been? I mustn't stop. He will live.
Keep resuscitating, keep resuscitating, keep resuscitating.
"Grace, stop. He's dead." I feel a hand resting on my shoulder. "You need to stop."
"He needs a doctor, he still has a chance," I whisper.
"Grace, stop. He's dead." She keeps talking to me, and I think it's Head Nurse Blanche. Her uniform is covered in bloodstains, and she leans next to me. "Are you okay? Were you injured?"
And I just shake my head in denial, releasing my lips from the mouth of the wounded man lying on the grass, gazing at the sky with a surprised look.
"You need to go back to your place." She rises, and I hear her shout to the soldiers to come take the wounded I tried and failed to save. Where's John? He was under my care, is he okay?
I look around, but I can't see him. The garden is almost empty now, just a few upside-down white chairs and empty glasses of juice thrown on the grass, and nurses and doctors bending over a few wounded men still lying on the grass, carrying them out on stretchers to the operating rooms. All the wounded who weren't injured have disappeared, they must have been brought back into the main hall. I don't see my crutches either, someone probably picked them up.
"Where's John?" I whisper.
"Grace, we'll send someone to help you get in and clean

up, you're covered in blood." One of the nurses approaches me, leaning beside me.

"Where's John?" I whisper again.

"Grace, he's fine, he's in his bed."

"Where's John?" I whisper again and again, looking up at the blue sky, now quiet.

<hr />

"John, are you okay, were you injured?" I sit on my bed and try to get closer to him, but he turns his back to me.

"John, are you okay?"

"Did you lie on top of me? Did you try to protect me?"

"Yeah, I think that's what I did." I want to stroke his hair, but I don't think it'll be pleasant for him now.

"It's not supposed to be like that. I was supposed to protect you, not you protect me."

"But you can't see. You couldn't see them."

"That's exactly the point. I should stay here, in bed." He turns to me suddenly. "What's the point of all this?" He looks at me with his bandaged eyes.

"The point of what? You're the one who first heard them." I want to stroke his hand.

"Going out, trying to act normal. What's the point? I'm in the dark anyway, whether I'm lying in bed or sitting on a bench in the garden, waiting for you to come take me for a walk, listening to my stories out of pity. What's the difference? What's the point?"

"I don't feel sorry for you."

"You weren't injured like me. You don't know what it feels like."

"Yeah, I wasn't injured that badly." I don't want to tell him how I was injured. What does it matter now? Will it help him feel better? He needs encouragement, not to pity me.

"So what's the point?"

"There's a woman waiting for you at home, isn't that a good enough reason to recover?" I keep talking, glad I didn't tell him about the letter then. Maybe it'll be the right time later, but not now.

"Recover for her? Do I think I can recover?" I notice his trembling hands. "I've been turning my back to you every night for days, afraid you'll offer to write me a letter. What will I write her?" he asks, and I don't answer him.

"What shall I write her? 'I love you, but surprise, I'm blind'?" He leans back in his bed. "Isn't it better to be silent and not write anything? Let her think I've forgotten her, or maybe that I was killed. Maybe it's a mistake I stayed alive today, and you shouldn't have thrown me on the ground and tried to protect me. Maybe God sent them to finish the job where the German shell failed?"

"Don't talk like that. I care about you."

"You just feel sorry for a blind wounded man sitting in bed next to you. You shouldn't have protected me. It's not your job."

Without saying a word, I grab my crutches and hobble away from him.

Bag, bag, bag, bag, thirty-eight steps to the exit and the dark garden at night, passing through the upside-down deck chairs. I make my way to the cliff overlooking the sea.

"Enough," I scream at the sea. "Enough with all this pain around me. I'm running out of strength." I sit bent over on the bench, ripping the chain with the cross from my neck and throwing it at the rocks. "How much longer can I be in pain and fail at everything I try?" I whimper as I light a cigarette in the dark, breathe in the smoke, and cough, not wiping the tears from my cheeks.

But the waves and the sea don't answer me. They're just waiting for me to jump into them, as I once wanted to when I realized I'd lost my leg. Back then, I didn't the courage.

"I need some courage," I whisper to the rock as I light another cigarette. But finally I turn around and go back to the dark building and the bright doorway looking at me mockingly. I'll try to beg the one who likes me, maybe she'll agree to give me a dose of morphine and I'll be able to fall asleep tonight. But she's not on duty, just another nurse I don't know who refuses me.

"Eight days, I was in Italy as a whole person for only eight days," I say to Francesca the next day. "Eight days and a few months without a leg and two German plane attacks."

We both sit down to rest in our hiding place, and I take out a cigarette and light it, inhaling the smoke and feeling myself suffocate. But I don't stop smoking.

"After the first time, I stayed like that." I touch my amputated leg and exhale the smoke into the blue sky. "The first time, when I heard the airplane engine and the shooting around me, I didn't understand what was going on, what all those flashes were." My fingers play with the dry leaves.

"By the second time, I understood, but it didn't change anything." I keep talking slowly, looking at Francesca, but she looks at the sea and says nothing.

"Eight days and two attacks, and I only lost one leg, that's not so bad, is it?" I look down, seeing her fingers also playing with the dry leaves, crushing them.

A few more minutes pass, and I light another cigarette for myself, feeling my trembling hand. I can't tell her about the flashes of the bombs hitting the ground, the air filling with dirt and a burnt smell, the screams that were all around me. The worst was the screams. They keep me awake at night as my fingernails scratch my leg, wanting to feel some pain. How much more should I suffer?

"And you know what's the worst thing?" I ask Francesca, but she's silent. "The feeling of helplessness, that I can do nothing." I take a deep breath. "And now, with these crutches, it's even worse. I depend on them and can't even try to escape." I push them with my hand and drop them to the dirt, enjoying the sound of them hitting the hard ground.

"I hate you," I turn in their direction and kick them with my single foot. "I hate you," I keep shouting, ignoring my tears. "Better to lie next to John in bed all day and look at the wall than be 'the crippled woman with the crutches,' the one everyone is always staring at when she passes through the aisle between the beds." I kick them over and over, pushing them away from me. "When will the ship arrive to take me from this bleeding place?"

Francesca

"Wake up." I feel someone touching my shoulder, waking me up. I open my eyes and examine the new scratches on the wall in front of me.

"Wake up. Come with me." I feel the hand again. I turn around and see Francesca standing over my bed. What does she want from me?

"Come with me." She pulls me to a seating position and hands me the crutches, placing them between my arms. I refuse to take them and lie back on my bed. I have had enough in the air raid. I will stay in my bed, like John.

"Come with me." She doesn't give up and pulls me back to sit up. She hands me the crutches, placing them under my armpits and closing my palms around them. "Come with me."

"Where?" I stand up and look at John. Maybe he'll say something to her. But he is silent. After what had happened, he fell silent again.

"Where?" I ask again. I don't want to go outside to the garden with her.

"I want to show you something." She holds my arm and walks by my side as we walk down through the hall of the wounded, as if trying to make sure I don't run away from her. Doesn't she know I'm a cripple who cannot run from anything? I lower my eyes to the floor while we walk through the aisle between the other beds, but she keeps looking ahead, ignoring the men who stare at us curiously.

"Francesca, I was just looking for you. I need you to start cleaning the nurses' station." Audrey says to her as we walk past her towards the entrance.

"I will be back in a few minutes." She answers her, still holding onto my arm. "Come with me."

I walk out with her into the garden and towards our secret place behind the warehouse. She probably wants to tell me something that would cheer me up after yesterday, not realizing she would not succeed. But to my surprise, she turns onto the hospitals' front driveway, helping me go down the front steps.

"Come with me." She continues walking on the gravel, passing the big Red Cross flag spread out on the ground, walking towards the cars parked at the side near the stone wall.

I pause for a moment to look at the torn Red Cross flag. It did not protect us against the German planes. I notice that it is full of bullet holes, probably from the German machineguns; a souvenir from the airplanes that attacked us.

"Where are you going?" I shout after her.

"I want to show you something." She doesn't turn around so I follow her, hobbling carefully through the gravel, paying attention to the ground lest I slip and fall.

"What do you want to show me?" I stand next to her on the side of the front driveway. In front of us are several green army supply trucks and jeeps are parked by the fuel barrels.

"Come with me." She removes a tarpaulin cover, exposing a red motorcycle that is covered with dust and mud. She lifts the hem of her black dress, tucks the soft fabric between her thighs, and sits at the driver's seat with her legs spread, motioning for me to sit behind her.

"What is this motorcycle?"

"This is my motorcycle. Have you ever ridden a motorcycle?"

"No." I stand embarrassed beside her. Still seated, she

kicks one of the pedals with her foot, and the motorcycle's engine ignites with a thunderous rattle. How can I ride a motorcycle without one leg? Doesn't she know I'm crippled now? Is she trying to make fun of me too?

"I can't go with you."

"Get up." She insists and motions for me to get closer to her. I take a step closer and place my hand on the back seat, supporting myself, as she takes the crutches from my hands. I carefully lift my amputated leg above the side of the back seat while holding it tightly. I can feel the engine shake and I'm afraid of falling.

"Hug me," She says while taking my hands and wrapping them around her waist.

What about my crutches? Will she leave them here? Where is she taking me?

Not a moment passes and Francesca places my crutches right between us. "Hold me tight." She yells over the engine's rattling noise.

"What?"

"Hold on tight." She starts driving slowly in the front driveway of the hospital. 'I hold on to her, pressing my body to her back ignoring the wooden sticks that are nestled between us.

Driving slowly, she passes the green army trucks and the jeeps standing on the siding, crossing the gate destroyed during the attack. I lower my gaze as we drive out of the hospital and onto the main road, worried that one of the nurses would see us.

"Are you alright?" She shouts after a few minutes as we drive down the road, and I can see through the trees on the sides of the road that the village houses are getting closer.

"Yes," I yell back and hold on to her a little tighter as the motorcycle shakes and jumps over the holes in the road. The road that was once well paved is now full of bumps and potholes, probably from the tanks rolling over it or the cannon shells that were fired during the fighting here. The wind on my face and the landscape around me feel so pleasant, and if only I could, I would spread my arms to the sides and imagine that I could fly like a bird, thinking of John and his stories of Tuscany.

"We're almost there." Francesca shouts to me as we approach the entrance to the village. In front of the first stone houses, on the side of the road, lies a destroyed tank. It is on its side blocking part of the road, and I can see the American white star that is painted on its turret.

My eyes follow the tank as we pass it, riding slowly through the village. I notice a group of children standing on it, playing with wooden swords.

"*La vedova en moto. La vedova en moto.*" They shout to Francesca as we pass them.

"What were they shouting?" I ask her, but she does not answer. Maybe she did not hear me.

Inside the village, Francesca slows the motorcycle and drives down a narrow road between the houses. As we pass by a pile of bricks that was once a house, I can see the single wall that had been left standing and the seawater that is clearly visible right through the wall.

"Hold me tight." She yells to me as the motorcycle jumps over the cobblestones road, and I hug her with both my hands.

We slow down again in one of the narrow streets, driving behind a cart strapped to a donkey. Suddenly, I notice people looking at me from the balconies and entrances of their houses, their eyes examining my hospital clothes and my missing leg.

"They're looking at me." I bring my lips close to her ear, trying not to raise my voice.

"They are not looking at you, they are looking at me. They call me 'Widow on the Motorcycle.'" She shouts back to me as she accelerates the motorcycle and bypasses the donkey and the cart. Still, not wanting to see their looks around me, I lower my head towards her back and close my eyes while holding on to her.

"We are here." I hear her voice and open my eyes.

The motorcycle is in the village square. Around us are several buildings and shops. In the center of the square I see the ruined fountain that Francesca once told me about. Several women huddle around the fountain, holding their water cans, and filling them from the tap. They scold the smiling children running around them, playing on the cobblestones. Near them, I see a single older man in a suit walking slowly, lost in thought.

"Did you bring me to your village to show me what we have destroyed?" I look around and see the abandoned building that must have once been a movie theater, the sky is now noticeably visible through its walls. A movie poster featuring a beautiful actress with a seductive look in her eyes still decorates one of the building's walls. Below it are torn posters glorifying Mussolini ,covered with red paint.

"Come with me." Francesca hands me the crutches ignoring my question. She walks down the square, cursing the children running towards the motorcycle shouting, "La vedova en moto, La vedova en moto."

Follow her and keep on looking down, beware not to slip on the pavement, ignore the looks of the women who turn around and stare and the children who run after us and shout, amputato, amputato. They're calling her names, not me. Where is she taking me? Does she want to leave me here alone in the square? Is she trying to teach me a lesson? I follow her as fast as I can, occasionally looking up, noticing her black dress against the white backdrop of the village square.

"Come this way." She enters one of the shops at the end of the square and says something to the older man who stands in the doorway. He answers something back and looks at me for a moment. Where did she bring me to?

The interior of the small workshop is dim and cool. All around there are carpentry' tools and small furniture. It smells of sawdust and varnish. Why am I here?

Francesca starts talking to the shop owner pointing at my leg. I can hear him talking, repeating the word 'Americana' and shaking his head. Francesca raises her voice in return. Meanwhile, I stand there looking at them not understanding a word they are saying.

"Wait here." She tells me before leaving the workshop, disappearing outside. I find myself all alone with the older Italian man. He stands there playing with his mustache, looking at me and smiling.

"*Americana*?"

"Si."

He comes closer and offers me a chair. I sit down and watch him as he goes back to his desk drawer. He takes out a measuring tape, approaches me, and kneels down by my leg. He raises his head to look at me:

"Si?" He asks.

"Si," I answer but I do not understand what he means nor what he wants from me.

Slowly and gently, he rolls up my hospital pants, exposing my amputated leg, examining it closely.

"Si?"

"Si."

His fingers loosen the bandages around my leg, gently removing them, and I close my eyes. I don't want to see the look on his face when he sees my ugly leg stump. My fingers grip the arms of the chair tightly as I feel his rough fingers gently touching my stump.

"Si?" I open my eyes and see him smiling at me from the floor, his hand touching my one single shoe.

"Si," I answer him, and he removes my shoe and sock, placing my bare foot on the wooden floor.

After examining the leg that remained and the one that I lost, he measures both of them, pulls out a pencil behind his ear, and begins to write numbers on a piece of paper that he had laid out on the floor.

A noise coming from the entrance makes me raise my head, and I see Francesca entering the workshop, followed by another older man wearing a gray robe.

The two men start talking or perhaps arguing, but I do not understand a thing. The man wearing the robe pulls out several strips of leather from his pocket and approaches my leg. He places the leather on my stump, and the two men proceed arguing. All I can understand is "Si" and "Americana." Finally they seem to agree on something. They finish their examination of my leg, sum up their lists, and rise from the floor. I can see them smiling at me, saying something in Italian.

"Stand up," Francesca tells me.

I hold on to the back of the chair and stand up. To my surprise, I can see the faces of some children who now stand outside the workshop, curiously peeking inside through the filthy window. They are smiling at me.

The two men bend at my feet again and continue to measure as I stand in the center of the small room, supporting myself with my crutches. I look down at their hands; they are drawing sketches on the pieces of paper lying on the floor in front of them. Still, my thoughts remain focused on the children and their questioning eyes outside.

"They are not looking at you, they are looking at me," Francesca tells me when she notices the direction I'm looking at, but I tend not to believe her.

"Andarsene," She walks out of the store for a moment and yells at them. I can hear them running away laughing, but not a moment passes until I can see their faces in the window again. Now I have no choice but to smile at them awkwardly, and I can see them smiling back at me, waving their hands.

"Cigarettes, do you have any cigarettes?" Francesca asks me when the two men stand up again, smiling at me and arguing with her. I pull out my box of cigarettes and hand it over to her. She then divides them equally between the two men as they shake her hand. The shoemaker nods towards me, leaving the workshop as we say goodbye to him as well as the carpenter.

"Get yourself some boxes of cigarettes, so we have something to pay them later." She tells me when we get back to the motorcycle, banishing away the swarm of children following us.

"Thank you," I whisper to her, my lips close to her ear, as we begin our ride back. I hug her tightly, but she does not answer me. Maybe she did not 'hear me.

"Where have you been?" Audrey yells at us from the hospital entrance when Francesca stops the motorcycle and turns to help me with my crutches.

"I felt ill. I asked the Italian to take me for a ride for some air." I shout back at her.

"Hurry up, there is still cleaning to do," she says to Francesca and disappears back into the hospital. I look at Fracescs who is waiting for me, to help me off the motorcycle.

"How long have you had this motorcycle for?" I ask her.

"It was my husband's motorcycle." She answers and strokes the handlebars for a moment. "He taught me how drive it the summer before the war began. Before the fascists forced him to enlist in the army and sent him to Russia to fight with the Nazis." She spits on the ground as she utters the words 'Fascists' and 'Nazis' and turns her back to me. Marching in her airy black dress, she enters the hospital white building, and heads to clean the nurses' room.

"Wake up." I feel a hand touching me. A few days have passed since our visit to the village. I open my eyes and see Francesca again.

"Are we going to the village?"

"Si." She nods at me.

"One moment." I sit in my bed, bending over and taking out my army duffel bag from the locker. I pull the bag onto the bed and empty all of its contents and hide them underneath my blanket.

"John," I whisper to him and touch his shoulder. I do not like to wake him up, but I need something from him right now.

"What, Grace?" He turns to me, and I suspect he's been awake for a little while now.

"Can I borrow your army duffle bag?"

"Yes." He answers me, turning around with his back to me again.

"Don't you want to ask why?"

"No."

"It's for a good cause."

"I'm sure it is." He replies, with his back still turned towards me.

For a moment, I want to hug him to cheer him up, but I know it's not my job. There is another nurse who takes care of him.

"I'll be back soon." I touch his shoulder and pull his duffel bag out of the locker. I empty his personal belongings and hand the bag to Francesca, who had been standing there watching us this whole time. "Let's go."

On the ground floor, instead of going out to the front driveway, I lead her to the kitchen supply cabin.

"Good Morning." I stand in front of the sergeant in charge of the kitchen.

"The Commanding Nurse had asked you to give me some food cans."

"And why does the Commanding Nurse need these food cans?" He answers, his tone slightly dismissive.

"Because she wants to have a surprise picnic for the nurses who have been working so hard."

"And do you have a request note from her stating that?" He approaches, looking down at me.

"No. Do you really want me to have to hobble back on

my crutches and get you a request note?" I raise my eyes and look up at him, hoping he will not send me back out of there.

"And who is this? Is she having a picnic too?" He looks at Francesca.

"Do you think I'm able to carry anything? That is why I brought the Italian along."

He thinks for a moment before entering the kitchen's supply cabinet, and yelled:"What do you need?"

"Canned meat, dried milk, orange juice powder, tea, coffee, and chocolate," I yell back.

This time, Francesca drives the loaded motorcycle much slower, careful not to roll over the potholes. "La vedova en moto!" The smiling children playing on the remains of the tanks decorating the entrance to the village shout to us. But Francesca doesn't answer them. The women on the street stare at us, and the square at the center of the village looks exactly the same as the last time, with the destroyed fountain and the movie theater where all you can see now is a glimpse of the morning sky shining through its ceiling.

"Bonjourno." The carpenter smiles at me as we enter. He hurries out behind his wooden desk, hands me a chair, and gestures me to sit down.

Then he bends down and takes out a wooden leg from behind the counter. My wooden leg.

It is made of light wood covered with varnish and has leather straps at the top of it. The straps are there so I can tie it to my stump. The wooden leg has a metal joint at the ankle area that allows for the movement of the foot.

Francesca disappears again and returns after a minute with the shoemaker by her side. As I look up, I can barely see the children' waving at me behind the filthy window through the tears in my eyes.

"Si?" The carpenter asks me as he leans by my foot.

"Si." I nod at him and wipe the tears away as he gently rolls up the ugly hospital pants and removes the bandages. He presses the wooden leg against the stump, examining the fit.

The wood is cold and smooth and hard against my skin, and I can feel a little pain. He turns around, says something to Francesca, and they start arguing. Again I do not understand a thing, but suddenly Francesca takes off her shoes and socks and hands the socks to him. The old carpenter takes one of the socks and puts it on my stump. Then he does the same thing with the other sock and examines the fit of the wooden leg once more. He says something to Francesca and she yells in Italian to the kids outside; I can hear them laughing, and after a few seconds, more socks are thrown from into the workshop. The carpenter puts them all on my stump, one on top of the other, then he places the wooden leg against the socks, ties it with the leather straps, stands up and smiles at me.

"Si." He gestures me to stand up. I hold his hands, and for the first time since that horrible day, I manage to stand up without the crutches. I'm still unstable, and still shaking while holding on to the carpenter's hands. But I'm standing up without my hated crutches.

Slowly, I manage to walk through the small room, holding on to the carpenter's hands. I look down and see the prosthetic leg pressed against my stump. Despite the socks trying to soften the wood, I can still feel the pressure. After a few steps, I feel myself needing to rest. It will take me time to get used to the new leg. But right now I'm trying to get used to the smiling children at the window and the two older men patting my shoulder, saying "bravo, bravo." I drag the two bags full of food cans and chocolates and hand them over together with the cigarette boxes. Suddenly, I look at Francesca standing near the shop's entrance and realize how inconsiderate I must seem. I take some food cans and cigarette boxes from the pile, get up, and give them to her. She refuses at first, but I insist, joined by the carpenter and the shoemaker, who also urge her to take them. She finally agrees and lets me fill her hands. The carpenter goes to the back of the counter, takes out a bottle of wine and passes it around. Everyone laughs as I bring the bottle to my lips and sip from it.

Still using my crutches, I walk slowly back to the motorcycle; the carpenter, the showmaker, and the children all follow me, walking by my side. Even some of the women pumping water in the village square, stop and join them. I can already feel myself stepping on the new foot as I walk.
"Grazie, grazie" I keep thanking them. It seems to me that maybe Francesca and I drank a little bit too much of that

wine, but it's hard for me to tell for sure. Every few steps, I pause and bend over to stroke my new wooden leg, while everybody smiles and cheers.

On our way back to the hospital, I seem to remember Francesca and I singing. I hug her tightly as the motorcycle changes its speed, depending on the song we sing. I do not really know what the songs are about as they are all in Italian. Maybe these are not songs at all, maybe she's trying to tell me a story. It does not really matter to me. The trees pass by us so fast, and I just want to spread my hands and fly, but I must hold on to her not to fall off the motorcycle. I notice a pleasant aroma of wine wafting from her.

It's almost sunset when we get back to the hospital. Francesca helps me climb up the stairs at the hospital's entrance, which now seem really high to me. I think I remember asking Audrey to help me go up the stairs as well, but she refuses.

"Good night, John." I whisper to him as I lie back in my bed, nauseous. "I have been fixed." But he does not answer me, maybe he is already asleep.

To Dance

"Dear John, the autumn winds are already starting to blow," I lie in bed late at night and read John a new letter from Georgia. He turns his back to me and doesn't respond. I don't even know whether he is listening to me or not.

"John, can you hear me? A new letter has arrived," I say to him again. I spent the whole afternoon sitting behind the warehouse writing to John, looking for the right words of encouragement. It's better than telling him she has left him for another.

"What is she writing? Is she missing me?" He finally answers. At least he's not sleeping.

"Yes. She writes that she's waiting to hug you and walk hand in hand through the main street of your town."

"So maybe you should tell her that blind people don't walk hand in hand. It seems to me that she doesn't know it yet." Then he turns to face me, "on the other hand, you already know how to lead me. Maybe we will write to her that she should find someone else, and you will stay here with me and continue leading me? You already know how to do it well. Unless another German airplane suddenly emerges out of the black sky…for me the sky is black even when the sun is shining."

"John, she's waiting for you." I hold the letter, looking at my handwriting. What else can I do to encourage him? Would it help if I wrote him more letters in her name?

"She's not waiting for me. She's waiting for another John to sit next to her by the fireplace and read her books. Do you think I can read books?"

"She will read books to you."

"Yes, just like you protected me when the German airplane arrived." His voice is so loud that it could wake up the other wounded sleeping in the hall.

"It's not the same."

"Really?" He sits up in bed and extends his hand in my direction, "Hand me the letter so I can practice reading."

"No, John, I'm not giving you the letter."

"It's mine, isn't it?" He motions his hand in the air, extends it forward, approaching me, touching my chest, stroking my breast for a second. I want to get away from him and his outstretched hand, but I'm afraid of falling out of bed.

"I apologize," he pulls his hand back and backs away in his bed, but the feeling of his warm fingers remains on my body.

"Take it." I crumple the letter and toss it at him, and in the dark, it seems to me that it hits his face.

"I'm sorry, I didn't know I would touch you. I didn't know you were so close."

"It's okay." I stroke the spot where his hand had just touched me, surprised by the feeling spreading through my body.

"No, it's not okay. A man should not behave like that. I apologize."

"John, it's okay," I want to get close to him and take the letter back, but I know it's not possible now. I shouldn't have thrown it in his face. "You couldn't see me."

"That's exactly the point. I'm blind."

"It's not the point. The point is that there is a woman who loves you and is waiting for you at home." I imagine his hand stroking Georgia.

"Tell me, Grace, when is your ship coming? Aren't you supposed to recover already and stop feeling sorry for me?"

"Is everything okay here?" I hear Audrey's voice. How long has she been standing there listening to us? Did she see what had happened?

"Yeah, everything's fine," John answers her.

"Because I heard noises coming from your direction." I see her placing a hand on his shoulder in the dark.

"I was just trying to get off the bed, and I accidentally bumped into the locker and woke Grace up." He answers her.

"So, she lit a candle on top of the locker?"

"She just wanted to see what happened. She's not blind like me."

"Grace, you can go back to sleep," she turns to me, "I will take care of him." It seems that she is smiling at me in the dark. I turn my back towards them and can hear her whispering something to him; he whispers something back.

I look at the wall, trying to count the lines I had drawn, but Audrey blows the candle out, and I can no longer see anything with the dim light coming from the nurses' station. It's going to happen soon, I know it.

Maybe a German submarine will hit the ship? Not hard enough to make it sink, but maybe only to cause some small damage that would delay its arrival? No wonder she thinks I love the Germans. I keep hearing them talking quietly in the dark, trying not to listen to what John is saying to her. Still, my body remembers the feeling of his hand on my breast.

"*Americana, Americana.*" I feel a hand shaking my body a few nights later. What do they want from me?

"*Americana*, wake up." The voice calls again. I open my eyes in the dark and gather that it's Francesca. Her face is close to mine, and she's whispering to me.

"What?" I answer her. The hall is dark and quiet, what time is it?

"The ship." She whispers to me.

"What about the ship?"

"It has arrived at the port. A telegram arrived." She keeps shaking me, "Wake up. I heard the nurses talking."

I sit up in bed and look at her. She is standing close to me, and I can notice her dark silhouette. What should I do?

"You have to run away. You're on the list." She keeps whispering to me, "I heard them talking about you," and I look at her for a moment and say nothing. I ran away once. They will not let me run away again. My time has come.

"Thanks," I whisper to her and lie back in my bed, looking in John's direction. At least he didn't wake up.

"*Americana*, wake up. You have to do something." She shakes me again, but I keep lying in my bed.

I wanted to return to be a nurse again so badly, but they won't let me, not in this place. Nothing can change their mind. My new wooden leg will accompany me on my way home.

"*Americana*, aren't you doing something?"

"There's nothing I can do." I have been trying to think of an idea for days without much success.

"You have to do something."

"Sorry," I answer to her in the dark, "it's time for me to go home."

"For an *Americana* who doesn't understand anything, you really don't understand anything."

"Sorry, you have a village to return to, and I have a ship waiting for me. I can't run away again; they wouldn't let me."

"And I thought you were my friend." She says, muttering something in Italian that sounds like a curse. I want to explain that I have no choice, but then I see her dark silhouette disappear behind the curtain, leaving me in the quiet hall with silent John and the black night.

Time passes as I lie in bed, watching the dark ceiling and the curtain that separates John and me from the rest of the wounded. What would John tell me to do? Would he advise me to try and do something? Escape again? For a moment, I want to wake him up and ask him for his opinion. But ever since he had touched me that night, we have hardly spoken. Every morning, I rush to get dressed and walk away from, and he doesn't try to get close to me either. At least I found the letter I had written in Georgia's name on the floor. It was torn and I taped it back together, even though I should have burned it. But it doesn't matter now, the ship is waiting for me, and I am on the list. A nurse will come in and read my name in a few hours. No one can save me from being shipped back home.

I get up quickly and get out of bed. While trying to grab its metal frame, my hand slips, and I fall to the floor, stifling a scream of pain and trying to stabilize myself.

Breathe, breathe. My fingers wipe away the tears as I sit on the floor. Why is this happening to me? How can anyone get used to falling like that from time to time?

"Grace?" I hear John.

Just get up, don't think about what just happened. My hand is searching for my wooden leg. I placed it on the side of the bed. Where is it?

"Grace, is that you?"

"Yes, it's me. Everything's fine."

"Are you sitting on the floor? I heard your voice coming from down there."

"Yes. I bent down for a moment." Where's my wooden leg? Here it is. I need to connect the straps. In the dark, my fingers search for the buckles.

"Isn't it nighttime right now? Did something happen to you? Do you need my help?"

"It's nighttime. I'm going out for a few minutes. Go back to sleep." I struggle with the buckles.

"I am worried about you. Are you sure you do not need help?"

"Tell me, John." One more buckle.

"Yes?"

"Would you be willing to lie in order to achieve something?"

I hear moving in his bed while I finish connecting the second buckle. I shouldn't have asked him that, these are my problems, not his.

"Yes." He replies after a few seconds, "If it is for a good cause."

"Thank you, John." I hold on to the metal frame of my bed and rise quietly reaching for my crutches, I still need them.

"Grace, do you need help with your lie?"

"No thanks." I smile at him and reach out my hand, but at the last second retract it as to not touch him. I must hurry now, I mustn't delay. I walk through the aisle between the sleeping wounded to the nurses' station.

"May I help you?" The nurse on duty looks up from the book she is reading and stares at me. I don't know her. She has never taken care of me. What do I tell her?

"The list, where is it?"

She hands me the sheet of paper, and I look at the names written on it. Francesca wasn't wrong. I'm on the list.

"I'm sorry." She tells me. She probably already heard the story about the nurse who lost her leg and wanted to stay but must go home tomorrow.

"Do you have a typewriter?" I ask her.

"What do you need it for?"

"I need a typewriter. Will you let me sit here for a few minutes?"

She smiles at me and gets up, takes a typewriter out of one of the closets and places it on the table. "Help yourself."

"What are you doing?" She asks as I shove the smooth paper in the paper guide and turn the knob, placing the list on the table next to me. What should I answer her?

"I am writing a letter."

"I can't let you do that." She looks at me, and I remove my hand from the keys, thinking the only idea I had just failed.

"Grace?" She tells me a moment later and gets up from the small table.

"Yes?"

"I can't let you do that, but I have to go out for a few minutes to check on the wounded. Can you please stay at the station and make sure everything is fine?" And she walks out the door and disappears into the dark, not waiting for me to answer.

My fingers type the list of names on the paper as fast as possible, hoping that the keystrokes do not wake anyone. I need to hurry, but I'm careful not to make typing mistakes. I never liked the typing lessons we had in high school; they were meant to prepare us for being helpful secretaries.

"A good secretary that types without mistakes is a crucial part of her boss's success." Mrs. Friesman lectured us as she walked through the classroom, holding a wooden stick in her hand, and hitting the fingers of those who typed wrong. "Grace, you would make a very bad secretary," she would say and hit my fingers.

"Grace, do you need help?" I hear the nurse a few minutes later.

"Read me the names," I whisper to her and type as fast as I can, making sure not to mix up the identification numbers of the soldiers going home tomorrow.

From the window, I can see the sun beginning to rise as I lay cowering in my bed, waiting for the nurse to enter the hall and start reading from the list. My fingers keep on peeling the plaster off the wall.

"Grace." I hear John whisper to me, "Did your lie succeed?"

"I don't know, but we will know soon enough."

"Adam." I hear the nurse voice and cower further in my bed.

"Going home."

"Arlo." She keeps reading.

"Grace, are you okay?" John whispers to me. I turn to him and place my hand on his fingers feeling their warmth on the white bed.

"Billy." The nurse keeps reading names off the list, and I feel John's fingers grip mine. I close my eyes and feel myself holding on tighter with each name being called off.

"Grace, I think she's done reading the list." I hear John's voice and open my eyes. I see the soldiers standing by their beds, saying goodbye to their friends, preparing for the voyage home, but I continue to hold his fingers tightly. I earned another month, but next time it will not be enough. If I want to be a nurse again, I must do more.

"Can you move fast?"

"No, Head Nurse Blanche." I'm standing in her office. I walked in a few minutes ago without knocking on the door. I want her to hear what I have to say.

"Can you run?"

"I helped the wounded when the planes attacked us." She would not let me into her office anyway. Her door is always closed.

"Yes, you definitely helped." She looks at me, touching and arranging her gray hair, even though it's already perfectly pulled back as if prepared for an army muster. "I have no idea how you did it without your feet. Lucky you weren't injured either."

"I want to be a nurse again." I hold my head high, repeating what I said when I had burst in two minutes ago. Before that, I stood outside her office for a long time, whispering to myself the very same words I would say to her. But now I have forgotten everything I wanted to say, and I'm repeating myself saying that I want to be a nurse again over and over.

"I'm sorry, but how exactly do you want to be a nurse when you were only an intern before, and now you can barely even walk?"

"I have a new leg." I take a step back and pull my pants up, exposing my prosthetic. I have been struggling with the leather strips all morning long and the wooden leg hurts me after a few minutes of walking, but she can't know that. I smile at her pleasantly as if it doesn't hurt at all, trying not to lean on my crutches, even though I brought them with me.

"Very impressive." She doesn't look at my prosthetic leg. "How did you manage to organize that?" She keeps reading from the paper lying in front of her on the table, the same one she was reading when I burst into her office.

"I had some help." I don't want to tell her about Francesca, but it doesn't seem that she cares about my leg either way.

"Yes, I heard that someone had organized a party for the nurses, supplied by U.S. Army food." She writes something on a piece of paper and without looking up at me, "I don't understand at all how you are still here. You were supposed to be on the ship on your way to Gibraltar, continuing to New York harbor from there." She finally raises her eyes from the paper and examines me as if looking for further information on my face.

"They didn't read my name." I look back at her. She mustn't suspect I had anything to do with it.

My leg starts hurting again, and I move a little, trying to get used to my new shoe. I have no idea where one of the nurses found me another shoe. For months now, I have been walking around with only one shoe. I had lost the other one somewhere, maybe during that day, amongst the burning and the screaming.

"So, when you are ready to walk, run, and carry the wounded, you can come again here and reapply to be a nurse. Until then, I will make sure you are on the list of the next ship leaving here." She lowers her gaze and looks back at the paper lying in front of her.

For a moment, I want to scream at her to look at me and see how hard I am trying, but I don't think she really cares. She is interested only in the papers on her desk and her tidy hospital.

"Thank you, Head Nurse Blanche." I turn and intend to leave. I will learn to walk and run and carry the wounded, and I will ask her again. I will not give up anymore.

"You're welcome, have a nice day."

"At least she didn't ask me to dance," I whisper to myself as I push on the door handle.

"Dancing is good too." I hear her mumble before I close the door behind me.

"Go ahead, *Americana*, catch me." Francesca walks away from me on the main road, holding my crutches in her hands.

"Stay where you are, La vedova en moto," I shout to her while walking slowly, keeping my eyes on the road in order not to fall but also to avoid the staring glances of the people standing at the entrance to the hospital.

"*Americana*, your wooden sticks are waiting for you." She lifts my crutches in the air and keeps moving away from me, making sure that I don't catch her. She's completely crazy if she thinks I can walk all that way. I can't walk more than a few steps in a row.

Despite the socks I wrap over my stump, it still hurts me. But I don't intend to give up. Step by step, I walk on the empty road. I will show them that I am not disabled.

"*Americana*, you are not allowed to rest." She calls me when I stop for a second and rearrange the socks over my leg. These are not the socks I received from the village children. I keep those as a souvenir, even though I know I must return them. They probably need them more than I do.

"You are very slow, *Americana*." I stand and look at her from time to time, but most of the time, I look down, trying to keep myself stable, swinging my prosthetic after my healthy leg, trying to move forward.

"Another step," I whisper to myself, ignoring the pain. Despite the pleasant afternoon sun, I'm sweating as if we are in the middle of the summer and not in early fall. "Another step." I'm looking at the road, careful not to slip. "Another step," and I finally reach Francesca.

"Come on, *Italiana*, you can't keep running away from me." I smile through the sweat and the pain. She stands still as I look up and see them.

From a distance, they look like a gray mass surrounded by a cloud of dust rising from the ground. They approach us in long, endless lines, walking on the main road, and I can hear their army boots hitting the broken asphalt.

"Let's move," I whisper to Francesca, but she stays standing in the middle of the road, watching them.

They wear gray uniforms, stained with mud and dust. They walk in two straight rows, followed by a few American soldiers aiming their guns at them, making sure they don't try to escape. They march and approach us, passing us by without stopping even for a second. Most of them have curly light hair and an indifferent look on their face. Some still have rank marks of the German army on their shoulders.

"Vorrei che tu morissi." Francesca says to a German officer. She approaches him, spitting in his face as he continues to march, looking straight ahead.

"Vorrei che tu morissi, I wish you would die." She approaches the next soldier, spitting at him as well.

"Vorrei che tu morissi, I wish you would die." She tries to push the next soldier as he moves away from her, looking forward and marching ahead.

"Vorrei che tu morissi. Bring my husband back!" She screams at the German soldiers, grabs my crutches, and attacks them, beginning to hit and spit at a German POW carrying an officers' rank. "Bring my husband back."

"Francesca," I scream at her as an American soldier from the guard runs up to her, holds and pulls her away from the center of the road. She tries to hit him and free herself, spitting at the German soldiers passing them by.

"Francesca," I shout at her again and walk carefully in her direction, lowering my eyes not wanting to see the Germans. They move out of the way for me, stopping for just a moment before they pass me by. I can smell their sour sweat and hear their labored breathing. I keep walking through the rows of soldiers, coughing and trying to reach her. I forcibly grab her hand and she clings onto me, while the American soldier drags both of us to the side of the road, finally releasing her.

"Bring my husband back." She breaks down crying on the side of the road while I bend down by her side, hugging her shoulders covered with wild black hair. We both sit on the side of the road, her black dress dirty with dust and tears. "Bring my husband back." She doesn't stop crying, as the column of German prisoners passes us by. Their light hair covered with dust, their eyes looking forward while their boots hit the ground at a steady pace as if they were thunderous drums.

"Let's get out of here," I whisper to her as the last of the German prisoners walks by, followed by two American soldiers armed with rifles. One of them stands for a moment and salutes us, even though I am not an officer and Francesca is an Italian.

"Let's get out of here," I whisper to her again, and we both get up. Holding each other, we walk slowly down the deserted road, picking up my crutches from the asphalt.

"Did you meet him before the war broke out?" I ask her after a few minutes. She looks back at the empty road, walks a few steps to the side, and sits down resting on a stone fence.

"You Americans think that wars start in one day, just as the Japanese attacked you in Pearl Harbor. You must think that wars have a start date and an end date," she replies after a few seconds. "But you understand nothing. Wars don't start with bombs and airplanes and explosions; wars start with silence." She holds out her hand, and I take the box of cigarettes out of my shirt pocket and hand her one.

"I was only a girl when my father went out one evening to demonstrate against the fascists." She lights the cigarette and starts talking, "He came back at night with his whole suit stained with blood." Her hands tremble as she holds her cigarette, inhaling the smoke. "My big, strong father who would pick me up on his shoulders and laugh out loud, could barely walk that night, his shirt was so bloody red." She stops talking for a moment, "Mussolini's bullies, the people in the black shirts." She says contemptuously, "would walk the streets, beating all those who dared to go out and demonstrate or strike." She pauses before continuing her story.

"Mother wanted to take him to hospital." She slowly exhales the smoke towards the setting sun. "But he refused. He said they would probably look for him there and arrest him. He recovered, but he never went back to how he was before that, my big, strong father."

"You know?" She turns to me. "The war started many years before the newspapers wrote about it starting."

I think of my home in Chicago, and my dad, who had never demonstrated against anything in his life, and lower my eyes.

"Then, they started to control and monitor us. In every way possible." She continues.

"If you wanted to study, you had to be a member of the fascist youth movement, and if you wanted to be a factory manager, you had to be a member of the fascist party, and if you wanted to contact a government official about a particular problem and actually have anyone listen to you, you had to be a fascist party member." She keeps on talking, "anything that you wanted to do, you had to be one of them. You had to bow down to Mussolini, the Duce. And you had to choose, to bow down, or live in fear."

"Fear of what?" I ask, lighting a cigarette for myself.

"Fear of the nights." She goes on pausing for a moment,

"in fear that someone will report you and then they will come at night to arrest you. They always came at night. They loved the night. It wasn't for nothing that they called themselves the black shirts and chose black uniforms." She spits on the dirt road. "For years, I lived in fear of the night. I hate the night. But that's how I met him too."

"Your husband?"

"Yes, my husband."

"At night?"

"Do you know how it is that you are young and stupid and believe that you will be able to change the world?" She looks at me.

"Yes," I answer her, remembering how I would run out of our house window and go out to meet my girlfriends. We would go to stand outside the dance halls in the center of town, watching the women dance, feeling so bold and free. Now, compared to Francesca, it feels so childish.

"It was before the 'real' war, before they started reporting on it in the newspapers." She speaks slowly, "we were a group of young people who believed we would be able to stop them, so we decided to rebel, like young people do. How naïve we must have been." She smiles to herself. "So we went to Rome, where no one could recognize us."

"And what happened?"

"We wrote a graffiti against Mussolini on some wall of a building. We didn't have the courage to do anything more than that. But we heard footsteps and feared it was the police or the black shirts and fled."

"And it was then when you met him?"

"They all disappeared. My friends and I, we all ran in different directions, and I walked alone for hours on the streets, imagining that I was going to be caught. It was already evening, and of course, I was late for the last bus back home." She points her head towards her village. "I was just standing between the platforms of the empty bus station, panting and worried I would meet a bunch of black shirt bullies, when he showed up with his motorcycle and took me back to the village." I notice her smiling to herself. "I asked him to take me. I had to ask someone, and it turned out I asked someone who would want to buy me a dress a year later."

"He sure is a lovely man."

"He said we would not be able to stop Mussolini's fascists, and I said we would succeed, and he was right." She puts out her hand, and I take the box of cigarettes out of my pocket and hand her another one.

"And he wanted to buy me a dress with flowers on it. I didn't agree because I told him it's bad luck when a man buys a dress for a woman. He didn't buy me the dress, but I was wrong; in the end, I was left without a floral dress and with bad luck."

"You couldn't possibly know." I exhale my cigarette smoke into the air, watching the sky getting darker.

"He hated the fascists even more than I did, but he had no choice. He had to draft into the army, otherwise, he would be hanged for treason. You see, we couldn't choose which side to be on."

I want to tell her something encouraging, but I can't think of anything as I wipe the tears from my eyes.

"So, he wasn't killed by the fascists. Instead, he disappeared in Russia and must have been killed by the Red Army." She looks at me, and I can see that she's crying too.

"You don't know it. Maybe he was taken as a prisoner of war and is still alive."

"Yes, you never know," she looks at the empty road where

the German prisoners of war had just passed. "The dress was so beautiful, and I wanted it so badly, but we just got married, and it cost so much, and I thought we should not waste so much money. You never know what the future holds. I hate Rome."

"You never know what the future holds." I lightly hit the stone terrace with my wooden foot.

"At least I have someone to smoke with."

"The lame with the wooden leg and the widow with the motorcycle." I smile at her when we get up, and she supports me as we walk back towards the hospital.

"Let's go around," I ask her, looking at the hospital entrance, as we enter through the destroyed iron gate. Near the wide steps of the entrance to the building, where once the landlord and his wife must have stood wearing their formal evening clothes, greeting the guests who arrived in their Rolls-Royce and Bentley cars, now stands a military jeep marked with the white American star. Instead of lavish dinner guests, nurses are now sitting on the steps, talking to the two pilots standing in front of them.

"Is everything alright?" She asks me as I turn towards the stone wall, looking for the gap in the wall that allows us to go through to the garden and the back entrance of the hospital.

"I just want to see the sunset," I tell her, but even though she doesn't answer, I think she doesn't believe me. One of the nurses laughs out loud and stands up in front of the pilots, swaying and making dance movements. I used to love dancing so much once.

"1944, the victory will happen this year." Back then, in the ballroom in Chicago, the sentence was clearly written on the poster that hung from the ceiling, spread wide from one side of to the other. This was less than a year ago, right before I boarded the train that would take me to New York harbor and then to the war.

"1944, look up." The announcer at the New Year's ball in Chicago shouted to the crowd, and a huge cloud of balloons fell from the ceiling to the sounds of our excited cheers.

"Look," I called happily and pointed to the red and white balloons that had fallen on our heads, ignoring the sweat pouring from me after hours of dancing. I think his name was Fred, the soldier who danced with me all through that evening. He was wearing a white navy uniform, and he hadn't yet received any war medals. He tried to kiss me, explaining that he was headed to San Francisco on his way to Hawaii the very next day. He promised to beat the Japanese and come back to Chicago to marry me.

"You don't know me at all." I laughed at him, raising my voice to overcome the loud music, as I held on to his broad shoulders, adjusted my steps to his, and let him put a hand on my waist. My eyes were looking around at all the soldiers dancing with their girls, maybe for the last time just like for Fred and me.

"I'll kill the Japs so fast that I'd be back before you have time to forget me." He brought his lips to my ears, hoping I would kiss him.

"I'm going tomorrow too," I said to him, and it seemed to me that he didn't hear me at all, but I didn't care. All I cared about was dancing with a handsome soldier that held me in his arms, with all the other soldiers and beautiful women surrounding us.

"Where are you going?"

"To the war." I laughed and let him hold me tighter, knowing that I would board the train to New York the next day to begin a new and exciting adventure.

He left me alone on the dancing floor for a few moments and then returned, holding two glasses of champagne. "To the war, for bringing people together."

"To the war and to all the adventures ahead of us." I smiled at him and sipped the sweet drink. And as we kept on dancing, he slightly lowered his hand resting on my back, and I didn't move it away. Still, I did not let him kiss me, even when the evening was over, and we said goodbye at the entrance to the ballroom. I promised to meet again, knowing it would never happen. I think I didn't even tell him my name, knowing that he would look for another girl to dance with in San Francisco or Hawaii the next day or the next week. I was okay with that. I knew that I would have many more chances to dance.

At the end of that evening, my legs hurt, and the high heels bothered me so much that I wanted to remove them and walk home barefoot. It was almost dawn, and I had to hurry and pack for the train, but I walked home slowly, smiling at the paperboys. That night, the war was so exciting.

But now, the hall of the wounded is quiet at night, and I'm reading a book to John, not knowing if he's listening to me or already asleep.

He has been letting me read to him since the day he held my hand while the nurse kept reading the names of the soldiers that were going home. But still, he lies in bed all day and refuses to go out to the garden. He also refuses to let me read Georgia's old letters. I'm afraid to tell him that she had left him. I'm also afraid to write him another letter that could somehow reveal that I'm lying, too. I close the book and look at him. I must stop thinking about that. He's not my problem. He has Audrey, who strokes his hair every morning and takes care of him, smiling at him constantly.

"John, do you like to dance?"

"I'm blind, Grace, blind people don't dance." He whispers towards the ceiling.

"John, I need your help," I whisper back to him.

"Are you offering me a walk in the garden? Actually, it could be nice." He says quietly while I approach him, "Maybe we could invite some German airplanes to attack us again. Then I could lie in the dark and wonder if this time the airplanes would finish what the previous ones had failed to do. I might try and think about where I could run and hide, but it doesn't matter either way." He keeps on talking. "Because either way, I can't run away from them even if I tried. I'm blind."

"John, enough with that. They were here and now they are gone. You survived, isn't that the important part?"

"Grace, have you ever felt helpless?" He reaches out into the air but doesn't move towards me, perhaps afraid of touching me again, like he did last time.

"John, we were all wounded by this war." I'm getting closer to him, placing my hand on his arm.

"No, Grace, not all of us are like those wounded who are in pain right now but will recover, keeping only the memories of their injury," he holds me too, and I feel the warmth of his fingers. "I mean, have you ever felt really helpless; that it doesn't matter what you do, it's not up to you anymore?"

"Yeah, John, I have felt like that. I have been feeling that way for months." I release his hand from my shoulder. He doesn't really listen to me, no matter what I say.

"Then you probably understand me." He leans back and looks up at the ceiling. What should I tell him?

I watch him lie motionless in his bed, as if waiting for me to assure him that he will recover; to assure him that nothing and no one else would attack him. How can I promise him that?

"I understand you," I finally say, "but, out of all of the soldiers and the nurses and walking in the garden that day, you were the first one to recognize the danger, and then you laid down and covered your head. You tried to do the best you could. You weren't helpless, you were never helpless, even now when you're blind." I try to find the right words, I keep looking at him as he looks at the ceiling instead of my direction, but I know I'm failing. "You're blind, and you're alive, and I'm just asking for your help, not because I feel sorry for you, but because I think you're the best person to help me," I whisper to him, trying not to raise my voice so that the nurse on duty doesn't have a reason to come and check on us.

But he doesn't answer, and I lie down in my bed and continue reading the book, wanting to take a pencil, mark and erase all the parts where the hero succeeds at the end.

"*Americana*, what do you need help with?" He asks after a while. "I heard the Italian woman calling you that name."

"It's dark outside now, so no airplane will be coming to attack us." I feel his hand gripping my shoulders as we walk slowly through the front driveway of the hospital, listening to the sound of gravel under our feet.

"We're standing in the front driveway. There's no one here to look at us." I tell him, looking around at the silhouettes of the military trucks and jeeps parked underneath the cypress trees. "There is a big Red Cross flag spread on the ground," but in the dark, I can't see the bullet holes left by the Germans' attack. If it was less dark, I could probably see the bullet marks on the building wall.

"There are only the two of us here." I stand in front of him.

"And I need you to dance with me." I let the crutches fall on the gravel and hold his hands, placing them on my waist.

I can feel the warmth of his hands through my hospital shirt as he holds me gently. I place my hands on his arms, feeling his shoulder muscles while we both begin to slowly sway from side to side, making sure not to step on each other. The only sound I can hear is the creaking of the gravel underneath our feet, while I try to stabilize my wooden leg, teaching myself to walk again.

What does he think of me? I look up at him, but in the dark, I can only see his silhouette looking towards the trees. I hold myself back from resting my head on his chest.

"Grace, is everything okay?" He asks after a while as we continue to move slowly in the center of the front driveway.

"Yes, everything is fine." I look up and smile at him even though he's unable to see me, not telling him that I'm in pain.

My wooden leg sinks into the gravel with every step, and I feel the pain of my injury. I hold John tightly to reduce the pressure on my stump, and I fight the urge to clench my palms into fists from the pain. It hurts so much, but I won't give up. I can feel tears of pain running down my cheeks; luckily, he can't see.

"Are you sure everything's fine?"

"Yes, I'm missing the music."

"We can hum."

"I'm too shy to be heard. We're so close to the entrance of the hospital."

"So, let's get further away from here, take me somewhere else."

I must hold his hand to pick up the crutches from the ground. We start walking, crossing the iron gate lying at the entrance of the mansion, walking to the main road in front of the hospital.

In the dim light of the moon, I can barely see the road and the trees around us, but there are no vehicles passing here tonight, and we are alone with only the dark trees looking at us.

"It's better here." I hold his waist again and start humming a song by Ella Fitzgerald, moving my feet on the hard asphalt, realizing it hurts me less over here.

It takes him a while to start humming the song along with me. His hands tighten around my waist, and I get a little closer to him. If someone were to pass by right now, they would think we were a loving couple, But John makes sure to hold himself far enough from me, as I try to adjust to his body movements, being careful not to touch his leg with my wooden leg.

"Are you comfortable?"

"Yes, thank you." I keep leaning on his body, my leg still hurts, but a little less now. I'll have to get used to the pain.

"Do you like this song?" He asks after a while.

"Yes, and you?"

"I'm not used to it."

"You're not used to dancing? I'm sorry, I did not think about that." I stop dancing and stand, still holding his waist.

"I apologize." I look around, searching for my crutches.

"I love to dance," he answers me quietly, "and I enjoy dancing with you," he pauses for a moment. "But I'm not used to dancing with another girl other than Georgia."

"I'm sorry, I didn't think of that."

"She's my girl," he stops holding me and takes a few steps back, leaving me to stand alone in the middle of the dark road. "We used to do everything together since we became a couple in high school. I had never danced with anyone else other than Georgia." He bends down, fumbles with his hands on the asphalt, and sits on the road. "I know I have to write and tell her about my injury and about what had happened to me. I've known this for days now."

"Oh, John." I approach him slowly, careful not to fall.

"Don't pity me." He looks up, "Just don't that, please. You told me before you didn't feel sorry for me."

"I don't." I stop where I am.

"Everyone feels sorry for me, especially the nurses. Audrey caresses my head as if I were a little boy, speaking to me in a motherly tone all day. As if one more caress would improve my blindness."

"I don't." I retract my hand, which was inches away from touching his dark hair.

"Please, at least you of all people, don't feel sorry for me." He keeps on talking while sitting on the empty road, "I know I need to write to her and tell her I'm coming home soon, but not as the John she is hoping to see. I'm a damaged man who can't do anything; I can't work, I can't walk alone in the street not knowing whether to turn right or left." His voice breaks, he starts crying, and even though I'm not supposed to, I take two steps towards him, manage to lean over without falling, and hug him.

"You're not damaged. There isn't a single flaw in you. You'll be okay, you'll see."

"How do you know?" His crying intensifies. "What will I write to her?"

"I don't know," I hug him tightly and whisper into his ear, "but you'll be okay." I feel his entire body trembling. "And as for Georgia, don't tell her you were injured, not yet. You don't have to tell her right now. You can wait on that."

"What does it matter if I wait or not? Do you think it would change her pain when she reads my letter?"

"I don't know what it would change for her," I stroke the back of his neck, "but maybe it would change your pain."

"You don't know a lot of things."

"Yeah, I don't know a lot of things." I keep hugging him, and his warm hands wrap around my body as if trying to hold on to me.

"Let's get away from here, let's go back to the hospital, to our corner," I whisper to him after a few minutes of silence, grabbing him and trying to get up off the road. My leg hurts, and I want to remove the prosthetic. I'm probably only hurting him with my words, either way.

"Can I invite you to dance?" He gets up and reaches out his hands, searches for me, and I guide his hands to hold my waist again.

While we continue to dance in the middle of the empty, dark road, he quietly sings a song by Frank Sinatra. I look up at his tender lips and ignore the pain in my legs. My head rests on his chest even though I know he's not mine.

In the distance, I can see the faint lights of a vehicle approaching. I can hear the engine sound, and we move to the side of the road. A A jeep, loaded with cheerful nurses, passing us on a slow drive before turning to the hospital. They get off, laughing, disappearing through the entrance of the building.

"Who were they?" John asks me.

"Audrey and her nurse friends coming back from visiting the pilots."

"They're having fun."

"Yeah, they're having fun." I feel his hands still holding my waist.

Later, I feel his hand on my shoulder as we walk back to the hospital, crossing the front driveway. I try not to limp as I feel the pain caused by the wood against my stump.

"Pay attention; three steps at the entrance to the hospital," I whisper to him. The nurses have already gone inside after bidding a loud farewell to the pilots. The jeep has gone too, passing us on its way back to the airfield.

"Three steps," John repeats after me, "are you okay?"

"Yes, I'm just a little tired. The entrance to the hall, you already know the hall." I don't tell him about my pain.

"Seventeen steps on the right."

"Exactly." I bite my lip.

"And then in the aisle between the beds of the other wounded."

"Thirty-eight steps" of humiliating stares from the other wounded.

"I used to count thirty-three steps."

"We'll go at your own pace." I need to take off the wooden leg rest my leg stump.

"Are they looking at us?"

"No, it's late at night."

"What are they doing?"

I stop for a moment and look around. I don't think I ever looked up from the floor at this point in the aisle. I must ignore the pain. John will notice if I show that it hurts me.

"Everyone is sleeping," I whisper to him as I look around, examining the quiet hall. "There's one person reading a book, or maybe a letter." I keep on walking.

"I haven't received any more letters from Georgia." I feel his grip around my shoulders tightening.

"I'm sure that she has written to you, and that the letter is on its way." I look down again, adjusting my gait to his pace. Fifteen more steps until we reach our beds. I'll have to write him another letter.

"We're at your bed." I take his hand and place it on the metal frame, letting him hold it.

"Thank you, Grace."

"Not at all." I sit down on my bed, rushing to release the leather straps holding the prosthetic, feeling the blood flow through my amputated leg, and scratching my foot hard with my toes. Quietly, not wanting to make any noise, I get out of bed and place the wooden leg on the floor. I sit myself down next to it, leaning against the wall, rubbing the stump as hard as I can, being careful not to injure the skin. I shouldn't have danced with John, it's too early.

"I enjoyed tonight." I hear him.

"Me too. I had a good time." I try not to sigh.

"What are you doing on the floor?"

"Just sitting." In a few minutes more, the pain will pass.

"Would you like me to join you on the floor?"

"No, it's okay," I'm trying to smile at him; he can feel it when I smile.

"Thank you for listening to me when we were out. Would you please not tell anyone that I cried?"

"I won't tell." My hand wipes the tears running down my cheeks. The pain isn't going away. Why did I try to dance?

"Some days are hard for me." I hear him whisper. "There are days I feel I can't go on like this," he speaks slowly, "I tell you this only because you're a nurse."

"I'm an injured nurse." I raise my head and lean it against the wall, close my eyes and let the tears flow.

"But you will recover soon. I can hear it in the way you talk, the way you walk, I can tell that your limp is improving."

"Yes, I'll recover soon."

"Sometimes I think I need to give up. All this darkness is just too scary."

"Don't give up," I whisper to him and caress the spot where my leg used to be, remembering how I screamed at Audrey when I had just arrived, and the pain overwhelmed me. She used to like me back then, before I had decided I want to return to being a nurse.

"Let me die, please, just three doses of morphine in one shot." I cried after finding out my leg was amputated, trying to grab the glass vial she was holding in her hand.

"It's okay. The pain will go away." Audrey hugged me, ignoring my sweaty body and my trembling hands.

"What will go away?" I screamed and cried, "Will my leg recover and grow back?"

"The pain," she continued to hold me tightly, "the pain will pass, I promise you."

"You had already promised it yesterday and the day before," I cried, trying to push her away from me. "Please give me more morphine, please."

"Don't give up. You must recover. You must overcome the pain."

"What for?" I cried loudly, my eyes welling up.

"Just get through the night, one night at a time." She kept hugging me until I finally fell asleep at the break of dawn.

"Don't give up, just go through the night, one night at a time," I whisper to John as I caress my amputated leg, take deep breaths, and pray for my pain to go away. Perhaps he had already fallen asleep. Perhaps his pain will pass with time, and one day he would find out that although she no longer likes him, Audrey was right.

"It's hard to feel helpless." He says quietly.

"I have a cane that I can give you," I look at my cane, which is leaning against the wall. Francesca brought it for me from the village a few days ago, so I could use it instead of my hated crutches, "You can try to walk with it by yourself." He needs it more than I do. I hope Francesca will understand.

"Thank you, Grace from Chicago."

"Good night, John from Cold Spring, New York."

"Do you think Georgia will accept me the way I am?"

"I'm sure she's going to love you the way you are." I'm scratching my thighs with my nails wanting to write to her and ask her why she had left him. How can I tell him he was left all alone?

"Good night, Grace from Chicago. I'll try not to give up."

"Good night, John from Cold Spring. Don't give up."

Herald

"Doctor, don't give up. We can still save him."

Just a few minutes have passed since Audrey approached our corner, telling me that Head Nurse Blanche was asking whether I was still capable of assisting the doctor with the surgery. "Yes," I answered her immediately, leaving the book I have been reading for hours, rushing to attach my wooden leg, and following her. I didn't even try to think why she was being nice to me again or why Blanche remembered me at all. It could be because the operating room nurses went out tonight to meet the pilots, or it could be related to the recent attacks on the German lines in the north and the stream of wounded soldiers that kept on coming.

And now, I'm the only nurse in the operating room, standing in front of the wounded soldier lying on the operating table.

"Save your breath." The doctor shakes his head, "It's a waste of time."

"Please, Doctor," I beg him, knowing that if he dies, Blanche will never give me another chance.

"I can try, but I don't think he will survive." He looks at me, "Are you new here?"

"Yes,"

Audrey agreed to give me a uniform set. I closed the curtain behind me and got dressed as fast as I could. I was standing with my back turned to John and had to remind myself that it didn't matter, that he couldn't see me either way. And now I'm standing in front of the wounded and trying to look confident. So much time had passed. Why am I the only nurse here? Why is there no one else here to help me?

"Clean and prep him for surgery."

"Right away, Doctor." I smile at him, hold the scissors, and start cutting off his blue-gray uniform, exposing his injured chest. I must not think about him. I must do everything necessary to keep him alive. This is my chance to prove myself.

"I wonder how he got here," I say as the doctor examines the light hairs on his chest while I disinfect his skin with iodine, making sure he is ready.

"I heard two guys brought him here on a jeep." He is holding the scalpel, "They left him at the entrance and hurried back." He examines his wound and starts cutting his skin, "He'd been waiting here for a long time, they couldn't find an available nurse. He might die of blood loss."

"I'm sorry," I don't even know why I'm apologizing.

"Ten blade." He reaches out his hand, and I hand him the scalpel.

"Vascular Scissors. Is this your first time with one of theirs?" He asks me after a few minutes.

"Yes." I hand him the scissors and turn around for a moment, examining his soldier's uniform laying on the floor. According to his ranks, he is an officer.

"Needle J shape. With us, the doctors, we always send the new one." He smiles at me under his surgeon's mask, "so I had no choice."

"I volunteered," I hand him the needle.

"You have a grace, even though they're not going to like you for that."

But I don't answer back, and he continues to operate quietly. Maybe I was wrong that I agreed to do this, but I had no idea, and no one had told me. What other choice did I have? I have to stay focused; this is my chance to be a nurse again.

"Should I give him more morphine?" I ask the doctor when he makes another incision, and the injured soldier sighs in pain.

"No, one dose is enough for him. We should keep the morphine for the rest of our wounded. I'm done." He looks up at me, "you can take it from here; continue closing to finish the job. Use the curved needle." He hands me the scalpels and backs away from the wounded soldier, cursing under his breath before getting out of the room. I'm left alone with the German wounded soldier lying on the operating table.

My fingers tremble as I try to prepare the thread to suture his wounds. It's been a long time since the last time I stitched an injury, and I have to hurry so that the wound doesn't get infected. But my eyes constantly wander from his pale chest to the floor, where his boots lay next to his torn German Air Force uniform. His eyes are closed, and his face is still covered with dirt and soot from a fire; a sign of him escaping a burning plane. Why did they bring him to us? Couldn't they just leave him exactly where they had found him?

I stop the suturing for a moment, take a clean bandage, wet it with some water, and clean the remnants of blood and soot from his face, feeling his skin and warm lips. He is still alive. I have to keep sewing him back up.

My fingers quickly run over his open wound, closing it as I try to ignore his uniform and boots staring at me from the floor. When I finally can't take it any longer, I kick them with my healthy leg, holding the operating table for support. Why did they ask me to treat him?

"I'm done," I call out into the hall after a few minutes. I make sure to wash my hands thoroughly, and go out into the hallway, looking for the soldiers who can take him wherever they take wounded like him.

"Can we take him?" Two soldiers approach us and hold his arms and legs, transferring him to a hospital bed.

"Carefully, where are you taking him?"

"To the end of the hall, behind the curtain, he should be separated from the rest of the wounded. Head Nurse Blanche said there are two wounded in recovery there, who need to be moved."

What do I tell John? I have no courage to help them move him to a new place.

I stand at the entrance of the hall and see the soldiers waiting patiently, standing by the German's bed, while Audrey approaches John, strokes his arm, and explains something to him. I'm not sure he understands.

What have I done? Now he will be even more alone. Why did I agree to help with the surgery?

John gets up from his bed and walks beside her, holding the metal frame of the bed as she pushes it to another spot in the hall. Someone else takes my bed and moves it along the aisle, placing it in another corner, far away from John.

The wounded German remains in the spot that was once ours; with the two soldiers standing on either side of him. I keep looking at them until one of them pulls the curtain closed obstructing my view. I need to go and get used to the new spot where my bed now stands., Maybe there's a wall I can stare at night, or another wounded soldier I can read a book to. Why do I care? It's not my job to help John recover.

"Grace?"

"Yes." I turn around towards the nurse calling me.

"Head Nurse Blanche wants to see you."

"I'm coming," I answer, but remain standing at the entrance of the hall for a few moments. This is the first time I have been invited to her office.

"It's good to see you walking in here without bursting." She raises her head while sitting behind her desk, looking at me.

"Yes, Head Nurse Blanche." I look at her and smile.

"Tell me, Grace, do you know anything about American army meat cans going around in the village?"

"No, Head Nurse Blanche." I lift my chin and look out of the window behind her back overlooking the bay. Even though I know she could punish me, I would have done it again if I had to.

"The surgeon said you did an excellent job."

"Thank you, Head Nurse Blanche."

"Let me tell you what we'll do until your ship arrives," she looks down at the paper lying on the table in front of her and then looks up at me again, as if expecting me to say something. I just stand there, not saying a word. Either way, she hates me already.

"We had to put the wounded German in your spot in the

hall," she says what I already know, ignoring the fact that I don't have my little corner anymore. "He's a prisoner of war." She carries on, "he should be separated from the other wounded. You can take your things and go find yourself an empty bed in one of the nurses' rooms."

"Thank you, Head Nurse Blanche." It takes me a second to register what she is saying to me, but I keep standing still.

"And make sure they give you a new white nurses' uniform." She holds a rubber stamp and presses it against the paper lying in front of her, handing it to me. "Here, this time you will have the right note of request."

"Yes, Head Nurse Blanche." I'm not daring to smile; afraid she might change her mind.

"And get out of my office so you can start celebrating, now that you've finally got what you wanted. Luckily for you, I have a shortage of nurses."

"Yes, Head Nurse Blanche."

I close the door behind me and lean against it. I succeeded. My hand is holding the note instructing them to give me a new uniform. I must tell John; he will be so pleased with me. I have so much to organize. Perhaps I'll invite him to dance with me again on the road tonight. I don't care if my leg hurts. I close my eyes and smile to myself. I'll tell him right away.

"John, hold on to me." I see Audrey leading him out of the hall toward the garden, guiding him to place his hand on her shoulder as they slowly walk out.

"Let's go outside. I'll lead you to the bench and come back to visit you later." She smiles at me when she notices me standing at the top of the stairs.

"Yes, Nurse Audrey, I like to sit outside and look at the sea." He answers her, and I cringe. How can I tell him I will no longer be by his side? Who will read to him every night?

My eyes follow them as they leave the hall and walk towards the garden, careful not to move or make any noise, thinking how lucky it is that he can't see.

After they disappear into the garden and I can't hear them anymore, I go down the stairs of the second floor and into the hall, limping to the corner that was once ours. I must take my things out of the locker; this is the German's spot now.

I count thirty-eight steps as I look around at the wounded, occasionally looking at the floor and being careful not to slip; my corner is waiting for me one last time.

The wounded German is lying in the spot that was previously mine, his eyes are closed, and his pale chest moves slowly with each breath he takes. The locker that John and I shared is by his side now, still filled with my personal belongings. The soldiers who had accompanied him disappeared, and he looked just like any other wounded soldier covered with bandages.

"Goodbye, wall," I whisper to my loyal wall, running my hand over it for the last time, pressing my fingers against the lines that counted the days of the approaching ship, looking at the drawings I had made and touching the peeling plaster that I had removed with my nails when I was in so much pain. "Thanks."

I bend over to the metal locker, pulling out my army duffel bag and small personal backpack, the only item that came with me to the hospital after the injury. All of my other equipment was lost. One last look to see if I had forgotten anything behind me, and I turn to walk away.

For a moment, I look at the German, thinking that not so long ago I was lying there, just like him. I managed to move forward; this is no longer my place. Suddenly, this corner of the hall and the man breathing quietly seem foreign to me; I have to get out of there and go to my new room.

An hour later, I place my bag on the empty bed in the nurses' room on the second floor. This is my spot from now on. All of the other nurses are on duty; I look at their iron beds covered with military wool blankets. I put the new white uniform I received right beside the khaki ones, folded on the bed.

Button after button, I button the white uniform up and examine myself in the filthy mirror attached to the wall. My wooden leg seems so noticeable. What can I do?

"You are Pinocchio," I whisper to myself, "you are a wooden doll who dreams of being a real child."

I sit down on the creaking iron bed and try to pull the white socks up as much as I can, but that's not enough, the yellow wooden prosthetic can be seen above them.

"Pinocchio, you will never become a real child. Your wooden leg will always stand out." I say to myself as I get up and try to pull the uniform dress down as much as possible, but it's not enough of course, everyone will be able to see that I am a wooden Pinocchio, a lame doll who struggles to walk.

I take off the white nurse's uniform and put on the simple khaki pants instead. They look like the ones I had at the hospital on the front lines. At least these ones are clean and not stained with mud and blood.

"Now I look just like a lame soldier," I whisper to myself as I look in the mirror.

"You can't tell I don't have a leg, nor that I'm a nurse." I wipe the tears from my eyes, open my personal bag, and turn its contents over on the stretched woolen blanket on the bed.

My fingers search through my things until I find two photos of myself that I had brought with me from home. The photos were taken on the day I finished nursing school. There I am, standing and smiling, both legs still attached. I hate these pictures, and I hate the leg I no longer have.

I take John's lighter, bring the yellow photos closer to the flame, and watch them burn with great satisfaction.

"Now I'm just the khaki Pinocchio, no more Grace with both legs," I whisper to the ash flakes scattered on the floor, crushing them with my wooden leg.

"Are you the new nurse, Grace?" A nurse I've never met before is standing at the door.

"Yes."

"I have been told to come get you, there's surgery, and they need you."

"I'm coming," I say to her, wiping my tears. I must stop with all this crying.

Careful not to slip, I walk into the operating room, tucking John's lighter into my pocket. I will tell him that I'm back to being a nurse in the evening.

I have been sitting in the dark in the garden for hours, looking at the hospital windows, waiting for everyone to go to sleep. Maybe John will fall asleep as well. I assisted in three surgeries today, working with two doctors who said I did an excellent job. Still, I hesitate to go into the building and look for John's bed and tell him that I am a nurse again.

The building windows go dark one by one until only two are left lit, looking like two eyes in the dark, staring at me. One of them probably belongs to Head Nurse Blanche, who never sleeps. I must get up and go search for his bed. I must promise him that I'll keep on coming to visit him.

In the pocket of my new uniform, there is a letter I wrote to him in between surgeries. She's telling him how much she misses their conversations. Still, I don't get up, it feels nice to keep sitting on the bench outside, all alone in the night.

Another window in the building goes dark, leaving only one to brighten up the blackness of the night outside; it's like a lighthouse showing me my way back home. It's time to go inside.

I keep sitting on the bench, playing with my cane. I asked Francesca to bring me a new one after giving John the one I had received from her as a gift.

"*Americana,* you do not give away my gifts, do you hear?" She said, still agreeing to bring me a new stick in exchange for a couple of canned meat and cigarettes.

"Americana, I don't need your charity." She looked at me, taking the things from my hands. "And don't think this is going to make me be nicer to you." She turned her back to me and walked to our spot behind the shed.

I take the cane she brought me from the village and use it as I slowly climb the stairs to the second floor, walking to the nurses' sleeping quarters. He must have fallen asleep already, I'll visit him tomorrow.

"Good afternoon, Gracie, I can recognize you by your walk." John says the next day as I approach and sit beside him on the bench overlooking the sea. He's never called me Gracie before, and I want to hold his hand resting on the bench, but I'm restraining myself from doing so.

"I wanted to come yesterday, but I was busy."

"It's okay, isn't it ironic?" He smiles at the sky.

"Why Ironic?" I feel sorry that I didn't come talk to him yesterday.

"Because at the end, the Germans did manage to separate between us." He looks in my direction, even though he doesn't see me.

"What did they tell you?"

"That there is a wounded German prisoner of war recovering in the hall and that he should be separated from the others."

"And that's it?" Did they tell him who helped operate on him?

"No," he moves his head and continues smiling into the horizon, "they told me that you have recovered and that I will no longer be sleeping by your side. That you have returned to being a lovely nurse wearing a white uniform. Well, they didn't actually mention the white uniform."

"Yes, I have recovered, but in the meantime, I'm staying here." I finally hold his hand resting on the bench. I won't leave him alone.

"Can you see the seagull?" He points his chin towards the horizon, and I look at the sky and the clouds in the distance but don't see a single bird.

"I'm sorry, I can't see it."

"It's because you're not blind," he smiles at me, "I can see what I want, and you look like a seagull. You're a lovely nurse in a white uniform."

"Yes, I'm a nurse wearing a white uniform." I don't want to tell him why I'm wearing the khaki pants instead of the white dress.

"It's time for you to start flying, spread your wings like a white bird." He looks in my direction, white bandages are covering his eyes.

"But I'll come visit you every day." I take the letter I had written for him out of my pocket, but after a second, I regret it and put it back. "I'll come visit you at night, I promise."

"You won't come, but it's okay." He turns his gaze back to the sea, "We're at war, you shouldn't make promises at war, and you're like the seagull that flies one place to another."

I want to tell him that he and Georgia had made promises to each other, but then I think of her and her broken promise and stop myself.

"I'll come in the evening." I get up and walk away from him.

"Goodbye, Gracie from Chicago." I'm glad he's calling me Gracie.

"Goodbye, John from Cold Spring, New York. I'll come visit." I'm walking away from him, knowing I'm not going to keep my promise as I've already registered to assist surgeries tonight.

The next afternoon, after finishing my shift, I see her sitting behind the shed, in the corner that belongs to me. She's leaning against the old wall, sitting on the ground like I usually do.

"Audrey, are you okay?" I stand at a distance from her.

"I know you tend to sit here," she looks at me, "this is the secret spot where the limping nurse usually hides at, isn't it?"

I stand and look at her while she takes a box of cigarettes out of her white uniform pocket and lights one, blowing the smoke slowly, "I haven't changed his bandages in two days." She looks up at me again.

"Whose bandages?"

"His."

"The German's?"

"Yes." She nods her head and continues to speak slowly. "For two days now, I've been approaching his bed, standing behind the curtain and doing nothing."

"Why?" I look at her trembling fingers holding the cigarette.

"I know I need to change his bandages." She motions for me to sit next to her, "and that if I don't change them, he will die, and I'm a professional nurse who knows how to do her job, but I just can't take care of him."

"Yes, there is an oath nurses take, and we must uphold it." I keep standing next to her. She's not my friend.

"Gracie, you can sit down. I won't bite you." She moves a little and makes room for me, and I sit down but keep some distance from her. I hate that she calls me Gracie.

"Do you believe in this oath?" She asks me as I lean against the old wall, feeling the rough plaster through my khaki uniform.

"I don't know." My hands play with the dry leaves scattered around me.

"I believe in this oath, that we should take care of all wounded, no matter what," she exhales the smoke, "and I'm a professional nurse." She continues to speak slowly, "but I'm standing and looking at him, unable to touch him. He's German."

"You know," she continues after a moment, not waiting for me to answer, "when they brought him in, Blanche specifically called me to her office and asked if I would be willing to take care of him because none of the other nurses are willing to do that. She told me that I'm the only one she can count on. I'm always the one that can be relied upon, even when it comes to taking care of a screaming intern nurse, who has lost her leg." She blows the smoke into the sky again and looks at me, but I lower my eyes.

"Thank you," I say after a time.

"And I told her I was ready," She ignores my 'thank you,' "because I'm a professional nurse and he's a wounded man just like all the other wounded. Except that he's not like the other wounded. He's German."

"Is that why you wanted me to assist during his surgery?"

"Not everything is about you, Gracie, I'm the one taking care of the German. When I stand by his bed and look at him, I can't stop thinking that maybe he's the pilot who shot at us that day?" Her fingers play with the leaves scattered around us, crumbling one of them.

"I don't think he's one of them," I answer, "there are far too many German pilots in the sky for it to be him."

"So maybe it's some of his friends? So why should we take care of him? Why does he deserve to live? Maybe he deserves to die?"

"I don't know," I answer her. What can I tell her? That she must treat him? That she took an oath? Does anyone even listen to the oaths and the promises in this never-ending war?

"You're probably one of those people who wanted to save the world, just like the woman at the recruiting center promised you would." She looks at me, and I smile a bitter smile back at her, remembering the woman at the recruiting center and the words she said.

"Girls, when you travel overseas, your white uniform represents the good, compassionate America, the one that extends a supportive hand to the Americans wounded and all of the wounded who are fighting in this difficult war." She spoke enthusiastically, then, at the recruitment conference in Chicago.

"Yes, I wanted to save the world," I answer her.

"I came here to be a professional, and I'm a professional nurse. For two years now, I've been a professional, tidy nurse, working according to the rules, smiling at the wounded, caring for them, stroking their hair." She doesn't look at me when she speaks, "I'm good to everyone, but suddenly there's this German."

I don't reply, I just keep playing with the dry leaves on the ground. What can I tell her to encourage her? Even though she treated me, she doesn't really like me. She used to like me only when I was helpless.

"But not with him," she continues, "Gracie, I think I shouldn't take care of him, you know." She looks at me again, "I stand by his bed and look at him and think maybe he should die. Maybe it's time for another nurse to take care of him. I shouldn't be taking care of the German, and it doesn't make me any less good of a nurse."

"No, it doesn't make you any less good of a nurse," I answer her and light a cigarette for myself, exhaling the smoke, looking up at the cloudy sky.

"Do you speak any German?" I ask Francesca when she comes in from the village the following day. She gets off her noisy motorcycle and covers it with a tarp to protect it from the dripping rain. It's been raining since morning.

"I won't help you." She answers me and starts walking towards the hospital entrance.

"You didn't even hear what I need from you."

"I know exactly what you need," she stands in front of me, her wild hair wet from the rain. "You need someone to help you with the German soldier because none of you speak German, so they sent you to try and talk to the cursing Italian and convince her to help you."

"Francesca, please, I need help." I try to keep up with her as she walks towards the hospital, but I'm having a hard time walking on the wet gravel.

"You don't need help. He needs help." She stops and looks at me angrily, "And yes, I know German, but no, I won't help him." She turns her back to me and walks towards the building.

"I'm the one taking care of him." I shout after her.

She stops suddenly, turns around, and comes back towards me even though the rain keeps getting stronger and we're both getting wet now. "I'll tell you what you're taking care of," she stands in front of me, "you're taking care of a German soldier."

"I know."

"No, you don't know, you don't know anything!" She continues. "Do you remember the destroyed tank at the entrance to the village, the one the kids always play on top of?"

"Yes," I say quietly, wiping the raindrops off my cheeks.

"At first, they were nice because we were on their side. They would even stop in the village sometimes, get down from their armored vehicles and buy groceries, paying with German reichsmarks. The wounded German is nice now, whispering danke every time you change his bandages. But when the Americans, started approaching, they became less nice." She pauses and breathes, "Then they started planting land mines on the roads, and in various places in the village. Believe me, it's a lot less nice. One of those mines hit and burned the American tank at the entrance of the village. A German gift."

"I didn't know," I whisper to her.

"You know nothing, Americana." She looks at me. "It took your soldiers weeks to locate the mines. And there were many injured people in the meantime. Who do you think treated them? We had no doctors left in the village. The only ones left were the old men. The fascists and the Germans took all the young men into their army by force; they took the doctors too. We didn't have any doctors to treat the wounded. And we definitely didn't have a magnificent hospital like you do now." She keeps on talking.

"I'm sorry."

"You know," she ignores my apology, "have you ever asked yourself why the children in the village love you so much?"

"Why?" I wipe the rain off my cheeks again, noticing that my whole body is wet.

"They think that you are a fairy, since you were wounded and survived, they think you must have some kind of magical powers. Because, in our village, after the Germans had left their presents, no one survived their injuries." She smiles at me a little, and I smile back at her.

"Do you understand? When the Germans left, I spat in their direction and went to church, praying that they would never come back. Then suddenly I see a convoy of German prisoner soldiers marching on the road from my village, followed by this wounded German pilot. What if tomorrow the Americans decide to withdraw their forces from Italy, or my village, and retreat? What would happen to us if the Germans return?"

"We will not withdraw," I answer her. I really hope I'm right.

"Yes, for an Americana who knows nothing, you sure are very confident." She turns her back to me again and starts walking towards the entrance of the hospital, soaking wet from the rain.

"I know I shouldn't take care of him." I yell at her, "and I know he deserves to die." She stops but doesn't turn back to face me.

"And I know you hate me too." I keep talking to her, "but every time I change his bandages, I think of your husband. Maybe he's in a Russian prison camp, lying in a bed wounded, while a Russian nurse changes his bandage and takes care of him, keeping him alive." I wipe my wet face.

"Don't bring my husband into this," she turns to me again and shouts.

"Maybe I'm naive," I reply to her, "but it gives me something to believe in, and maybe it's a small thing, but sometimes small is better than nothing."

"You're not taking care of him for me, you're taking care of him for you. You're willing to do anything so that everyone would see you as a nurse again." She shouts and turns her back towards me one last time, entering the building, leaving me soaking in the rain.

"*Danke,*" he sighs and whispers to me after I finish changing his bandages, generously spreading sulfa powder on his fair skin so that his injury won't get infected. Sometimes I think of dressing his wound without the disinfectant or putting only a small amount of it. But I try to banish this sort of thoughts from my head, focusing on my movements: cutting, removing, cleaning, spreading sulfa powder, and dressing the wound again.

He tries not to moan in pain, even though I know that it hurts him. Perhaps he knows that all the other wounded in the hall are staring at him from behind the curtain, wishing him dead. I was even instructed not to give him any morphine; it should be saved for our own wounded.

Sometimes, I stay standing next to him quietly in the corner where my bed once stood, watching him sleep, not wanting to go out and deal with the hateful stares of the other wounded. Those stares always accompany me outside as I pass in the aisle.

How does it feel to fly? I hold the iron frame of his hospital bed, close my eyes, and imagine my fingers gripping the control stick of an airplane. I never flew.

How does it feel when the engines roar, and the airplane lifts off from the ground? I open my eyes and look at him. He has light, short hair, and his bright face was unharmed in the plane crash. He's about my age.

What does it feel like to look through your airplane scope and engage the trigger that shoots streams of bullets at people? I once saw it in a news diary playing before a movie back home, in America. The pilot smiled at the camera as the announcer explained in an enthusiastic voice how our heroic pilots fire their machineguns at the enemy. How did you feel when you shot people? When you pressed the button that fired at me from the sky, did you smile too?

I open my eyes and look at his face and his light hair. He looks back at me and tries to smile. The air feels stifling here behind the curtain, I have to get out of here.

I say nothing as I cross the curtain back into the main hall, making sure to pull the curtain closed after myself. I'll come back later to see how he's doing and whether he's still alive.

Francesca stands outside the curtain as if trying to make sure that I don't talk to him or stay by his side for too long. It doesn't matter as I don't understand any German, even the few words he says as he moans. But she's not the only one that is watching me. It seems to me that all of the other soldier's eyes are staring at me as I walk across the hall, leaning on my wooden cane. As I walk by them, I keep my eyes on the floor; I must be careful not to stumble.

Knock, knock, knock, I hear the wooden stick hit the floor. I can also hear Francesca's steps right behind me. She's probably here because she wants to make sure I don't stay by his side.

Even though they're all staring at me, no one says a word, maybe due to Francesca's presence. "German lover," I heard someone whisper once as I passed by, but Francesca cursed at him, and he hasn't spoken to me since. I'll visit him again later when everyone is asleep.

"*Meine uniformen.*" He sighs and whispers to me the next time I come to check his wound, trying not to hurt him.

Before I came to see him, I thought about giving him a dose of morphine. This would have involved taking one syringe from the nurses' station and hiding it. But I couldn't do it. Was he a fighter pilot or a bomber pilot? Does it matter at all?

"*Meine uniformen.*" He whispers again and looks at me in the dim light of the lamp that is still on. I don't answer him. I don't want to talk to him. He's my enemy, and I don't want to see his human side.

"He wants his uniform," I hear Francesca. She stands in the corner, leaning against the wall, watching me, checking my every move.

"Why does he need his uniform?" I turn to her.

"He probably wants to wear it again and be a proud German soldier." She answers and crosses her arms over her chest. "I'm not going to ask him. He's your wounded German." She goes away, forcibly closing the curtain behind her.

"*Meine Uniformen.*" He whispers to me again. How many people did he kill while wearing his uniform?

"Where are you going?" Francesca asks me, following me as I walk through the hall.

"That's none of your business," I answer her, but she keeps on following me.

"You're looking for the German's uniform."

"That's none of your business." I go down the stairs, holding on to the railing, careful not to stumble.

"Are you actually trying to help him?" She walks after me to the back of the building, standing behind me as I start rummaging through the piles of torn uniforms tossed near the trash cans.

"I don't know," I answer her.

"Yes, I forgot, you're an Americana who knows nothing."

I don't answer her. She doesn't have to help me if she doesn't want to.

Finally, my hands pull his torn gray-blue uniform out of the dirty pile. I look at it, examining it carefully. Why did he mention his uniform?

On the uniform, I see his officers' ranks. I rip off the epaulets, and throw them back into the torn uniforms pile. I do the same with all of his war medals; he probably received them for killing American soldiers. My fingers open the buttoned pockets and search through them.

"I thought you wanted to give him his ranks back." I hear Francesca.

"I despise his ranks and what they represent." My fingers keep searching the shirt pockets.

I find a packet with a drawing of a German eagle and the word 'chocolate' written above it, and offer it to Francesca, but she looks at the eagle holding the swastika with its claws and throws it angrily back into the pile of dirty uniforms, looking at it with contempt. There is a holster of a pistol without the pistol, probably taken by those who got to him first, and a wallet. My fingers pull out some German banknotes, a military certificate with his name, 'Herald,' and a photo of a girl with golden curly hair.

The back of the photo reads "Elke, Summer 1942." Francesca looks at the photo without saying a word. She doesn't say anything even as I return to the German's bed and place the photo in his hand. He looks at the picture for a moment and whispers, "*Danke,*" turning his gaze back to the wall, his bandaged chest rising and falling gently with each breath.

I rush out closing the curtain behind me again and walk away looking at the floor. At least John can't see me, otherwise he might end up hating me like the rest of them. I haven't visited him at night since I started working as a nurse again, but I can't be thinking about that right now, I have a wounded German to care of.

Several days later, I pull the curtain that hides the German back, holding a packet of clean bandages and a jar of sulfa powder, but his bed is empty.

The German pilot no longer lies in his bed, and any trace of his existence has disappeared. The bottle of iodine I left on the locker next to the bed last night was also taken, as was the newspaper someone had left for him, the headline reading: "The German army has withdrawn from Belgium." What happened to him? Did he not survive the night?

I close the curtain behind me, not wanting to be exposed to the other wounded who are watching me, holding the hospital bed frame, taking a deep breath. Maybe it's better that he's not here anymore. My hand searches through the bed sheets, but the picture of the girl I gave him a few days ago has also disappeared.

"The German, where is he?" I walk to the nurses' station, take the patients' list, and go through it, looking for his name, but he's not on the list anymore.

"Good morning, Gracie." Audrey smiles at me, "I was wondering when you would notice that the wounded soldier you were responsible for no longer exists."

"The German wounded, where is he?"

"I thought you would be interested to know what happened to him." She looks at me with her red lips.

"What happened to him?"

"He ended up going to the right place for enemies like him."

"Did he pass away last night?"

"Unfortunately, no." She goes back to the newspaper she is reading, "they came and took him to a POW camp. They decided that he recovered enough to be sleeping behind barbed wire."

I look at her and think whether to ask her who took him and which POW camp they took him to, but I decide to say nothing. She's right, that is the right place for him. He's a German pilot who killed American soldiers. Even if he has a face, a name and a woman who's waiting for him at home, he's still my enemy, and I shouldn't think about him anymore. I must be just like Audrey, believing he deserves to die, and maybe everyone would forgive me for keeping him alive.

"You can always go visit him there." She continues to talk to me without raising her head from the newspaper, "I'm sure he will be very happy if you do."

"Yes, I'm sure you'd be happy too. Nothing can stop you from being a professional nurse who takes care of all of the wounded in this hospital," I tell her and walk away, not waiting to hear what she has to say to me. I should go ask John if he wants me to take him back to his previous spot.

"Grace?" He turns to me as I approach him, hearing my cane hitting the floor.

"Yes, it's me." I hate that he recognizes me by my walk. "How are you?" I approach and stand by his bed.

"You should meet Edward. He is the wounded man lying next to me," John extends his hand in the air, aiming to the bed beside him, "I have to admit that Edward doesn't read as nice as you do; he should really work on his reading tone." And I look at Edward, who is smiling at me, and reply with a polite smile.

"I'm happy to hear that." I get closer to John and lay my hand on his bed.

"He also agreed to keep reading right where you left off from, even though he didn't know the beginning."

"Luckily, I have dog-ears all over the book," I say to John, want to stroke his hair, ask him how he feels.

"He's one of those old-school people who claim we shouldn't dog-ear books. He insists that it destroys them."

"I promise to stop destroying books." I smile at Edward and remember all the times this book had been thrown on the floor in the recent months, "I was thinking of reading you a little."

"That's nice of you, but there is no need. I'll continue reading with Edward later." He said, as I removed my hand from his bed. I wanted to sit close to him and give my foot some rest, but now it seemed inappropriate.

"Our corner at the end of the hall has become available again. I thought you might want to go back there."

"No, thank you, it's nice for me to be here together with everyone around. They treat me very well." Edward smiles at me again.

"We promise to take care of him and thank you for the book, even though you're tend to ruin books with your dog-ears." He says.

"You're welcome," I reply and begin to walk away, thinking of all the things I have ruined. "Bye John, I'll come visit again soon."

"Goodbye, Grace. It was nice to meet you." Edward waves his hand at me.

"Goodbye, Grace." John waves his hand as well. He could have asked me to stay longer. He could have also call me Gracie.

Although it's not my job, I go back to the corner of the hall to make the German's bed.

My fingers check between the sheets to see whether he had forgotten something, but he took everything with him. There is nothing on the floor or in the locker, no memory of anyone ever sleeping there; neither me nor John nor Herald the German.

For a moment, I am tempted to lie on the bed and look at the wall, as I have done so many times before. For a few minutes, I want to go back to the time when this place was my home. But I know that things have changed, I'm already wearing a nurse's uniform instead of the hospital clothes. I had made a promise to myself that I would move forward.

My fingers run over the peeled wall, feeling the plaster and the cracks still familiar to me, but then I notice there is something new there.

'Herald war hier 1944.' Someone had engraved the letters on the wall with a sharp object. As I approach and touch the letters with my fingers, feeling the grooves, I notice the writing below, in smaller letters: 'Danke Grace, Danke Italiana.'

I sit on the bed for a few minutes and lie down on the white sheets, looking at the ceiling. I don't care if any of the wounded or the nurses see me now. I don't care if they talk about me, they hate me either way.

"Were you taking care of him as well?" I ask after finding her in the garden, leaning against the shed wall.

She sits and smokes, looking at the autumn sky without answering me.

"Were you taking care of him as well?" I ask her again and sit down next to her.

"It has nothing to do with you, Americana," she says at last, looking at the sky and returning to her silence.

But after a few moments, she speaks again, whispering to herself. "Maybe it has something to do with me hoping that there might be someone in Russia who is taking care of my husband if he's lying there injured."

I hold her hand, feeling the warmth of her fingers.

Several days later, I can feel the pleasant afternoon sun as I turn onto the main road and head back to the hospital. I must practice walking without my cane, even though my leg hurts.

I slowly pass the broken gate, enter the front driveway, and turn around to make a detour behind the parking trucks to the garden at the back of the hospital. Today, like all days, they sit on the steps at the entrance talking to each other.

"Hi, German lover, come join us." Audrey waves and signs for me to come closer.

I ignore her and keep on walking, pretending that I didn't hear her, but another nurse calls my name, and I stop and approach them.

"Come, sit with us," one of the nurses moves a little, making room for me on the white stairs. I think it's the nurse who helped me then with the list. I bend down carefully and sit between them, and they all look at me as if I were an exotic animal that escaped the zoo.

"Weren't you afraid of him?" One of them finally asks.

"The German?"

"Yes."

"No, I wasn't afraid. He was injured." He was also in pain, like our other wounded, I think to myself.

"And how did you feel? Didn't it bother you that you were taking care of the enemy?" Someone else asks me.

"I didn't think about it." I turn to her, wanting to tell her how hard I tried not to think about whether he likes Hitler or not, or whether he was drafted into the army by force. I want to tell them how hard it was not to think about whether he likes to kill American pilots, or was he scared when he got into his plane every morning. But I'm not sure they would understand me if I told them all of my thoughts and fears. I'm not sure I understand myself either.

"And you just volunteered to take care of him?" She asks me, and I look at Audrey, who lowers her eyes.

"No, I was asked to do that," I answer her and look at Audrey's red lips, "Head Nurse Blanche asked me."

"You're kind." The nurse smiles at me.

"Thanks." I smile back at her and look at Audrey.

"Would you mind it if he died?" Audrey joins the talking. What should I answer her?

"I don't know," I look at her, "I just know that I'm no longer the same Grace who boarded the ship in New York Harbor almost a year ago."

"It's because you have no leg." She laughs, and I look down, struggling to keep myself from getting up and walking away.

"I'm also not the same person I used to be before I arrived here." Says one of the nurses, "I helped so many soldiers, and I saved lives, but I saw things I shouldn't have seen, and sometimes I don't know if it was a clever idea to get on the ship that brought me here or maybe I should have run away."

"Me too," says another nurse.

"Luckily, the German was transferred to a POW camp. At least he won't be able to kill anymore," Audrey says, and another nurse nods in agreement.

"Grace," one of the nurses turns to me, "you're one of us now. You're a nurse, aren't you? You should come with us to visit the pilots at their club."

"She's an intern nurse," Audrey replies, "and besides, how will she come with us wearing those khaki uniforms she's wearing while limping? Why would anyone even look at her?"

One of us

The hospital's front driveway is quiet in the fall afternoon as I sit on the stairs, gasping and catching my breath after walking on the main road. I must keep practicing so no one will notice my limping.

I carefully lift my khaki pants and scratch my sore legs, cautious not to bruise the sensitive skin. For a moment I think of loosening the prosthetic leg's leather straps and rubbing the stump. But when I raise my gaze, I hear an army jeep approaching from the main road, swiftly entering the hospital's front driveway, and I pull down my khaki pants and watch as it stops near me.

"Good afternoon." Two officers are sitting in the green and noisy jeep, and one of them is talking to me. They are both wearing leather aviation jackets, visors, and sunglasses, as if they've just come out of a pilot recruitment ad, like the ones I used to see back home.

"Good afternoon," I reply, gently stroking my sore leg through my pants and lowering my gaze, feeling my sweat.

"Can you please call Audrey and her friend, and tell them we've arrived?"

"They'll be out soon." I keep on sitting on the stairs. If I start walking, they'll see my limp.

"Then we'll wait for them," he answers and smiles as he gets out of the jeep. He leans against the hood, placing his hand on the white American star painted on the jeep's green and khaki camouflage.

Should I say anything to them? Be nice to them? I look at the cypress trees on either side of the entrance to the mansion, searching for something to focus on, anything but them.

"Nice to meet you, I'm Henry." He holds out his hand after a while.

"Grace. Nice to meet you." I look and smile at him, reaching my hand out without getting up. He approaches me and we shake hands, not before he takes off his sunglasses for a moment. He has a tanned face and short brown hair, several medals and decorations are pinned to his chest, and he is smiling at me.

"Are you new here?" he asks.

"Yes." I don't want to tell him about my past here. Why are Audrey and her friend not coming out already?

"We're from the airfield beyond the hill."

"I've heard about you."

"Are you one of the female truck drivers here?" He continues the polite conversation, pointing to my khaki uniform and the army trucks parked on the side.

"Are you one of the bomber drivers?"

"Yes, I think so," he laughs, still holding the sunglasses in his hand. "I've never thought of myself as a bomber driver."

"What plane do you drive?"

"A B-17 bomber. What truck do you drive?"

For a moment I wanted to tell him I'm driving a wooden leg, but I was ashamed.

"I'm not really a driver," I look down.

"And I'm not really a pilot," he replies, despite the leather jacket and pilot wings attached to it. His friend, who got out of the jeep, smiles.

"You're obviously a pilot, you have pilots' sunglasses."

"Here, take them," he hands them to me. "I'm just using them to show off."

"And what will I do with them?"

"You could say you're an army truck pilot."

"I'm a nurse," I finally reply, looking into his eyes. He has brown eyes. Why are they not coming out?

"Sorry, my mistake, I apologize," he smiles at me. "I didn't think you were a nurse because of the khaki uniform."

"Yes, she likes to be different," I hear Audrey laugh as she comes down the hospital stairs and walks over to greet Henry, rising to kiss him on his cheek. "Have you been waiting for us long?"

"I'm always willing to wait for a beautiful woman," he laughs as she takes his hand, pulling him after her and into the jeep waiting for them.

"Have a nice flight," I whisper to them, watching the other nurse hugging her pilot too.

"Being different is good," I hear Henry before he climbs into the jeep, smiling at me.

"Being different is great," I reply. If he only knew how much I hate being different.

"Your glasses," I shout to him, trying to overcome the jeep's noise.

"It's okay. Give them back to me the next time we meet. In the meantime, you can drive your truck."

"Drive what? She's just an intern nurse," I can hear Audrey as the jeep starts moving.

"It was nice to meet you, Grace," he yells towards me as the jeep moves away. "Come visit us at our club," I can still hear him say, but his voice is already mixed with the sound of the girls' laughter.

"I promise," I quietly say to him and look at the sunglasses in my hand, knowing I'll never have the courage to visit them.

"Come on, Pinocchio's leg, let's go to the room," I whisper to myself after the jeep disappears behind the trees, and I slowly get up and limp to my room. I have a long way to go before I'm accepted to the Pilots' Club.

The following days, I'd avoid sitting and resting on the hospitals' front stairs when returning from my walks on the main road. I don't want to see how Audrey hurries to get into that pilot's jeep again, determined to remind me of my place. I also avoid visiting him; he has Edward, who reads to him from the book without destroying the pages with dog-ears, and I have a job as a nurse in an operating room. But I have something for him in my uniform pocket, and I'm careful not to break it. I must go see him.

"Grace, we're done for today, it's actually tomorrow already," the surgeon takes a few steps back from the wounded soldier lying on the operating table, removing the white mask covering his mouth. "Go rest. It's already midnight. You're working too hard." I finish bandaging the wounded soldier, who is sleeping in a cloud of morphine, and then leave the operating room, washing my hands and wiping the sweat off my face.

At the bottom of the stairs, before going up to my room, I stop for a moment and look at the hall of wounded men, trying to get used to the darkness. He must be sleeping by now, I don't see candlelight from where his bed is, nor can I hear Edward reading my book to him. The next time we meet, I can say it was night when I visited him, and he was asleep.

"Gracie, is that you? With the funny steps?" he whispers to me in the dark as I approach him, and although I hate that he can recognize me, I smile.

"How are you?" I touch his fingers. "I'm sorry I haven't visited for a long time."

"Did you come to read to me? You're lovely, but there's no need. Edward reads to me every morning." John doesn't move the fingers I'm touching.

"I didn't come to read to you. I just passed by." He doesn't need me and doesn't miss our conversations.

"And how are you? Did you fix a lot of wounded soldiers?"

"I brought you something." I sit down on the edge of his bed. I must let my leg rest a little. I'll give him what I brought and go to my room, it's late.

"What did you bring me? Isn't it the middle of the night?"

"Come closer to me."

He sits up in bed, and I light a candle and gently remove the bandage covering his eyes. They've been there for too long by now, and the nurses only keep them there now to hide his injured eyes. My fingers touch and feel the scars on his closed eyelids, and his fingers join mine as he gently caresses his eyes and my fingers.

"It's a strange feeling," he whispers and keeps stroking his eyes, keeps touching my fingers as well.

"You've recovered well." I take what I brought him from my uniform pocket, carefully placing it over his eyes.

"What's this?" He touches the thin frame. "Glasses?"

"Yes, glasses."

"Blind-people glasses?"

"No, pilots' sunglasses." I set them over his eyes.

"Is this the German pilot's glasses?" he asks, and I tense up and cringe. What does he know about the German and me?

"What did you hear about him?"

"Was it you who took care of the German?"

"Where did you hear about that?" I get up from his bed. It's time for me to go.

"Everyone was talking about the nurse no one likes, the one who walks funny," he quietly says. "They say she likes them, the Germans, that she's the only one willing to take care of him, unlike all the other patriotic nurses who refuse to cooperate with the enemy."

What should I tell him? What does it matter anyway? He knows who this limping nurse is. How many limping nurses are there in the world?

"Yes, it's me," I say to him after a while, getting ready to go to sleep in my room. I've had a long day.

"Please sit down." He touches the bed with the palm of his hand, moves a little, and gives me some space.

"Thanks," he quietly says after I sit, reaching his hand out and holding my fingers.

"For what?" I feel my tears flowing, even though I promised myself I wouldn't cry anymore.

"I sat here in bed and listened to them, how they talk about you," he slowly says, as if searching for the words. "And I thought to myself that I fought against them, and I could fall in battle and be captured by the Germans." He is silent for a moment. "And if that were to happen, I would want a German nurse like you to take care of me."

I hold the palm of his hand tightly and press it to my teary cheeks, feeling the warmth of his fingers and holding myself back from kissing them, while still touching his fingers with my lips.

"Do you know she's waiting for me, back home, to marry me?" He doesn't move his palm.

"Yes, I know," I answer and move his hand away, releasing it and shedding even more tears. What else could I tell him?

I'm silent, I want to keep holding his hand, or lie next to him on the bed, just for a moment, but I know I mustn't. He thinks someone is waiting for him back home, but the silence between us becomes uncomfortable, it's time to say good night.

"So now I have pilots' glasses, and I can imagine that I'm flying?" He finally says, and it seems he's smiling at me.

"Yes, you have pilots' glasses." I don't want to go upstairs to the room I share with the other nurses, Audrey is there. "Have you ever flown?"

"No, just in my imagination."

"Tell me." I hold his hand again, just for now.

"When I was in the desert, in North Africa, lying in my ditch at night, I would imagine I was a grain of sand escaping from the hot days and cold nights, and flying over the Atlantic," he says to me. "I imagined landing in my small town, just for a moment, glancing at Georgia, watching what she does, how she quietly lives her life in a warless place." He strokes my fingers, or maybe I'm imagining it while listening to him talking.

"And only after imagining it for a few moments would I go back to the desert again, to the trench I was lying in, to the weapon I was holding in my hand and the soldier lying next to me. You see, we were both waiting for the enemy to come." His palm touches my foot resting on his bed, perhaps by mistake. "And I had to think about her, or I wouldn't have been able to go on fighting."

"Good thing you thought of her." I stroke his fingers, even though I should stop.

"And what about you, what were you thinking of?"

"When you were in the desert, I was probably still in Chicago." I don't want to tell him about all the glittering dance rooms I went to and all the men who held me in their arms.

"I especially loved looking at all the people moving through the street or the train station," I finally say, trying not to think about all the dance halls I've been in.

"The train stations are the center of the world." I see him smiling in the dark, his palm still touching my thighs. "In New York, inside Grand Central Station's main hall, there's a golden clock above the information booth, and every time I went to the big city, I'd stop at the hall and watch the people pass by and stop for a moment to see what time it is, and whether they are on the right path. I'm sure this clock is the center of the world."

"I was there once, on the way to the ship that brought me here."

"And were you on the right path?"

I want to tell him that I don't know anymore, and that if I could only continue to hold the palm of his hand, which is touching my thighs, maybe I'll have an answer. But he has Georgia, he thought of her when he was in the desert, and I have my bed waiting for me upstairs, wrapped in an itchy, woolen military blanket with all the other nurses around. I have to be one of them. This is the place for me.

"Good night, John of Cold Spring, New York, thinking of his beloved Georgia."

"Good night, Gracie," he moves his hand away and lets me go.

"You need to hurry, they're coming to pick us up soon, we're late. I need to use the mirror too."

"Do you think it's okay if I wear khakis?" I move aside and sit on my bed, watching as she stands in front of the small mirror in the room, her fingers buttoning the white dress one button at a time. My white nurse's dress is spread out on my bed, waiting for me.

"You'll stand out anyway, so it doesn't really matter." Audrey moves in front of the mirror, examining herself and making sure the dress fits to her satisfaction. I wish I had beautiful breasts like hers. "You can't go with us looking like that." She looks at me.

I've been walking around in my underwear for a long time now, trying to ignore my wooden leg while looking at myself in the mirror. I shouldn't have asked to join her tonight.

"And what does this club look like?"

"This isn't Chicago, don't set your hopes too high," she says while combing her hair, curling it fashionably. I used to do the same when I had two legs and dance clubs to go to in Chicago, when I loved myself so much, but I mustn't think about it now. I promised myself I wouldn't change my mind.

"Is it a big club?"

"They're pilots, but they live in corrugated iron huts and tents. I think you'll fit in." She's putting on her red lipstick.

"And will there be more girls there?"

"I always see more girls there, maybe from the Transportation Corps, I think they're truck drivers but I'm not sure. You can always be one of them with your faded khaki uniform," she smiles to herself in the mirror.

I look at my dress again, lying on the bed. I have to decide.

"You should put on some lipstick, that way no one will look at your feet." Audrey tosses her red lipstick tube on my bed, and I look in the mirror, trying to keep from crying. But when she bends down to put on her shoes, I take her lipstick, approach the mirror, and put it on, applying a thick layer on my lips. Maybe everyone in the club will just look at them.

"You'd better hurry, this isn't Chicago where men are waiting on girls for a date," Audrey says to me and walks out of the room, leaving behind a trail of rose-scented perfume. I stand and watch the simple khaki uniform thrown next to the white nurse's dress. I have to decide.

"Here's Grace, who stole my sunglasses." Henry stands in the dark next to his jeep, and jokes with the girls already sitting inside the crowded vehicle, all of them lit by the dim light emanating from the hospital's front entrance. "Nice to meet you again," he watches me as I carefully go down the stairs, hoping I won't slip without the cane Francesca gave me.

"Nice to meet you again, Henry the plane driver," I smile and approach him. How am I going to take the sunglasses back from John now? "I thought you bomber pilots have everything you need, and if something's missing you write a note and get it a second later," I add, and he laughs.

"First of all, you have to teach us how to write." He gives me his hand and helps me get in the back of the jeep, huddled with the other two girls already sitting there.

"So, you finally decided to stay simple?" Audrey smiles at me when she returns to the front seat next to Henry, after getting out and letting me get in the back with the rest. "What were you two talking about?" she asks.

"About how good the bomber pilots have it," Henry replies

as he sits in the driver's seat and starts the engine. "Are you all holding on tight?" He laughs as the jeep accelerates, and I grip the metal frame so as not to fall back, placing my other hand on my khaki pants. I can't let everyone see my wooden leg.

"Is it comfortable in the back?" Henry speaks loudly, trying to overcome the engine noise.

"Very comfortable," the two other nurses crowded beside me in the back are laughing, and I laugh with them. I have to be one of them.

The jeep crosses the village at high speed, stopping only for a moment to bypass the ruined tank at the entrance, and I look at its black silhouette. In the dark, there are no children playing wargames on its turret. The village streets are empty, and I notice faint lights in the windows here and there.

"This is the village square," Henry turns to us for a moment while driving, and shouts, pointing to the ruined fountain, momentary lit by the jeep's headlights, as if he's the tour guide for the new girl. "This is where they gather and talk all day, sitting and waiting for the war to over."

"And pumping water into their houses and helping people with amputated legs," I whisper, making sure they don't hear me through the noise the jeep makes over the village's cobblestone streets.

"Too bad they fought against us," says one of the nurses, and it seems to me that she's watching me in the dark.

"Yeah, they deserve to suffer," I say, and hold on to the side of the vehicle as it quickly goes down the hill and away from the village, passing the winding dirt road between boulevards of cypress trees, ahead in the dark, towards the airfield.

"Our humble home," Henry turns and smiles at me as he stops the jeep, tires screeching, near one of the huts. I'm unpreparedly thrown from my seat, holding onto his shoulder for a moment so as to not fall.

"Sorry, I'm sorry."

"It's okay." He helps me stabilize myself, holding my hand a moment too long than needed before turning off the engine.

In the silence around us, I can hear the music coming from the dark corrugated iron hut, along with the sounds of frogs and other nocturnal animals from the fields nearby. Even the control tower standing above us is dark, its silhouette the only visible thing in the moonlight.

"Shall we go in?" Henry goes to the other side of the vehicle, holding Audrey's hand while she comes out and thanks him by getting closer to him. The other girls follow her, thanking him with a smile and a touch of their hand. But when he reaches out his hand for me, I thank him and insist on getting out on my own, supporting myself and carefully stepping onto the gravel. I should've brought the cane with me.

"Are you okay? Were you injured in the war?" he asks as he sees my steps on the way to the hut, and I want to turn back and go into the jeep. I should've stayed in the hospital.

"That's what war is like, isn't it?"

"Are you coming?" Audrey calls us from the hut's entrance, standing together with the two other nurses, and Henry turns towards them.

"Good evening, ladies, and welcome to our club," he smiles at them as he opens the door with theatrical movement and an outstretched hand, remaining in that pose with the door open until I reach the doorway.

"Thanks," I smile at him.

"We're not just bomber drivers. We're also gentlemen." He removes his visor and laughs, closing the door behind me.

The Squadron Officers' Club is nothing more than a simple hut made of corrugated iron, filled with loud jazz music and cigarette smoke. Some officers are standing by the wooden bar in the corner, talking to each other. A few others are sitting at the small wooden table to one side, laughing with several women. I've already seen some of the nurses and I don't know who the others are, dressed like me in khaki uniforms – maybe army drivers, as Audrey said. One couple is dancing in the center of the hut, holding each other, and when I raise my eyes, I notice the flags hanging on the hut's ceiling. The first is a US flag, next a flag with a wing painted on it, probably their squadron flag, and a torn red Nazi flag next to them.

"A trophy from North Africa, we took it from a German officers' club after they retreated. We love souvenirs," Henry explains to me as he sees me looking at the swastika flag. "Does it bother you?"

"Why would it bother me?" I step inside. Everyone thinks I love them anyway. "Aren't we all souvenir collectors?" I reply and think that I have for example collected a wooden leg called Pinocchio, but I don't tell him that.

"Come join us around our luxurious dining table," Henry accompanies me to the nurses' table, where they're all wearing white.

"Thank you, Your Highness, Prince Pilot, for bringing me to this magnificent palace," I walk to the simple wooden table. For a moment I want to join the army drivers in their khaki uniforms, sitting in the other corner. At least with them I won't stand out as much.

"Compared to the tents we sleep in, it's a magnificent house," another pilot laughs as he joins us, introducing himself and shaking my hand. "But your mansion is above all, we call it the palace," he adds while bringing me a chair and inviting me to sit.

"We're such spoiled nurses," Audrey replies, smiling at him with her red lipstick.

"Girls, what would you like to drink?" Henry asks us as he pulls a cigarette from his jacket pocket, lighting it for himself.

"I'd love to have some whiskey," Audrey asks as she reaches for his jacket pocket. Her fingers pull out the box of cigarettes, and she also pulls out a cigarette for herself, putting it in her mouth and waiting for Henry and the other pilot to offer her a light. "Thanks," she says as she blows the smoke up and smiles at me.

"And you?" The other pilot turns to the other nurses and me.

"Gin, please," I awkwardly smile at him.

While waiting for the men to bring the drinks, I look around at the small dance floor that now has three couples on it, moving to the sound of the swing music, moving their hips and hands to the rhythm of the trumpet. I need to smile more, all the women around me look so perfect. Only the color of their hair and eyes sets them apart. We even all applied the red lipstick the same, as if it came from the same military bag.

"Here you go, girls," the men arrive and put the drinks on the table, to the sound of the other girls' laughter.

"Let's toast the nurses of the United States Army," one of

the pilots who joined us raises his glass in the air.

"Let's toast our heroic pilots," the girls reply, and sip the whiskey.

"May the war and the beautiful nurses go on forever," Henry smiles at all the girls at the table, drinking his whisky.

"May you continue bombing German cities and destroy them," Audrey replies and raises her glass in the air, and everyone joins.

"Let's toast the planes that guard us," he says.

"Let's toast the ambulances that bring us the wounded so we can take care of them." She picks up the drink in her hand and smiles at him, and I turn my gaze away from them and look at the couples on the small dance floor. I have to imagine I'm one of them.

"How were you injured?" Henry yells at me from the other side of the table, trying to overcome the music.

"What's it like to fly?" I ask back and empty my glass of gin in one gulp, feeling the heat of the drink in my throat.

"Flying's like a dream." He leans in my direction while one of the girls puts her arm on his shoulder, and all the girls watch his lips as he talks to me. "The plane takes off, and at that moment you feel like a bird, you see everything from above, clearer, sharper. And everything looks smaller, like you're a giant looking at the world from the clouds. Want a cigarette?" He pulls out the box of cigarettes and offers me one, and I notice Audrey and the other girls looking.

"No thanks," I smile at him and make sure to smile at the other pilots listening to us as well, as I move my body slightly to the beat of the music, trying to sip from the empty glass again, imagining that I'm dancing.

"And then," Henry continues to talk to me and the other girls, leaning back and spreading his hands to the sound of the girls laughing. "And then you feel how small we all are, and how big and amazing this world is. It's just you and the noise of the engines destroying the peaceful silence around." He looks at the other girls, smiles at Audrey, and they all smile back at him. "And of course, my co-pilot George destroys the silence by telling me bad jokes on my headphones, even when the Germans are shooting at us with their anti-aircraft cannons." He points to one of the pilots standing by the bar, and all the girls look at him. "George, come join us," he yells. "There are beautiful women here who want to meet you." And George smiles at us, bringing a chair and joining the table crowded with nurses and pilots.

"Another gin," one of the pilots hands me a glass, and I smile at him and take the drink from his outstretched hand, even though I didn't ask for it.

"Would you like to dance?" he asks me.

"No thank you, I don't like to dance, but you can go invite someone else." I look at the other nurses at the table. It seems to me that they're eager to dance. The lipstick tastes strange to me mixed with the taste of the gin.

"I'll dance with you." Audrey gets up and holds his hand as she smiles at Henry, and we all watch them as they turn their backs to us, stepping onto the small dance floor.

A new song begins, and Audrey and the pilot dance and wave their hands in the air, touching and holding each other as they swing together, until his hands grip her waist while he spins her in the air. Despite the loud music, I can hear her laughter, her hands on his shoulders while everyone looks at their moves and cheers, until the song is over. They're both standing in the center, laughing and panting, while she smiles at Henry.

"Audrey sure knows how to dance," Henry says to me during the applause.

"Yes, she sure knows how to make the right moves." I also used to know how to make those moves.

Two more women join her in the center of the hut, expelling the men from the dance floor and standing in a line. They start dancing to the sound of a new song and try to move at a steady pace, looking at each other to coordinate their feet and smiling at the men around them.

"Bravo," everyone shouts and applauds them as they stand and bow to the small crowd, hugging each other before returning to our table, panting, and smiling.

"Bravo," Henry raises his glass. "You dance wonderfully." And we all raise our glasses to toast Audrey, who turns her gaze around and smiles at the pilots.

"A toast to the war that brought us together," Henry raises his glass again.

"To the war." We all drink, and I bring the second glass to my lips too, even though it's already empty.

The music turns quiet, and a few more couples fill the small dance floor, hugging each other while moving slowly, leaving the tables around me abandoned. I'm the only one left sitting, watching them, politely refusing when another pilot approaches and asks me to dance, occasionally sipping from the drinks left on the table even though they're not mine. I'll never be able to be one of them.

"Can you take me back to the hospital?" I finally get up from the table and turn to a pilot standing at the bar. I have to ask someone.

"Are you okay?" He keeps holding the whiskey glass in his hand.

"Yeah, I'm sorry, I just don't feel well." At least I tried to be one of them.

"I'll take her," Henry leaves the girl he's dancing with and holds my hand.

"No thanks, I'll manage. I think I drank too much." I don't want him to feel sorry for me. I saw him dancing with Audrey before dancing with this girl, hugging each other and whispering. She's probably already told him about my leg.

"It's okay," he says, still holding my hand.

"You're dancing with a girl," I look at him.

"I'll be back soon." He strokes the girl's shoulder and whispers something in her ear that makes her smile at him before he turns to the door with me. If he takes me and hurries back, maybe he'll still have time for another slow dance with her.

We walk side by side to the jeep, and I try to stay steady, lowering my gaze so I don't stumble. He should've danced with his girl now, not pity me. He could laugh and hold her in his arms, spin her in the air.

"Thanks." I let him hold my hand as I climb into the jeep, watching him get into the driver's seat and start the engine. Why did he volunteer to take me, leaving that beautiful girl he was dancing with? But he says nothing as we start driving in the dark, and the jeep lights are the only visible thing on the dirt tracks of the airfield.

"I want to show you something," he finally says, raising his voice to overcome the engine noise as he changes direction to another dirt road, and we begin passing by the heavy bombers. They stand dark in the night, in an endless line, like good-natured whales patiently resting on the ground, waiting for the morning to come so they can be loaded with heavy bombs and make their way towards the enemy.

One, two, three, four, I quietly count them, but soon lose count and just watch their silhouettes; another and another, they don't stop appearing in the jeep's lights for a second before they disappear in the dark again, until he stops next to one of them. Henry turns the engine and car lights off. "Come with me." He gets out of the jeep and gives me his hand.

The sound of our footsteps in the dirt is the only thing heard as we slowly walk towards the dark plane, and in the moonlight, I look up at the huge wings and the large propeller engines hanging on them. The cockpit shimmers in the moonlight, and the machineguns stand out from the bright plexiglass canopies, as if they were black sticks facing the dark sky.

"Come closer," Henry says again and approaches the plane, stroking the metal, and I do the same, feeling the smooth, cold fuselage.

"Is this your plane?"

"Yes, this is my plane."

"Do you like flying?"

"It's the most wonderful feeling in the world, but you already know that; you asked me before, when we were sitting inside the hut, now I can ask you something?"

I'm silent, knowing what he's going to ask me. "Yes," I finally reply.

"How were you injured?"

"A plane shot at me." I don't want to tell him anything more.

"So, I guess you don't like pilots," he chuckles.

"I try not to be afraid of them," I smile at him.

"Are you scared of me?"

"You don't look scary to me," I look up at him. Even in the dark I can see that he is handsome. "It seems to me there are a lot of girls who aren't afraid of you."

"We're just enjoying ourselves at the club. They want to collect some pleasant moments, as we all do."

"Yes, we're all collecting pleasant moments in this war." I want to tell him that I haven't had any pleasant moments since I arrived here, but I say nothing. Maybe I'm collecting things too. My hand feels the smooth metal fuselage, and I think of John's lighter in my shirt pocket and Henry's sunglasses, which he'll never get back.

"We're at war," he finally says. "There's enough fear around us for a lifetime." He keeps talking, and for a moment I think that if I were Audrey, I could stroke him now, tell him that war sometimes hurts your body and your soul. But I'm not Audrey or one of the other girls waiting for him, and I keep stroking the side of the cold plane, running my fingers over it.

"And aren't you afraid of flying towards Germany?"

"I can't allow myself to be afraid. This is why I came here, to win this war. If we don't do this job, no one else will."

"Yes, you're right. You can't be afraid." I look at him. We all mustn't be afraid. We're at war.

"This banishes my fears." He takes something out of his jacket pocket, and I see his face in the faint moonlight, smell the leather scent of his pilot's jacket.

"What is it?" I reach out and feel the small, flat metal whiskey flask.

"This is my mascot. This is my guardian angel of whiskey."

"Your mascot?"

"To overcome the fear." He sips from the small bottle and offers it to me, but I refuse; I've already drunk too much. "I got it from the previous captain of this plane," he keeps on saying.

"And what happened to him?"

"He flew too much," he quietly laughs.

"And what's this?" I run my hand over the fuselage. There's something painted on it.

Henry pulls a lighter out of his jacket pocket and lights it, bringing the flame closer to the fuselage, and I notice a drawing of a girl painted on the plane's nose. She's lying in a seductive pose, wearing a red swimsuit and a perfect smile, with her hair painted in waves of blond, spilling over the name 'Betty,' written in rounded letters. A row of bombs and three swastikas are next to her almost-naked body.

"Is she watching over you too?" I turn to him, watching his face in the light of the faint lighter flame.

"Do you see the swastikas?" His hand rises and brings the lighter closer to the three curved crosses painted in black on the silver plane's body. "Every time we fly, their fighter planes try to kill us," he continues while I remain silent. "This is when we managed to kill them. So yes, she's probably also watching over me." His hand holding the lighter passes over the girl's drawing in the red swimsuit, while I reach out and touch the black-painted swastikas with my fingertip.

"Do you have someone waiting for you back home?" He turns off the lighter, and we both return to the darkness, with only the moonlight above us.

"No, I don't have anyone. And you? Do you have a girl waiting for you?"

"No girl is waiting for me."

"So, who do you belong to?" I think of the women in the

club who wonder where he's gone. Why did he bring me here?

"I don't belong to anyone."

"Except Betty, who's guarding you?" I lay my hand on the drawing of the girl in the red swimsuit.

"Do you smoke?" Henry asks as he pulls out a box of cigarettes and lights one for himself.

"No, I don't smoke."

"We're moving from one place to another, she's far away, and I'm far away, and I keep her close to me, drawn on the plane I use for fighting, but we're at war," he quietly says, and I can barely see his lips in the dark. "You and I, and everyone in this damn war, move from one place to another. We are all war wanderers." The cigarette momentarily lights his face as he inhales from it.

"You're right." I extend my fingers and feel my way to his jacket pocket, feel the soft leather and pull out the box of cigarettes and the lighter. Henry says nothing at the touch of my hands wandering over his body. In the dark it seems like he's smiling as I put a cigarette between my lips and light it, momentarily seeing my fingers lit by the lighter as he also sends out his hand to wrap around mine, protecting the flame from the soft evening breeze. "You're right," I say again and exhale the smoke into the cool sky. "We're war wanderers." Above me, in the dim light of the cigarette and the moon, I notice Betty's flowing hair painted on the nose of the plane.

We both stand in the dark and smoke in silence under the shadow of the bomber, as if knowing what's going to happen in a few minutes. I count the cigarette inhalations, but I can't be like the other girls, even though I know I should. The lipstick is weird to me, and my leg bothers me. All I can think about now is John, even though I don't have to think about him; he believes he has his Georgia waiting for him back home.

"Will you please take me back?" I step away from him and breathe the night air, touching the cold metal of the plane.

"Yes, of course." It takes Henry a few seconds to answer while standing in the dark, watching me, and I hope he doesn't try to kiss me. What will happen after the kiss? Will he dance with me after finding out I'm disabled? What would he say if he knew about the wooden leg?

"I apologize," I say as he walks to the jeep, and I follow him, climbing into the vehicle and sitting next to him. This time he doesn't offer me his hand.

"It's okay. I just wanted to ask how you got injured. I thought you'd like to talk about it."

I don't believe him, but I'm happy for the jeep engine noise and the wind during the ride, which eases the silence between us as we pass through the dark village on our way back to the hospital.

"Good night. I had a pleasant evening." He politely kisses my cheek as I get out of the jeep, and we say goodbye at the hospital's driveway next to the huge Red Cross flag spread out on the ground, barely visible by the moonlight.

"I had a pleasant evening too, thank you," I smile at him and turn my back to the jeep, walking as upright as I can and hearing the noise of the jeep receding on the gravel. He has to hurry, one of the girls is waiting for him at the club.

I sit on the hospital stairs and look at the night outside. I can still hear the jeep's engine moving away and see its lights in the distance, like two small streaks of light in the dark.

My hand grips Henry's lighter, which I didn't return, and

I compare the engraving on it to John's lighter. Is this my destiny? Will I never dance again? To always sit and watch other girls be hugged by handsome men? Will I always live in fear that someone will find out about my leg at the end of the evening? Will I sit alone on the hospital stairs?

I toss the cigarette and get up. I have to do something.

<hr />

"John, get up." I touch his shoulder.

"John, get up." I reach my hand out again, stroking his hair.

"Gracie?"

"Yeah, it's me," I smile. At least he didn't mention my limp. "John, get up."

"Gracie, are you drunk?"

"Not enough," I grab his shirt, trying to lift him into a sitting position.

"It seems to me it was much more than enough. You smell of gin."

"I like gin," I whisper to him. "John, I need you to come with me."

"Gracie, what time is it?"

"It's the middle of the night outside, but it doesn't matter. I need you to come with me." I pull his hand. Maybe I drank a little too much.

"Where to?" He sits on the bed.

"Somewhere, to do something; take me to the beach."

"We can't go to the beach; you're drunk and I'm blind."

"Please, John." It seems to me that I'm starting to cry. "I have to do something."

"What happened?" He searches and places his hand on mine.

"This war happened," I whisper to him while his warm hands stroke my fingers, and I want him to continue. I no longer care to stay here by his bed all night, I just need him to caress me like that until I fall asleep.

"Let's go," he says after a while, pulling his warm fingers away from my hand. He gets out of bed, placing his hand on my shoulder. We quietly leave the hall of the wounded, careful not to make noise and draw the night nurse's attention; she's sitting in her tiny room reading a book.

The hospital garden is dark, and I walk towards the cliff and the path leading down the beach, even though I know I'm not supposed to and that I'm unsteady. I can feel John's hand resting on my shoulder, letting me guide him, but it seems to me that sometimes he holds me so that I don't fall, until I no longer know whether he's following me or if I'm leaning on his arm.

"Gracie, are you okay?"

"I've been okay for six months. A few more steps, we're close."

"To the beach?"

"To go down to the shore." I can already hear the sound of the waves crashing against the rocks at the bottom of the cliff, but I feel John's hand tighten on my shoulders.

"I think we'll stop here." He holds me back.

"A few more steps, we've almost arrived at the path."

"I think we'll stay here." He holds my arm and prevents me from walking further.

"John, the beach is waiting for us." I get my arm free, grab his hand and try to pull him after me. There are only a few more steps before we can go down the path. It's somewhere here, even though I don't see it in the dark. I know it's there. If I can only find it, we can go down the cliff and the beach. I need the sea; the waves are calling to me. But John holds me tightly and doesn't let me move any further, his hand wrapped around my body, shaking from the cool night breeze.

"Please, John. I have to do something." I turn to him and place my hands on his shoulders. "Let's dance, like we danced then, on the road." I try to move my body to the beat of imaginary music, start humming in a whisper, as we did that time.

"Gracie, what happened?"

"I'm full of lies, John. I'm a liar." I let go of him and bend to the ground, clinging to his legs so as not to fall, and whimper as I hit the grass.

"Gracie, what lies?" He bends over me, touching my pulled-up hair.

"I've lied to you," I start to cry. "John, I don't have a leg, I don't have a leg." I lay down on the grass and look at the dark sky. "I wasn't just injured, I lost my leg, it was amputated." I whimper, feeling his fingers caressing my hair. It seems that he's sitting down next to me on the grass.

"A German plane shot me, and I'm disabled. I'll never recover. I'll never dance again. I'll always be disabled," I cry and look at the stars twinkling in the sky, but maybe it's because of my tears.

"Sh… it's okay…" he continues to stroke my hair.

"What will I do?" I keep crying, hating myself so much for breaking down again. "Everyone is watching me all the time, staring at me, the limp girl with the wooden leg."

"Then you'll have to learn to be Grace again." His hand keeps stroking my hair and shoulders.

"I can't learn to be myself again. It doesn't pass, it'll never pass, the pain, the looks around me, the pity."

"I don't pity you." He keeps stroking my cheeks, and I want to tell him it's because he can't see how ugly I am.

"Because you're injured too." I don't wipe my tears away.

"Yes, because I'm injured too, and it won't pass for me either."

"So come with me to the beach, let's go together." I look away from the cliff into the dark, where I can hear the waves of the sea. Maybe we can both walk there.

"We'll stay here together." I feel the touch of his hand as he hugs me. His fingers are warm on my quivering body.

"I can no longer be so different, hiding myself so much, trying to imagine what they're thinking of me."

"Why does what they think of you matters to you?" He hugs me tightly.

"Because you don't see their looks."

"That's true, I really can't see their looks."

"John, I'm sorry, I didn't mean that." I start crying again. "You're the only one who doesn't feel sorry for me."

"Because of your amputated leg?"

"Yes," I nod my head, even though he can't see it.

"Can I feel it?"

"My leg?" I turn my gaze to him.

"Yes, can I?"

I try to examine the expression on his face, but I fail to do so in the dark.

With both my hands, I pull my khaki pant leg upwards, lifting it above my knee, then I hold his hand and guide it to my stump, placing his fingers on my prosthetic leg.

With our hands held together, I slowly let him feel the smooth wooden prosthetic leg, down to my shoe and then back towards my knee and thighs. I feel his fingers caress the strips of leather that tie the stump to my leg.

"What is it?"

"These are leather straps. They tie the wooden leg in place, so it doesn't slip, and stays stable." I stay lying down, looking at the stars, not daring to look at him.

"And is it comfortable?"

"I have to get used to it, and sometimes it hurts. I also can't walk with it for a long time because the wound is still sensitive, but it's kind of a leg, better than nothing." For a moment I want to take off the wooden leg and let him feel the stump, but I don't have the courage.

"Your leg is like Pinocchio, who wants to be a real boy," he whispers and continues to caress the strips of leather that harness my leg.

"Yes, like Pinocchio the liar." I keep looking at the sky. I also have no courage to tell him the truth about the woman he loves.

"You're not the only one who hides things and lies." He stops stroking my leg after a while and leans back. "I hide things too." I turn my gaze to him.

"I lie to her. Can you help me write a letter to Georgia and tell her?"

John bends over the small metal locker by his bed, looking for a candle, and I put my hand on his shoulder and look around the dark hall. All the wounded soldiers are asleep, and the shift nurse is sitting in her room. How can I write a letter to Georgia?

"Do you have a light? I had a lighter in my bag, but I lost it," he asks me as he gets up and gives me a candle. "It must've fallen off when I was injured in Florence or when I was evacuated here." I tuck my hand into my pocket, feeling his lighter beside Henry's. I have to give them back; I'm both a liar and a thief.

"Why do you have a lighter? Do you smoke? You don't smoke." I light the candle, placing it on his locker. I'll find a way to return the lighter to him.

"No, I don't smoke." He sits in his bed. "The lighter isn't mine."

"So, whose is it?"

"It belongs to Private Robert Walker of Iowa, who dreamed of growing corn like his father," he whispers into the dark. "Shall we write the letter?"

"Wait a minute," I say. "I'll be right back." I get up, hurry to my room, and take my pad, the one I never use to write any letters.

"I'm ready," I say to him a few minutes later, sitting down on the edge of his bed, holding the pad and pen in my hand. I'll write the letter and not send it; it won't matter to John anyway.

"He gave me the lighter when we were on the landing craft, a few minutes before we stormed the beach at Anzio, when we were all shaking with fear," he quietly says, and I put my hand in the pocket of my uniform and feel it.

"This was our third landing, after Tunisia and Sicily," he

continues. "And we were already really scared, we felt twice as lucky, and this time it wouldn't happen again. He was with me from the beginning, when we joined the army in 1941, right after Pearl Harbor. He slept on the bed next to mine at boot camp." John holds my hand in the dark. "And that's it. He gave me the lighter for luck, even though I didn't want to take it from him. There was an engraving on it, *To Hell and Back*, that he somehow managed to engrave. Maybe he found some engraver in the nearby Sicilian village when we prepared for the invasion of Anzio. In the boat he told me he felt he'd made a mistake and that the lighter would bring him bad luck from now on. He asked me to take it, so that at least one of us would return from the beach alive." John stops talking but keeps holding my hand tightly until I feel pain in my fingers, but I don't move my hand.

"You know," he continues after a while, "on stories, we always expect some dramatic ending, like in the movies, with music in the background or some wonderful ending sentence, but there was nothing." He releases his grip, and I stroke his trembling fingers. "One moment we're running between the houses in Anzio, storming a German bunker, and that's it, a moment later he was no more; such shitty luck." I think I can see tears streaming down his cheeks in the dark. "I kept wanting to return the lighter to him, to tell him it's damn bad luck to visit Hell in Anzio, but I couldn't." His hand trembles on the blanket, and I hold it tightly. "Then we had to keep fighting, moving forward, and they took him. I wanted to go back to him, give him back his lighter, but there are places you can't go back to, like that place – Anzio." I wipe the tears from my eyes, hoping he doesn't notice.

"Don't cry," he says. "It's just a silly story about a lousy lighter. Maybe it's better that it's lost."

"Let's write your loved one a happy letter, not something sad," I say. "She loves you and is waiting for you back home."

"I can't. I tell you stories that make you cry so as to not write that letter. I'm a coward."

"You're not a coward." I want to hug him, knowing I'm much more cowardly than he is.

"You're a woman, can you perhaps write to her and tell her what happened to me? So, it'll be less painful?"

"Yes, I'm a woman," I say, even though I don't feel like a woman. I'm a coward and a liar Pinocchio doll with a wooden leg.

"Hey, wooden leg, come help me," she calls me the next day, and I follow her to the driveway, walking behind her to the truck parked at the entrance. "We have a shipment from Naples. We need to get it inside." She walks to the back of the truck and removes the green tarp cover, revealing small wooden crates marked with seals.

"What are those?"

"Medicine, Gracie. The kind that made you so feel so good when you were on the wounded side, lying in your white bed and whimpering in pain." She grabs one of the crates and throws it at me, and I hurry to grab it, even though I almost stumble. "Blanche decided I should help with the interns' dirty work." She also grabs one of the crates and takes it off the truck, walking into the building. "Blanche must feel sorry for you."

"Why do you hate me?" I stay, standing and looking at her, holding the wooden box.

"I don't hate you, Gracie." She keeps walking, and I start following her, grabbing the crate, and trying not to stumble as I climb the stairs.

"Yes, you hate me. Once I thought we could be friends."

"We can't be friends." She keeps walking and places the box in the corner of the little medicine room.

"Even though you don't like me, we can try and be friends. You helped me when I was injured, and I helped you with the German." I place the crate I brought on top of hers.

"You didn't help me with the German." She turns to me and brings her lips closer to mine. "You did him a favor and left him alive. If he wants, he can thank you." And she turns and walks away from me, out to the truck parked outside.

"So, I didn't help you. You just helped me," I follow her, not telling her that he already thanked me on the wall in my corner. I need to erase what he engraved.

"Exactly." She takes another crate from the trunk. "And we can't even be close to calling ourselves friends."

"Why?" I'm holding another crate, like her.

"I'm too veteran in this business, and you're too young, we can never be friends. You wouldn't understand."

"What wouldn't I understand?"

"I've been wandering in this war for three years." She walks ahead of me. "You have no idea what three years means."

I walk after her and want to tell her that even a few months are enough in this place, but she stops again and turns to me.

"Do you receive letters from home?" She looks into my eyes.

The letters to John, did she see them in my locker? Is she rummaging through my things? Or does she remember the time I told her I have someone back home? I must return the letters to him.

"Yes, I do receive letters from home." I look back at her. What does she know?

"I no longer receive letters, no one still writes to anyone after three years." She keeps walking, holding the crate in her hands. "And that's okay, it makes sense that this happens, the difference between us is that you still think it won't happen to you."

"Letters are not the most important thing in the world." Sometimes at night, I sit and read Georgia's letters, trying to imagine what John would've written to her.

"You have someone waiting for you back home, I no longer have anyone, but I don't care." She places the crate in the small cubicle and turns to the truck again, and I follow her. I shouldn't have told her that I had someone.

"Audrey, where are you from?"

"From New York. Why does it matter?" She collects a new crate. "I'm from North Africa, from Morocco, from Casablanca, from Kasserine Pass, from Sicily, from Italy, I'm from the war."

"I was in New York, albeit only for a few hours," I reply. "On the way here, I didn't get to see the city, I just passed through Grand Central Station, and I was in Italy. I was in some other places too, I'm not young and naïve." I struggle with the heavy wooden crate. My leg hurts.

"'I was in New York,'" she imitates me. "You're like a woman who's never been with a man and wants someone to love her. Just so you know, I hate New York and Grand Central Station, there are seven million people in that city, and everyone passes by that station without smiling to each other once. It's a city of lonely people."

"And none of them are waiting for you?" I'll never tell her that I've never been with a man.

"It's none of your business, wooden leg. I asked for help carrying crates, not for you to ask me about my private life and not for you to be my friend." She takes another box. "And to be honest, you have to do this job, not me. This is the new one's job." She puts the box back in the trunk. "You can keep unloading the truck. You wanted to be a nurse, didn't you?" She stands aside and lights a cigarette for herself.

"Yeah, I wanted to be a nurse." I grab the crate she put in the back of the truck, ignoring my sore leg, and start walking to the medicine room. I won't let her mock me anymore.

"Don't try to be my friend. You'll never succeed," she says as I go back to get another crate.

"You don't have to be in this war for three years to understand it. You made that very clear," I reply and take another one, ignoring my sweat.

"Okay, Gracie, don't be offended." She tosses the cigarette and comes to help me with the crates. "We'll be friends if you want it that much."

But even though I smile at her, I don't believe her.

"Gracie, you should join us too. Don't you want to be one of us?" She turns to me a few days later as I enter our bedroom after my shift is over. She's standing in the center of the room, trying on a yellow dress. "It's nice out there. There won't be many more days like this before winter." She looks at herself in the mirror. "Join us. No one cares if you come in your simple khaki uniform."

"And where are you going?" Does she want to make fun of me again?

"Why do you care where? Just be thankful for being invited." She lets her hair down and combs it.

"Who else is coming?"

"Your Henry's coming," she smiles at her figure in the mirror. "And a few more pilots too."

"Henry isn't mine."

"I was wondering why you let him take you back that evening."

"I didn't want to, he insisted."

"I thought you had someone waiting for you back home." She examines herself, spinning around.

"Yes, I have someone waiting for me back home." I sit down on my bed, sorry I lied to her that time, but I can't back out now.

"I'm waiting for them outside with the other girls. You'd better hurry up. No one's going to wait for you." She finishes combing her hair and throws me her red lipstick. I stay sitting on the bed and look at the lipstick laying on the woolen military blanket.

I need to fit in. I also need to wear red lipstick so that no one looks at my limp or my khaki uniform. My leg is too ugly for me to wear dresses.

A pleasant autumn noon sun warms the stairs of the hospital's entrance, and the other girls are already sitting on them in colorful dresses, looking at the road leading to the hospital entrance, waiting for the pilots.

"At least I look like the stalk among all the flowers, I belong too," I whisper to myself as I exit the main entrance towards them. I sit a few feet away, enjoying looking at them from the side. They're so beautiful as they chat and look at the main road in anticipation.

Like the gurgling noise of smug cats, three jeeps emerge behind the bend of the main road and enter the mansion's gate, stopping in front of the girls, who go down the stairs and walk towards them, spreading out like colorful petals.

"Good morning, girls. Our convoy is about to leave soon," I think I hear Henry's voice among all the pilots laughing and hugging the petal girls. Although I'm advancing towards him, by the time I get to his jeep it's already full of girls, and Henry is busy bowing and talking to one of them. I turn to the last jeep in the convoy and step inside. It doesn't really matter to me anyway. He was nice to me that evening out of politeness.

"Nice to meet you," the pilot who huddles with me in the back of the jeep introduces himself, and I smile at him, shaking his hand.

"Are you a nurse too?" he asks as the jeep starts moving, looking at my uniform.

"No, I'm just an intern," I reply. "And intern nurses aren't allowed to wear white dresses. I'm hardly allowed to measure blood pressure for the wounded." It seems to me that if he wanted to hold my hand before, he's changed his mind.

We stayed completely silent for the rest of the drive, looking at the nurse sitting in the front seat, how she laughs with her pilot and places her hand on the back of his neck, stroking his short hair. I think the pilot next to me in the back of the jeep is sorry he only got an intern nurse. I should be nice to him.

"Where are we going?" I ask and smile at him, wearing Audrey's red lipstick.

"Haven't you been told?" he asks. "We found a lovely sandy bay on the seashore, so we decided to invite you for a picnic." He smiles back at me and almost holds my hand.

"I love the beach." I look out of the jeep and think it would've been nice if Audrey had told me where we were going.

"It's probably hard to be the new one with all the veteran nurses."

"No, they're nice to me."

"I'm sure you'll have fun at the beach."

"I'm sure I will." I think of the soft sand and smile at him, forcing myself to place the palm of my hand on his arm. I must learn to fit in.

The jeeps go down to the bay and stop at the end of the dirt road, and I look out to the shore and the distant sea. The water is clear turquoise, and the sandy beach strip is empty and clean, as if inviting us to walk on it. But not me, I can't walk on the soft sand with my prosthetic leg.

"Let's go to the sea, lovely girls," Henry's voice roars. "The last one to reach the water's edge is making coffee for everyone." The girls hurry out of the vehicles, taking off their shoes and running on the soft sand while laughing.

"Here you are, the girl in khaki," Henry approaches me as I get out of the jeep and stand, looking at them running ahead of me. "I thought I saw you when we arrived earlier, but you disappeared."

"I chose someone else. Your truck was already full of lovely girls."

"I always have room in my truck," he bows and kisses my hand chivalrously. "Though you chose excellently." He taps the shoulder of the pilot standing next to me, unpacking blankets, and a picnic basket from the jeep. "'Aren't you competing? I think you'll have to make us all coffee. "

I look at the impossible strip of sand and the distant sea. Audrey and the other girls have already reached the water, walking barefoot between the waves, splashing on the sand. What can I tell him to sound funny and not make him suspect that I can't walk in this place?

"Are you coming?" the other pilot asks, starts walking towards the others.

"I'm sorry, I have to stay here. I'm not feeling well, feminine issues," I finally say to Henry, knowing it's not as funny as I wanted it to be. "I'll stay here to keep an eye on the jeeps for you."

"Are you sure?" Henry looks at me. "There's no one here except a few seagulls, and what will they steal from the jeeps, our sunglasses?"

"Yes, I'm sure I'll stay here and watch the jeeps. Go join them, they're waiting for you." I look at Audrey and another of the nurses, standing and watching us. "I'll wait for you all in the jeep. I'm having fun here."

"Are you sure?" he asks again. "The sea is still warm this time of the year."

"Yes, I'm sure." I want him to go already, so he won't notice the tears on the sides of my face and pity me.

He smiles and touches my arm for a second, before he turns his back and runs to join his friends, taking off his military-issue shirt while I look at his muscular back, as he goes to talk to the other girl. I turn my face away from them and wipe my tears.

"I'm sorry, I'm not feeling well. I have some feminine issues," I whisper contemptuously to myself as I sit by the driver's seat of the silent jeep, playing with the steering wheel and trying to press the pedals with my wooden leg. "I definitely found an amusing sentence. I'm the amusing nurse everyone feels sorry for."

"I'm actually a Transport Corps driver, I'm here at the beach by mistake," I talk to a convoy of ants transporting wheat grains to their underground nest.

"I patiently wait for them to finish having fun," I explain to the nail I hold in my hand, using it to engrave the side of the jeep.

"I need something to hide my Pinocchio leg, so I can wear a dress," I whisper to the distant sea and the group of women and men sitting on the water's edge, laughing and splashing water on each other. I can never be one of them if I can't hide my wooden leg.

The Voyage to Rome

"*Americana*, we're at war, he says he doesn't have enough leather for boots, certainly not for a boot as tall as you want," she turns around and says to me.

We're both inside the shoemaker's small shop in the village square, surrounded by the scent of leather, shoe polish, and wooden shoe forms that hang on the walls in pairs, with names engraved on them, probably those of all the villagers.

"*Americana*," he walks over and hugs me as I enter his store, a few minutes before, following Francesca and looking around at all the tools spread on his small wooden table. But since then, He and Francesca have been arguing and pointing at my leg. I look at them and occasionally turn my head to see if the kids peek out the window again. But this time, the filthy glass is empty of their smiling faces. The falling rain must've driven them away.

"All the leather went to the army, to the soldiers' shoes," she tells me. "He says it's impossible to get leather these days."

"Rome," he says to her. "Rome." And she turns around and argues with him again.

"What is he saying?"

"He says he hates Rome," she turns to me.

"So why is he mentioning Rome?"

"Because in Rome, there are the luxury shops that he hates, the ones that never care if there is a war in the world, they always have nice leather."

"Does a pair of boots there cost a lot of money?"

"*Americana*, don't you understand that you are an Americana? With your cigarettes, you can buy whatever you want here, so with your money, you can buy even more of whatever you want."

"*Americana*, Rome," the shoemaker smiles at me, and I take out the box of cigarettes I brought especially for him, placing it in his hand, but he refuses to take it, even though I insist.

"I'm not going with you to Rome," Francesca snatches the cigarette box from my hand, places it on his desk, grabs my hand, and pulls me out of the shop.

"Why won't you go to Rome?"

"Because I hate that city, and I'm not going away from my child," she walks to her motorcycle, which is standing in the square, wet from the rain.

"Do you have a child?" I stand and watch her. Why didn't she tell me?

"Yes, *Americana*, I have a child," she turns to me.

"And why didn't you tell me you had a child?"

"Because you don't know everything, Americana," she turns her back and continues walking towards her motorcycle.

"How old is your child?"

"What are you implying?" She turns to me again, her hair wild and fluttering.

"I'm not implying anything."

"Do you want to know who the father is? Do you think I was like all those women who met German soldiers after my husband disappeared in Russia? Impressed by their glittering ranks?" She raises her voice.

"No, Francesca, I don't think that."

"I had one husband, and I hated his uniform, and I hate

the Germans. When he would come back home on vacation, I wanted to cut his uniform to pieces and throw them into the fire," she turns away from me and starts walking. "And my name is not Francesca, my name is the widow with the motorcycle."

"Francesca, I don't think that. Will you let me meet your child?" I follow her and raise my voice.

"No."

"Why not?"

"Because you're *Americana*, who understands nothing, and wants to go to Rome."

"Then I'll go there with someone else."

"It's exactly what you should do," she lifts her black dress and presses it to her thighs, before sitting on the motorcycle's wet seat, dripping with rain. "You should find an American soldier like you, who'll take you to Rome, and you'll be lovey-dovey in front of the Colosseum."

"I apologize," he tells me a few days later, when I go out to the hospital's front driveway. He leans against his jeep and holds a small bouquet in his hand.

"What exactly are you apologizing for?" I look at the flowers. He must've picked them on the way, stopped by one of the bougainvillea bushes at the entrance to the hospital, the ones that climb the giant cypresses.

"About last time, we went to the sea, leaving you alone in the jeep."

"It's okay. It didn't bother me at all," I'm turning my back to him and stepping back into the hospital, I have a lot of work to do.

"Grace," Henry runs and catches up to me, touching my shoulder. "I really apologize," he hands me the bouquet of bougainvillea flowers, which are sprinkled with purple petals, on the hospital stairs. "I know you think I don't care and that I had fun on the beach with the other girls while you sat alone," he takes the palm of my hand and places the flowers in it. "I was insensitive. A gentleman shouldn't behave like that. I should've stayed with you in the jeep," he gently closes my fingers on the stems with his palm.

"I hate the beach. If I'd known you were inviting me to the beach, I wouldn't have come." I hold the flowers in my hand, wondering if he and Audrey have a new idea for humiliating me. A few minutes ago, she came and told me that someone was waiting for me outside, refusing to say who it was.

"I didn't know you hated the beach," he smiles through his new sunglasses. "Come with me, join me for a trip, just you and me."

"Thanks, but I'm busy," I turn to the entrance. I've already heard about these trips. The nurses tend to giggle about them in our room at night, telling each other what the pilots are trying to do and where they're reaching their hands when they invite them on these trips.

"Grace, I brought things for a picnic. I won't try anything, I promise."

"Why me?" I turn to him. "There are so many nurses here who'd be happy to go out with you."

"I don't know," he takes off his sunglasses and looks at me, and I take one step towards him, examining his brown eyes.

"Who does?" I look at him. Does he feel sorry for me?

"No one knows. We're at war. This isn't the time to ask

tough questions, especially when a nice guy like me offers a lovely lady like you a picnic in the open air. Come with me, a little escape from this hospital," he smiles at me and bends down to the floor, collects some of the bougainvillea petals that have fallen on the stairs, and attaches them to the bouquet I'm holding, wrapping my hands. "You lost some of your flowers."

"It's because you're a bad suitor and don't know which flowers to bring a girl."

"Will you teach me?" He keeps smiling at me, his brown eyes sparkling.

"And you won't try anything?" I examine his face.

Henry bows and removes his visor, holding it with his stretched hand. "Would you be willing to join me in my carriage jeep?"

And I go downstairs, stop for a moment, look at my shoes and the limp leg covered by my khaki pants, and walk to his carriage. If I want to be like them, I must learn to fit in.

"Can I pour you some orange juice or wine?" He asks later, as we sit on a blanket spread out in a field by the side of the road, and I nod. Henry pours some orange powder into the metal cups, filled with water, from the military canteen he brought, mixes them, and hands me one.

"Thanks," I smile at him.

"Can I offer you a small reinforcement?" He smiles at me as he pulls out his small whiskey flask, and I nod my head again as he pours some for both of us, sipping his drink and leaning back, looking at the blue autumn sky.

"So, why me?" I look at him and all the food he has spread on the blanket. Such a picnic will win any girl's heart.

"Does it matter?" He laughs. "We are two people who

barely know each other, sitting on a brown military wool blanket in a field of weeds and crickets in Italy, during this never-ending war. Do we have to look for logic and reasons in what we are doing?"

"You're right," I reach for his whiskey bottle, which rests on the blanket, and pours more of it into my synthetic orange juice. "We shouldn't look for reasons."

"And besides," he speaks to the sky and points to a flock of migrating birds passing south. "You can always get up and run away with the jeep if you don't like my behavior."

"Not really," I follow the birds in the sky with my eyes. "Did you forget I injured my leg?" I don't want to tell him I can't drive. Dad didn't have money to buy us a car. Back home, in Chicago, we never had enough money.

"Do you know how to drive?"

"A little," I drink more of the reinforced orange juice.

"Let's go," he gets up and holds my hand, lifts me up until I almost fall, and must hold onto him to support myself, placing my hands on his hips. "Let's see how fast you can drive."

"I'm not driving with you," I follow him to the jeep and rest my hand on the metal frame of the jeeps' window. I must tell him I can't drive at all.

"I promise not to look," he laughs, pulls me to the driver's seat, and stands beside me.

"What about all the food and the picnic blanket?" I look at the slices of toast, drink, and meat from the boxes he brought with him and spread out on the blanket.

"Leave them to the birds, they'll thank us," he runs to the other side of the jeep, sitting in the passenger seat. "Do you see the silver button? Press it to start the engine, and these are the clutch, brake, and accelerator pedals," he shows me with his hand, inadvertently touching my legs.

My fingers grip the steering wheel. I should tell him that he's completely wrong about me and I can't drive, or I should I press the silver button? I must decide.

My fingers reach the button, and I press it, hear the engine's vibration as it turns on, and my hand grips the steering wheel even more tightly.

"Now, gently press the clutch pedal," he leans towards me and points, and I lift my leg and press it as gently as I can, and he shifts gears.

"And now release," he whispers to me, and I move my leg, and the jeep immediately shuts off.

"Again, push the silver button," he takes my finger and makes sure I don't regret it. I press the clutch again and rerelease it, this time trying to be gentler, and the jeep starts to drive slowly in the field. I want to scream in fear and joy; I'm driving.

"Great, keep the wheel steady," he leans close to me, giving me directions, but I'm not focused on his body odor and the fact that he's so close, my eyes are fixed on the dirt road we slowly drive on, and my whole body is tense.

"It's too fast. We'll turn over," I whisper to him.

"It's a low gear, the jeep won't overturn. I'll close my eyes, I won't look," he covers his eyes with his visor while the jeep advances slowly down the road.

"Henry, everything's shaking."

"Grace, you're the pilot. I'm the blind co-pilot."

"What direction should I turn?" I yell at him as we approach a blue road sign with the name 'Anzio' written on it.

"It seems to me that we are going to Anzio," he lifts his visor for a moment before returning it and covering his eyes.

"Henry, we'll roll over," I shout at him but want to scream with joy, and despite the slow speed in which I drive, I can feel the wind trying to let my hair come undone. But as we approach the small town, I stop the jeep and don't want to go further.

Many houses, on both sides of the street are ruined, and far away, at the beach, I can see gray wrecks of landing crafts standing in the water, as the waves hit them with white foam. Along the main road, leading to the town, stands several German ruined tanks with their cannons pointed at the sea, as if still threatening the shore, even though the Germans had already been chased away from here.

"Let's go a different way," I say to Henry and get out of the jeep.

"It's not a place for us. Let's go look for a happier place," he says as we change seats. We're passing the Germans tanks, searching for the exit from the town, continuing to drive between houses perforated by bullet holes, and destroyed Americans tanks, but I'm trying not to look at them.

"Stop here," I say and put my hand on his shoulder, hurrying to get out of the jeep once he has stopped.

The flat field on the side of the road is full of white crosses, in straight lines, and I start walking between them, ignoring my leg, even though it's difficult for me to walk on the soft ground.

"Grace, what are you looking for in this place?" He yells at me from the jeep, but I don't answer him. I keep on walking between the white crosses.

"Robert Walker, Robert Walker," I whisper the name again and again, searching line after line, white cross after white cross with my eyes.

"Grace," he shouts again, but I don't answer him. I must find him, know if he's here.

"Robert Walker," it's written on the simple white wooden cross, along with his personal number, and I stand and look at the black letters. Trying to imagine him storming the shore from a landing craft. What did he look like? Was he afraid?

"Did you know him?" Henry asks me, placing a hand on my shoulder, and I shake my head in negation. I didn't even hear Henry as he approached me.

I take John's lighter out of my shirt pocket, look at the engraving 'To Hell and Back' one last time and place it at the foot of the white cross.

"No, I didn't know him, but I pay him final respects," I say to Henry, who's taken off his visor and looks at me.

"Grace, do you have my lighter?"

Without saying a word, I take out his lighter from my pocket, give it back to him; I know I must apologize. I'll apologize to him later.

"Final respects," Henry places his lighter next to Robert Walker's, stands up, and salutes him.

Later, we slowly return to the jeep, pass by the crosses, and read the names.

"You know, Grace," he says, as we lean against the jeep and look at the beach and the shipwrecks. "Sometimes I'm scared to take off and fly on a new bombing mission, but really scared," and he takes the whiskey flask out of his leather jacket pocket and sips from it, not stopping.

Only in the evening does he drop me off at the hospital entrance, saying goodbye.

"I apologize we didn't manage to reach Rome," he says. "I wanted to take a photo with you in front of the Colosseum."

"At least you taught me how to fly a little," I smile at him and remember my hands tightly holding on to the steering wheel. I know I need to kiss him now, as the other nurses do, but I still can't.

"At least we fed some birds in the field," he smiles at me.

"At least I retrieved your lighter; thank you," I say to him and turn my back, start climbing the stairs to the hospital.

"Goodnight, Grace, you're a good woman," he says to me as he gets back into his jeep.

"And a liar, too," I whisper to myself as I enter the hospital. "At least you didn't discover that I have no leg. Unless Audrey's already told you, and you pity me."

"Tell me, Grace, isn't your man back home sending you more letters?" Audrey asks me two days later, as we lay in our beds in the nurses' room at night. She's reading a book, and I'm reading one of Georgia's letters again, the part where she misses riding a bike with John by the river. I already know this paragraph by heart. It always makes me cry.

"No new letters have arrived, but I'm waiting," I stop reading and look at her. Does she suspect something and is testing me?

"And don't you miss him? Don't you write to him?" She asks as she returns to reading her book.

"I write to him," I answer and show her the notebook I have, cover it by my hand, so she won't notice I didn't tear any pages from it. "I really miss him," I keep saying to her, not telling her how much I miss someone to love; she'll laugh at me.

"Maybe you don't miss him enough," she raises her head from the book.

"What do you mean?"

"I heard Henry took you on a picnic."

"Yeah, he was nice. I didn't want to, but he insisted."

"Yes, he's a kind-hearted man," she replies and returns to her book. "Once, he took me for a picnic in the fields and we saw a bird with a broken wing," she pauses, looking at me. "He wanted to save her, but I said to him that it has no chance and that it'll die anyway."

"Did he save it?"

"I was right," she closes her book and blows on the candle by her bed. "Good night, Gracie."

"He didn't take me to a picnic," I say to her after a few minutes. "He took me to Rome to show me the Colosseum," I fold the letters and put them back in my locker, blowing off my candle, keep talking to her in the dark. "I've enjoyed Rome so much."

I place my finger on the jeep's silver starter button and close my eyes, silently saying a prayer. That there's enough gas in the fuel tank for this trip, that no one will stop me on my way out of the hospital, and that I know how to drive well enough to get us to Rome and back.

The engine rattles, and I lift my wooden leg and press the clutch pedal, releasing it gently, feeling the jeep starting a slow and bouncy ride.

"Are you sure you know how to drive?" John asks me and laughs as the jeep rattles again and shuts down in the canter of the front driveway.

"There was a stone here," I reply and start the engine again, trying to concentrate on the pedals and the steering wheel. I need to succeed. I also have to get out of here as fast as I can before someone notices I took a jeep without permission.

One more round of test drive in the front driveway and one more gear shift training, which is answered with tormented engine noise, and I turn onto the exit, passing the ruined metal gate and the two main cypress trees, starting our journey towards Rome.

The autumn wind makes me quiver, and I'm sorry I didn't bring coats for John and me, but I mustn't think about it now, I have to concentrate on the gear shifting, even though I drive as slowly as I can. It took me such a long time to convince him to join me. I'm too afraid to make this trip myself, and I'm responsible for him, even though he won't be able to help if anything happens to us, but he's the only one I could ask.

After he agreed, I woke him up early in the morning, put his army uniform I had managed to get on the bed.

"Close your eyes," he whispered to me as he took off his hospital pajama.

"I'm a nurse. Have you forgotten?" I didn't mention to him that I'd already seen his body when he lay wounded beside me when he had just arrived, and I thought he wouldn't live.

"Close your eyes."

"They're closed."

"I don't believe you," he undressed in front of me, quickly put on the khaki uniform while I looked at him, at his chest hair, that was removed when he was wounded, didn't grow back yet, and there were scars all over his chest, which will darken one day. Still, he looked so handsome to me, and I was sorry when he buttoned the shirt of his khaki uniform.

"Let's go," he took his little backpack, put on his sunglasses, reached out his hand, and placed it on my shoulder.

"Where are you off to so early?" The nurse on duty asked us. "Grace wants to show me something," he smiled at her, and I touched his hand, that was placed on my shoulder, wondering why he was so good to me.

And now we're driving on the road heading north, and I'm afraid of Rome. Afraid I'll fail and that something will happen.

At the entrance to the village, near the ruined tank, I slow down the jeep even more and bypass it gently, smiling at the children sitting on its turret.

"*La vedova en moto, la vedova en moto,*" they yell and wave as soon as they recognize me. "*Americana, Pinocchio,*" they jump out of the tank, and I stop the jeep, smiling at them awkwardly.

"What's going on? Who are they?" John turns to me.

"We're at the entrance to the village," I say to him. "And there's an American destroyed tank thrown by the side of the road that the children like to play on, imagining they're at war. "

"*Americana, Americana,*" they surround the jeep and smile at me and John, who smiles through his sunglasses. How can I explain to him how they know me?

"They love American women. I have no idea why, maybe because of our accent."

"How many are they?" John laughs and extends his hand in their direction, while they laugh at him and hold his hand, theatrically shaking his hand.

"They're five of them, four boys and one girl, and they're lovely." I look at their wild black hair, simple clothes, and big smiles.

John turns to them and spreads his hands wide, as he is a great magician, and they stand in anticipation, occasionally laughing at the sight of his hands and moving fingers.

"Abracadabra," he waves his hands in the air again and then turns to the back of the jeep, groping for his leather backpack, revealing a military chocolate bar from the bag.

"Chocolate," he whispers, while waving the military rationed chocolate in the air, announcing as if he created it out of nothing.

"Bravo," they clap their hands while he opens the package and breaks the chocolate into cubes, fumbling in the air for their outstretched hands. One by one, he gives them the sweet cubes, and they push them into their mouths, chewing and smiling.

"Il circo con il cioccolato," they shout and return to climb the tank.

"Bye, bye, Pinocchio," they wave to me as I start driving, and I wave back at them. John also raises his hand and waves in the direction of their voices as we slowly enter the village.

"Where's the chocolate from?"

"It was a surprise."

"What kind of a surprise?"

"A surprise I prepared for us for a journey," he says as his head is turned back to the children, even though we cannot see them anymore. "Now it seems to me that the surprise is in their belly."

I want to tell him that he's a good man and that he moved me, but I have to concentrate on driving on the narrow stone streets inside the village, to be careful that my leg does not slip, even though it does every now and then, causing the jeep to jump.

When we arrive at the square, I slow down again and stop, even though it's empty early in the morning and no one is standing by the shattered fountain.

"This is the village square," I describe to John. "In the center stands a white marble fountain and a statue of a proud lion spitting the water to the pool at his feet," I try to imagine what it was like before the war. "Around the square, there are shops and a café, where the men sit for a morning coffee and read the newspaper, soon they'll probably come and greet each other. And at the far end, there is a cinema. Once a week, in the evening, all the men and the women go to see a movie. Now the movie playing is a romantic one," I look at the destroyed billboard in front of the cinema, covered with Mussolini posters.

"Thanks," he smiles at me as we drive out of the village and his hand a little closer to my thigh, but he's not touching me.

'To Rome.' A blue sign, attached to a wooden pole and perforated with bullet holes, shows us the way, and I turn the jeep and continue driving on the dirt road down the hill, between the cypress avenues.

"Grace, is everything okay?"

What's going on? Something's wrong with the jeep, it's going down the hill too fast, what happened to the breaks?

I'm pressing them, but my legs keep on slipping to the side. What's wrong with my wooden leg?

"Grace, what's going on?" I hear him while my hands hold tightly on to the wheel, trying to stabilize the jeep. Something's wrong with my wooden leg, and the jeep is too fast. My leg slips again and again, no matter how hard I push it against the breaks.

"Grace," he shouts, and it seems to me that he's holding on to me, or trying to protect me, as the jeep keep on driving as if it has a life of its own, continues to turn, and goes down the hill to an olive grove on the side of the road, while I shout and keep pressing the brakes with all my might, holding the steering wheel. I then think something hit me and I scream again.

"Grace, are you okay?" I can feel his hands around me, his warm body leaning on mine. I open my eyes and look around.

We're still inside the jeep, which is lying in a ditch on the side of the road, in an olive grove. My hand slips on my leg, trying to arrange the leather strips through the khaki pants. They've slipped and caused the wooden leg to loosen and change position.

"Grace, are you okay?" I look at him again, his face close to mine, and I examine his eyes, the sunglasses are gone from his face, and I reach out and touch his closed eyes, stroking them gently.

"Yes, I think I'm fine," I reply slowly. Why did this happen to me? Why did I think I could take us to Rome?

"Can we get out of the jeep? It's safe," he continues to hold me as if guarding me, and I look around.

"Yes, I think we can manage to go out," I stop stroking his eyes. The grove is quiet, and the dirt road is behind us.

John leans back as I carefully get out of the jeep, helping him out, and looking at what I did. Why can't I succeed? Why do I fail in everything I do?

"John, are you okay? I'm going to get help," I say and walk away, limping over to the dirt road and start walking.

"Grace," he's calling after me.

"I'm going to find help," I shout at him and don't turn around.

Go, just keep on going, you mustn't think that you are responsible for what happened. Just keep on walking and look for help. Walk, walk, walk, don't stop walking. It's not you, it's the wooden leg. I limp up the dirt road, and it seems to me that I hear him still calling me, but I can't stop now, I must find help, I'm responsible for what happened, I'm the one who destroyed everything, me, and my leg. I must fix what I did.

I'm ignoring the pain in my leg, my limping, or the sweat covering my body. I'm also ignoring his calls that I almost can't hear anymore. I'll find someone to help me and return things as they were before, when I had a leg; when I had a leg, and when I believed in myself. Another step and another one, I keep going up the hill, I won't give up, I won't stop walking, I must succeed, I'll find a solution.

Just at the top of the hill, I sit down on a rock, raise my khaki pants, remove my wooden leg, rub my sore stump, and start crying.

The sun in the sky is heading west as I finally get up from the rock, at the top of the hill, and start going down the path again, slowly limping, looking for John and the jeep, trying to think what to tell him. I'll tell him I went to the village to seek help, and no one was willing to help me. But I know that even he, who can't see, won't believe me. The village is too far away.

The jeep is parked on the side of the road, as if it had never been in a ditch, and John is sitting on the wild weeds next to it. His backpack is open, and he's eating canned meat. I slowly approach, making a deliberate noise and standing in front of him on the wild weeds.

"Are you hungry?" He raises his head at me.

I shake my head, but after a moment I realize that he cannot see me, and I sit down in front of him, reach out my hand and touch his arm. John hands me the canned meat and his fork, and I hungrily eat it. I haven't eaten all day.

"I'm sorry," I finally say.

"It's okay."

"I apologize for leaving you alone here."

"I'm blind. I have to learn how to manage by myself," he takes the can of meat from my hand and continues to eat.

"How did you manage?"

"I got help."

But as I continue to ask him, he refuses to tell me more, and we resume eating in silence. I watch his hands groping for the food cans lying in front of him, occasionally raising my eyes to the jeep, standing by the side of the road. How did he manage it alone?

"Thank you for bringing food," I finally say.

"It was the second surprise I brought with me. I wanted us to sit on the side of the road, on the way to Rome, and eat. The first one was taken by the kids on the tank."

"It's too late. I don't think we'll get to Rome."

"No, we won't get to Rome."

"We need to get back," I say and think that, despite everything I have done, I want to stay and sit with him here under the olive trees, even though I know he's angry with me.

"Can you drive back?" He starts collecting the empty cans, searching for them with his hands.

"Do you trust me to?"

"I'm blind, and we're the only two people here."

I want to keep asking him how the jeep got back onto the road, but I'm ashamed. Maybe soldiers with a truck passed by and helped him, perhaps a tank, connected a cable to the jeep, easily pulling it out of the ditch, but I don't ask again, and he doesn't tell me. Quietly, we collect the empty food cans into his backpack and get into the jeep.

"Start the engine. Everything's okay," John puts his hand on my arm for a second, and I reach for the silver start button and press it, hearing the engine gurgle as the vehicle starts. On a slow ride, while my feet are constantly ready to press the brakes, and the leather straps are tightly attached to my leg, until I have to ignore the pain, I start driving. We return through the village, and I overlook the shattered fountain and the ruined cinema, not stopping near the tank at the entrance to check if the children are still playing.

"Thank you for this day," he finally says as I park the jeep at the hospital's front driveway, behind one of the supply trucks.

"John?"

"Yes?"

"I'm sorry," I say instead of asking how he felt after I abandoned him.

"It's okay," he puts his hand on my shoulder, and we enter the hospital. He goes to his corner and I to my room, waiting for Blanche to call me and punish me for stealing the jeep. Maybe no one noticed.

"Grace," he says before we part.

"Yes? I really do apologize," I approach him.

"Don't give up on Rome," he's walking away from me, groping his way through the hall to his bed, and I don't follow him.

"I need a jeep to go to Rome," I stand in her office and watch her. I've been waiting for her to call me to her office since yesterday, and this morning I didn't hold back and went into her room.

"And why do you need a jeep to go to Rome?" She leans back behind her brown wooden table and looks at me.

"So I can practice driving," I want to put my hands on the table and explain to her that I must stop being different, but she won't understand me.

"Tell me, Grace, do you belong to the U.S. Army Transportation Corps?" She looks at me with an amused look.

"No, Head Nurse Blanche."

"And are you a girl from a respectable family, say from the Hamptons, with a really rich daddy, who woke up one morning and decided to rebel against daddy and be a racing driver with my jeeps?"

"No, Head Nurse Blanche, I don't have a rich father," I think of my drunken dad and my mom, who work all day, never home. What punishment will I get?

"And do you have any experience driving jeeps, say from North Africa?"

"No, Head Nurse Blanche. I wasn't in North Africa. I arrived from New York to Italy," I say to her, but she already knows that.

"And if I give you a jeep, who will accompany you on your way to Rome?" I look at her and think of the jeep stuck in a ditch and John's arms protecting me.

"I'll find someone," I raise my eyes and look at the gray sea I can see from her window, knowing that there's no one to accompany me on the way to Rome. I abandoned the only person who trusted me. I should've stayed with him.

"So, you can't take a jeep to Rome, with or without my permission," she once again leans forward and begins to write something on the paper laid on her desk. "And get out of my office. I have a complaint to take care of. Someone took one of my jeeps yesterday."

"Yes, Head Nurse Blanche," I hurry out of her room, closing the door gently behind my back and praying she won't call me again in a few minutes. I won't give up Rome. He also told me not to give up. I have to get boots to cover my wooden leg, that I won't stand out so much.

Francesca stops the motorcycle at the side of the road, next to the blue, bullet-riddled road sign, painted with an arrow in the direction of Rome.

"*Americana*, wait for me here," she leaves me sitting on the running motorcycle and gets off, approaches the sign, lifts the hem of her black dress, kneels at its feet, and pees.

I blush and avert my eyes in the other direction, too shy to look at her, watching the road. I'll warn her should a car come, but no vehicle approaches, and I don't think it bothers her at all.

"*Americana* let's keep going to that city," she says as she climbs back onto the motorcycle, lifts the hem of her black dress again, and wraps it around her thighs.

"Thank you, *la vedova en moto*," I grip her waist tightly and cling to her as the motorcycle continues its bouncy ride on the dirt road. She's the only one who agreed to take me to Rome.

"I don't need your chocolate, *Americana*," she said to me a few days before, when I approached her as she was sitting in our corner, placing a paper bag full of American Army sweet chocolate bars in her lap.

"Please, take it," I asked her, as she tried to return the bag to me. "I need to get to Rome."

"And that's what you think of me? That some chocolate will make me go to that ugly city?" She tore the bag, and all the yellow packages scattered on the ground between us.

"I have to get there."

"So ask your new friends, who walk around in their fancy white uniforms all day and call me the cursing Italian," she held out her hand, and I gave her a cigarette.

"Please, you're my only friend here. I'm tired of being so different, that everyone's looking at me."

"And how do you think I feel?" She lit the cigarette and looked at me. "*La vedova en moto*, the widow on the motorcycle. I keep hearing these words wherever I go in my village. Do you think that they won't speak behind your back if you have boots? *Americana*, you know nothing."

"Please, *la vedova en moto*, let's go together."

"This city is the devil. Only bad things happened to me when I arrived there."

"But you met your husband there."

"And what did I get out of it?" She blew the cigarette smoke into the sky.

"Please, I have no one else to ask."

"All right, *Americana*," she looked at me. "We'll go to Rome," her hands collected the chocolate bars from the floor and tucked them into the torn paper bag. "And this is for my child. He deserves a little sweetness in his life."

And now we're driving to Rome on the ruined road, between cypress and olive trees. I'm wearing my khaki army uniform and hugging her waist, and she's in her black dress, as we both ride on her rattling, red motorcycle.

When I recognize the place where the jeep went off the road, into the olive trees, and notice the tire tracks, I look away to the other side, holding her tightly and closing my eyes. How could I leave him alone like that?

"Americana, is everything okay?" She yells at me, trying to overcome the sound of the motorcycle.

"I was in charge of him," I whisper, knowing she won't hear me.

"What?"

"Tell me something about your child. How old is he?" I shout back at her. I'm ashamed to tell her what I did.

"No," she yells back at me.

"Why?"

"Because it brings bad luck, you listen to me, and then you'll leave one day, and it'll bring bad luck."

"Not everything brings bad luck," I hug her tighter, even though I've only had bad luck since I got to this place.

"Believe me, *Americana*, in this war, everything brings bad luck," she twists the gas handle even harder as we get on a new dirt road with another blue sign pointing to Rome, and I try not to think what people will say when they see us riding on her noisy red motorcycle.

"Viva Italia," a group of soldiers sitting in the back of an army truck shout at us when we bypass them on the dirt road, and I look to the other side so as not to see their smiles. But when we get on the main road and approach the city, the army convoys moving north are endless. One by one, we need to bypass the khaki trucks and the whistling soldiers, and I hug Francesca and close my eyes, letting her lead us through the streets, entering the busy city full of green army trucks and jeeps with the American white star painted on their hoods.

"This is the place where you *Americanos* take photos," she stops the motorcycle at a large square in front of the Colosseum. I look at all the soldiers standing and holding cameras, taking pictures of their smiling Italian girls.

"Let's take a picture," I say to Francesca as I get off the motorcycle, even though I don't have a camera. I raise my eyes and watch the Colosseum standing above me.

"I'm not taking pictures with you. I thought you wanted to come to Rome to buy boots, not to be like all the Americans, who bring here their new Italian girlfriends they bought with cigarettes and chocolate," she looks around at all the soldiers and their girls walking around us, wearing floral dresses, and laughing.

"Smile," I move away from the motorcycle and act as if I'm photographing her.

"I'm not smiling," she looks at me but smiles a little.

"Now I have a photo of you from Rome," I smile back at her and look around. Everyone around us seemed so happy and cheerful, as if the war was over and there were no more battles against the Germans in the north.

"Will you take a picture of me?" I ask her.

"Smile, *Americana*, and look at the Colosseum, like all Americanos," she finally raises her hands as she takes a photo of me. Still, when I'm looking aside, I can see a soldier passionately kissing his girl while she hugs him tightly.

"Let's get out of here," I slowly limp back to the motorcycle.

"*Americana*, don't you want a photo?" She looks at where I looked before.

"No, I've changed my mind," I'm trying to lift my leg and get on her motorcycle, ignoring the stairs around me."

"*Americana*, she has an ugly dress," she whispers to me as I climb back on the motorcycle, and we continue to ride the city streets. I know she's lying but won't stop hugging her.

"What is this?" I ask her as we pass in front of a vast white building, made of marble columns and sculptures of bronze horses at his fronts.

"It's this city's wedding cake," she replies as she rides between the military trucks and the local men wearing suits and riding bicycles "We once had King Victor Emmanuel, who wanted to be remembered, so he built himself an ugly white wedding cream cake."

"It looks like a typewriter," I yell at her, trying to get over the noise of the motorcycle and the trucks driving around us.

But she doesn't reply and steers through the narrow streets, bypassing military jeeps or small armored vehicles, cursing at their drivers. Finally, she stops on a street full of luxury shops, and we both get off the motorcycle, looking around.

It seems like the war had never visited this part of the city, there are no bullet holes in the walls of the buildings and none of the building are destroyed, the cafés are full of soldiers and civilians sitting around small tables, and the air smells of real espresso. Women in fashionable dresses stand by the shop windows. Only the newsboy walks down the street, holding a bunch of papers under his arm, and shouting that the Russian army has occupied Prussia. But it seems to me that no one here is interested in the war around, while he keeps calling out the news loudly, hoping, in vain, that someone puts a coin in his hand and buys a newspaper.

"Let's buy my boots and get out of here," I say to her as we walk down the street, examining the shoe store windows.

"*Americana*, where's your money?"

"Why?" I place my hand on my backpack, feeling my wallet inside.

"*Americana*, where's your money?"

"Here, in the backpack," I look around, checking to see if anyone is trying to approach and pickpocket me.

"Where is it? Give it to me."

I take out my wallet and hand her the bills I brought, and she takes most of it and walks away from me.

I start walking after her, watching how she goes to one of the house's entrances, approaching a young woman talking to a soldier standing with his back to us. Francesca starts talking to the soldier in Italian, and it seems to me like she's cursing him while he curses her back in English. Still, she starts yelling and pushing him away from the other woman until he walks away down the street, keeps on cursing Francesca.

The other woman is wearing red lipstick and a black dress, but simpler than Francesca's, and one of her dress shoulder straps is dropped, exposing her white bra.

I begin to approach them, but when she notices me, she starts moving back into the shadows of the house's entrance.

"*Americana*, wait there," Francesca turns to me, going back to talking to the young woman, placing a hand on her arm for a moment. She wears torn black tights and worn-out high heels.

"Let's get out of here," Francesca comes back to me after giving her something. The woman has disappeared into the dark stairwell as if she'd never existed.

"Where is my money?"

"Let's get out of here. You don't need it."

"It was my money."

"You don't need it. She needs it more than you do. We'll buy you boots elsewhere," she keeps walking towards the motorcycle, and I limp after her, passing the café full of smiling soldiers and Italian girls. They sit next to the boot shop, whose fancy boots are displayed in the window. These were supposed to be my new boots.

"Stay here," Francesca says to me, after a few minutes of driving through the narrow alleys, between peddlers 'carts and cyclists; she passes in places where vehicles can't enter and parks the motorcycle next to several peddlers' carts.

The small square, surrounded by reddish buildings with peeling plaster from their walls, is full of people standing and talking to the merchants, who spread their wares on blankets in the middle of the street— silverware, shoes, clothes, matches, and cigarettes.

From the side, I see how she approaches one of the merchants and starts arguing with him, pointing to a pair of boots. He answers her, and for a moment, it seems to me that they'll start hitting each other, but finally, they smile and shake hands while he hands her the high boots in exchange for what's left of my money, and she approaches my hiding place, behind one of the peddler's carts.

"Your new boots, Americana," she hands me the second-hand boots, and I feel the smooth brown leather and the buckles, wanting to hug her. Finally, I won't stand out as much.

"Thanks, *la vedova en moto*."

"Let's get out of here. I hate this city," she climbs on the motorcycle and starts it, and I sniff my new boots for another moment before tugging them into my backpack, climbing on the motorcycle, behind her.

Only when we drive away from the city, towards the exit, and pass the signs pointing the way back to the south and Naples, does she park the motorcycle on the side of the road, next to a ruined building. We both sit on the ground and lean against an old wall, and I take out a lunch box I brought with me.

"I'm afraid of Rome," she says after a while. "This city scares me."

I look at her and say nothing.

"What scares me the most is that I'll become like that woman in the alley," she takes out a cigarette and lights it. "A woman without a husband and with a small child, a woman that's willing to do anything to get some money to buy her child food."

I place my hand on hers, thinking of what to say.

"Don't feel sorry for me, Americana," she looks at me and blows the smoke into the sky. "But for me, it's the scariest thing, having to be like her."

"You won't be like her."

"This is what is left at the end of a war, widowed women who're selling their bodies to soldiers," she whispers.

"Let's finish eating and go back to your village. Your child is waiting for you," I stroke her arm. I wish someone was waiting for me.

Henry

"You don't come to the club anymore," he watches me as he stands next to his jeep, his hand holding a bouquet of bougainvillea. He had probably picked them from the bush near the ruined gate while he stopped for a moment as he was coming over.

"Yes, I had a lot of work to do," I look at him. He has a nice smile. John also has a nice smile, but I don't have the courage to come to his bed at night again.

"Didn't you enjoy our last trip? Did visiting Anzio sadden you?" He comes closer, walks up the stairs and gives me the flowers.

"I really enjoyed that day," I take the colored branch from him. I don't have to think about John. I am trying not to think about him ever since.

"The birds in the field whispered in my ear that they're grateful for the food we left there. I met them the last time I flew, and they asked me to tell you that in person."

"So that's the reason that you came over, to tell me about the birds?" At least Henry is interested in me, unlike John, who loves a woman back home that no longer loves him.

"Of course that's why I came over, and also to give you a formal invitation."

"What formal invitation?"

"Dear Ms. Grace, the honorable transport driver in the khaki uniform, will you kindly come and visit me at our glorious club? You don't come anymore," he smiles and bows. I'm still in my khaki pants. I don't have the courage to wear my nurse dress and new boots.

"And if I refuse, will you offer the flowers to some other girl?"

"If you refuse, I'll have to invite you to a picnic again, or maybe I'll take you on a trip to Rome. Have you been to Rome?"

"I've not been to Rome," I look at him, reminded of the soldier who kissed his girl in front of the Colosseum. I shouldn't think about John, he'll never kiss me. I have to believe in Henry.

"Mr. Henry, the honorable bomber pilot, I promise to come," I bow and smile at him, but my fingers play with the flowers I'm holding, scattering them on the white floor of the front steps.

"Bye Gracie, I'm waiting for you," he gets back to his jeep and exits the ruined gate, and I think that only two other people call me Gracie, one of them I hate, and I shouldn't get attached to the second one.

I keep standing and watching the jeep move away until it disappears behind the bend and the cypress trees, leaving a slight cloud of dust and a pungent scent of burnt gasoline at the front driveway.

Does Henry really like me, or am I some funny amusement on his way to the next girl? I need to talk to someone. I also need to apologize to John.

I finally get inside, throw the flowers in the parking lot. I'm not a pilot that can pick a branch of bougainvillea flowers and present it to him wrapped in tempting words. I'm a woman who's left him alone and now hasn't dared to apologize. I look for him around the hospital, thinking of what to say, but he's not there.

He's not in the garden among the other wounded, sitting in white chairs covered in woolen blankets, the white bench overlooking the sea and the sun before sunset is also empty. He's not in his bed either, and Edward, the wounded soldier lying next to him, doesn't know where he went. I ask the on-call nurse where he could be, but she tells me she only saw him taking his cane, hitting it on the floor, and going out of the hall.

Only when I go out to the hospital's front stairs and look around do I see him. He's standing by himself on the ruined road, far away from the hospital. What is he doing there?

I hurry down the stairs and cross the large parking lot, ignoring the pain in my leg from walking on the gravel, crossing the iron gate, getting close to him.

He stands in the middle of the road and moves from side to side; his hands are raised as if embracing an invisible lover while dancing with her to the sounds of an imaginary melody.

I try to walk towards him, as quietly as I can, approaching him slowly and reaching out my hands to take his, but a few steps before I can hold on to him, he stops dancing and turns to me.

"Hey, Pinocchio, how are you?"

"I came to dance with you," I approach a few steps further, touching the palms of his hands.

"I enjoy dancing alone," he releases his hands from my fingers.

"Would you invite me to dance with you in the autumn sunset?"

"I'd be happy to keep on dancing by myself," he bends down to the road and searches for his cane with his hands, lies down, picks it up, and turns his back to me. He slowly moves away, further down the road, hitting the ruined asphalt with the stick.

"I thought you'd be happy to dance with me," I shout at him from a distance, not approaching anymore. "And I also have new boots; I wanted to tell you."

"So, you told me," he starts dancing with his imaginary loved one again, hugging her in his arms.

"And I also want to dance with you."

"What's changed?" He turns to me. "Did you come to pity the blind soldier and clear your conscience?"

"No," I cringe. "I wanted to see you."

"No, you didn't come to see me. You wanted to tell me how nice you were recovering and that you have new boots."

"But I also wanted to see you," I feel the leather of the boots tighten on my feet, and I try to move from side to side, standing on the road.

"You wanted to see me before or after you left me there alone, in the ditch, with the jeep?"

"I'm sorry, I thought you were fine," I say, holding my hands together. "When I came back to you, you weren't angry with me."

"You left me alone in the dark, Grace, alone. You abandoned me. I'm blind," he feels his way towards me with his stick but stops at a distance and doesn't get any closer. "Shall I tell you how long it took me to find the jeep after I tried to chase you when you ran away? Shall I tell you how many times I fell in the dark, scratched from the thorns and the rocks as I felt my way back to the jeep?"

"I apologize. I'm so sorry," I look up at him and feel the tears coming down. "I was stressed. It's all my fault. I wanted to find a way to get the jeep out of the ditch," I want to get close to him, but I know I can't, he'll reject me again.

"Why were you stressed? Because you were with a blind man? Is that what you do when you're stressed, run away?"

"I didn't run away. I went to seek help. I wanted to rescue you."

"I don't need you to rescue me, and you didn't rescue me. Someone else rescued me.

"What happened there?"

"What does it matter?"

"Please tell me," I can feel the tears on my cheeks.

"A man, I don't even know who he was, helped me," he lowered his hands. "He and his two donkeys. An Italian man who probably passed by and saw me sitting on a rock and felt sorry for me, because that's how it is, everyone feels sorry for me, you too."

"I don't feel sorry for you," I say to him quietly, but he keeps talking.

"I don't even know what he looked like and how old he was, but from his slow speech, I think he was an old man," he stands close to me and gasps.

"You know," he continues after a moment, "I didn't understand a word of what he said to me, but he approached and kept on talking in Italian, putting a rope in my hand, and together we tied the jeep to his donkeys. He and I, and his two Italian donkeys, pulled the jeep out of the ditch — an old Italian man, who patted me on my shoulder and probably greeted me. I have no idea because I didn't understand a word of what he said before he disappeared into the darkness and left me alone again. Shall I tell you how my hands were scratched when I pulled the ropes with him?" He raises the palms of his hands, and I see the scratch marks on his hands and want to stroke them but remain standing in my place.

"An old Italian man helped me, and now you came to show me your new boots? So, if you didn't notice, I'm blind. I can't see your new boots."

I want to tell him that I wanted to let him feel them, see them with his fingers, but it's too late now. My boots don't matter anymore.

"John, trucks are coming," I yell at him as I hear a noise approaching, turning around and seeing them. The army trucks approaching us beyond the turn are driving fast, and I want to help him move away from the road, but John already hears them and walks to the side while I follow him and stand a few feet away.

One by one, the khaki trucks with the white star on their sides pass us in an endless convoy heading north, and I stand and watch the soldiers sitting inside them. They're wearing steel helmets and holding their weapons, smiling at me as they pass.

"Come and join us, be our mascot," someone yells at me from one of the trucks, and I just smile at him, but after him, there are a few more who whistle and shout at me to come join them in the war, and I stand and watch, smile back at them and wave my hand, not answering and looking at John. He just stands with his sunglasses, away from me on the side of the road, and looks at them until it's impossible to know that he's blind.

"You can join them. You've already recovered, you've heard them, they're looking for a mascot to take care of them," I hear him tell me as the last truck has passed, leaving behind only a cloud of brown dust that slowly sinks onto the road.

"You too have recovered and can go back to who you were before. You dance wonderfully on the road and manage fine on your own," I shout at him and turn around, starting to walk back to the hospital.

"Grace, I'm a teacher. I can never go back to who I was before," I hear him yell at me and stop in my tracks.

"I'm a teacher," he says again, and even though I want to keep walking away from him, I turn back.

He stands on the empty road and looks at me, "Back there, at home, I'm a teacher, an elementary school teacher."

"I used to go into my class every morning, pat my schoolchildrens' shoulders and watch them, see who was tired because he had to get up early and help at home, and who didn't bring a sandwich, offering my own food, telling them I'm not hungry," He keeps on talking, standing on the road and looking in my direction.

"Grace, I'm a teacher. I listen to children, even if I've only met them once," he continues to look at me. "That time, at the entrance to the village, near the ruined tank, there were five of them. One was a little taller and bigger than the others, holding my hand tightly. And there was one there with dirtier hair, but I heard his laughter, he's a happy kid, and there was the girl there who quickly snatched the chocolate from my hand, walked away and laughed, but then went back to get more," he pauses for a moment before he continues. "I even keep a chocolate bar in my pocket to give you for them, for the next time you go there," he puts his hand into the thin coat that he wears and pulls out the bar of chocolate, throwing it towards me, but it falls on the road, stays there laying between us, stands out in its yellow packaging on the ruined asphalt.

"I didn't know."

"Because that's who I am, I'm a teacher. An elementary school teacher at Cold Spring, New York, and now I'm here in this country and no longer know who I am."

"You're still the same person you were before you came to this place. You told me that, at nights, when we used to talk."

"No one here stays the way they were, even if they try as hard as they can, but it doesn't matter anymore. You have pilots to go meet, I heard the other nurses keep talking about them, and I have to wait for a letter from the woman I love and, in the meantime, keep dancing with myself," he returns to the center of the road and continues his dance moves, ignoring my presence. I walk back a few steps, stand and look at him, trying to guess which song is playing in his head as he dances and step on the chocolate bar thrown on the road.

"Nurse. I was a nurse back home," I yell at him. "I was an intern nurse at Mercy Hospital in Chicago, and I took care of patients. I'd just graduated from nursing school, but I wanted more, I wanted to see New York, the world, I wanted to see the war that everyone was talking about on the news."

"I was in Italy for eight days before I was injured," I keep shouting in his direction, seeing him stop dancing and look at me. "Four days of which in a hospital tent, helping perform surgery on wounded soldiers who kept coming in, one after the other," I can't stop talking. "The other nurse fell apart after two days and was evacuated, and I was left alone, a new nurse, to work with the doctor. I have no idea what happened to him in that attack. Eight days John, I saw the world and the war I so wanted to see for eight days," I wipe away my tears. "And now I'm not sure what's left of me, after this place."

"You stayed the same as you were before," he slowly approaches me.

"No one will take me back at home, I'd never recover, I have no leg."

"I didn't notice, except for your funny walk."

"I hate my funny walk," I scream at him, turning and walking back away. "You're right, you have to wait for letters from the woman you love, and I have a pilot to meet."

It takes me a while to find the corrugated iron hut at the dark airport in the evening. The other girls had already gone there ahead of me, and by the time I entered our bedroom at the hospital, it was already empty. I still managed to see them from the window, giggling and getting into the pilots' jeep, but I didn't want to shout at them to wait for me.

It took me a long timeo to put on my white nurse's dress and my new boots, look at myself in the mirror, and take it off, fold it back into my small metal locker and put back on my loyal khaki pants and regular shoes. And it also took me time to sit in the hospital parking lot, in the stolen jeep, wiping off the sweat from my forehead despite the cool breeze and forcing myself to press the small silver start button.

And now I'm sitting in the jeep, outside their club, having driven slowly through the village, making sure not to shift gears, that my wooden leg won't slip again, holding the steering wheel tightly and sigh in relief as I turn off the engine in front of the hut.

Jazz music emanates from the hut club, and I look up to the sky, watching the silhouette of the dark control tower. I need to get in.

My finger touches my lips and feels the thick layer of red lipstick I applied, trying to make them as prominent as I can, hoping that no one will look at my feet. I had to bring the lipstick with me in case I had to fix it, but I couldn't.

For a second, I'm struggling with the urge to stay here and listen to the crickets outside and the music coming from the lit door, or maybe turn around and drive back to John. But what's the point in that? It won't change a thing, he has a woman he misses, and I have a pilot to meet.

Slowly I get out of the jeep and walk on the gravel, towards the open door, that invites me in. This is the right place for me.

At the entrance, I stand for a moment and look inside. There are fewer pilots and girls in the club tonight. The Transportation Corps female drivers have also disappeared, maybe they're bringing more ammunition in endless convoys, feeding the war monster in the north. Only a few pilots stand by the bar, and a few more sit at the small tables, entertaining the nurses, or maybe vice versa. No one's noticed me yet, I still have time to regret and turn back.

"Grace, come and join us," Henry notices me standing at the door and waves at me, invites me to come, and I see him bend over and say something to the other girls, but I can't hear what he's whispering to them.

"Meet my date for the lovely picnic," he announces and gets up from his chair as I approach, bringing me a chair from a nearby table, and I sit with the others, lowering my eyes.

"Do you hear?" Henry raises his voice over the music as

he places new glasses of whiskey on the table. "It's for you, special delivery of gin," he puts the glass in front of me. "It's not every day that someone goes out to try and persuade a girl to go with him on a trip to Rome, and in the end, completely fails in his attempt to reach his destination."

"Maybe she just made him linger on the way," one of the other pilots say, making everyone laugh.

"Or maybe you choose different destinations," another girl adds to the sounds of laughter.

"I like the red lipstick you're wearing," Audrey leans over and whispers to me, "That's exactly the color I have."

"Thanks," I smile at her and grab my glass of gin, sipping it in one gulp. I won't tell her where I got it from.

"She told me she wanted to see Anzio," Henry keeps talking loudly.

"A toast to the ground infantry mice that fought in Anzio," another pilot joins us, stands behind me, and I hear his loud voice as he picks up his glass of whiskey.

"I'd rather be an infantry mouse," laughs one of the pilots sitting at the table with us. "At least if I'm injured, such a beautiful nurse will take care of me," he puts his head on one of the nurses' shoulders while everyone laughs.

"He's right," Henry declares, raising his voice again. "If the German Krauts hit our plane, what will happen to us?" He pauses for a moment and looks around. "If we were lucky and managed to get out of the burning plane, and if the poor parachute has opened, and if we were lucky enough to reach the ground alive, where will we land? On German soil, and who will take care of us? Ugly Inge from Berlin, what kind of justice is that? Friends," he stands up and keeps talking. "I want to be an infantry mouse, too."

"Just like that," one of the girls answers him, and everyone laughs. "We want to treat you, if you're injured, not some Kraut Nazi pilots."

"The right place for German pilots is in a cemetery, not under the caressing hands of beautiful nurses like you," another pilot replies, and the sounds of laughter increase while the girls are looking at me and laughing. I reach for one of the full glasses on the table and drink it too, sipping the burning drink. I don't care who's it is.

"So why didn't you reach Rome?" Audrey asks and leans over Henry. "Did the lady detain you?" She looks at me, and I lower my eyes, searching for another drink for me.

"The lady didn't detain me," Henry touches the pilot's wings attached to his uniforms with his finger. "The lady wanted to learn how to fly."

"I want to learn how to fly too. Why don't you teach me?" Another nurse leans against his other shoulder.

"Girls, this is just a legend," another pilot laughs. "Our jeeps are meant for operational missions only. They're not meant for travel to Rome and certainly not for amusement."

"True, you're just having fun inside your bomber planes. That's the reason they were designed so big, you don't really care about the bombs you are carrying," one of the nurses replies, snatches his hat from his head, wears it, and salutes him.

"Miss," he salutes her back. "We're just fighting in our planes, I swear," he puts his hand on his chest to the sound of the audience laughing, and I look up and see that more pilots have joined and stood around our table, holding glasses of drink and laughing. I must get up and walk away. I'll never be one of them.

"And now, let's dance in honor of Anzio's ground infantry mice," says someone, and the pilots reach out to the women, inviting them to dance. I see Henry asking Audrey, and she willingly rises from her chair.

"Can I invite you to dance?" Someone is asking me.

"She doesn't like to dance," Henry tells him, and the pilot pulls his hand back, looking around, but I get up from the table and smile at him, hold his hand and lead us to the small dancefloor, which is already filled with pilots and other nurses wearing white uniforms. I'm tired of sitting alone in the company of empty whiskey glasses and cigarette smoke.

Gently, his hands are holding my waist, and I'm getting closer, smelling his clean uniform and looking at the medals on his chest. He has a pleasant scent, and he holds me tightly as we dance while I try to follow his lead.

I missed dancing so much, and I don't care about my pain, it'll wait until the end of the evening. For now, all I care about is the soft music and the muscular hands holding me. I don't even remember his name, even though he told it to me a moment ago, when he introduced himself. It seems to me that my body is trying to remember movements I'd forgot, and I hope he doesn't notice my limp, but I know he does, even though he's polite and says nothing. I close my eyes and place my head on his chest, smelling the scent of his cologne. He surely noticed my limp, everyone did.

"Can I dance with your girl?" I open my eyes and see Henry standing next to us, holding his hand.

"I thought you had another girl," he replies, and I look aside to see Audrey leaning against the bar, sipping a drink, and looking at us.

"Please. One dance, then I'll give her back to you, I promise," Henry smiles at him. "She promised me a dance back then, on the trip to Rome that ended in Anzio, and did not keep her promise."

"The lady is all yours," the pilot smiles at me goodbye before walking to Audrey, asking her to dance, and I smile back at him, letting Henry hold my hand, but make sure to put some distance between us.

"I thought you didn't like to dance," he whispers to me, trying to bring us closer.

"I thought I didn't promise you a dance on our trip," I keep my distance from him.

"I was thinking of a reason to put you back in my arms."

"You thought of a bad one. I've never been in your arms, and I think there are other girls who enjoy being in your arms."

"I think you enjoy being in someone else's arms too."

"Yes, I enjoyed it," I stand in the center of the dance floor, between the other dancing couples. "He was nice, and he didn't make fun of me and our trip together. I'm sorry, I had a long day, and I'm nauseous," I turn to leave the club. Maybe after I go, they'll be able to continue telling jokes about the intern nurse he tried to take to Rome or about the time they let her take care of the German pilot, hoping she'd kill him by mistake.

"Grace," I hear him calling, but I don't stop and walk out of the club, feeling the cool breeze blow in my face as I get out to the silence of the night.

"Grace, I'm sorry, I'll take you back," he walks after me.

"Thanks, but I'm fine," I keep walking slowly, careful not to stumble on the gravel. My leg is in pain, I shouldn't have danced.

"But how will you get back?"

"Did you forget that you taught me to drive? Did you forget why we didn't get to Rome, and you didn't get that photo you probably wanted, another souvenir of you kissing a nurse in front of the Acropolis?" I say and keep walking.

"Grace, I'm sorry for what happened inside," he approaches me. "The trip with you was special to me, but I didn't want to say it in front of the others," he stands close to me as I lean on the jeep, and I smell his leather jacket mixed with the smell of cigarettes. I so want to believe him but I know he's lying.

"Sorry, but I have my own carriage to take me to my castle," I smile at him. He means no harm. This is the man he is, wandering between women. He said it from the beginning, and I knew exactly who he was. I'm just a comic relief for him, to pass the boring time between the other nurses.

"Please, give me just one moment. Don't run away, please," he touches my arm for a second and disappears into the club, and even though I didn't reply, I keep on standing and looking at the open door of the hut. He's probably promising Audrey a trip to Rome in the near future. I lean against the hood of the jeep and hug myself. The last few nights have become cold. How long do I have to wait for him?

"Problem solved," Henry gets out of the club and holds my hand. "Your jeep will return to the hospital safe and sound. One of the pilots will return it. Now, will you please let me apologize for my behavior and drive you back?"

I don't answer but let him hold my hand, and we walk to his jeep, hand in hand, start driving in silence on the dirt roads of the airport. I run my fingers over my lips, feeling what's left of the lipstick covering them. I shouldn't have taken Audrey's lipstick. I need to get my own red one.

The big bombers flicker in the jeep lights before disappearing in the dark as we pass them, but this time I'm not counting them, I just keep thinking about my lips. I haven't kissed anyone for so long, and now the only one who wants me is the man who's taking me in his jeep. He'll probably take Audrey or someone else in his jeep to Rome tomorrow. At least someone wants me and doesn't leave me sitting alone at the table in front of the whiskey glasses.

Henry says nothing but also doesn't put his hand on my thigh or try to touch me. He's just focused on driving, like counting the planes. If he tries, I'll let him put his hand on me. I'm so pathetic.

"Please come with me," he says as we stop the jeep near one of the planes, and I can already recognize Betty with her red swimsuit painted on the bombers' nose, lying in her seductive position, with her flowing hair drawn on the silver fuselage.

Only the sound of our footsteps is heard on the gravel as I follow him towards the plane, and I know I need to turn around and get back in the jeep. Maybe it's better to sit alone at the table and watch everyone else dance.

"Feel it," he gets close to me and takes my hand, brings it to the metal fuselage of the plane, and I feel his warm fingers, and once again smell the scent of the pilot jacket he's wearing, as our fingers slide on the cold, smooth metal until I feel a hole and sharp torn steel.

"What is it?" I release my hand from his grip and turn to him, leaning back on the plane and feeling the sharp metal scratching my back.

Henry takes a lighter from his jacket pocket and lights it, brings it closer to the plane's fuselage, and I see that the whole side of the plane is full of holes and torn metal pieces.

"Bullets from a German plane," he says quietly and turns the lighter off as we keep standing, facing each other in the dark. "Over Munich, from yesterday. But we managed to return. Tomorrow or the next day, they'll fix the holes, and we'll set out on a new mission."

I stroke his jacket and reach for the pocket, take out the lighter and turn it on, look at the shell holes again, touch them with my fingers, examine the torn metal. I then give it back to him, enough, I've already taken one lighter from him.

"You can take that one too," he smiles at me in the dark, "So you have a souvenir from me if something goes wrong."

"Keep it with you," I don't want to take a souvenir from him, and I don't want anything to go wrong, but the palm of his hand closes my fingers on the lighter, refusing to take it back.

"You know," he says after a while "Even though we fly at high altitude, and it's cold outside, sometimes it's so hot inside the plane, and I feel the sweat dripping inside the overall I'm wearing, feel suffocated by the parachute and the yellow lifejacket tied around my body. And all around me is the noise of the engines that I pray won't stop working, or that the Germans won't hit them, and that they'll keep working until I land safely. And there's the radio going off in my ear, that I hope won't become the screams of a wounded gunner from my plane or that a plane flying next to me won't become a ball of fire. And the sky around us is full of black clouds of anti-aircraft shells waiting for us to go inside, to our destination, and I can't escape, I must fly straight to the black hell of German planes and anti-aircraft canons that are waiting for us," Henry keeps talking, and I feel his hand holding my arm as if looking for some support. I search for his jacket pocket, pull out the whiskey flask, and serve it to him.

"Most of all, I'm afraid of the pre-flight briefing," he sips his drink and serves it to me, and I make myself drink; I don't want him to feel alone "When the intelligence officer stands inside the briefing hut, in front of his maps and aerial photos, explaining the target we need to bomb to us," he sips again and keep talking "He points to the big map hanging on the wall, reviews the anti-aircraft canons and the German fighter squadrons waiting for us, looking to blow our planes up to balls of fire. In order to get the plane down, they always aim at the engines or the nose, to hit the pilots," he sips again. "You know, Grace," I think he's trying to smile at me in the dark of the plane "I've been in this business for two and a half years. I started in England, and I bombed in Germany, and I continued in North Africa, and I bombed in Germany again, and now I'm in Italy, and I still take off every other day to bomb over Germany," I touch his jacket, look up and reach out my hand, stroking the back of his neck.

"Thirty-four bombing missions so far," he pauses, and I'm not sure if he's shivering for a moment or if it's the cold of the night "My plane was hit Five times, two of my machine gunners were killed by anti-aircraft fire, and once my co-pilot was seriously injured by bullets from a German fighter," I stroke his cheek "That's a pretty fair total relative to the number of missions I did, isn't it?" He picks up the bottle, sips from it again, and gives it to me, but it's empty when I put it to my lips.

I lift my head and start kissing him, my hand gripping the back of his neck, stroking his short hair. He has pleasant lips, and despite the smell of whiskey and cigarettes that remains between us, I can still smell the cologne from his neck. I'm glad I'm also wearing some cologne. At first, he hesitates, but then, his hands tightly wrap around my body, and he leans on me, and I feel the cold plane's metal in my back and through my uniform. I keep on kissing him as hard as I can, ignoring the scratches of the torn metal on my back. I need to keep kissing him. He deserves the touch of my lips, and maybe they'll banish his fears. I don't care now if he tells this story to every girl he brings here, to his Betty. Still, I so want to believe that I'm special.

"Thank you for listening to me," he says to me later, as we sit in the jeep at the hospital entrance', "If I were injured, I'd like you to take care of me."

"Thanks," I reply, hoping that he'll never come to this place as a wounded soldier.

"I'll be happy to meet you again, to show you my plane," he strokes my arm.

"Me too," I reply to him as I get out of the jeep, stand on the front steps and watch him as he drives, my eyes following the lights of his jeep moving away until they disappear behind the bend.

Despite the late hour, I couldn't sleep; he kissed me. Will he want us to do more than that the next time we meet? What will I do then?

I can't sleep, and I walk to the back of the building, stepping into the dark and empty garden. The white deckchairs stand on the grass waiting for the wounded soldiers to sit on them tomorrow, and I pass through them and sit on the bench that overlooks the sea, letting my hair down after it's been up all evening.

What will he want us to do the next time we meet? Will he want us to do what the other girls giggle about as they whisper to each other in our room at night?

The cool night wind blows the hair onto my face, and I have to pick it up again, even though I want to leave it as it is. I searched for someone who'd like to be with me for so long, but now, I feel my stomach aches.

"He likes me," I turn around and whisper to the few windows of the building that are still lit, watching the faint yellow light emanating from Blanche's room. "And I like him," I add, taking a few hairpins out of my pocket, tightening my hair back to its place.

My fingers loosen the leather straps holding the prosthetic leg, and I am scratching my stump, massaging it and trying not to hurt myself. Why would he want a damaged women like me?

"He's not making fun of me behind my back. He told me I was special," I say to the bench and clean what's left of the lipstick I applied at the beginning of the evening with my fingers, rubbing hard and also wiping the taste of his lips.

"And he wants to be with me. That's all that matters," I light a cigarette and ignore the taste of the smoke that makes me nauseous.

"He'll be my first," I talk to the bench and take the scissors out of my military coat pocket, open them and hold the scissor's blade tightly with my hand.

I carefully start engraving on the bench, to the light of the lighter I'm holding with my other hand. My hand grips the scissors' blade as I try to hurt the wood as much as I can, creating in it a drawing of Henry's bomber with its propellers and wings. At least he wants me, even though I'm crippled.

"I have to accept what others are willing to give me," I

whisper, again and again, making another scrape and another scrape in the hardwood of the bench; I must be able to hide my damaged leg. No one else will want me. I don't have to think about John, he doesn't think about me either.

My fingers pull sharp pieces of wood from the scraped bench as I continue to engrave his plane, cutting the cockpit and the black machineguns jutting out in every direction.

"It must be at night, in the dark," my fingers close the lighter, turning the flame off. I look around at the darkness with only the moon and the stars above, trying to spot the lounge chairs on the grass, I then look at the sea, trying to see the foam of the waves. What about my wooden leg? Can I see it in such darkness? What about inside his closed jeep or inside the dark plane? It must be really dark. I'll keep his lighter so that he doesn't make even a tiny light.

"The boots, I'll wear my boots," I bend down and fasten the leather straps to my amputated leg, forcibly tightening them and checking through the khaki pants with my fingers. Without the boots, I can feel the straps and the leg. I'll check again while wearing the boots. When he touches me, he mustn't think that something's wrong.

I won't let him touch my leg. I'm holding the scissors' blade on my thighs, feeling the sharp metal hurt the skin and create a stripe of pain. He mustn't touch me under this line.

"He always brings me back in his jeep. He likes me," I inhale the smoke one last time before I put out the cigarette and toss the butt to the ground. I'll kiss him a lot, so he thinks about my lips.

When the other girls in the room talk about the pilots and laugh with one another, they always whisper about spreading their legs, I'll spread my legs as wide as I can.

I lie back on the bench and try to spread my legs. How will it feel when he lies on me like that? Will his body be heavy for me? Will I like the feeling like the other girls who whisper about it at night? But the most important thing is that I like him and that he wants to do it with me.

The other girls in the room are already asleep when I enter, and I undress in the dark. They must've come back when I was with Henry by his plane or when I was sitting on the bench, facing the sea. My fingers search for my locker, and I place my clothes in it, loosen the prosthetic leg's leather straps, quietly placing it on the floor.

"Tell me, Grace, did you use my lipstick?" I hear Audrey whisper to me, but I don't answer her.

"Did you think it would make him fall in love with you?" She continues without waiting for me to reply. "You're so naive."

I lie down on my bed and cover myself with my military wool blanket, trying to be as quiet as possible.

"They always take new girls like you to show them the planes at night," she continues. "Letting them feel the smooth fuselage, saying something about the girl painted on the nose in a swimsuit or revealing dress, confessing about longing for the women they left behind, back home, when they went out to fight for our nation."

My fingers massage my amputated leg, pressing it firmly.

"Then they tell you how magical it is to fly," I keep hearing her. "How wonderful it is to be in the sky, like a bird, to see everything so small, and how brave them pilots are, defeating the Germans, showing you the drawing marks of the bombs painted on the side of the plane, proud of themselves for destroying Berlin and Munich," I keep looking at the black ceiling in the dark.

"Then you let them kiss you," her words continue. "You'll be his great prize. Sure, he'll never stay with you, don't worry, you're neither the first nor the last one, surely a new nurse will arrive soon and take your place," my fingers wrap around the rough military wool blanket, gripping it tightly.

"If you're good enough," I hear her slightly laugh. "He'll even draw you on his plane, writing your name on the nose, replacing the previous one, so he can remember his conquest before the next one in line will replace you," I don't move, I want her to think I fell asleep, still, I'm wiping the tears from my cheeks with my hand.

"But at least you'll be like the rest of us, just the way you always wanted to be," it seems to me she's smiling as she whispers, and I scratch my thighs with my fingernails.

Finally, she pauses, and I turn to the wall, trying to peel off pieces of plaster.

"Don't worry," she says after a while. "I didn't tell him you don't have a leg. I wanted to let him find out for himself."

"Americana, this is not your church; it brings bad luck," she replies when I ask her to take me to pray. I'm ashamed to tell her that I hardly went to church back home. I don't want her to think I don't believe. I so need to believe in something.

"La vedova en moto," I shout as I follow her to our corner, behind the old shed. "Do you have another place where I can pray?"

"Go to the sea to pray to the lord of the waves," she turns around and answers me, reaching her hand out, asking for a cigarette.

"I can't," I protect the match's flame from the wind with my hands while she lights her cigarette. I can't pray in the sea after I threw away the cross that was on my neck. He must be waiting for me for revenge.

"You're Americana, you can do anything," she exhales the smoke and stomps her feet. For several days now, the rain hadn't stopped, and we cannot sit on the muddy ground, just stand close to the old shed wall and hide from the rain under the protruding roof.

"Okay, Americana," she says after a while, throws the cigarette into the mud. "Let's go."

"I knew it would be bad luck to take you to church," she yells at me as I hold her waist tightly and try to ignore the pouring rain falling on us, as we ride on the rattling motorcycle.

Her black hair is glistening from the rain and blends with her sodden black dress, which clings to her skin, dripping water on the road, and I have to hold her with all my might as not to slip, feeling the rain penetrating through my military uniform, also getting me wet.

The motorcycle drives slowly through the village paved streets, and I'm afraid we'll slip and turn over at any moment. Maybe I was wrong when I asked her to take me to pray.

"Come on, *Americana*," she yells at me as she parks the motorcycle on the side of the square and starts running to the church entrance, trying to avoid the rain. But I can't run after her. I have to carefully walk on the smooth pavement and use the stick she once gave me. At least the square is empty, and no one can see how miserable I look; one wet woman walking alone in the dripping rain, crossing the abandoned square.

"Come on, *Americana*," she shouts at me and goes down the stairs to the rain again, accompanying my slow steps and trying to protect my head with her raised hands, even though the rain is dripping between her fingers and gets both of us wet.

"Come here," she holds my hand as we reach the top step and pulls me inside the church, crossing the heavy brown wooden door.

It takes some time for my eyes to get used to the darkness inside. Still, in the center of the nave, I notice a bright light going down from the roof, down with the dropping rain to the floor, falling on the ruined, wet wood pews that are scattered on the floor, and when I raise my head, I notice a big hole in the church's roof.

"Another gift from some bomber," Francesca says as she notices where I'm looking at and walks inside, bypassing the broken pews towards the apse, looking up at Saint Mary and Jesus and crossing herself, and I do as she does.

Then she goes to one of the rows of unharmed pews, sits, and starts praying in a whisper, and I also sit on one of the wooden pews, but in another row, not wanting her to hear my prayer.

"What shall I do?" I whisper and look up at the saint? "Shall I do with him everything the other girls are laughing about at night?" I try to peek at Francesca, it's just the two of us in the abandoned church. I have to concentrate on my prayer.

"At least there's someone who wants me. Shouldn't that be enough? Even though I didn't tell him that I'm disabled. He mustn't know," my hands are crossed as I keep on praying. "I couldn't tell him. He thinks I was just injured. Is it a terrible sin to lie like that when no one else wants me without a leg? Why do I keep thinking about John, who loves another woman? Is it awful that I'm lying to him, too?"

But Saint Mary doesn't answer me, and only the rain continues to make a noise, falling from the hole in the roof and hitting the stone floor and the wood fragments lying in the center of the church.

My eyes follow Francesca as she approaches the apse again, holding a candle, lighting it, and crossing herself. I follow her, holding a candle and quietly light it.

"*Americana*, that's not how you light candles," her cold and wet fingers hold mine as she instructs me on how to place the candle among all the others, and I take another candle and light it, followed by another one and another one.

"*Americana*, why are you lighting so many candles? Do you think we have a candle factory here?" She whispers to me, but I just look up at Saint Mary, who's watching me from above, and whisper another prayer. For Henry, please make him not be afraid of flying over Germany, asking her to protect him from the German bullets, and for Francesca's husband, asking her to bring him back alive from the cold Russian winter. I also ask her to make John forgive me after I hurt him so much and I don't know how to fix it; and for me, that I'll find someone who'll love me, even though I have no leg.

After I finish and cross myself one last time, I follow Francesca, who's waiting for me at the door, leading me to the corner of the church, to the curved stairs going up to the bell tower, and we both sit on them, waiting for the rain to stop.

"Long before you arrived," she says after a while. "There was another woman like me here, in the village," I watch her fingers arrange her wet dress, trying to separate the black cloth that sticks to her thighs.

"Her husband was drafted into the army, like my husband. Together, they went to Russia," she pauses for a moment. "Then we heard that the Russians had won at Stalingrad and that the Germans and Italians had frozen to death in the Russian winter. The fascist newspapers from Rome said we won, but one person in the village was listening to the BBC, and he told us the truth. And the letters had also stopped coming," she combs her wet hair with her fingers, arranging it.

"I'd see her a lot in the post office when I'd go to the old clerk every day, asking him if a letter had arrived from my husband," she wipes the raindrops from her cheeks. "Or I'd see her here," she gestures at the church with her head. "When I'd come to pray. There was still no bomb hole in the church's roof at that time. And one day, I think after about a year, she stopped praying and started dating a German officer."

I listen to the rain fall and lean against the stone wall, saying nothing, watching her fingers play with the wet fabric of her dress.

"I think she needed to feed her child and had no more money left," she continues. "And she went and prayed to

Saint Mary and asked her what to do. She had to choose between standing in the alley in Rome and the gray uniform of the German."

"And what happened to her?"

"I stopped talking to her. Everyone stopped talking to her. Everyone hated her, me too. I would go to the post office and beg the clerk to look at the mailbag again. Maybe he didn't notice, and a letter had arrived, and would see her getting out of her German officer's military car, dressed in beautiful clothes, wearing white leather gloves."

"And is she still here?"

"No," Francesca looks at me. "She disappeared when you arrived. First, the Germans stopped walking around the village in their clean uniforms, and only soldiers' trucks would cross the main street, on the way south to Naples, carrying German soldiers holding their rifles and staring at us in hatred. And then, before they were really gone and left their mine presents, one day she disappeared. She must've feared revenge. Maybe her German officer took her with him to Berlin. Let's go. We can get back on the motorcycle. I think the rain has stopped."

"Maybe she didn't understand what Saint Mary was telling her," I say to Francesca and get up from the cold stone stairs.

"Maybe, I don't know anymore," she stands up and again arranges the fabric of her dress that clings to her thighs. "I chose to wear a black dress, she chose the Germans," she smiles at me. "She probably didn't think she was worth much."

The boots are tightly fastened to my feet. Earlier, when I got dressed, sitting on my simple bed in the nurses' room, I tied the laces as tight as I could, so he couldn't take them off if he tries to, when we'd be together. I'm also wearing a bigger sized dress, so it'll be easier to roll it up.

I take out the lipstick and try to wear it again in the dark, that my lips will stand out as much as possible, even though it's not the red lipstick I wanted. Earlier in the evening, as I was getting ready to go to the club, I looked for the red lipstick in Audrey's locker, but it was gone. I eventually managed to find my old pink lipstick tucked in the bottom of my army duffel bag. I'll have to settle for it.

I lean back in the jeep's seat and look at the darkness outside the pilots' club. He accompanied me to the jeep and asked me to wait for him for a minute, returning to the hut and the music emerging outside, into the night, through the open door. For a moment, I think of the woman in the alley in Rome, and I feel of nauseous, but maybe it's because I drank too much. I'm ready for what we're going to do. That's what I want. And he wants me. I'll never find anyone better than him.

"Sorry for the delay," Henry returns to the jeep and smiles at me, and I smile back, holding the jeep's metal frame tightly. All evening he laughed and smiled and was nice to everyone, and when I got up to go, he volunteered to drive me back.

"No thanks, I'll manage on my own," I replied, knowing he'd insist.

"Let me be a gentleman," he laughed, and some girls laughed along with him while I agreed for him to take me. But Audrey wasn't among them. Tonight, she didn't come at all.

"Shall we go?" He sits in the driver's seat and looks at me.

And I turn to him and smile, saying nothing but feel my stomach cramps as the jeep begins to drive fast on the dirt road. At least the rain stopped, and it isn't as cold outside.

His plane is waiting for us in the dark while Henry parks the jeep in front of it, shuts off the engine, walks over to my side, and gives me his hand, without saying a word. We both know why he brought me here.

"Do you have a cigarette?" I ask him next to Betty's nose, trying to buy some time, even though I have my own. Henry hands me the box and protects the flame with his hands as I lit myself one, and for a moment, his face is lit by the yellow light. He has a pleasant face; he'll be gentle with me.

We smoke in silence, and I run my hand over Betty's fuselage, feeling its smoothness. The torn metal holes that he'd shown me the previous time had disappeared and had been replaced with shiny new boards. It's nice to stand outside like that, in the cold air.

"That's where we get into the plane," he pulls a handle on the side of the plane, opens a door in the metal body, and I toss the cigarette to the ground and slide my hand on Betty's fuselage and her red painted swimsuit one last time, which looks almost black in the dark.

"Be careful," he is touching my hair as I'm placing my feet on the small metal ladder and climb, bend, and enter the plane. The small space is filled with crates, seats, hydraulic pipes and handles, and I'm carefully feeling around me, trying to see in the dark, noticing the black machineguns.

"This is our real home," he climbs after me, and I can feel his presence close to mine. I'm ready.

"Grace," he's bending over next to me, showing me where

to sit with his hand, and handing me his whiskey flask while I lean back against the side of the plane and feel the iron pipes through my dress.

"No thanks," I return the flask to him, feeling his body next to mine on the cold metal floor. I'd already drunk a lot when we were at the club.

"Grace," he tells me again after drinking by himself. "You're different from the other girls, I don't know why."

"It's okay," I answer. I don't want him to keep talking about how different I am.

"No, it's not okay," he says, and it seems to me that he also had too much to drink. "Just so you'd know, there is a Betty. The real Betty exists."

"We're war wanderers, aren't we?" I feel his body heat through his uniform as we both sit close together, in the narrow space behind the cockpit and the pilots' seats.

"Yes, we're war wanderers," he sips from his whisky again and places his hand on my knee, and I tremble for a moment. Did he feel the leather straps of the prosthetic leg?

"There's only here and now," I place my hand on his fingers, holding them tightly, preventing him from stroking further down to my feet.

"Is everything alright?"

"Yes, everything is fine," I look at his dark silhouette and I can see the moon through the pilots' canopy above us. I'm just like all the other girls.

"You're not like everyone else. I didn't tell anyone about her," he says while stroking my thighs, just as he stroked all those who sat here before me.

"Thanks," I reply, even though I don't believe his nice words.

"I know we're at war and that I may die tomorrow, and

that for us there is only here and now, but it was important for me that you know that there is a Betty for me, one Betty," he drinks again, and I can smell the whisky.

"And what are you to her?" I ask and feel his hand stop stroking my thigh.

"To her I'm just a spoiled and arrogant young man with a sports car and rich parents," he sips from his little bottle again.

"You must be wrong," I whisper to him.

"No, I'm not mistaken," he reaches out and strokes the black machinegun next to him. "That's what I am to her."

"Is that what she told you?"

"She didn't have to," in the dim light of the moon, I can see his hand playing with the bullets belt that is swallowed up in the black machinegun, hearing the rustle of metal under his fingers. "Back home, we always had a lot of money, and a big house, and cars, and I'd go out to parties and hang out. But most of all, I wanted to go with her. She said I was making her laugh."

I try to think what to say but can't, and I put my hand on his thigh.

"But her parents, and my parents as well," he continues. "Always said that nothing would come out of me. Until finally, she refused to go out with me anymore, saying that for in order to get married, one needs a person who takes life seriously."

"And what happened then? Did you try to change?"

"Nothing happened. I kept going out and hanging out and laughing with girls that I can't even remember their names, because that's who I am, a spoiled and arrogant young man that will never take life seriously; even she told me that. And people don't really change," he puts his hand on my thigh again, and I touch his warm fingers.

"After that, Pearl Harbor happened," he sips again. "And I was sitting in the living room of our house and heard the announcer on the radio. I think he was crying. The next day, I ran away from home and went to war," he offers me the whisky again, and I sip from it as he continues to talk slowly. "My dad had a big black Cadillac, he always made sure it was clean and tidy, and he never let me drive it. He once told me that I have to earn the right to drive this car and that I probably never will," I hold his hand tightly, caressing him.

"That day, I took his black Cadillac without asking his permission," he continues. "And drove to one of the Long Island train stations and left it out there in the parking lot, without saying goodbye or even telling him I was going to war. It wasn't even the closest train station to our house," he laughs to himself as he drinks from his whiskey.

"You know, Grace," he strokes my hand in return. "I went to the army, and learned how to fly, and became a captain of a B-17 bomber, but I still drink and smoke and go out with girls I don't remember their names, telling them that war is one big adventure. So, what does that say about me? Does that mean I changed? Or did I stay the same spoiled and arrogant young man?" He sips again.

"I didn't know you then," I stroke his neck, wanting to hug him.

"Deep in my heart," he continues to caress my hand. "I want to hope that the day I get back home, my dad's black Cadillac will still be waiting for me at the train station, right where I left it three years ago, and I'll go in and drive home, and my dad will shake my hand, telling me I've changed. "

I keep stroking his warm hand.

"And I hope," he places his hand again on the black machinegun at his side. "That maybe Betty will wait for me and see that I've changed. But I know it won't happen, people don't change."

I want to tell him that people do change and that he's not the same arrogant young man who got on the train at Long Island station three years ago, but maybe he's right. Maybe people don't change.

I look at his fingers, gently caressing the machineguns' bullet belts, - awaiting tomorrow, for the German planes that would come from the sky - and wonder how many women he did bring here before me, huddle with him in the dark, inside the plane, between boxes of ammunition and machineguns? How many women did look at the black sky through the plexiglass canopy of the cockpit as he told them this story and made them want to fly to the stars with him?

But isn't that the reason I'm here? At least I'm not different from them.

"Will you ever teach me to fly?" I force myself to say. I must do it. He's the only one who wants me.

In the dark, I can notice his smile as he hands me the whiskey again, and I sip from it, emptying what was left, and reach out my hand, shoving the silver bottle in his leather jacket pocket, my hands shaking.

"You're different than everyone else."

"I'm not different," I grab his pilot's jacket and bring my lips closer to his, smelling the whiskey.

"Come with me," he doesn't kiss me back, and to my surprise, he opens the door of the plane, and I feel the cool night breeze penetrating inside.

"Spread your hands as wide as you can," he puts his hand on my back for a moment as I stand in the open jeep, leaning against the windshield and trying to stabilize myself.

"My arms are spread," I shout at him.

"Now, close your eyes."

"I'm scared," I feel the cool night breeze blowing in my face.

"Trust me."

"They're closed," I say to him, even though I keep them open.

"Now lean forward, so you don't fall backwards," he shouts at me and starts driving with the jeep on the dirt runway, increasing his speed. I feel the cold wind hitting my face and ruffling my hair, and only the jeep headlights flicker on the white dirt as he increasingly speeds up, and I look up at the sky and see the stars.

"I'm flying," I shout at him, holding my hands against the cold wind, fighting her back, and not giving up. I want to tell him that he did change and should go back to his Betty, but I'm too embarrassed. I also have to tell my feelings to another soldier, even though he has a woman he thinks is waiting for him back home.

"Dear John, even though I didn't receive a letter from you, I know that you'll write to me as soon as you can," I quietly read the words to myself as I lie in my bed. What would Georgia have written to him if she still loved him?

My notebook is laying on the bed, lit by the dim light of the candle. All the other girls in the room are already sleeping, and I must be quiet. I even left my book standing open to hide the small light from the others. If anyone asks what I'm doing, I'll tell them I'm writing a letter home.

As I write down the words, I occasionally put down my pen and look at Georgia's old letters, the ones I keep in my small locker by the bed. Now they're spread out in front of me on the bed while I'm trying to mimic her rounded and perfect handwriting, though it doesn't really matter. He can't see anyway.

'I keep reading the news that comes from the front every day, trying to guess where you're fighting. All the newspapers are writing about the liberation of Paris. Still, I don't care about Paris. I know you're in Italy, and when the war is over, you'll take me to Tuscany to show me the places where you were.' I look around the dark room, thinking of John lying in the dark, 'Everyone here in town is asking about you,' It takes me a while to remember where he lives, and I finally delete and correct.

'I love and miss you, Georgia.' I sign the letter and look at it. Shall I kiss the paper as she used to do when she loved him?

I bring the letter closer to my lips, kiss it and try to imprint what is left of my lipstick on it, but then I'm once again reminded that he's blind. I'm ashamed of myself for a moment, I almost kissed Henry tonight with those lips.

My fingers forcefully rub the paper, trying to erase my lipstick marks, but it smears until it becomes an ugly stain and I think maybe I should burn this letter and start writing a new one instead, but it's too late, and if I don't give it to him now, I'll lose my nerve.

"It's so hard to be so alone. He has to believe she still loves him," I whisper to the candle as I fold the letter. "I'm not doing it because I miss him. It's for his own good. He misses her letters so much," I keep whispering, hoping no other girl is awake. Still, I don't hold back and kiss the folded paper one more time before I quietly get out of bed and blow out the candle.

"Dear John, even though I didn't receive a letter from you, I know that you will write to me as soon as you can," I stand by his bed and quietly start reading to him, lighting the letter with the lighter I'm holding in my other hand, not stopping to check if he's awake at all.

"Gracie, is that you?"

"Yes, it's me," I keep reading the letter to him, placing my letter-holding hand on his bed, hoping he won't notice my trembling fingers.

"Is that a letter from her?" He puts his hand on my palm, touching the paper. His fingers are warm.

"Yeah, John, it's from her," I keep reading to him. "Summer will be over soon, and I'm already feeling a chill in the air, remembering how we used to walk together, hugging," I mustn't think of his hand touching me.

"She didn't like it when we hugged in public," he whispers to me. "She used to say that it's embarrassing to hug in front of other people."

"Maybe she misses your hug," I have to move my hand off his bed.

"Maybe," his fingers still touching mine, stroking my hand. I have to think of something else.

"John, what does she look like?"

"Georgia?" He stops moving his fingers.

"Yes."

"She has light hair, slightly curly. And she has bright eyes,"

I see him move his hands in the dark as if trying to describe her. "We've been together ever since we knew each other, when we were kids," he smiles at me. "I have a picture of her. Do you want to see?"

"Yes, please," I grab the sheet with my fingernails. Why didn't I tell him she didn't want him once that letter had arrived?

"Look in my backpack, in one of the pockets," he gets up and extends his hand, touching my body.

"Sorry, I'm sorry," he leaves his hand on my waist.

"It's okay," I keep standing next to his bed.

"And you, what do you look like?" I can feel the warmth of his fingers through my uniform.

"I have dark hair, almost straight," I look at him. "And I have dark brown eyes."

"Can I touch your face? to get to know you?"

What shall I reply?

I step back and bend over to his locker, grabbing his backpack, once again looking at the picture of Georgia smiling at me, wearing her summer dress, the same picture I looked at before, when I thought he'd die and that she misses him so much.

"Yes, you can touch my face," I say after a while, returning Georgia's picture into his backpack and locker, approaching him again. She doesn't want him anymore.

His hand fumbles in the air as I bring my face closer, feeling his warm fingers touching my neck gently, then they climb up to my lips, and I let him feel their softness, open my mouth a bit. I mustn't do that; he just wants to get to know the woman he's talking to. My eyes close as his fingers continue to walk up to my nose and then to my cheeks, gently caressing them, and I want to hold his hand but stop myself, gripping the metal frame of the bed tightly. He longs for someone else. I mustn't think of his fingers touching my closed eyes, passing over my lashes and eyebrows like a butterfly fluttering its wings against my skin.

"Your hair is pulled back," he quietly says as he strokes it.

"Yes," I pull back from his touching fingers, take out the hairpins and spread my hair, approach him again, place his hand on my unbound hair, let him feel its smoothness.

"Now I know what you look like," he continues to stroke my hair, goes down with his hand to my neck again, and further down towards my breasts, I mustn't let this go on, he loves someone else, not me.

"I apologize for the previous time, on the road," I'm moving back from his warm hand.

"I have to apologize too, all you wanted to do was show me your boots, and I was angry at you," he leaves his hand in the air. I mustn't get close to his hand again.

"It's okay. I have boots that cover my prosthetic leg."

"So you're no longer Pinocchio? Have you become a real boy?"

"Yes, I became a real boy," I approach him just a bit, lift my legs to his bed, and place his hand on my boot, letting him feel it.

"Pinocchio, you have human legs," his hand caresses the boot and climbs up, touching and stroking my thighs. I want him to keep his hand there, but I know he mustn't go any further.

"Yes, I almost have human legs," I place my hand on his, stroking it back.

"Describe them to me," he leaves his hand on my thigh, gently stroking me, my fingers following his.

"They're brown, and they have laces and buckles," I think

of his hand touching me. "And I'm comfortable walking in them," he slides his hand down to the boot and climbs back to my thighs again, I want him to continue, he also knows we shouldn't go on.

"I missed our conversations," he keeps on stroking my legs, and I feel I'm starting to breathe slowly.

"I missed our conversations too. I shouldn't have yelled at you," I get a little closer to him, placing my hand on his waist. Why does he love someone else?

"Did you give the chocolate I threw on the road to the children in the village?" His lips are close to mine.

"I haven't been to the village yet," my fingers caress his cheeks, and I don't tell him that after he left, I walked to the road and threw the bar of crushed chocolate to the weeds, at the side of the road.

"When you go to the village again, will you give it to them?" He brings his lips closer to mine and touches them gently.

"I promise," I cling to him as he kisses me, first gently and then with passion, his fingers caressing my hair, and I try to be as quiet as I can in the dark hall, among the other wounded soldiers sleeping. I can feel his hand stroking my hips as my hands unbutton his shirt, caressing his chest as we kiss deeply, and I breathe heavily. I mustn't do that, If I continue, I wouldn't be able to stop myself.

"I'm sorry," I push him with my hands, trying to calm my breathing quietly and arranging my uniform shirt. Still, the feeling of his hands on my breasts remains, even after I manage to calm myself down.

"I'm sorry, I shouldn't have done this," he puts his hand on my leg again, but I move it away and place it on the sheet, still holding his fingers. We mustn't continue. I won't be able to fall asleep tonight anyway.

"I shouldn't have kissed you. You love someone else."

"Yes, I love someone else," he removes his hand from mine. "She's waiting for me back home. I was told the ship would arrive soon and that they have to decide whether or not to send me back."

"I have to go. I just came to apologize and read you a letter that arrived from her anyway," I run my finger over my thighs, scratching it with my fingernails, not telling him that this time the ship's for me. I'm tired of running away from this ship.

"Thanks for the letter."

"Good night, John from far away Cold Spring," I force myself to get up from his bed. My bed is waiting for me in the room, with the other girls, covered with a dark, itchy wool blanket.

"Good night, Gracie from Chicago, the big city beyond the horizon," I hear him whisper, and I'm not replying.

"Gracie?" I still hear him as I walk away.

"Yes?" I stop and turn to him.

"Will you come visit me again?"

"I Promise."

I have to stay away from him. He, too, loves someone else.

Naples

"Grace, Blanche wants you in her office," Audrey says, entering one of the treatment rooms as I change a soldier's bandage.

"What does she want?"

"She didn't say." Audrey smiles at me and disappears behind the door. My fingers grip the white bandage tightly as I keep wrapping it around his hand.

"You're hurting me." He looks up at me.

"Sorry," I release the bandage and start wrapping it again. What does she want from me?

"Grace, how are you doing here, among all the other nurses?" She looks at me as I stand tall and tense in her office.

"I'm doing fine, Head Nurse Blanche."

"I understood from Audrey that you assisted in the German pilot's surgery."

"Yes, I did, and she took care of him afterwards. I'm doing fine here." I don't want to mention that Audrey has been calling me a German-lover since the day I started taking care of Harald. Some of the soldiers call me that as well.

"Well, I'm happy to hear that. Audrey is a good nurse, and works by to the book."

"Yes, Head Nurse Blanche." I examine the bench in the garden overlooking the sea, I can see it from the window of her office.

"It's a shame all my nurses don't follow the rules like she does."

"Yes, Head Nurse Blanche."

"Do you have anything to tell me about the jeeps that disappeared from my hospital parking lot at night?"

"No, Head Nurse Blanche." I keep looking straight ahead. What would she do to me if she found out?

"You know, Grace…"

"Yes, Head Nurse Blanche," I say as she keeps talking.

"There are always those who think they know better than others, that they can always manage on their own."

"Yes, Head Nurse Blanche."

"Well, those who think that are wrong."

"Yes, Head Nurse Blanche." What does she mean? Is she going to punish me? I keep my head up and look through her window.

"Grace, early tomorrow morning you will accompany one of our trucks to Naples, and help the driver with the medical supplies."

"Why?" I look at her for the first time since entering her office. As usual, she's busy with the lists of names placed on the table in front of her.

"Because that's what intern nurses do – the dirty jobs no one else wants. Maybe that's what you deserve as a reminder, since you seem to have forgotten, that this here is the US Army and you can't do whatever you want."

"Yes, Head Nurse Blanche."

"Now get out my office."

"Yes, Head Nurse Blanche," I answer her and turn around. It seems as though she'll never be happy with me.

"Grace?" she calls after me. I turn around and see her looking up from the page she's holding.

"Yes, Head Nurse Blanche?"

"I appreciate people who keep their humanity during wartime, like those who change bandages for wounded

German soldiers after a senior nurse refuses to take care of him."

"Thank you, Head Nurse Blanche."

"That'll be all. You can close the door behind you." She returns to her papers.

"Yes, Head Nurse Blanche." I walk out slowly and close the door behind me. At least there are no severe consequences to my actions.

"I'm to escort you on the drive to Naples," I tell the truck driver standing in the parking lot, smoking and rubbing his hands to keep warm.

It's early dawn. He mutters something under his breath, clearly displeased about them sending him a woman with a cane. He probably thinks he'll have to do all the work himself. He gets in the truck and starts the engine. Honestly, I don't care what he thinks. If this is Blanche's way of punishing me, I can live with that. I've been through worse than being a companion to an unpleasant truck driver, I think to myself. I get inside the truck and slam the metal door behind me.

"To Naples" reads the road sign placed by the American army. Next to it is another sign indicating that the road and its surroundings have been cleared of mines and bomb remnants. Both signs are attached to a wooden pole above a sign that reads 'Naples' in German. Below it is a bullet-hole-riddled Italian sign, 'Napoli.

"It's going to take us a while, the road is badly damaged," the driver finally says after driving in silence for a while, but I don't answer him, I just look at the potholes on the road and try to remember the only other time I drove this way. Back then I was coming from the other direction, from Naples to the front. It was when I had just arrived in Italy, and the war still seemed so exciting. Only a few months have passed since then, but the road seems so different to me.

I look around at the trees and road signs. Still, I can't seem to remember the road. Maybe it's because I was too busy looking at the soldiers sitting next to me in the back of the army truck. I was assigned as a nurse to an infantry brigade on its way north to fight the Germans. It seems to me that a whole life has passed since then.

"Hey there, newbies," a sergeant wearing a dust-covered uniform shouted when he saw us trying to find our way through the crowded Naples port a few months ago. It was already noon, long after we disembarked from the ship, and we had been trying to find our way through the commotion around us. I think it was right after I gave all my cigarettes to the begging children, since I remember the sergeant driving them away, but I don't remember clearly now.

"Yes, sir," the new female soldier and I answered, approaching him and holding our duffelbags tightly.

"Throw your lifejacket there," he instructed us and pointed to a pile of yellow lifejackets lying on the platform.

"Yes, sir," I answered and rushed to remove the lifejacket, placing it on the top of the pile.

"Do you have your documents?" he shouted, his voice trying to overcome the engine noise of several Sherman tanks that had descended to the dock from a tank carrier, and rolled by us with deafening noise.

"Yes, sir," I shouted back and handed him the folded papers in my pocket.

"Wait there," he instructed us after a moment, pointing to a corner of the dock. We dragged our duffelbags next to a pile of diesel-smelling barrels and stood there watching the neverending convoys of trucks full of soldiers and tanks that kept unloading from the landing ships.

Every now and then I looked at the other female soldier: she wore a clean white nurse's uniform like mine, and she too appeared unbothered by the noise and vehicles passing around us.

"Hey nurses, will you take care of us if we get injured?" I heard a voice and looked up at a group of soldiers sitting in the back of an army truck that had been unloaded from one of the ships. I smiled at them in response.

"And what about us?" I heard a few soldiers from another truck. They smiled at us under the green helmets they were wearing, but I didn't have the courage to answer them.

"Hey you, nurses, the new ones," the sergeant approached us and we both stood up straight.

"Yes, sir."

"There's a problem with your transportation north to the front lines. All vehicles and drivers have been taken by another division."

"Yes, sir," we both said, not knowing what else we could do.

"Let's arrange a ride for you to the war zone. Follow me."

"Yes, sir," we said at the same time and grabbed our duffelbags, rushing after him as he walked between the transport trucks.

"After me." Now he was talking to one of the truck drivers, showing him our papers as we stood there waiting.

"You two, get on this truck," he instructed us while he climbed into the back of the truck.

"Good morning, Infantry Brigade 141," he said to the soldiers sitting in the back of the truck.

"Good morning, Sergeant," they answered him at the same time, straightening up.

"Joining you are two lovely guests traveling north to the front lines."

"Yes, sergeant."

"Treat them nicely."

"Yes, sergeant."

"You two," he turned to us, "where are you from?"

"Sergeant, I'm from Chicago," I shouted as another tank convoy passed by us, shaking the truck.

"Sergeant, I'm from New York," the other nurse answered him.

"That's great. Chicago, New York, I hope you have a safe journey and save a lot of lives in this bloody war." He helped us lift our duffelbags onto the back of the truck, and disappeared behind the other armored vehicles standing on the platform, waiting for their drive up north.

"Miss New York, please sit down." One of the soldiers got up and made room for the nurse on the wooden bench at the back of the truck.

"Miss Chicago, please sit." Another soldier smiled at me under his helmet and moved, making room for me too. I sat down, huddled between them. I could smell the sweat wafting from their army uniforms, the result of the long voyage at sea. I probably smell that way too, I thought to myself.

More and more army trucks joined the convoy, until it seemed like the whole port was full of them. I looked around the truck and noticed the soldiers staring at us curiously, so I lowered my gaze.

"Where are you going?" the other nurse asked them.

"We're on our way to conquer Rome," they answered her and laughed. "And you?"

"We're on our way to a field hospital near the front lines," I answered, looking up and examining their uniform.

"Are you new here?" One of the soldiers asked me.

"Yes, and what about you?" I looked into his black eyes.

"Yes, we're here as reinforcements."

"Straight from America?"

"Straight from faraway America." He smiled at me.

"Me too." I smiled back at him.

"I'm also here as reinforcements," the other nurse said.

"We're the reinforcements everyone's been waiting for. We've come to beat the Germans and finish the war," one of the soldiers said to her and laughed.

"We'll be celebrating Thanksgiving in Berlin," another one joined in.

"The Germans should consider surrendering before your arrival," she smiled at them.

"Move out," shouted one of the commanders standing on the dock, and the convoy of trucks began to slowly drive away from the port and onto the road along the coastline, moving away from the city. The townhouses kept getting smaller behind us until they became tiny dots in the horizon, like a pile of shells spilling into the blue bay.

Suddenly the road got rougher, due to the potholes probably caused by passing tanks and cannon shells that ruined the asphalt. This caused the truck to drive slower, and as for me, I kept my gaze on the green fields and trees until I saw it.

The tank was lying on the side of the road, black and sooty, its cannon pointing towards the ground as if surrendering to the war. I could still see the black German iron cross painted on the sides of the tank.

The other soldiers also followed the tank with their gaze until it disappeared from their view, but after a while another damaged tank appeared on the side of the road along with a destroyed American tank. I looked at the faces of the soldiers sitting on the wooden bench in front of me.

Serious looks replaced the smiles they'd given us at the beginning of the drive. Their eyes that had been focused on the other nurse's lips until now were surveying the surrounding fields, while their hands gripped their guns a little tighter.

The truck slowed down as we passed by another damaged tank blocking a part of the road, the American star still visible on the front of its destroyed turret. The soldiers stared at it intently, even as the truck continued on its way. No one was smiling anymore.

"Where are you from?" I asked the soldiers sitting in front of me.

"Atlanta," one of them replied, turning his gaze away from the wreckage and facing me. "Charlotte, North Carolina," continued the one sitting next to him. "Charleston," the next added, "Jacksonville." One by one, they said the names of their hometowns in an endless list I couldn't possibly remember, and slowly the smiles returned to their faces.

"Please, Miss Chicago," the soldier who had made room for me earlier pulled a box of cigarettes from his uniform pocket and offered me one. "Thanks," I said, and took a cigarette in order to be polite, not telling him I don't smoke.

"Keep the pack," he smiled at me as I handed him the box back.

"Thanks, but it's yours."

"After we kill all the Germans, we'll have as many cigarettes as we want," he said, and everyone nodded in agreement as I leaned towards his outstretched hand holding the metal lighter.

"Maybe you'll need them," I said, and tried not to cough as I inhaled the bitter smoke.

"Please take them so you have a souvenir from me." He took out a pen and wrote his name on the box of cigarettes. "And I'll have a reason to come visit you." He smiled at me. I smiled back at him, stuffing the cigarettes in my pocket and examining his face, which was barely visible under the green helmet he wore.

"Take mine as well," another soldier pulled a box of cigarettes out of his uniform pocket, wrote his name on it, and handed it to me.

"And mine." More soldiers added their names to the cigarette boxes they handed to me.

"Miss New York, do you want a cigarette?" Some soldiers turned to the other nurse, and she laughed and refused them. Still, they didn't give up and kept talking to her, offering to marry her when the war was over and promising to visit. I looked at the road and the destroyed tanks that occasionally appeared on the side of the road.

"This is where your hospital is, behind the hill," the truck driver shouted to us as he stopped the truck on the side of the road. We rushed to get out, so as not to delay the endless convoy of trucks on their way to the front.

"Good luck, Miss New York; good luck, Miss Chicago," the soldiers on the truck exclaimed. The soldier with the dark eyes just nodded his head without saying a word. I nodded back, saying goodbye to him.

"Don't forget us," the soldier with the boyish face added while smiling at the other nurse.

"We're waiting for you," she said, and waved goodbye as the truck continued on its way.

We both stood there waving goodbye as the trucks passed us one by one.

"See you in Berlin," some of them shouted to us, and I smiled at them, trying not to think about the burned American tanks I'd seen on the road.

Finally the last truck in the convoy went by, and the quiet fields around us replaced the noise of the engines and dust. We stood alone next to a road sign full of bullet holes, looking for the right way to the hospital.

I bent down and put my duffelbag back on my shoulders, and two boxes of cigarettes fell on the ground. I picked them up and looked at the names written on them. What if they did get wounded and ended up at the hospital? Would I be able to save their lives?

"What are you doing?" she asked me as I walked to the side of the road.

"Nothing," I answered as I took the cigarette boxes out of my uniform pockets and threw them as far as I could into the bushes by the side of the road.

"Aren't those the cigarette boxes they gave you as a present?" she asked.

"I don't smoke," I said to her and looked at the empty road, praying silently they would never have a reason to arrive at the hospital. I had to tell them I was just an intern nurse.

"I thought there was a shortage of cigarettes."

"You heard what they said. After they kill all the Germans, they will have as many cigarettes as they want," I answered, and watched her light a cigarette from one of the boxes the soldiers had given her, even though she'd claimed she didn't smoke.

Two days later, the battle of Rome began in the mountains. The other nurse cracked under the pressure of the neverending stream of wounded and couldn't function anymore. They evacuated her, and I continued my job in the operating tent all by myself.

Although I tried to recognize their faces while examining every wounded soldier, I couldn't remember any of them.

Maybe the fact that I had thrown their cigarette boxes into the bushes had kept them from coming to visit me after all.

Maybe I should have cracked under the pressure as well, then I would have been evacuated back home. But that was a long time ago, in a different lifetime. Now I'm on my way to Naples on the medical supply truck.

"Want a cigarette?" the truck driver asks me as I stare out the window. The road is still badly damaged and full of potholes, but the wrecked tanks lying on the side of the road are gone. Someone must have transferred them along with the rest of the war wreckage. Maybe my leg ended up there as well.

"Want a cigarette?" the driver asks me again, and I turn my gaze towards him.

"Yes, thank you."

"We'll get to town soon." He hands me the lit lighter, and I lean towards his hand, inhaling the bitter smoke and thanking him.

"How were you injured?" he asks.

"A plane."

"During the attack on the hospital?"

"No, before that."

"Was it painful?"

"War is a painful thing, isn't it?"

"Yes, war is a painful thing," he agrees.

"Have you been here long?" I ask him.

"Two and a half years. I haven't been home in two and a half years, is that a long time?"

"Yes, two and a half years is a long time." I exhale the smoke out the truck's open window.

For a few minutes we slow down, driving after a convoy of refugees headed south on the main road. I want to give them something, but I have nothing, so I just watch them walk slowly, their clothes covered with dirt. For a moment I see a family walking among the crowd; the woman is holding a suitcase, and next to her is a man in a suit that must have meant something back in the day, carrying a little girl in his arms. They don't stop, ignoring us as the truck passes them on the road, they just move a little to the side, continuing their neverending journey. The little girl in his arms looks at me and smiles with her white teeth, and I avert my eyes.

"It's their fault they joined Hitler and let the fascists rule them," the truck driver says to me.

"Yes, it's their fault," I answer and think of Francesca's husband, who was forced to enlist in the army by the Fascists. What would I have done had I been in their shoes?

"May I?" I ask him a few minutes later as we continue on the road, leaving the refugees behind us. I point at a photo of a smiling woman tucked in the dashboard of his truck.

"Yes, of course" he answers and hands me the picture. I look into the woman's happy eyes, turn the photo and read 'Juliana, 1941.'

"She's beautiful."

"I'm a lucky man, she's waiting for me at home, we'll get married when I come back."

"Does she write to you?"

"All the time."

"You're a lucky man," I say, and toss the cigarette out of the window, looking at the Naples townhouses that look like a pile of colored seashells spilling towards the blue bay.

At the end of the day, after we fill the truck with medical supplies and drive back from the supply base near Naples, I ask the driver to make a detour and pass through the port.

"Why do you want to go through the port?"

"Just feeling nostalgic, I was there not so long ago and wanted to see it again."

"Before the war?" he asks. "The port has really changed since then. The Germans destroyed it."

"No, I've never been to Italy before the war." I look around as we drive through the city. The narrow streets are no longer full of brick fragments from collapsed buildings as they were the last time I passed here. More people are walking the streets, and I can see the clotheslines stretched between the buildings filled with colorful laundry drying in the autumn sun. But there are still damaged buildings everywhere, some with a mere wall left standing, and some missing their façade, showing remnants of broken furniture.

"They shouldn't have fought us," the driver says, glancing at a ruined wall. But I don't answer, I just look around for the children I saw when I first arrived here, the ones who snatched the cigarette boxes from me.

At the entrance to the port is a new gate with a guard. The port seems to be in order and not too busy. There are no longer damaged ships laying in the water near the docks, with their red bellies towards the sky. And the water, once stained with huge black spots of oil and fuel, has returned to its usual greenish color. The cranes that were in the water have been taken out, and soldiers in coveralls were now working to repair them, illuminating the afternoon with welding sparks that flew into the water like fireworks.

"Please stop," I ask him, and get out of the truck right as he parks it. I walk carefully towards the green water. Everything has changed so much. The last time I was here I had a leg, and everything was so busy and loud. The kids were gone too. Where are all of the children?

I look around and search for the children who were here then, the day I arrived, but they're no longer here. Maybe the sergeant finally managed to drive them away for good, maybe the new fence and gated entrance is stopping them from entering the port. Or perhaps they wandered somewhere else, searching for other things to exchange on the black market in return for food.

My fingers touch the cigarette boxes I had tucked into my backpack in the morning. I'd been saving them for the children. Now I'm sorry I didn't give the cigarettes to the refugees we saw on the way. I think of the father wearing his suit, carrying the little girl in his arms, and the woman walking beside him, holding the suitcase. All searching for a new home, a new beginning.

"Look, the ticket back home," the truck driver stands beside me, pointing to the horizon. A white ship with a large

Red Cross painted on its side slowly sails out of the harbor, leaving behind a trail of white foam. The ship's bow faces west towards the setting sun.

"What is it?" I ask, even though it seems to me I already know.

"It's a return ticket, my dream, a small injury that will take me home to my beloved lady. The ship carrying the wounded to New York Harbor," he says.

"Yeah, a little injury, that's all it takes," I agree with him, but he keeps talking, and it doesn't seem to me like he's listening.

"The ship just arrived yesterday, and today it's already sailing back. Too bad I'm not standing on its deck waving goodbye," he says, looking at the white ship and the seagulls surrounding it.

I say nothing. I just light another cigarette for myself and take a few steps on the dock, thinking of Head Nurse Blanche who probably hates me.

"They must have emptied the hospital of the wounded. They're waiting for another major offensive against the Germans in the north," he keeps talking, and I turn to him. John, what about John?

"Did you say something?" he asks me.

"No," I answer and throw the cigarette butt on the ground. "Let's go back." I open the truck door and climb into my seat, rushing the drive to hurry up. What about John?

The way back is taking longer in the dark. The fully-loaded truck drives slowly, as the driver takes care to slow down before any pothole in the road. What will I do if John has gone with the ship today? Why is he driving so slowly? We should have been back at the hospital by now.

"Do you always smoke this much?" the driver asks me when I light another cigarette.

"Yes," I answer and exhale the smoke outside the open window, unable to have a conversation with him. Why didn't I know the ship was coming?

"Can I have one?" he asks, and I give him one, seeing his face by the light of the lighter for a brief moment. I didn't have time to say goodbye to John. Why didn't I go up to say goodbye to him in the morning?

"It's nice to have company driving this way at night," the driver keeps talking and smiling at me.

"Yes, it's nice." I look out the window, trying to locate the village lights and the hospital, but I notice only a few lights in the dark and I can't spot the hospital. When will we get there?

"Good night," I say goodbye to the driver as soon as he stops the truck in the hospital parking lot. Finally I can hear the silence after hours of driving, surrounded by the engine noise and the smell of burnt diesel.

"Good night," I think I hear him reply, but I'm already rushing towards the hospital stairs. I have to find him.

"Where were you? They've been looking for you all day," Audrey asks me. "Even the hospital commander was angry with Blanche when he heard you weren't here. I don't know what she told him."

"I don't know either," I reply to her. I need to get the list of the wounded soldiers that were shipped back.

"Where were you?"

"I went to see refugees."

"What do you mean, 'I went to see refugees'?"

"You wouldn't understand." She also wouldn't understand if I ask her to give me the list of those shipped back home.

So I enter the nurses' room, searching for it and seeing it hanging on the wall.

"Please get out. It's my shift now. You can't disturb me right now."

"I need to see something."

"You're bothering me. Please get out."

"I just need a minute, and I'll go."

"Get out of here. You've already done enough damage," she whispers to me and gets up from her table.

"What damage?"

"You wouldn't understand." She smiles at me with her perfect red lips.

"Please," I step back, "I only need a minute."

"Gracie, you used to be a nice person once, and it was worth helping you. Now please stop bothering me." She sits back down at the table and opens the book she's been reading, trying to return to the page that was lost when she got up.

"My name is Grace. You have no right to call me Gracie," I answer her, turn around, and exit the light-filled room into the dark hall. I have to find him.

Bed after bed, I'm walking in the dark, touching the white metal bed frames and looking for him. Most of the beds are empty, and my hands feel the smooth clean sheets waiting for the next wave of wounded to arrive. John's bed is also empty. I didn't even get to say goodbye to him. That can't be right. He's in no condition to be returning home.

I walk as fast as I can, checking the beds in the hall again, looking closely at the sleeping men still in the hall, trying to find John in the dark. I don't want to turn on the light, fearing Audrey will come and kick me out of here. I have to find him.

"John?" I whisper and touch the palm of a wounded man in the third row.

"Um?" I hear him saying. He's not John.

"Sorry, go back to sleep," I touch his shoulder and move to the next bed.

"John?" I whisper to another wounded man who smells a little like John, stroking his fingers.

"Gracie wooden leg?" His fingers caress my hand.

"Yes, it's me, Gracie wooden leg." I stroke his hair.

"Didn't you get on that ship? I thought you left without saying goodbye."

"No, I didn't go," I wipe away a tear, not telling him that's exactly what I thought.

"They read the list in the morning, you were on it, and I heard people asking and searching for you. I sat on the bench in front of the sea all day, and thought you went with the convoy without saying goodbye." He sits up in bed.

"I wouldn't have left without saying goodbye to you." I touch his chest, feeling it through his open hospital shirt.

"Gracie." He touches my hand and brings me closer to him. "Let's do something, let's get out of here."

"Where should we go?" I have to stop touching him even though I can feel his hand gently stroking my hair.

"Let's go somewhere where I'm not an injured soldier, and you're not a nurse."

"It's midnight and it's completely dark outside." I'm holding his hand. We shouldn't.

"What does it matter?" He laughs quietly and gets out of bed. "The night is my companion all the time." He leans over to put on his shoes, touching me by mistake but keeping his hand on my waist. I really shouldn't stand so close to him.

"Come with me, Gracie wooden leg." He stands up, takes my hand, and starts walking through the hall. I follow him, holding his hand tightly.

"I can't see in the dark," I whisper to him as we search for the exit to the garden.

"Then be like me." He feels his way along the wall, still holding my hand.

"But you don't have a wooden leg."

"Right," he holds my hand and pretends to limp, "here, I do now."

"I hate my limp," I whisper to him as we walk in the empty garden outside the hospital even though, there's no longer a reason to whisper.

"But I love it, it makes you special, part of who you are to me," He pauses for a moment, still holding my hand. It seems as though he wants to hug me but changes his mind at the last moment. What have I done? Why did I start this thing with John? Why did I lie to him about the letters?

"Let's go to the sea." I take his hand and walk towards the cliffs and the path that goes down to the shore.

The Sea

Once we're at the bottom of the trail, I turn around and look up at the path we just came down from, using our hands to cling to the rocks and each other, being careful not to slip. In the dark I can't really see the path, and the silhouette of the black cliff above us seems so threatening. I gasp and smile at it. We've finally reached the strip of sand leading to the sea.

"Do you hear the sirens? They're singing to us from the sea, inviting us in," John whispers to me.

"We really shouldn't get closer to them. We must stay where we are," I whisper back to him. I'm a cheat and a liar, just like those sirens, but I don't want to lie to him tonight.

"What could possibly happen to us? I'm blind, and you're missing a leg." He takes my hand and begins finding his way towards the waves we hear in the distance. The sand underneath our feet seems bright even in the dark.

"I can't." I release my hand and stand still, looking at his silhouette walking away from me. Why did I bring us here? I'm a cripple.

"Is everything okay? Did I say something wrong?" John stops and turns around, walking back to me. What should I tell him?

"I can't walk on the sand," I finally say.

"Why? It's so pleasant and soft."

"That's exactly the problem," I breathe deeply. I have to face it. I will always be the handicapped woman, who can't go to the beach, nothing can fix that.

"What's the problem? You don't like sand?"

"I like the sand, I like its touch on my feet and its softness," I say quietly, hoping he won't hear me over the sound of the waves, "but I'm unable to walk on the soft sand."

"Can the sand damage your prosthetic?" He walks towards me.

"No." I don't bother wiping my tears away since he can't see them.

"Or is it the sea water that can damage it?" He gets even closer to me.

"No, I'm just not stable enough on the soft sand. I can't walk on it."

"Come with me." He bends down and takes me in his arms, walking on the soft sand towards the water.

"John, you're crazy, you're injured."

"All I am is blind, so please point me towards the water," he laughs.

"A little to the left," I laugh and wipe away my tears, "you're crazy and blind." I hug his neck and cling to him, feeling his warm body and his breath as he carries me towards the white waves gently hitting the shore.

"Welcome to Italy." He lowers me once we reach the water, and I feel the soft sand and cold water around my legs as he suddenly presses his lips to mine. "You have a pleasant laugh."

His hands grip my waist tightly, and I cling to him, feeling his warm lips against mine. My hand caresses the back of his neck as I kiss him again and again, feeling his hands touching my body and stroking my breasts through my uniform, while his fingers search for the buttons.

Button by button he opens my shirt, and I tremble and breathe heavily at the touch of his warm hands. My hand opens his shirt and caresses his chest, feeling his scars with the tips of my fingers. I remember changing his bandages over those wounds. Back then I thought he was going to die. We have to stop, I have to tell him the truth about the letters and the woman he thinks is waiting for him at home.

"We need to get back," I pull away from him and gasp for air, feeling the cool water on my feet.

"Yes, we have to go back." He doesn't try to kiss me again. "This sea isn't safe for us."

"Will you take me back to reality?"

Without saying a word he hugs me for a few moments, wrapping his warm hands around my body to protect me from the cool night breeze.

"Hold me tight," he lifts me up in his arms again, and I keep stroking his chest, feeling his body through the open hospital shirt.

"Gracie, if you don't point me in the right direction, we'll never reach the cliff," he whispers to me.

"I don't care," I whisper back, resting my head on his chest, inhaling the scent of his body. I'm so pathetic.

"Wait for me here. I'll be right back," I say to him as we get back to the top of the cliff and sit down on the white bench overlooking the black sea. I want to be with him a little longer, even though he's probably dreaming of another woman, but we're both shaking in our wet clothes.

I quickly enter the dark building, climb into the nurses' bedroom and take my woolen blanket with me. All the other nurses are asleep. Only Audrey's bed is empty, she's probably on call. I hope she's not looking for John.

"Gracie, I'm sorry I kissed you like that," he says when I sit close to him and cover us both with the blanket. "I shouldn't have done that."

"It's I who should apologize." I hug myself under the blanket.

"I have to be loyal to the one who's waiting for me at home."

"Yes, she's waiting for you." I know it's time to tell him, but I can't.

"I got carried away. But I have to think about her. She's the one who's waiting for me."

"What if she wasn't?" I take a deep breath.

"I don't know, Gracie, I don't know." I feel his warm body under the blanket, but I suddenly lose my courage.

"Sometimes I think we're all wanderers in this war, moving around from place to place, without meaning," I say and close my eyes. Now I'm thinking how it might have been better for him or me to go back home. I wish we could just keep the good memories between us and leave the lies behind.

His hands wrap around my cold body and hug me, but we don't kiss this time, and I struggle to keep my eyes open and not fall asleep. No one has hugged me this way in a very long time.

"Gracie, are you awake?"

"Yes, John, I'm awake." I open my eyes for a moment, still resting my head on his chest.

"I think someone engraved an airplane onto this bench. I can feel it with my fingertips. I've been trying to figure out what it is for a few minutes."

"He must have wanted to fly to the stars," I whisper to him, but he doesn't answer me.

"John, are you asleep?"

"No, Gracie."

"I feel lost."

"Why?"

"I can't say."

"Not to even a blind soldier?"

"Not to even a blind soldier. I don't really know what to do."

"Don't worry. You'll find the answer."

"I'm not so sure anymore."

"Do you remember I told you about the clock at Central Station in New York?"

"Yes."

"It's right above the information booth, right in the center of the hall," he slowly whispers. "I remember when I was a kid, every time I came to the big city with my parents I would look at the golden clock and all the people standing in front of the woman behind the information desk. Once I asked my mother who she was," he says, and I find his voice so pleasant. "She told me the woman behind the counter was a great magician who had the answer to every question you could possibly think of. And all the people in line were there because they were waiting for her answers."

"Do you think she'll know the answer to my questions?" I want to touch his body under the blanket.

"If you suddenly feel lost, you can always go there and ask her. I'm sure she'll have the answer." His warm body makes me feel comfortable, and I struggle to keep my eyes from closing.

"I feel like I should have said some things that went unsaid, and now it's too late."

"I feel like I'm cheating on her."

"Don't feel that way. You haven't done anything wrong."

"I seduced you."

"I wanted to be seduced, and in any case, I'm the liar and the cheater."

"Me too. I need to write to Georgia and tell her that I've changed."

"Yes, you should write to Georgia." I'm a liar and a coward, and I don't have the courage to tell him that I faked the letters from Georgia. I'll tell him tomorrow. Now I'm just going to close my eyes for a few minutes.

What's the time? I look at the sky, which is turning reddish. Did I fall asleep?

"John, are you awake?"

"Yes, Gracie, I'm awake."

"We need to go back inside. They'll probably be looking for you soon, not knowing where you went. And I need to start my shift. New wounded soldiers will be coming in from the front. I have to be ready for them."

I want him to say something or to kiss me, but he says nothing, he just puts his hand on my shoulder and I feel his warm fingers through my rough uniform. Maybe I should have been the one to kiss him or say something. I should have probably said a lot of things to him.

On the way inside, as we cross the driveway, I stop for a moment on the hospital stairs and look back. I can see some army ambulances approaching on the main road, but in the morning light they look almost black, their front lights shining like yellow flashlight eyes.

"Cold Spring, New York? Is there anyone here from Cold Spring, New York? Does anyone know someone from there? Cold Spring, New York?" We're standing at the entrance to the hall, as I hear a newly-wounded soldier shouting. He's supporting himself with crutches and walking between the beds, asking loudly about Cold Spring, New York. I suddenly freeze.

"I think John is from there. John?" I hear Audrey's voice.

She helps the wounded soldier get settled into his new bed and places his backpack in the metal locker. "John?" She gets up and turns to us, looking at John and me.

"Yes, I'm from there, John Miller," he answers the soldier, and I feel his fingers letting go of my shoulder.

"John Miller? How are you? I haven't heard from you in so long. What happened to you? Where were you injured? Edgar Foster, remember me? I was two years under you in high school. I remember you joined the army in the first wave." He approaches John with his crutches, making his way between the beds and extending his hand to shake John's. I make room for him and move back, watching Edgar's hand as it remains raised in the air, while he looks at John. Finally he realizes John is unable to see him. I have to stay away, let them talk.

"I remember you," John smiles at him and extends his hand in the air towards the voice, "so you're here as well? When did you join this bloody war? How were you injured?"

"I'm new here, it's just my rotten luck, a bullet in the foot from a German sniper, but the doctors say I'll fully recover."

"And how are things at home? How's my Georgia?"

"Georgia? Your fiancée Georgia? Didn't you hear?" Edgar keeps talking. "She's marrying someone else, some substitute teacher who came from the city because of the war, Gerard something, I don't even remember his last name."

"Georgia Griffin?" John pauses the handshake. I want to run out of the hall, my head full of the sounds of beating drums.

"Yeah, Georgia, from your class, I remember her. You were together all the time. She told everyone you broke up and that she wrote to you about it, and now she's with someone else."

"I don't understand," I hear John. I must escape this place, but I can't move, my hands are trying to support myself by holding one of the iron beds.

"Didn't you know? I'm so sorry," the wounded soldier, I think his name is Edgar, looks around as if searching for something to say.

"I don't understand." John turns in my direction, looking at me through the sunglasses he's wearing.

What should I tell him?

"Maybe she wrote to you and the letter didn't arrive? You know some letters are lost. We're at war, after all," I say, and try to get closer to him. It seems to me that Edgar and the other wounded men in the hall are looking at us. I have to get out of here.

"But you've been reading me letters from her that she sent recently. She wrote about the coming fall, preparations for Thanksgiving, she wrote that she misses me, I don't understand." He keeps looking in my direction, and I look around, searching for help, but the hall is empty of nurses. Even Audrey has left me alone with my lies. Only Edgar, John and the other soldiers are looking at me as I stand in front of them in the center of the hall, feeling as if I'm being hit by a ton of bricks as I search for the right words.

"*Dear John,*" I hear Audrey's voice behind my back and turn around. She's standing at the entrance to the hall, reading a letter.

"*It's been so long since I've written to you,*" she continues to read, and I already know by heart what the following lines are. "*There's no easy way to say this, but I've met someone else, and we're together...* Should I continue?" She approaches John, and I take a step back, holding onto another bed frame.

"Grace, what's going on here?" he asks me, but I'm out of words.

"I'll keep reading then," Audrey smiles at me with her red lips. "*The distance between us, the longing, and the loneliness were unbearable for me. I've met someone else who was there by my side during those difficult times. I'm so sorry, but we're together now. You will always be special to me. Bye, Georgia,*" Audrey reads the last line slowly.

"John, Georgia wrote to you," Audrey keeps talking to him, ignoring me. "But Gracie here hid the letters from you." She puts Georgia's letters in his hand, and I want to turn around and run from this place, but I'm trapped between the iron beds and the peering eyes of the wounded soldiers.

"But why? I don't understand?" He turns to me, and I can see the tears flowing from his eyes through the sunglasses.

How can I explain to him that I did this to protect him when he was lying in bed, severely injured? I try to find the right words.

"I'll tell you why," I hear Audrey's voice again. "Because she wants you to love her."

"That's not true," I say, but Audrey gets even closer to

him, standing by his side as I take another step back.

"Are you still trying to decide who to believe?" she says to John. "Ask your soldier friend from Cold Spring to read you Georgia's letters."

"I don't understand why." He continues to stand there, holding the letters in his hand and looking in my direction. I want to wipe the tears coming down his cheeks, to explain that I care about him, but I can't, Audrey is holding his hand now.

"All she wants is for people like you to love her," she continues, "but don't worry." She looks at me for a moment and smiles. "You're not the only one. Has she told you yet that she's dating a pilot who shows her his plane at nights?"

It seems to me the entire hall is quiet now and that everyone is staring at me. Even the newly-wounded soldiers who just arrived are whispering back and forth with the older ones, asking them about the nurse standing in the center of the hall with her hands shaking.

"Are you seeing someone else? Is that where my glasses came from?" John turns in the direction he thinks I am, but I'm not there anymore, I'm walking away, I need to get out of here.

"You're not the only one she's been lying to, and neither is the pilot," Audrey strokes his hand. "She's been lying to me as well. She told she has someone waiting for her at home, but no one ever writes her. She took your letters and told me they were hers."

"Is that true?" he speaks into the empty air near him, the spot where I was just standing, and I hear a loud noise as John steps on the sunglasses, crushing them with his foot. Why didn't I return the letters? I must explain to him. He must know my feelings for him.

"I didn't want you to get hurt. You were so wounded," I manage to get the words out of my mouth, and he looks at me, surprised at how far away I have gone.

"You didn't want me to get hurt so you hurt me even more by lying to me? I thought you were my friend."

"I am your friend," I struggle to get the words out.

"I thought she was my friend too, at first," Audrey interrupts me. "Until I realized who she really was."

"I think I don't have to be afraid of going home anymore," he says in my direction. "No one is waiting for me anymore, and the only one who's been by my side through it all did it out of pity, lying to me all this time."

"John, please." I start to walk towards him.

"Don't come near me."

"John, please, let me explain. I'm not seeing anyone else." I keep walking, ignoring the looks from the other wounded and their whispers, trying to get closer to him. It seems as though one of the soldiers is trying to trip me and I almost stumble, grabbing on to the metal bed frame and John's hand so as not to fall.

"Don't touch me," he whispers to me, "your lies and pity are the worst thing I could have asked for. Luckily I'm blind and can't see the look in your eyes."

***

My room, I'll go to my room, there's a wall I can peel there. I turn around and limp to the exit, holding the beds' metal frames while walking, afraid someone will make me stumble. Step by step I advance towards the entrance in the quiet hall while keeping my eyes on the floor. *Ignore all the looks and the whispers burning my back. The most important thing is to escape from here.* I climb the stairs to the second floor, enter the nurses' bedroom and freeze. Audrey's revenge is visible here as well.

The metal locker next to my bed is open, and all its contents are scattered on the floor. She has ripped my notebook, thrown the crumpled pieces of paper along with my clothes on the floor, and stepped all over them with her shoes. My pink lipstick is smeared on the floor, creating an ugly stain, and the wooden stick I got from Francesca lies broken in pieces. Fighting tears, I look at my leather boots, the ones that hide my wooden leg. Each of them has a large cut from a sharp knife, and they lie on my white bedsheets as if they were bodies whose life-saving surgery had failed.

What did I do to her? Why does she hate me so much?

I leave of the room, unable to stay inside. I must find out why she did this. I've already ruined everything, and it doesn't matter to me anymore. I must find her and find out. I carefully go down the stairs, occasionally wiping the tears, being careful not to slip, but I don't dare re-enter the hall. Everyone there knows what happened just a few minutes ago. I'm the one to blame, and they will blame and curse me. I stand at the entrance and peek inside the hall, but she's no longer there. I have to find her.

The hospital garden is almost empty. Only a few wounded choose to go outside after the sun has disappeared, making way for clouds that cover the sky. Where can she be?

"Why do you hate me so much?" I finally ask her, standing, shaking in front of her. She's in my spot, sitting on the wooden board Francesca and I laid on the ground a few days ago in order to avoid getting wet from the dirt. She's sitting in my hiding spot, leaning against the shed wall.

"I was wondering when you'd get here, Pinocchio," she looks up at me and exhales the cigarette smoke.

"Why? Why do you hate me so much?"

"Yeah, I thought about it. You're right. I really do hate you." She inhales from the cigarette in her hand.

"What did I do to you?" I stand in front of her, my body shaking, and I can feel the tears streaming down my cheeks. "You used to take care of me, you used to be nice to me."

"Yeah, back then, when you were so injured and helpless, you were nice back then," she looks up at the clouds. "Back then, it was worth being nice to you."

"What changed? That I wanted to recover and stop being helpless? Aren't we nurses supposed to be compassionate towards each other?" I wipe my eyes, wanting to sit but unable to bring myself so close to her.

"I thought we already agreed that we don't have to keep the oath and everything we promised ourselves before we came to this place. Aren't we at war?"

"Why are *we* at war?"

"Don't you understand?" She looks at me and exhales the smoke towards me again, and I keep standing there looking at her, saying absolutely nothing.

"It's all about what you choose, Pinocchio," she continues. "In the beginning you were wounded and nice because you needed me, but then, when you started to recover, you started choosing, and you never chose my side."

"What are you talking about?"

"Do you really not understand?" She takes scissors out of her dress pocket and throws them in the mud. "This is my gift for your boots, because you always choose the other side."

"Which other side?"

"You chose the cursing Italian who hates me, and you chose John."

"What about John?" I wipe my cheeks again.

"He was my wounded soldier, but you stole him from me, taking care of him at night, making him like you more than me."

"But he was blind and almost dead. Someone had to take care of him."

"Yes, and that someone was me. I'm the senior nurse, and I took care of him until you showed up, like a compassionate angel, and at the end of the day they all like you more than me." She threw her cigarette into the mud. "And what about Henry?"

"What about Henry?"

"I wanted him, and he preferred you."

"All the other girls wanted him, but you chose to hate me for it?" I yell at her. "Couldn't you hate someone else?"

"All the other girls want him, that's right," she speaks to me indifferently. "But in the end, he chose to invite you to his jeep. The lame intern in the simple khaki uniform." She looks at me and I see she has tears on her cheek. "What exactly did you say to him that he chose you? There's nothing to you but lies. "

"I'm sorry Henry invited me."

"You don't feel sorry Henry invited you, you're always nice to everyone, lying to them as you see fit, and in the end they like you. And you always choose the ones I care for, making them like you more. You even treated the German pilot with a smile on your face."

"But you had asked me to take care of him," I shout at her, trying not to shake.

"I didn't ask you," she shouts back at me. "He was supposed to die, he's our enemy, don't you understand? But you took care of him and kept him alive. You chose Francesca the Italian, the blind man likes you more, the pilot likes you more, even the dying German likes you more. In the end, that's how it is, you're either with me or against me. And you're definitely not with me."

"Really?" I scream at her. "Do you think everyone likes me? In case you hadn't notice, I am an amputee without a leg," I ignore the tears on my cheeks, "and if you hadn't noticed, John hates me, and Henry probably doesn't like me at all, and yes, I lie to everyone. I'm a liar. What is there to like about me anyways?" I support myself leaning against the wall, struggling to stay upright.

"You're right. There really is nothing to like about you. I don't understand how you can even tolerate yourself." She turns away from me and lights another cigarette for herself.

"*Americana*, stop," she follows me.

"Leave me alone," I yell at her and keep walking, trying to get away from her.

"*Americana*, you can't go there," she continues to shout at me.

"It's none of your business. It's between him and me." I look back for a moment and see her behind me, her black dress fluttering in the wind. "Go back to your village." I turn my back on her and approach the rocks. It's time for me to search for the cross I threw into the sea back then.

"*Americana*, it's dangerous. You can fall."

"That's none of your business." I start walking down the rocks. It's time I give up the path that goes down to the beach. It would have been better if I hadn't gone down there last night with John.

"*Americana*, stop," she yells at me, but I don't listen to her. I bend down and hold onto the smooth rocks, sitting at the edge of the cliff and looking at the angry gray waves below.

"What did I do wrong to you? Didn't I try hard enough to keep him alive? Didn't I care enough about him? What did I do so wrong that you punish me over and over?" I scream at the waves below me.

"*Americana*, be careful." I hear her, but I don't care anymore. I'm tired of getting up and falling, only to get up and fall again.

"Why is this so hard?" I shout at the seagulls screaming above me.

"Because that's how it is, Americana, it's hard sometimes," she yells at me. "Nothing is waiting for you there."

"I don't care," I turn around and yell at her, looking at her holding the hem of her dress with her hands while the wind hits her. "Nothing is waiting for me here too. I'm a liar."

"*Americana*, we're all liars," she stands up and shouts back at me.

"Really, *la vedova en moto*? What are you lying about?"

"Everything, Americana, I lie about everything." She looks at me and comes one step closer.

"I'm a liar, and I'm disabled, and I'm afraid to go home," I shout at her, standing and taking another step towards the edge. The sound of the waves at the bottom of the cliff invite me to join them.

"I'm lying to myself that my husband will come back one day," I hear her.

"You don't know that," I answer without turning my head, still looking at the white foam and the waves.

"You don't know that either," I hear her.

"Who could ever love me like this?" I turn to her and scream, trying to overcome the noise of the wind and the waves. "Who would want a crippled woman without a leg?" I fold and collapse on the sharp rock at the end of the cliff. "Who would want me?" I sit on the rocks and cry. "I'll never have someone that loves me."

"Shhh... *Americana*, it's okay," she approaches and bends over me, hugging me with her warm arms.

"How am I going to get back home like this?" I sob. "What I've done is so awful." I turn around and scream to the sea, wanting to break free from her arms that surround me. "All in all, I tried to help him. He was going to die. I wanted people around me to live. I wanted to be a nurse who saves people. Why did I come here at all?" I can't stop weeping.

"Shhh... *Americana*, it's okay, you're amazing, Americana, you saved a life, and one day you'll find some nice Americano."

"How would anyone like a crippled liar like me?" I look at her through my teary eyes. "I stole his letters and read them to myself, trying to imagine that someone loved me."

"Shhh... *Americana*, your *Americano* will come one day."

"You don't know that," I sob into her embrace.

"You're right, *Americana*, I don't know that." She sits down next to me and holds me tightly. "But I do know one thing, that you're the most special Americana I have ever met, and I know one more thing, that you have to believe that one day the right man will come, as I have to keep believing that one day my husband will return from Russia." She strokes my hair with her fingers, releasing the hairpins, letting my hair flutter in the cold wind. I look at her and notice that she's crying too.

"Everyone hates me, and I'm a liar." I hug her.

"Everyone hates me, and I'm a liar too." She hugs me back. "But don't go to the sea. It is disgusting and cold." She wraps her arms around me, making sure I don't get any closer to the edge of the cliff.

The cold autumn wind continues to whistle around us as we huddle on the rocks above the water. I try to ignore the cries of the seagulls flying over us, screaming and waving their wings as they struggle against the wind.

I lift my head and look down at the gray sea. How will I enter the hospital again, when everyone knows what I've done?

"How will I go back in there?"

"I don't know, *Americana*."

"For *la vedova en moto* who always knows what to do, you sure know nothing."

"Yes, *Americana*, I know nothing too." She gets up and holds my hand, helping me off the ground. We both smile at each other, wipe away our tears and hug as we walk back to the hospital.

Now they can hate us both.

The Thanksgiving of 1944

"Lord, Thank you for your blessings over us." Audrey stands in the center of the hall and reads from a page she holds in her hand. "Thank you for saving our lives on the battlefield of Italy." I watch her reading from the entrance. All of the other nurses are gathered around her in front of the wounded sitting in their beds and listening to her. I'm more comfortable standing at the entrance of the hall. I don't usually go inside except during my shifts. I don't want to deal with the looks and curses of the wounded soldiers.

"Lord, Thank you for helping us recover," she continues her prayer, and I can see him from a distance. He's wearing new sunglasses. Probably a gift from Audrey. I wonder what she had exchanged them for.

"Thank you for bringing us together here." I keep looking at them from a distance. I prefer to work in the operating room; the wounded lying on the table, sedated by morphine, don't care about what I've done.

"Thank you for the food you bring to our mouths." She points to the food cart standing beside her. The supply ship was delayed, and no turkey arrived at the hospital. Still, some nurses went to the trouble of decorating the hall with colorful blue, red, and white ribbons. They didn't invite me to join them.

"Thank you, Lord, and may we return home soon." She finishes her prayer, and the wounded nod their heads as the other nurses begin to move between the beds, handing them out the holiday meals. One nurse enters the nurses' station and turns on the radio. Pleasant music spreads through the hall. I like Thanksgiving, even though I have nothing to be thankful for this year.

"Happy Thanksgiving." They smile at each other, and I can see Audrey stroking John's hair, handing him his holiday meal. "Have a good night," they say to them later and leave the hall. They look right past me when they leave, as if I don't exist. Only one of the nurses smiles at me and touches my palm, as if accidentally; they have to prepare for a Thanksgiving party with the pilots.

I've stopped going to the pilots' club, and I don't know whether Henry is looking for me. I no longer go out to the front stairs to sit with the nurses while they wait for the pilots to visit them either.

I can't go to the party even if I wanted to. The boots Audrey ruined are gone now, she must have thrown them away. I must wait until the nurses leave and then go up to my room.

"Grace," Blanche calls me later from her office, as I walk down the quiet hallway to the nurses' bedroom. I'm going to lie in bed and read a book, marking the pages with dog ears until I fall asleep.

"Yes, Head Nurse Blanche." I enter her room. I have to thank her for the trip to Naples that helped me escape the ship going home, but I'm scared; she must have heard what I did with John.

"Aren't you going out tonight with the other nurses?"

"No, Head Nurse Blanche."

"And may I ask why?"

"I don't think they like me very much, Head Nurse Blanche."

"Since when do you care what others think of you?" She

gets up from her chair and turns to a metal cabinet. She opens one of the drawers, pulling out a bottle of whiskey. "You have a lot of things to be thankful for," she looks at me, "like, for example, the ship you miraculously didn't board again." She sits down in her brown chair and pours herself a glass.

"Thank you, Head Nurse Blanche."

"And maybe, despite what you've done, you should also be thankful for one of the wounded you treated with so much care." She pulls another glass from the drawer of her table and pours me a drink.

"He doesn't want to talk to me anymore, Head Nurse Blanche." I approach the table and take the glass, holding it in my hand. I tried to talk to him several times while he sat in the garden on the bench overlooking the sea, but he pretended not to hear me. The other times I tried, Audrey saw me and asked me to leave. Even at night, when I approached his bed, he pretended to be asleep.

"Since when do you stop yourself from trying to fix something that went wrong?" She raises her glass of whiskey. "Cheers."

"Cheers, thank you, Head Nurse Blanche." I sip the whiskey.

"You know, Grace, it would be nice if you could stay with us a little longer."

"Yes, Head Nurse Blanche."

"So get out of my office and go and have some fun, it's Thanksgiving."

"I don't have too much to be thankful for, Head Nurse Blanche."

"Grace, I received confirmation today that you're one of the permanent nurses on my staff. You no longer need to keep dodging the ship going home."

"Yes, Head Nurse Blanche."

"So you have at least one thing to be thankful for."

"Thank you, Head Nurse Blanche." I place the glass of whiskey on the table and leave her room. I have many other things to try and fix.

"And don't touch my jeeps." I hear her as I walk down the hall.

"Yes, Head Nurse Blanche."

My fingers caress the steering wheel of the jeep. I've been sitting here for a long time. Although I try to listen to the crickets' sounds out there in the dark, I hear only the sounds of music and laughter from inside the hut. Sometimes it seems to me that I can hear Henry's laughter amidst all the other voices. Should I go inside?

The white nurse's dress feels strange on my body. My lips are pale, lipstick-less, they aren't even painted with the simple red lipstick, which Audry had ruined. I hadn't gotten myself a new one, the type of lipstick that would make the pilots gawk at my lips. All I have is a wooden leg and simple shoes, not even boots to hide my prosthetic.

A dress and a wooden leg, that's me.

What will they think when they see me?

I look up at the dark control tower feeling as though it's looking back at me. It's now or never.

I let go of the steering wheel, and get out of the jeep. Maybe I will return humiliated in a few minutes. Twenty-two steps, and I stand at the entrance of the hut, looking inside.

The club remains as it was, the same flags that hang on the ceiling, the same pilots in khaki uniforms and leather jackets embossed with the squadron emblem, the same nurses dancing in their arms or sitting by the small tables covered in cigarette smoke. Nothing changed, except that everyone was staring at me as I stood at the door.

I can't tell whether they've all stopped talking because of me, but it seems as though the couples have stopped dancing while the music keeps on playing. The nurses sitting by the tables are now looking at me. I need to go inside.

My eyes scan them as I pass by the whispering couples on the dance floor. I notice Henry among them, holding a beautiful girl with wavy gold-colored hair and fair skin; she's from the transportation corps. She hugs him tightly as he whispers something in her ear.

"Just go inside," I say to myself, but I stay standing in the doorway and smile awkwardly. It was a mistake to come here.

Just a few steps. I breathe deeply. I'll sit at the table and drink gin, even if I have to sit here by myself all night. I won't give up. This is me, Grace, with a dress and a wooden leg, and this is what I've decided to do, no matter what. All through the drive here I encouraged myself, again and again, driving slowly through the dark village.

Just a few steps to the small table in the corner of the hut. I start walking.

"Can I ask you to dance?" Henry leaves the transportation girl with the golden hair and walks in my direction.

"I think there's already a lovely lady dancing with you."

"And now someone else will dance with the lovely lady. Can I ask you to dance with me?"

"Not if you're going to pity me."

"Why should I pity you?" He looks into my eyes. "For not wearing lipstick?"

"My lipstick was lost in the war." I hold his arm. Can I trust him?

"You're lovely with or without lipstick." He puts his hand on my waist and leads me to the small dance floor. I place my hands on the back of his neck and get closer to him, smelling his cologne, but before I close my eyes and let myself go with the music, I see Audrey walking out of the hut. She probably doesn't want to be in the same room with me. We haven't spoken at all since that day.

"Thanks," I whisper to him later as we dance between the couples. He gently leads me through the dance, ignoring my limp as if it doesn't exist.

"What?"

"Nothing," I say to him and let myself open my eyes.

"Can I dance with your girl?" I hear someone say and see another pilot standing next to us.

"Would you like to dance with him?" Henry asks for my permission. I smile at him and say thanks as he walks away to the other girl. I hold the pilot's hands and dance with him, and then another, and another, until my legs hurt. Still, I don't care, the pain can wait. One dance is followed by another as glass after glass of gin is served to me by the pilots. I focus on the music and move to its rhythm and enjoy the hands holding my body, ignoring the looks around me until I gasp and ache. I say goodbye to the last handsome pilot dancing with me and go stand in the corner, letting myself have a little rest. The dancing couples are no longer looking at me, and neither are the women sitting by the tables. They were once again smiling at the pilots around them. I look down at my wooden leg. I have so much more to fix.

"See you later," I finally say to Henry from a distance, waving at him as I turn to the door.

"Grace, wait." He leaves the golden-haired girl hugging him and walks over to me. "I'll take you back."

"No thanks, I have a jeep, and you have a girl to dance with."

"You already know me," he smiles. "You know how I am with women."

"Yeah, I already know you," I smile back at him and walk towards the door, but suddenly I stop and turn around. Walking over to him and grabbing his waist, I say to him: "You know, you have to stop trying to prove to everyone who you are and how you are with women. You're a good man, and you're a good pilot, and you've paid enough in this war. We've all paid enough. I gave up my leg, and I gave up the idea that anyone will ever want me again. But we're allowed to go back home and be who we are."

"You have a lot of grace in you," he smiles at me, and it seems he wants to kiss me, but he needs to kiss someone else instead.

"This war will end one day," I continue to hold him, "and you'll go back home to the same train station you left three years ago. Your dad's black Cadillac, the one you stole, will be waiting for you, and you'll get in and drive home. Your dad should be proud of you and everything you've done in this war. He should be proud of the insignia on your shoulders." I look up and smile at him, touching the medals on his chest with my fingers. "And you'll go to Betty's house, you'll knock on her door, holding flowers, and ask her to go out with you. And it'll be her win if she accepts your invitation. There's nothing wrong with you, and frankly, there's nothing wrong with me either."

I kiss him goodbye on the cheek and turn towards the door. But then I see Audrey follow him inside.

He follows Audrey into the club, his hand on her shoulder, wearing a military uniform that she must have given to him.

"I'm sorry," I walk over to him.

"He doesn't want to talk to you," Audrey says to me.

"I'm blind, not deaf, and I can speak for myself," he says and lowers his hand holding her shoulder. Then he turns to me. "You hurt me."

"I'm sorry."

"You hurt me the most by pitying me."

"I didn't pity you, I cared about you." I want to tell him that I have so many feelings for him.

"You did pity me, so you lied to me. You thought you were allowed to lie because I'm weak and vulnerable." He stands and looks in my direction, and I touch his arm, wishing he knew I was listening to him.

"Yes, I was injured," he removes my arm from his, "but the last thing I needed was pity. I got it from everyone else." He points with his head in Audrey's direction. But I don't think she notices; even though she's holding his hand, her eyes are looking around. Maybe she's looking for Henry.

"I didn't mean to hurt you."

"I needed someone to believe that I was strong enough to recover. You know how it is, you were there once. Of all people, you're the one who should have known pity would hurt me the most. Because that means you didn't believe in me."

"You were the wounded soldier lying in bed next to me, and I tried to take care of you. I didn't think of it as pitying you or lying to you. I just wanted you to have enough strength to recover, isn't that enough?" I say to him.

I want to tell him that I think about him all the time and miss our conversations, but I can't say that next to Audrey. She's staring at us, holding his arm trying to move him towards the club.

"It's too late, Grace. You can't take back lies and pity."

"You're right," I say to him and step out of the club, walking towards the jeep. I wish he would have called me Gracie, then I could still believe there was a chance for forgiveness.

"What are you doing here at this hour?" I ask her as she exits the hospital and sits down next to me on the white stairs. I couldn't go to sleep after I came back from the club, and I was sitting alone, looking at the stars, and trying not to shiver in the cool air.

"Americana, I want to make sure I'm not like that woman in the alley in Rome." She puts her arm on my shoulder, and I offer her a cigarette, but she refuses. I was going to light one for myself, but I change my mind and put it back in the box. I need to stop with all this smoking.

"Would you let me meet your son?" I ask her after a few minutes.

"He's asleep now, Americana. You should go to bed too." She gets up from the stairs and starts walking down the dark parking lot towards her motorcycle. I can hear the sound of her footsteps on the gravel.

"Good night, la vedova en moto."

"Americana," She suddenly turns to me. "Come meet my son."

"Wait one minute." I go up to my room and get a coat. I rush back to the parking lot and sit behind her on the motorcycle hugging her tightly.

"One look and that's it, Americana, don't disturb his sleep. He dreams of angels," she says as she starts the motorcycle, slowly exiting the parking lot towards the dark road leading to the village.

We reach an alley in the village, and she stops and gets off the motorcycle. I follow her, walking slowly on the cobblestones, careful not to slip.

"Shhh... *Americana*," she whispers to me as she stops in front of a wooden door, opening it quietly.

Inside the house, she whispers to an older woman, and all I can understand is the words bambino and Americana as she looks at me and smiles before disappearing into the corridor, she then returns after a moment holding a three-year-old boy in her arms. He hugs her and rubs his eyes, looking at me suspiciously before putting his head on her shoulder.

"Tea?" the older woman asks me. Perhaps she is Francesca's mother, or someone who takes care of her child while she's away.

"*Americana*, why are you crying?" Francesca asks me after a moment.

"It's nothing," I wipe my tears. "If I ever have a child, I wish he'll be exactly like yours."

"Thank you, *Americana*," she says to me on our drive back to the hospital.

"Good night, *la vedova en moto*," I say to myself as I stand on the hospital stairs and watch her drive away back to the village and her son.

"Allen."

A few days after Thanksgiving, I hear a nurse walking in the hall, reading names off the list she's holding in her hand. I knew this day would come soon.

"Going home." Allen gets up from his bed and starts packing.

"Garrett."

"Going home."

I watch him shake his friends' hands, and I lower my eyes back to my book. This isn't about me anymore.

"Jeffery."

"Friends, I'm going home. We'll meet again on the other side of the Atlantic."

I should concentrate on the words in my book. I'm just a nurse who sits in the nurses' station reading a book. I don't have to be worried about the ship going back home. I got what I wanted.

"John."

"Goodbye, friends, you've been great, even though I can't see you." I can't help myself and lift my gaze. I can see John hugging Edward, who has been reading to him after I left the hall. The book I'm reading now is much more interesting.

"Kenneth." She continues to read.

"Home awaits."

At least I know that it's over. No matter what I try, he's not willing to talk to me anymore. It's fine, I don't have any feelings for him either way.

"Lester."

"Going home."

I see Audrey approaching John's bed, helping him pack his things. I need to stop looking at the hall, I have a book to read. He's not different from any other wounded soldier I've treated.

"Raymond," the nurse continues to read, but I no longer follow the names on the list. I watch the soldiers as they begin to walk towards the ambulances waiting for them outside, and John leaves as well, putting his hand on Audrey's shoulder and following her. I get up from the nurses' station and walk past him, trying to be as loud as I can with my wooden leg on the floor. Maybe he will hear me and say something about my limp. But he says nothing, while Audrey smiles at me with red painted lips. Perhaps he didn't hear my footsteps.

I come out of the building and look at them from the stairs. One by one, they get into the white ambulances parked in the front driveway, waiting for them. I try to locate John, but I can only see Audrey walking towards me. He's already in the ambulance, it's too late now. It's been too late for days, but now I can't even wave goodbye.

"I'll always remember his kiss goodbye," Audrey pauses next to me, but I don't answer her.

I cross the parking lot and go past the white ambulances, past Francesca's motorcycle parked behind the supply trucks, reaching the stone fence I crossed when I ran away the first time. I don't need to watch him leave; he doesn't want me anymore.

One by one, the ambulances drive out of the parking lot. I grab onto the stone fence and climb over it, remembering that day I fell. This time I'm not injured, and I just need to be careful not to slip. I rush and walk through the trees and manage to see the white vehicles moving away towards Naples. I suppose I can still get to the road and try to stop them, but there's no point. He's made his choice, and I tried to apologize and failed.

I watch as the ambulances become white dots in the horizon, like a flock of white birds flying to the hot south in the winter. I have to return, there's no point in standing here and looking at the empty road.

"Did he leave, *Americana*?" She sits in our corner and hugs me as I sit down next to her and rest my head on her shoulder. I'm not going to cry, I've cried enough in the last few months.

"Now that John is gone, you can try to be my friend again," I hear a voice and see Audrey standing near us. She holds a box of cigarettes in her hand, about to light one for herself.

"No," I say to her, "I'll never be your friend again. You'll never be able to understand Francesca and I. This friendship corner doesn't belong to you, this corner belongs to us flawed and strange women."

Audrey tries to think of an answer while lighting her cigarette, but Francesca turns to her and starts yelling at her in Italian, and Audrey backs away and leaves.

"Go find yourself a pilot," I shout after her, "but not Henry, he's too good of a man for a woman like you."

She pauses for a moment, perhaps thinking about turning around and answering me, but Francesca curses at her, and she walks away, leaving us alone.

"*Americana*, today it is a pleasant sunny day," Francesca says after a few minutes.

"Yes, *la vedova en moto*, it is a pleasant, sunny day, " I answer and hug her.

The newspaper headlines say that the army has broken through the German defense line in the north and is advancing towards Bologna. For several days now, transport trucks have been arriving at the mansion and the soldiers have kept loading them with all the non-essential equipment we had at the hospital.

"Grace, come into my office when you're done." Blanche walks past the operating room and pauses for a moment before disappearing in the hallway.

"Yes, Head Nurse Blanche," I mumble through the medical mask I'm wearing. What have I done now?

"Artery surgical forceps," the doctor says quietly, "did you make a fuss again?" He looks at me for a moment, but I don't answer him. Since John's departure, I've only been focused on work, trying to forget him, even though I know no one has forgotten what I've done to him.

At night I keep reading the letters Georgia wrote to him, imagining that I was the one who wrote them. I managed to grab the letters from the floor that night, but I need to forget him. We're at war, people keep coming and going, we're all war wanderers just like Henry told me.

"Grace," the surgeon says to me, "I'm done. Finish dressing him, then go, the intimidating Blanche is waiting for you."

"Yes," I smile at him as I open a new bandage and begin to dress the wound.

"So what should I do with you now, Grace?" She looks at me seated behind her desk.

"What do you mean, Head Nurse Blanche?" I stand and look at her.

"We're leaving. In a few days, the hospital is moving north. What do you want to do?

"I want to keep working with you, Head Nurse Blanche." I look at her. I don't care what people think of my wooden leg anymore.

"You know Grace, someday you'll have to return home, the war will end one day."

"There will always be another war, won't there? You're still here in this hospital."

"Yes, there will always be another war, and I'm still here." She looks up at me and goes to her metal locker, taking out the whiskey and two glasses. "But don't be like me." She pours both of us a drink and hands me a glass.

"When did you become an army nurse?"

She remains silent for a moment as if thinking whether to answer me. "In the previous Great War," she smiles to herself and sips her whiskey. "I was very much like you back then, twenty-two or twenty-three, so excited to sail overseas and save lives. In the spring of 1917, I came to France with the wave of American soldiers."

"And why did you stay for so long?" I sip my whiskey.

"Even though I wasn't injured, after what I saw in the war I couldn't return home. I felt that whoever didn't fight wouldn't be able to understand me." She also sips her glass of whiskey. "So I stayed, because there's always another war, and I went to the Philippines, and I went to Spain to fight Franco's fascists, and now I'm here to fight the Nazis. I think I just got used to this way of life," she smiles at me and pours more whiskey into our glasses.

"You've saved a lot of lives." I look at her. There is a lot of grace in her gray hair.

"Yes, I've stopped counting by now," she hands me the glass. "But I don't want you to be like me. It's good to go home. In the end, peace will come." She raises her glass and we both take a sip.

"Anyway," she says, "if you'd like to continue with us, I'd be very happy to have you."

"I just need a jeep for half the day." I place the empty glass on the table.

"Why are you suddenly asking for permission?" She looks at me. "Get out of my office. I don't want to know about this."

"Yes, Head Nurse Blanche." I get out of her office and hurry to the parking lot, get into one of the jeeps, and pray quietly.

I hope that there is enough gas, and I hope I'll find what I'm looking for.

The pleasant afternoon sun is blinding me as I slowly cross the village on my way from Rome. Suddenly I change my mind and turn around, slowly driving back to the village.

"*Geppetto, Pinocchio,*" the children playing on the tank call out to me and wave their hands as I stop beside them.

"Francesca," I raise my voice over the jeep's engine noise, and they jump off the tank turret and surround me.

"Francesca," I say to them as I pull a bar of chocolate out of my bag, breaking it into cubes. The tallest one, holds my hand tightly, while the boy with the wild hair laughs and chews on the chocolate cubes, and the girl quickly snatches the cube from my hand but comes back for more, smiling at me with a mouth full of chocolate.

"Francesca," I say to them again, but they don't seem to understand me.

"La vedova en moto," I finally say, and they yell "Si, Si" until one of them jumps into the jeep and points at me with his hand. Everyone else joins him and climbs inside, and I drive through the village streets in a jeep full of children, laughing and pointing me in the direction of Francesca's house.

"Grazie," I wave to them as I park the jeep. They wave back and run away through the narrow street, their mouths filled with more of the chocolate they found in my bag. I hold the package wrapped in brown paper and walk carefully on the cobblestones, searching for the wooden door. Finally I see a red motorcycle parked outside and I know she's home.

"Americana, this brings bad luck," she tells me after a few minutes.

"It's not bad luck. It's a gift."

"*Americana*, it's bad luck when a woman buys another woman a dress."

"It's not bad luck. Sometimes bad things happen to us without a reason at all."

"It's a lot of money, you stupid *Americana*." Her fingers caress the soft fabric.

"*La vedova en moto*, I bought it on the black market."

"Did you give the money to the girl in the alley? Like I taught you?"

"Yes."

"I don't believe you."

I wipe away a tear, not telling her about the meat and milk cans. I carried the duffel bag with me and gave to her. At first she ran away from me, like a suspicious cat. She hid at an entrance to a building as I approached, and I placed the food cans on the floor and walked away, looking at her. She came out from the shadows, collected the food cans, and disappeared again. I hope Blanche won't hear about the missing cans.

"Wait here, *Americana*," she tells me and leaves the house. I'm left alone, sitting and smiling awkwardly at a toddler peeking from one of the rooms.

"*Americana*, the shoemaker almost cried when he saw them," she walks in and hands me the boots that Audrey had ruined, "but he managed to sew them up. I took them without asking you."

"Thank you, *la vedova en moto*." I hug her, "Thanks for everything. Even though I can get along fine without them. Walking on a wooden leg; that's who I am."

"*Americana*, this is for the day when you meet a nice *Americano* like John and want to dress up like an Italian."

"I'm an *Americana*, have you forgotten?"

"Good thing you're going. I won't need to clean up after you."

"I'll come visit, you're my only friend."

"Go already. I knew that in the end, you would go and leave me alone." She wipes away her tears.

"I'll think of you all the time." I have tears too.

"You're a liar. You'll forget me as soon as you drive away."

She hugs me and then removes the cross from her neck, "Take it, *Americana*, It will protect you."

"I can't take it. It is yours."

"*Americana*," she puts it on my neck, "it didn't do me any good, but I'm sure it will take care of you."

"Thank you, *la vedova en moto*," I whisper and feel the little cross with my fingers. It hangs on a delicate necklace around my neck. I so want to believe she's right.

"Go already, *Americana*. It brings bad luck to cry so much." She hugs me in the alley for a long time before I get into the jeep that awaited me.

Chicago, Sep. 1945

"I see you recently returned from Europe." She sits behind her dark wooden desk and peruses my discharge papers spread out on the table, while I stand tall in front of her.

"You can sit, you're no longer in the army." She points to the wooden chair in front of the desk, and I sit down. Her nurse's cap is tightly fastened to her black and silver-striped hair, and she is wearing black-framed glasses.

"I see you were here as an intern before you went to Europe, and now you want to come back since the war is over," she continues to read from the pages.

"Yes…" I want to continue the sentence and correct myself, "Yes, Head Nurse Marie."

"I also see that you were injured."

"Yes, Head Nurse Marie, but I also recovered and continued to work as a nurse, taking care of the wounded."

"There is no full recovery from such an injury." She speaks to herself while reading the papers. "This is a civilian hospital. I'm not sure how patients will react to such a nurse."

"Head Nurse Marie, I'll deal with it. In the end, people will get used to my leg. It's who I am."

She keeps on looking at the papers for some time. Then she gets up from her desk and goes to the big wooden cupboard on the side of the room, checks one of the drawers, and returns, putting two letters on the table. "They arrived some time ago, no one knew what to do with them, I kept them with your old personal documents. I don't know how they knew you would come back here."

"Thank you, Head Nurse Marie." I hold the letters and my

fingers gently tear the first envelope, even though I'm sitting in front of her and it's not polite. She's just looking at my papers and not at me. She won't hire me anyway.

The first envelope is empty and contains no letter, just one picture of a woman with long, scattered black hair wearing a flowery dress, standing next to her motorcycle.

"Grace, is everything okay?" she asks me. "Bad news?"

"No, Head Nurse Marie, great news," I answer as I wipe away a tear and my fingers open the second envelope. I couldn't learn not to cry.

'Dear Gracie,' my eyes go over the words.

'I said a lot of bad things to you that day when I found out what happened, and I can only tell you that I'm sorry for each and every one of them.

I wanted to write to you on the ship home to New York Harbor, but it took me a while to gather the courage to admit I was so wrong. And then, wanting to apologize, I forgot the name of the hospital where you worked in Chicago before the war, even though you shouted it loudly back then when we were standing on the road.

Twenty-seven such letters have been written by good people who helped me, to twenty-seven hospitals in Chicago. Maybe one of them will find its way to your hands and heart. But that's not what I wanted to write to you.

You didn't hurt me. You were my lifeline in the darkest times, my shield from further pain, covering my wounded body with your whispering words at night. Only my pride prevented me from admitting that I needed you more than you needed me, not because I was blind, but because your company was so pleasing to my injured soul. Grace, the touch of your fingers stirred my imagination, even though I've never seen the color of your eyes or your hair, I didn't need to, you were always beside me. You were the one I thought about every night, waiting for your words, and you were the one I fell asleep with every night in my imagination. But in the end, of all people, you were the one I wasn't willing to forgive, even though the one who had to apologize was me.

I went home to Cold Spring, but after a while I realized that the small and familiar place was too suffocating for me, surrounded by Georgia and Gerard-something. Finally I left the comforts of home for the big city of New York, even though it's more complicated there. I no longer wanted to be pre-war John, I wanted to be a John who danced with you on the ruined road, holding your waist and feeling your body close to mine.

I am learning to be blind, and I've started teaching children in a school for the blind. Who knows, maybe I'll also be able to go back and teach in a regular primary school here in the big city one day.

I don't know where the war took you. I think you told me then that we are all war wanderers, and you were probably right, and our paths have parted. Still, at the end of every day, when I'm on my way home, I enter Grand Central Station, and before I get off the train platform I stand for a few minutes near the clock in the center of the hall, the one above the information post.

The woman at the counter, the one who knows the answer to every question in the world, didn't know where I could find a woman with a pleasant touch, smooth skin, and soft lips, who wears military uniforms and whispers to me at night. And I was ashamed to tell her that this woman saved me with her words and the touch of her fingers, and that I lost her with bad words.

So every day in the evening, on my way to the train, I stand for a few minutes under the clock and listen to the footsteps of all the people who cross the hall, trying to imagine that I can hear the sound of your funny walk.

I don't know where this war took you, but I so hope that wherever you are, you've found your love.

Sorry for hurting you,

John.'

"Grace, are you sure everything's fine?" Head Nurse Marie asks me. "You're crying."

"Everything's fine," I answer her and get up from my chair, not bothering to wipe away the tears.

"Grace, where are you going?"

"Sorry," I reply to her, "but I have a train to catch."

The End

To my daughter, who asked for two more pages:

Grand Central Station, New York

"Train 1503 to Philadelphia will leave platform five in three minutes," I hear the speaker announce in its metallic voice as I get off the train from Chicago.

"Train 2210 from Atlanta arriving at platform seven in two minutes," it says as I walk along with the crowd towards the stairs to the departures hall, holding my cane in my hand. I don't care if they're looking at me.

"Train 3148 to Pittsburgh will leave platform four in two minutes," I can still hear the announcer as I climb the stairs and enter the golden hall, looking up at the high ceiling and stopping for a moment. The painted stars look down from above on all the people walking around me on their way home at the end of the day. None of them stops and stares at the cane I hold in my hand. Here I'm just one woman standing in the crowd. How will I find him?

The golden clock above the information booth in the center of the hall shows five and seventeen minutes, and I want it to tell me whether I'm early or late, and maybe this letter sent months ago is no longer meant to be.

I already know most of the words he wrote to me by heart. I haven't stopped reading the letter throughout the trip, since yesterday when I arrived at the Chicago train station and hurried to buy a ticket for the first train to New York, not stopping for a moment to think that maybe I should take a bag of clothes or at least toiletries for the long journey. Line by line I read the words as the train passed through forests and villages. Even when the sun went down and the night outside replaced the green fields, I continued reading by the light of the little lamp above my head, until the woman sitting on the bench in front of me remarked that the light was interfering with her sleep. I took out the lighter I'd kept in my bag since Italy, even though I no longer smoke, and kept reading his words.

What will I do if he doesn't come? Who keeps waiting every day for months in the same place, for a letter he sent without knowing where?

"Excuse me, Miss," a handsome Navy soldier turns to me, "how do I get from here to Times Square?"

"Sorry, I'm new here," I answer him, feeling weird to be out of uniform, and he smiles at me and hurries to ask a man in a suit who points him to the right exit.

There are still many soldiers in the crowd, rushing from and to the train platforms, but there are fewer than two years ago when I first arrived here, on my way to New York Harbor and a journey that would bring me to Italy and John. The big sign hanging on the wall, calling for the public to buy defense bonds to support the war effort, has been removed. The war is over.

I hold the letter in my hand and slowly walk to the clock in the center, surrounding it and searching, but I don't see him. The woman at the information booth doesn't know a tall man with warm fingers and a charming smile who hid a chocolate bar for picnics in his backpack and handed them to children at the village entrance. She politely smiles at me and turns to the man standing in line behind me, who asks her about the train to Baltimore.

Could it be that I'm late? Maybe he's no longer standing and imagining the sound of my footsteps?

I walk to the bookstore at the side of the hall and buy myself a travel book, one about a heroine looking for love and finding her man at the end. Did he also write her a letter?

I stand at the side of the hall, flipping through the book randomly and looking at the clock in the center. Six thirty-six, how long will I wait?

"Excuse me, miss, do you want to buy a ticket?" asks the saleswoman sitting behind the barred window of the box office where I stand.

"No, thank you, I've arrived at my destination."

"So can you move aside? You're disturbing the other people in line who haven't yet arrived at their destinations."

"Sorry," I answer her and move a few steps, leaning against the white marble wall and folding dog ears in the pages. I will count to three hundred, then I'll decide.

I'll count to another three hundred, then I'll decide.

But then I see him.

He's not in uniform or the white clothes of the wounded, but brown trousers and a button-down shirt. He walks through the crowd wearing sunglasses, maybe the ones he got after breaking what I brought him. Still, he holds my wooden cane in his hand, groping his way through the people to the clock in the center of the hall, and standing next to it. In small steps he starts dancing, as he did on the ruined road, ignoring the people waiting in line for the information booth and the woman who knows everything but didn't understand that this is the man I'm looking for.

"Miss, you forgot your book," I can still hear the girl from the ticket office calling after me, but I ignore her and walk towards him, making noise with my legs and the cane I hold in my hand.

"Gracie?" He turns in my direction, his hands waiting for me.

"Yes, it's me." I hold them, feeling his warm fingers.

"I love your limp." He puts his hands on my hips and continues to dance with me. I don't care about all the people around us.

"I hate my limp, but it's part of who I am." I come close to him and bring my lips to his, touching them and kissing him.

The End

Printed in Great Britain
by Amazon